Gone: Surviving the Zombie Apocalypse

SHAWN CHESSER

ISBN: 978-1-7325695-0-8

CONTENTS

ACKNOWLEDGEMENTS

For Maureen, Raven, and Caden ... I couldn't have done this without your support. Thanks to our military, LE and first responders for your service. To the people in the U.K. and elsewhere around the world who have been in touch, thanks for reading! Lieutenant Colonel Michael Offe, thanks for your service as well as your friendship. Larry Eckels, thank you for helping me with some of the military technical stuff. Any missing facts or errors are solely my fault. Bud Ableman: Your help with four legged critters is appreciated. Beta readers, you rock, and you know who you are. Thanks George Romero for introducing me to zombies. To my friends and fellows at S@N and Monday Steps On Steele, thanks as well. Lastly, thanks to Bill W. and Dr. Bob ... you helped make this possible. I am going to sign up for another 24.

Special thanks to John O'Brien, Mark Tufo, Joe McKinney, Craig DiLouie, Armand Rosamilia, Heath Stallcup, Saul Tanpepper, Eric A. Shelman, and David P. Forsyth. I truly appreciate your continued friendship and always invaluable advice. Thanks to Jason Swarr and Straight 8 Custom Photography for another awesome cover. Once again, extra special thanks to Monique Happy for her work editing "GONE." Mo, as always, you came through like a champ! Working with you over the years has been nothing but a pleasure. I truly appreciate having a confidante I can trust. If I have accidentally left anyone out ... I am truly sorry.

***

Edited by Monique Happy Editorial Services
www.moniquehappy.com

Prologue

Cade Grayson was staring straight out over the wide, gore-streaked hood at the remnants of the lopsided ambush he, Duncan, Jamie, and Lev had sprung on an unsuspecting band of cannibals. Caught sticking their noses where they didn't belong, the marauders, based north near Bear Lake, had been dealt a massive blow from the encounter and subsequent military action levied against them. The two-lane stretch of State Route 39 Cade was inspecting through his Steiner binoculars fell away from the Ford F-650's rounded front end at a shallow angle and continued for roughly a hundred yards before transitioning into a long, flat straightaway before finally ending at a sharp left-hand turn nearly two-thirds of a mile away. In the gutter on the left where the shoulder was wide and guardrail nonexistent, a full-size SUV rested on its roof. Having burned until all that remained was bare, soot-blackened metal and rims minus their tires, the bullet-riddled shell looked more like an insect in repose than the massive Ford Excursion it once was. Behind the destroyed Ford and trapped in the ditch was a pair of SUVs. Once shiny black Chevy Suburbans, both were now soot-coated, their sheet metal skin cratered from absorbing massive amounts of gunfire. Both sat on flattened tires and were listing hard to their passenger sides. With all of their windows blown out and just the skeletal tube and wire remains of what once were leather-clad seats showing in the openings, the vehicles conjured in Cade's head images of the Arizona and Nevada foundering on Pearl Harbor's Battleship Row.

After spending a few seconds glassing the kill zone, he paused and framed the vehicles furthest from him with the Steiners. One was Charlie Jenkins' Jackson Police Department Tahoe. Its front end was mangled considerably and most of the windows were cratered by bullet strikes. The second vehicle was a black van with a body-length red stripe and roof-mounted spoiler. Though it had also suffered considerable damage from the guns of Cade and the Eden crew, it was still clear it was tricked out to resemble the ride from the A-Team television show. Out back, the shot-up double doors were open wide, exposing the bodies stacked inside like cordwood.

Satisfied nothing living was present, Cade grunted, then turned his attention to the bottom of the hill where five zombies ambled down the center of the two-lane. They were arranged nearly shoulder to shoulder with a pair of adult Zs on the left and three preschool-aged boys of equal stature taking up the eastbound lane. Ground-hugging mist swirled as an assortment of ratty shoes and road-worn bare feet struck the rain-slickened blacktop. The wet slaps of the latter meeting the road could be heard clearly over the ticking of the Ford F-650's rapidly cooling engine.

"Looks like they turned rather recently," Raven said. She had hitched herself up to the front edge of the seat and was balanced there. One small hand was wrapped around the A-pillar grab-bar. The other hand had ahold of the collapsed stock on her M4, her nimble fingers slowly opening and closing on it. Nestled between her knees, its short barrel planted on the floor by her boots, the stubby carbine was a hand-me-down from her late mother. An item that represented more than just protection from the new monster-filled world. A world slowly collapsing in on her. Tightening like a metaphorical noose that with each passing day was gradually purging from her memory the last vestiges of a happy childhood. She had adopted the inanimate object as a sort of talisman. A physical thing linking her to her mom. And though she wouldn't tell her dad even if asked, it represented an unspoken promise from the grave. The promise of her survival, if only she took proper care of it, kept it cleaned and oiled, and most importantly, at all times, locked and loaded.

A gust buffeted the slab-sided pickup. The stench of decaying flesh wormed its way in through the open windows, easily overpowering the sweet smell of Hoppes #9 gun oil emanating from the weapons scattered about the cab.

Cade watched the steam wafting from the mug perched on the dash and wished he could instead smell the aroma of the weak coffee.

Leaning closer to the windshield and squinting, Raven said, "I think they're a family."

Cade looked sidelong at his twelve-year-old. Her jaw was set, the muscles there well-defined from months of apocalypse-induced stress. Add a high ponytail and a ball cap and fast forward two decades, she'd be Brook's doppelganger.

Though Cade was in agreement with her hypothesis, he said, "What brought you to that conclusion?"

Chin now resting on the flat of the M4's buttstock, Raven replied, "The boys are triplets. They're all the same height. They have the same oval faces. Their hair is the same color and looks like they all had it cut in the same style."

Pleased to see his girl relying on powers of observation, he nodded. Then, after reflecting on the way their brindle Australian Shepherd, Max, had come to be a member of the Grayson family—having adopted Brook and Raven after showing up outside the wire at Schriever with a similar-looking band of walking corpses—he said, "I think you're on to something. But I'm pretty sure they don't remember each other."

She nodded this time. "And they don't have feelings anymore. All they want to do is hunt and eat what they catch. I know all that, Dad."

"What else do you make of them?"

"Well," she said, squinting again, "I'd guess they died during the same attack and then reanimated together. Probably been hunting in a pack ever since."

Smiling inwardly, Cade said, "The woman and man are about the same age. What do you think? Mid-thirties ... like me?"

Raven regarded her dad. Let her eyes roam his newly clean-shaven face. "Naw," she said. "Those two are in their forties. Even on the newly dead, wrinkles take a while to stretch tight."

"Parenting triplets did that to them. Would have aged me prematurely if there were two more just like *you*." He smiled and shook his head at the glare he received. "Kidding, sweetie. Those two are mid-thirties … tops," he insisted. "Want to bet on it?" He held out his hand. "I'll do your dish duty for a whole week if I'm wrong."

Raven pursed her lips. After a moment of contemplation spent staring at her dad's hand, she said, "What do I have to do if I lose the bet?"

"Twenty-five pushups and seventy-five sit-ups a day for a week."

She looked at the dead things, now about fifty yards off the Ford's bumper and just beginning the long uphill slog.

Shrugging, Cade gripped the steering wheel two-handed, regarded the dead and began humming the *Jeopardy* theme song.

After a long ten-count, Raven let go of the grab bar and offered her hand.

Making her wait, Cade made a show of looking at his nails. There was reddish-brown dirt caked under them. Along with sore arms, a tight back, and a number of blisters on his palms, the clay-rich grime was a byproduct of digging the newest graves in which three of their own now rested for all of eternity.

"Well?" she said. "They'll be at our doors before long."

Cade gave her hand a firm shake. "Deal," he said. "Blades only."

Bone-handled Arkansas Toothpick already clear of its sheath, she said, "Let's do this. I'll take the kids."

Gerber dagger in hand and shouldering open his door, Cade said, "Don't you forget they're fresh turns—"

Interrupting, she called back, "And the smaller they are, the faster they move."

That's my girl, he thought, closing his door with a firm shove.

Chapter 1

Duncan came to crunched up in a fetal ball and facing a wall clad with faux-wood paneling. Above his head was a dinner-table-sized window. Slivers of light probed the bottom of the mauve curtain, painting the queen bed from head to foot with vertical stripes. If there was a prison for the man, this was it. A cold bed wedged into an even colder Winnebago. One that still smelled of bleach and death, the former waging a losing battle over the latter. He rolled over and felt his brain seemingly come into contact with every sharp-edged bone inside his cranium. It was as if the organ currently waging a war against him was untethered. Floating free in a sea of spinal fluid shored with razor blades.

Rimed by crystalline gunk, his eyes were slow to open fully. So he grabbed blindly at the water bottle perched on the narrow shelf behind his head. It was light in his hand. Not a sound when he shook it. The bottle next to it was empty, too. *At least I hydrated before passing out*, crossed his mind as he tossed the bottle to the floor. Either he'd finally learned his lesson after nearly sixty years on this unforgiving rock, or the empties were days old. Judging by the world class case of cottonmouth, he put his money on the latter.

Rubbing the crust from his eyes, he spotted the squared-off form of a vessel all too familiar to him. It was upside down due to the viewing angle, but still unmistakable. *Jack Black. Old Number Seven out of Lynchburg, Tennessee.* For a split second he wondered what had become of the distillery there. Was it still standing? Did the warehouses get looted as the country went through its initial death throes?

A knock on the door. No urgency. Just two soft raps.

"Keep your pants on," Duncan called as he hinged up and swung his legs off the bed. A bad move on both accounts. The initial action resulted in a barrage of laser-like tracers clouding his vision. The weight of his dangling boot-clad feet continuing their pendulum swing to the left made his upper body yaw in the opposite direction. Grasping the shelf the Jack Daniels rested on steadied him in a sitting position that afforded him a clear view down the center of the recreation vehicle. He saw the far tree line where the concealed entrance to the subterranean Eden compound lay. His dead baby brother, Logan, had done a superior job of laying the place out and stocking it for the Y2K collapse that never came. The camouflaged blind shielding the dirt ramp leading down to the entry door was expertly positioned so that it remained in shadow even with the changing light of day. And judging by the pewter smudge above the towering firs, he pegged the hour somewhere between breakfast and lunch. Going with nine, he stood and discovered he'd passed out fully clothed in woodland-patterned camouflage pants, red flannel shirt, and wearing the stocking cap Daymon had lifted from the ski shop at Powder Mountain before he and Oliver tore up the slopes above Eden, Utah—twenty some-odd miles west of the compound. Having contributed to the aching in his lower back, the trusty Colt Model 1911 pistol was still in the leather holster riding high on his right hip.

The simple act of his left hand brushing against the liquor bottle's smooth surface started within Duncan a craving he'd been battling off and on for more than three decades. As if on autopilot, his hand moved up the bottle and his fingers encircled the stubby neck. With a practiced motion, he brought the bottle to his lips, the plastic cap already spinning off thanks to a single flick of his thumb. He gulped the whiskey, thick bubbles forming in the neck.

Wiping his mouth on his sleeve, he ambled toward the door, empty bottle still in hand. "Whatcha want?" he called.

Nothing.

"Glenda ... that you?"

Only silence.

Forgoing lifting the curtain over the single window in the door, he threw the lock and took hold of the knob. "Daymon? You back to claim your casa? If you are, you better sit down. I have really bad news to relay to you." With a vision of Heidi in his head—the medicated, smiling visage, not the sullen post-Jackson Hole version of the blonde—he opened the door slowly.

At once Sasha said, "You're drunk." Full head of red hair adopting the tilt of her head, she stood there by the short stack of stairs, hands on hips and directing an accusatory glare up at him.

Duncan leaned against the jamb and surreptitiously reached over and placed the bottle on the counter. Fingers drumming the door frame over his head, he said, "I'm not drunk yet, missy."

"You're still tanked from last night's activities. You were so loud in here, I thought Zombie Brook had come back again and was tearing up the place."

She's only fourteen, Duncan reminded himself. "I was cleaning my guns," he said through clenched teeth.

"With dynamite?"

He let it go. Changed the subject, saying, "Where are the others?"

"Captain America and Raven took off in Black Beauty. Said they were going to bury Heidi and the Thagons up on the hill. After that, they're checking the tree roadblock before heading back toward Woodruff."

"They have radios and a phone?"

She nodded, her posture a little more relaxed.

"Tran?"

"He's probably watching us right now from the security pod. Seth is out tending to the solar panels. Said on the way back he was going to decant some water from our collection and check fuel levels on the generators." Expecting more questions, Sasha made a beckoning motion with both hands.

Duncan said, "Jamie and Lev ... they head north yet?"

Sasha looked at the big black diver watch on her wrist. "They set out in the Raptor at the butt crack of dawn."

He shot her a *watch your language* look that seemed to go unnoticed.

"How about the other half of the infamous 'Kids' gang?"

Making air quotes, she said, "My brother and Taryn are out *exploring*. If you know what I mean."

Ignoring the implication, Duncan coughed into his shoulder.

She said, "They took radios with fresh batteries."

Smart kids, thought Duncan. Last thing he wanted to do was mount another rescue mission. Seemed to be happening all too often in this new environment. He didn't bother to ask if they were armed. It was the new gold standard. Alone, or in numbers, *nobody* went outside the wire without a blade and a gun.

Sasha sensed Duncan was saving the obvious questions for last. So she took the initiative, saying, "Still no word from Daymon. And, yes, Glenda is still pissed about last night."

Duncan hung his head and inspected the knuckles on his right hand. They were swollen and crisscrossed with lacerations. Without making eye contact, he said, "Where is she now?"

Sasha leaned close and inspected Duncan's hand. "Shouldn't be punching holes in walls. You could have broken some bones, you know."

Still staring groundward, he said, "Where is Glenda?"

"Don't know," Sasha replied. "She changed Raven and Jamie's dressings while breakfast was cooking."

Duncan stood straight and sighed. "Suppose I should go and find her."

Sasha made a face. "Glenda's gone."

He grimaced. One hand went to his head. Started worrying the wisps of gray hair there. "You said you didn't know where she was."

"I don't."

"Spit out the details. What *do* you know?"

"She had a pack and rifle when I saw her last."

"Which direction did she go?"

12

Sasha pointed over her right shoulder. "She said 'goodbye' to us and stalked right up the feeder road."

"Didn't she say where she was headed?"

"Nope."

Throwing his hands up, he said, "And nobody thought to ask her?"

"She didn't appear too receptive to an inquisition."

"Shit," he drawled. "Looks like I've got some packing to do."

Incredulous, she said, "Now *you're* leaving because *she's* mad?"

He looked at Sasha like she was crazy. Then he remembered she was just a teen and still saw some things in black and white. Apparently detecting nuance was not her strong suit.

"That's not like you to cut and run."

"X gets a square, little lady. I'm not scooting with my tail tucked. I'm fixing to mount a search and rescue mission."

"For Daymon?"

He shook his head. "That's what Cade's doing, I reckon."

She looked a question up at him.

"It's Glenda who needs saving," he said. Absurdly enough, *From herself,* is what he was thinking.

Chapter 2

State Route 39

The black F-650 filled up most of the two-lane, its headlights cutting a swath through the fog tendrils rising up from the shadowed dip in the road.

The moment Cade had stepped outside the hulking truck and shut the door behind him, Raven's *family* of Zs had picked up their pace and struck out on two divergent courses. Both adults and one of the triplets angled for him at once, the female quickly taking the lead. As if some snippet of memory demanded it, the males fell in lockstep on her heels.

The other two undead tots were locked onto Raven.

Barely a yard of blacktop separated the trio of fresh turns as they tackled the incline left of the centerline. There was a bit more separation between the kids as they neared the transition a few feet right of the centerline. It looked to Cade as if the laggard of the group was operating on a bad wheel—something he had been dealing with off and on for months since injuring his ankle in the helo crash in Draper, South Dakota.

Just making the transition behind the adults was one of the triplets. Barely a yard tall and partially obscured behind the male Z's filthy ski parka, the undead tot was near to overtaking what more and more looked to have once been his parental unit.

A quick flick of the eyes allowed Cade to pick up Raven. Pressed in tight against the Ford's right front fender, all that was visible of her from his angle was the pointed tip of her slender six-inch blade and the bobbing red tassel atop her black stocking cap. Inching up onto his tiptoes allowed Cade to see her magazine-clad arms. As if sensing she was being watched, she

14

turned her head and they made eye contact. If the girl was scared, it wasn't showing. He did, however, detect the grim determination projected by her clenched jaw and tightly coiled upper body. Three-plus months of this new reality, coupled with the irreversible losses heaped upon her slender shoulders over the last few days, had her inching dangerously close to being one of those walking time bombs so prevalent in the news before the collapse. Only his girl wasn't on the verge of committing an atrocity against unarmed helpless members of society; she was undergoing a sort of metamorphosis brought about by the crucible she was put through on a daily basis. Though Cade had no crystal ball, his gut told him Raven was going to give more than she got for a long time to come. Hell, wasn't that why they were out here together in the first place? To further hone her survival skills so that when he was gone she could roll on. Maybe even live long enough to find someone with whom to settle down and raise kids of her own. His eyes misted over as the reality struck him that he would likely not be around to witness any of this, should it happen. A lump formed swiftly in his throat as he was struck by the thought that Brook would *definitely* never know any of it.

If he was being honest with himself, the reason they were dismounted and about to confront the Zs instead of just driving around them and continuing east was a direct result of his wife's passing. It pained him to admit that finding Daymon alive was a very distant second on his give-a-shit radar. His plan, going forward, was to expose Raven to as much controlled adversity outside the wire in as short a time as humanly possible.

After surreptitiously pinching the tears from his eyes, Cade said, "Always choose where you want to engage your enemy." He raised the black dagger to eye level and pointed to the guardrails lining both sides of the road. "If possible, learn the lay of the land before any engagement. What are you going to do here?"

"When I make contact," she said, "I'll use the truck and guardrail to my benefit. I'll let the boys come down the chute toward me. Stick and move so long as my back … uh, my *six* is clear."

Cade glanced behind them. Saw only open road and white-painted guardrails and verdant forest stretching away to the west.

"Do one of them and backpedal," he instructed. "And don't forget about having an escape plan." *Or three*, he thought.

On the opposite side of the Ford, Raven cast a glance at the trio of identical-looking zombies. Their unblinking sharks' eyes were locked with hers. Head tilted back slightly and with teeth bared, the boy in the lead was close to cresting the hill a dozen yards from the truck's right front fender. Coinciding with the Z's guttural moans increasing in volume, the Z's lolling head came level with the flat and he somehow found a higher gear.

Cade's eyes never left the female Z as he said, "Be loose. Fluid, like water. And stay on the balls of your feet, keeping most of your weight forward. Just don't get ahead of your skis."

No stranger to the slopes, the last part of her dad's instruction painted the picture. So she bent her knees, rolled her shoulders forward, and bounced up and down a couple of times. Tightening her grip on the Toothpick's bone handle, she took up station beside the Ford's right front tire. It came nearly to her shoulder. She could feel heat radiating off the engine tucked somewhere up inside the darkened wheel well.

Suddenly the clouds shifted and bars of light painted the landscape all around in a soft tone of gold that made Raven think of a Hallmark card. But this was nothing of the sort. This was hell on earth in lipstick and a wig and the pale-faced kids lurching toward her wanted to bite her neck and wallow in her blood as they stripped the flesh from her bones.

Now to her fore, maybe five or six yards distant, it looked as if the little monsters would barely come up to her sternum. The one in the lead was missing most of his fingers. The thumb on his outthrust left hand had been severed with a blade, or, more likely, chewed off by a feeding Z. The gray winter coat the kid wore was now a short-sleeved item, tatters of fabric flicking to and fro as he tackled the last few feet of hill.

The undead kid behind the leader was dragging one bare foot. The narrow bones running from the toes to the base of his gnawed-on ankle were showing. Like ivory keys on a pianola, they pistoned up and down with each labored step. On the opposite foot was a yellow rubber boot. The sole up front was worn completely through, the heel but a rounded nub of rubber that went *scritch-thunk* with each footfall. Now and again the zombie kid's matching gray coat would part and allow Raven fleeting glimpses at the torn dermis and hamburger-like flesh ringing a hollowed-out chest cavity totally devoid of anything resembling an internal organ.

"I have a plan," she finally said.

Cade leaned forward and peered past the headlights. Breathing in the sharp tang of spoiling flesh coating the bumper and grill, he said, "Hit me."

"If things go sideways …" She paused to think, but kept her gaze locked on the first little rotter. "What do you call that guy? The one who's always messing things up for you?"

"Murphy," Cade said, his eyes never leaving undead Mommy who, with less than a dozen feet to cover before reaching the truck, was beginning to look closer to thirty in age than forty. "What about him?"

"If he screws it up for me, I'll drop and roll under the truck," answered Raven. "And when I pop up on your side, I'll just wait for the little dudes to crawl after me. When I see the whites of their eyes, I'll set their souls free."

Remembering a similar situation in which he was nearly trapped inside a hardware store east of Schriever, Cade nodded to show his approval. The snarls and moans and stink coming from the approaching dead made the memory of that near-fatal foraging mission snap into sharp focus. In his mind's eye he saw the pack of dead things that had been hunting him that day worming their way underneath the F-650. He heard the tearing of fabric and chatter of teeth as the flesh-hungry first turns crushing against each other dragged themselves forward, the sharp items protruding from the truck's undercarriage ripping clothes and flesh with equal impunity.

Quick shooting, a bit of blade work, and a hell of a lot of luck had gotten him out of that mess.

The scratching sound of shoes on blacktop sharpened his focus. The woman Z was now two, maybe three arm's lengths away and staring the meat off his bones when the radio on the dash came to life. Over the clicking of teeth, Cade heard Tran's voice, but couldn't make out the words.

Ignoring the call, he grabbed a fistful of the creature's coat and locked his elbow. With the Gerber held in a reverse grip, black pommel facing him, he stabbed down, head-high, the blade at a forty-five-degree angle to the ground. His aim perfect, the dagger buried inches-deep into the Z's right temple. There was a soft squelch and Mommy Z went limp for the final time. When Cade let go of the jacket, the trip to the ground was instantaneous. Reduced to nothing but dead weight, the corpse rolled once, then came to rest, elbows and knees jutting every which way, directly in the path of the others.

Tran's unintelligible voice was still coming from the radio when the male zombie reached the Ford's front bumper, where a streamer of fabric trailing behind the tattered and torn parka somehow got snagged on the battered angular bumper, arresting all forward movement as if the proverbial hook had been administered from stage left.

Taking advantage of his good fortune, Cade lunged forward and delivered a well-aimed kick to the arrested Z's sternum. Ribs crunched and the sole of his Danner soaked up the shock. With its coat still hung up on the bumper, the force of the kick spun the Z clockwise away from Cade, sending its head rocketing on a one-way trip to the truck's grille.

With the solid *thunk* from skull impacting steel echoing across 39, Cade turned his attention to the final threat. As he was getting into a combat crouch to meet the undead kid at his level, a gloved hand shot out from the right and latched onto the gray coat.

Raven?

18

Newton's Law in full effect, the undead kid was yanked off his bare feet and, without announcing her presence, Raven emerged and stood over him. She planted a boot on each flailing arm, pinning the kid to the road. Then, brandishing the Arkansas Toothpick two-handed, its blade aimed groundward and just inches from the squirming triplet's face, she flashed Cade a look that screamed *I got this*.

Incredulous, he shot, "You're finished with your two *already*?"

Slowly driving the blade into the Z's darting eye, she said, "Finished the dad for you, too. His head hitting the grille didn't do him in."

Different but familiar voices joined the conversation on the radio with Tran. The exchange was brief, then the voices trailed off and the radio in the truck went silent.

Cade cleaned the Gerber with the kid's coat and sheathed it. Looking Raven in the face, he said, "Thanks for getting your old man's six. I must confess, though. I *was* half expecting to see you pop up behind me with the little demons in hot pursuit."

"But I didn't," she said, her tone relaying a level of confidence commensurate with the deeds committed.

He said, "You dispatched them, Bird. That means you get to dispose of them."

Raven cleaned her blade on the undead boy's jacket sleeve and returned it to the leather sheath on her hip. "No way I'm going to be able to budge the dad," she said, glancing at him.

Cade looked at the corpse lying face up and perpendicular to the Ford's bumper. "I'll take care of him for you."

After scanning all points of the compass—a move that did not go unnoticed by Cade—Raven looped around front of the Ford.

Cade started with the mom, rifling through her pockets and finding only a small leather-bound notebook, a thick stack of trading cards still sealed inside colorful foil wrappers, and a multifunction pocket knife with the words *Grand Teton National Park* seared into its wood handle. After removing the Patagonia coat from the corpse, he searched the kid, finding in his pockets only Pokémon cards and colorful wrappers from small Halloween-sized Snickers and Three Musketeers bars. The cards were dog-eared. The one on the top was scuffed, the foil leaf rubbing off in places. The card on the bottom of the inch-thick stack was dotted with tiny bloody fingerprints, the papillary ridges on some clearly defined. That the cards were kept together with a thick rubber band spoke of their importance to the boy.

He rolled the tiny corpse out of the way then dragged the dad closer to the guardrail. In the pockets of the bloodstained parka he found some cereal bars as well as dozens of unopened packs of cards adorned with a cute yellow dragon-like looking creature. In the front pocket of the corpse's damp Levi's was a bi-fold wallet. It contained no cash. But it did have some of the proof necessary to settle the friendly father/daughter wager.

Cade put the booty in a pile then proceeded to manhandle the adult corpses off the road. It was clear to him the family wasn't starving for food prior to whatever befell them. The woman, whom he figured to be at least six feet from toes to nose, weighed just south of what would be considered obese by the medical profession. He guessed her to be two, maybe two-twenty-five. Then there was the fact that she was fully clothed and *dead*. Cold corpses always seemed to weigh more than the living.

Though fairly thin at the wrists and around the waist, the man was tall and rangy. Taller than the woman by an inch or two. All arms and legs with a long neck and massive head that lolled around as Cade dragged him across the fog line to the narrow shoulder.

It took some doing, but after a minute spent nudging the corpses with the toe of his boot, the couple was through the narrow gap and sprawled atop each other at the bottom of the roadside ditch.

The boy weighed less than a big bag of dog food. Which was near the top of the foraging list for the day. Cade grabbed an arm and leg, lifted the body over the top of the guardrail, and flung it atop the other corpses.

By the time Cade had finished his morbid task, the low-hanging sun was again shrouded behind fast-moving clouds and a sheen of sweat was forming on his brow.

Her disembodied voice nearly drowned out by the rising wind, Raven said, "Too bad we don't have the time to bury them."

Cade turned to see her standing equidistant to him and the Ford. She had retrieved her M4 from the truck and was holding it at a low-ready, her muzzle discipline exemplary.

Speaking loud to be heard over a strong gust, he said, "We only bury our own."

"Every one of these we put down deserves better."

Rubbing his lower back, Cade said, "I know they do. But there's *waaay* too many of them." He paused and turned toward the ditch. Saw that the boy had settled face down in a puddle of water, hair matted to the back of his head. Mom was laying spread-eagle beside him, head rolled at an unnatural angle, mouth open and already the attraction of a single black fly. To add insult to injury, Dad had ended up face down with his gaping mouth precipitously near to the female Z's crotch. Cade grimaced at their unfortunate final repose, then added, "And far too few of us."

"We can say a prayer for them," Raven said.

"That we can." Cade surveyed their surroundings. Seeing nothing moving save for the tall grass beyond the ditch, he closed his eyes and bowed his head. "You doing it? Or do you want me to?"

"All yours," Raven responded.

Cade cleared his throat. "*God* our *Father*," he began in a soft voice. "Your power brings us to birth, Your providence guides our lives, and by Your command we return to dust. Lord, those who die still live in Your presence, their lives change but do not end. I pray in hope for my family, relatives and friends, and for all the dead known to you alone. In company with Christ, Who died and now lives, may they rejoice in Your kingdom, where all our tears are wiped away. Unite us together again in one family, to sing Your praise forever and ever. *Amen*."

"Amen," said Raven.

When Cade opened his eyes, he saw his daughter looking up at him.

"The bet," she said. "I think I won."

Already privy to the dad's age, Cade said, "How do you figure?"

Raven was holding the journal in one hand.

"You were reading *that* while I was praying for their souls?"

She shook her head. "I picked this up right before you started. I heard something fall out about the time you were at the *we return to dust* part. Still, I didn't open my eyes. That would have been very disrespectful to both you and the family."

Cade looked to the ground. Splayed out like a hand of playing cards near Raven's boots were a number of rectangular sheets of paper. The one on top was folded over. Visible on the corner was a single tiny footprint, the black ink standing out starkly against the yellowed paper.

Raven knelt down and scooped the papers off the road. They were wet and sticking together. "These are their birth certificates," she stated. "I saw the mom's name and year of birth as soon as I opened my eyes." She put her finger on the top sheet. "It's right here beneath the footprint. Bad news for you, Dad. Rose Campion was born March 13, 1972. Makes her older than you." She glanced skyward, mouth moving, no words coming out. Finally she leveled her gaze at her dad. "She was thirty-nine … point five … ish."

"You win," Cade said. *That woman was too imposing to be a Rose,* was what he was thinking.

Raven worked at the corner of the stack of papers with her thumb. "If I can get these apart without them ripping, we might be able to see how old the dad is."

"Was," Cade said. "Don't bother." He took the wallet from his pocket and handed it to her.

She tucked the birth certificates inside the journal and handed it to her dad. She flipped the wallet open and stared at the driver's license tucked behind a yellowed plastic window gone cloudy around the edges.

"Bryan McGowan from Cambridge, Massachusetts *was* forty-three," she said, casting a smug look Cade's way.

"Guess I have dish duty for a week," Cade said. "Sasha's going to *love* that."

Raven giggled. Adjusting the slung rifle, she said, "You won't have to get your hands all pruney, Dad. Consider it a gentleman's bet you just lost. I'll go ahead and keep doing the dishes."

Cade was conflicted. Though he was happy to see her powers of observation hadn't failed her, he still wanted her to lose and have to do the daily exercises. She could surely use the additional upper body strength. He said, "You sure about that? You'd get a week-long break from Miss Motor Mouth."

"I'm positive," she said. "I went outside the wire and put the people looking for me in danger. I earned the punishment and I aim to serve out my sentence."

Cade scanned their surroundings. *Still clear.* Fixing Raven with a stare, he said, "Very noble of you."

She crossed her arms over her chest. "Even though I won the bet, I'm going to start doing the exercises tonight."

Cade looked a question at her.

"I couldn't budge the dad. I figure the exercise will help me improve my abs and upper body, not to mention my core strength." She scrutinized the license, thinking how the man with the sideburns, wide forehead, and high cheekbones looked nothing like a Bryan. Joel or Wade, maybe. Bryan? Heck no.

My Bird is channeling her mom, thought Cade.

"Why do you think Mr. McGowan was still carrying a wallet?"

"Hope," said Cade. "That and the fact that old habits die hard. Especially for us guys."

"Do you carry your wallet?"

Cade shook his head. "I leave all that behind when I go outside the wire." Tapping his chest, he added, "I carry a picture of you and Mom in my pocket. Been doing that since day one of this madness."

"You think hope alone got them this far?"

"It was a good chunk of what kept them alive this long. Especially with three little kids to have to look after."

"Four," corrected Raven. "There was a fourth birth certificate stuck to the third. The boys' names all started with a B. There was Brody, Brandon, Brock, and Bryce."

"Four or a hundred," said Cade. "A little hope and resourcefulness go a long way."

"They kept the kids quiet with the promise of Pokémon cards, didn't they?"

Cade nodded.

Parroting her dad, Raven said, "Hope and resourcefulness," and stared at the bodies in the ditch. "Sure didn't see them far enough." She looked the road up and down. "Now what?"

"Now we drive down this hill to that van." He pointed across the hood. "There's something in back I want to get."

Now she looked a question at *him*.

In response, he handed the journal back to her and dragged some cereal bars from a pocket and divvied them up.

With a tilt of her head, Raven said, "What do you want me to do with these?"

"Read the journal. Eat the bars."

Chapter 3

After speaking with Sasha, Duncan had entered the tree line on the pretense of visiting the outdoor latrines. Muttering about everybody always leaving him behind, he reversed course and picked his way through the trees, careful to steer clear of the pit traps set previously by he and Logan, all the while avoiding the areas covered by cameras watching over the clearing and feeder road.

Still on the pity pot and grousing about recent transgressions against him, most minor and not committed purposefully, nor directly, he arrived at the Eden compound's hidden entry confident he hadn't been seen or followed.

He tried the door handle. Incredulous at finding it unlocked, he directed a reluctant thank you at the last person through. Protocol was to have the person manning the monitors in the security station throw the lock behind anyone leaving the compound—most likely Sasha in this instance. The same routine was to be followed for anyone returning to the compound. Cade had instituted this weeks ago. To the best of Duncan's recollection, lapses had been few and far between, but usually were attributed to the kids who were the lesser experienced among the group. Luckily for him the *far between* period had just reset.

He lifted the handle and pushed on the steel plate door. Though recently spritzed with WD-40, the years of accumulated dirt and fine metal shavings from months of constant use caused them to emit a soft grating noise as the door swung inward.

Duncan stopped inside the foyer, where he drew a deep breath and closed the door behind him. Hanging on hooks to his left were a dozen coats in different styles and sizes, a chest rig bristling with spare thirty-round magazines, and binoculars. A half-dozen pair of muddy cold-weather boots were lined up toes to the wall below the coats. On the right, propped up in the corner, was a pair of AR-style carbines. The short barrel model equipped with an EOTech 3x scope and stubby suppressor belonged to Tran. The other was a nearly new extra they'd found when looting the prepper compound at the nearby hilltop quarry.

After a couple of yards, a hall branched off to the left. There was no sound coming from that direction. To Duncan's fore was the heavy curtain separating the foyer from their security station, basically just a plywood desk holding a monitor and ham radio. Above the desk were plywood shelves piled high with radios, satellite phones, and charging cables.

Hearing only the wheels of the rolling chair grinding against the plywood floor beyond the curtain, Duncan slipped around the corner. He heel and toed it down the hall, stopping when he reached the door to his former quarters.

Unlocked. Not surprising, considering Glenda was out and about.

He entered and found the chain on the hanging light by feel.

The flare of light from the 60-watt bulb instantly renewed the banging in his head. Squinting, he raised a hand against the light and swept his gaze the length of the cold Conex container.

Two sets of bunkbeds—formerly pushed together to make one queen-sized bed—were now pulled apart, the bedding taut and tucked in at all the right places. Atop the army surplus woolen blanket was a thick blue book, its spine creased, the corners of the cover bent and rounded from use. Leaning against the book was a single white envelope. It was sealed and bulging. Written in a familiar flowing hand was his full name: Duncan Wayne Winters.

At first glance he knew exactly what it was.

"Might as well put *Dear John* on the damn thing," he spat. This wasn't his first breakup letter. He'd collected two of them during his stint flying Hueys in Vietnam. Nearly a dozen of the breakup letters had landed on his proverbial lap in the years since.

Call this thirteen, he thought as he snatched it off the bed, ignoring the A.A. book altogether.

To read or not to read? was the million dollar question banging around his head.

"Time's a wastin', you old coot." He collected the book. As he did so, he noticed his old combat shotgun hanging by its sling from the bed support. After staring at it for a beat, he decided to leave it.

He listened at the door. Heard what sounded like potato chips crunching. In his mind's eye he saw Tran sitting before the monitor, an open bag of Lays potato chips on the desk. That vision was fleeting. Seth, maybe. He loved junk food. More than likely it was Tran munching one of the misshapen carrots harvested from his garden.

Walking slow and deliberate, Duncan retraced his path down the hall and through the foyer. Standing before the door to outside, he snatched up Tran's M4, a pair of spare magazines, and slung the Bushnells over his head. "Munch away, Bugs," he whispered, the sound from him opening the door barely audible over the noises coming from beyond the curtain.

***

Duncan had already navigated around the clearing and was standing alone by the second set of fencing when Tran's muted voice emanated from the radio in his pocket.

"This is Tran. Duncan, can you hear me?"

Duncan ignored the call. He was shimmying between the taut wires when Tran came back on.

"Cade? Can you hear me, Cade?"

There was no answer. Only a few seconds of silence.

Standing on the other side of the fence in the trees where he was well clear of the cameras watching the inner gate, Duncan listened to Tran report that the quarters he shared with Glenda had been cleaned out of most of their belongings. After a short silence, voice full of worry, Tran added, "I think maybe Glenda and Duncan went outside the wire without telling anyone."

"X gets a square," Duncan drawled. "Just not together." He studied the ground by his boots. The pine needles scattered about were mostly dry. He looked behind him and noted damp spots mottled with mud left there by his passage. Then he crouched and scrutinized the game trail snaking away in the direction of the hidden exit fronting the distant State Route. Though the light wasn't optimal, he could still see similar traces of mud and disturbed needles on the ground he had yet to tread on.

Miss Gladson came this way on foot.

A closer look revealed a partial print with a pattern he recognized.

Hi-Tec hikers.

The depression was shallow, which Duncan took to mean she was traveling light.

"Where are you going, Glenda Gladson? Visiting your boy's grave up on the hill? Or are you going home? All the way to Huntsville?"

If he were wagering on one of the two, his money would be on the latter. Still, he needed to rule out the former.

Sticking to the path paralleling the feeder road, he ducked low to avoid the cameras, then popped back out to the gravel road once he was beyond their range.

The M4 banged against his backside as he trooped toward the camouflaged gate. A couple of hundred feet from the gate he reacquired Glenda's trail. The gravel was dry in places where she had crossed. He followed the subtle scuff marks to the gate and paused beside a run of knee-high grass growing next to the gate. As was his custom any time he approached from the blind side of the gate—which he secretly considered a rotter magnet—he raised his nose to the air and drew in a deep breath.

Nothing.

No sickly-sweet pong of carrion hit his nose.

No lingering odor of gun smoke from a recently discharged weapon was evident.

Confident he was all alone, he edged around to the west, one-eyeing it past the screen once he reached the spot the gate ended and a chest-high barbed wire fence began. Looking across the two-lane, he focused on a spot a couple of hundred feet uphill. The grass covering the half-knoll had grown very tall and, presumably, was as heavy with dew as the grass bordering the feeder road. There was a trail bisecting it horizontally from west to east. Just as he suspected: Glenda had walked to a spot where a lone person crossing the road would blend in nicely with the fencing and foliage cluttering the background. For someone watching the camera feeds in the security center of the compound to pick up the movement, they'd practically have to be looking at the correlating pane on the flat panel and be keyed in on the exact spot in the road. And that was acting on the assumption the watcher was expecting the crosser. Which he had no reason to believe. Glenda had made a quick and quiet escape. Furthermore, he figured her run-in with Sasha was calculated. Eventually, he gathered, someone would start asking questions and pry the facts out of the fourteen-year-old whom he didn't include among the sharpest tools in the shed. A little too much bluster on her part. In his experience, the ones who barked the loudest had less to add to the conversation.

The route Glenda had taken to the graves on the hill presented as a barely distinguishable line a shade darker than the rest of the vast green expanse. It arced up slightly from right to left, finally stopping a few yards past the old overwatch post where Phillip had been bitten and turned prior to Duncan granting him second death.

In his mind's eye, Duncan saw a couple of wildflowers arranged on the unmarked patch of sod containing Oliver Gladson's last earthly remains. Everything, that is, save for the lower portion of his leg that Adrian and her brainwashed followers had amputated.

Duncan leaned against the weathered fencepost marking the corner of the Eden property and loitered there for a few minutes, watching and listening.

***

Though the two-way radio's volume was turned to the lowest setting without being totally muted, Duncan had been able to pick up most of what was being said over the open channel.

He grimaced when he heard the Kids report back that they were still roaming the outskirts of the property and had yet to see any signs of Daymon.

Though the signal had been weak, he'd gleaned that Lev wasn't too concerned about he and Glenda leaving the wire. He smiled when his friend shot back at Tran, reminding the likable fellow of their collective ages and that he figured a couple of *fifty-somethings* would be just fine on their own. Then his mood turned dark when Lev reported that so far he and Jamie had found no trace of the dreadlocked firefighter north of Woodruff.

Duncan did the math in his head and concluded the radio in his pocket would be at the outside edge of its maximum range before he reached Huntsville. He guessed he would get to the burned-out Shell station east of Huntsville, and then find he was on his own. Which was fine by him. It was how he came into the world. And more and more it was becoming evident to him it was how he was destined to leave it.

As Duncan neared the stretch of SR-39 where deciduous firs and mature oaks crowded it from both sides, creating a creepy flora tunnel, he unshouldered the M4 and thumbed the selector to Fire.

Chapter 4

Cade fired up the F-650 and turned on the defroster. He took his mug of tepid coffee from the dash and drank it down in one long gulp.

"Made quick work of that," Raven said. She stowed her rifle muzzle down in the well near her feet and fastened her seatbelt.

"Speaking of work," Cade said. "How'd you do the kids?" He tossed the mug into the back seat and directed a thoughtful look toward his daughter. "Let me rephrase that. How did it go down on your side of the truck?"

"That's better," she said. "I did it just like you said to. Light on the balls of my feet. I let the first one get ahold of my arm and draw it toward his mouth. All it took after that was a little poke to the eye." Pretending to brandish a knife, she extended one arm horizontally over the dash and curled the other over her head and held it there. Holding the mock fencing pose, she added, "Number two was a bit different. He went for the blade and got it in the neck before I could get him straightened around for the killing blow." Now Raven was shooting her dad a thoughtful look. "I can't believe you let me out of your sight."

"Neither can I," Cade admitted. "Then again, you held your own against the adult Z that attacked Dregan's oldest."

"With a *gun*," she reminded.

"The Dregan fella's own gun, no less. Made me proud how you handled yourself when I wasn't around. So did Mom. She diffused that situation with the elder Dregan perfectly." He paused for a beat. "When you keep your calm, the rest falls into place."

Entering uncharted territory with her dad made Raven squirm a bit in her seat. Changing the subject, she said, "We're burning gas. Shouldn't we be going?"

Cade shifted his attention to the ribbon of road reeling out in front of them. In the span of a few minutes the emerging sun and steady breeze out of the east had scoured the morning fog from the shallow depression.

"Astute observation," he said matter-of-factly. Dropping the transmission into gear, he eased up on the brakes and let gravity pull the truck forward.

"Seatbelt," she said.

Apple doesn't fall far from the tree. He said, "Why bother? We're stopping by the van, remember?"

Raven made a show of tightening her belt.

Sighing, Cade clicked his seatbelt home. Feeling the truck pitch forward and pick up speed, he grabbed the radio off the dash. It had been silent for a few minutes now. "You were closer to the open window than me. Did you hear what Tran wanted?"

"He was wondering if you knew where Duncan was. He called your name a few times, then tried the others again." She went on, recounting the entire conversation to him.

"Going by everyone's reporting, I have a feeling Daymon continued eastbound on Center Street last night."

Raven didn't have anything to add. She wasn't there when Daymon showed up out of the blue. So she kept quiet and focused her attention on the dense woods to her right.

The F-650 reached the transition from hill to flat with a decent head of steam. Cade steered what Raven had taken to calling "Black Beauty" around the destroyed SUVs, avoiding a debris field consisting of pebbled automotive glass, spent bullet casings, and the burned corpse of one of the attackers. Legs bent at the knee and arms reaching skyward, the charred husk barely resembled a human. The skull was hairless, the eye sockets shadow-filled. The intense heat had cooked off most of the fat and flesh, leaving a shrunken carcass with sharp-edged bones pressing against what little of its blackened, leather-like dermis remained.

Raven had loosened her shoulder belt and was balanced on the edge of the seat again. Rising up for a better look, she said, "You did this?"

"Yep," Cade said unapologetically. "With a little help from my friends." He drove them the length of the straightaway, keeping the passenger tires tracking along the right fog line. A dozen feet from the black van, he slowed and parked broadside to the open rear doors. On the driver's side was a pair of corpses. Both were obese by anyone's standards. Only one had turned before death. Its belly was ripped open and maggot-filled, the fly larva causing the taut gray skin to undulate subtly.

The bodies stacked halfway to the ceiling obscured most of the detail from a distance. Up close, however, it was clear the van's once vibrant shag carpet was soiled with dried blood and God only knew what other bodily fluids that had leaked from the corpses. A sheet of metal perforated with holes—some machined and perfectly round, dozens more jagged and created by bullets—separated the cargo area from the front seats. It was splashed with blood long ago dried to black. Like the apparatus on a set of monkey bars, chain, cable, and steel cuffs attached to the van's roof cut up the gloom.

Crinkling her nose, Raven said, "What's all that for?"

"Did Taryn or Wilson mention the booby traps the cannibals were leaving in some of the places they looted?"

A gust blew down the road at them, whipping the grass atop the berm to their left into a wild frenzy. Shell casings propelled by the sudden blast skittered along the blacktop.

Raven swallowed hard.

"I'll take that as a 'yes'," he said. "They were transporting Zs in this." He motioned to the left side of the van. "That one almost got me."

Parroting Duncan, she said, "Almost only counts in hand grenades and horseshoes."

Cade shook his head. Marveled at how the old guy was rubbing off on everyone. At how steady of a presence he had become—when he wasn't drinking.

Though Raven knew the basics, she said, "What did they do with the Zs?"

Cade made a face. Said, "The bastards would clip their vocal cords and drill out their ear canals. Leave them in places where unsuspecting people would run into them. The traps they set were pretty elaborate."

"Taryn said she didn't hear the one that got ahold of her hair."

"Which one?" Cade said in front of a soft chuckle. "She has a knack for letting them get a jump on her."

"Wilson, too," she answered, tucking her pigtails up inside her stocking cap. "Operation Arm Removal. Remember?"

Wearing a half smile, Cade shook his head. "I've only heard the story a *dozen* times." As he was talking his eyes were roving Raven's face. He noted her slightly upturned nose. The freckles on her cheeks, all but faded now along with her tan. Then he stared into those dark brown eyes. Brook's eyes.

Raven snapped her fingers in front of her dad's eyes. "Are you going to get whatever you came here for?"

"Right," Cade said, blinking back to reality. His cheeks felt hot. No doubt they had gone red. Ears burning, he shouldered open his door and stepped to the road.

Raven watched her dad pause at the rear of the van and waver there for a second. Head moving slightly side to side, he reached into the van and grabbed an ankle. He pulled the first corpse hard and stepped to the side as it slithered from the van and banged the bumper on the way out before settling stiffly on the road. He removed bodies until he had cleared a path to the apparatus. After recoiling from what she guessed was a wall of stench, she saw him wipe the gore from his hands on a clean patch of shag carpet, then dip a hand into a cargo pocket of his camouflage fatigue pants and come out with a shiny multi-tool.

After a short three-count during which he stared into the interior, he grabbed ahold of the handle on the bullet-riddled door, stepped up onto the bumper, and disappeared inside.

Raven rose up off her seat and checked the road fore and aft. Seeing they were still all alone, she opened the journal and thumbed past a small calendar going out three years, several pages filled with phone numbers and addresses all written in the same hand, and a couple of pages listing all of the recognized holidays.

The heading on the first page beyond the front matter read *January 1, 2011*. Raven skimmed the entry—a ramble of words scrawled in the same hand as the contacts. Apparently Rose and Bryan had attended a New Year's Eve party at the headquarters of Raytheon, Bryan's employer. Rose complained of a hangover and how the quadruplets just wouldn't listen when she asked them to play quietly.

Quadruplets, thought Raven. "What happened to the fourth brother?" she said aloud. She lifted her gaze and saw movement inside the van. Judging by the dark camo pattern of the pants, it was her dad hard at work trying to remove some part of the interior. As his hips and upper body rotated back and forth, the van moved in concert, swaying on tired shocks. Eyes touring the mirrors, she found the road behind still clear all the way to the rise. Whipped up by the wind, the only thing moving was the mohawk of grass and ground-hugging vegetation atop the dirt berm to her left. Regarding the bend up ahead where the road swept gently left, she saw only the half-dozen festering corpses lined up on the right shoulder.

Satisfied they were alone, Raven buried her face in the journal. Thumbed all the way ahead to that last Saturday in July when, as Duncan was wont to say: *The shit hit the fan.* The Saturday her stay with Grams and Gramps in Myrtle Beach, South Carolina was cut short by a worldwide viral outbreak whose scope and devastation she was yet to fully comprehend. Her jaw nearly hit her chest when she read the entry for that day.

Bryan called home from work this morning saying a friend of his high up in the DoD urged him to take that vacation to Yellowstone ... *yesterday*!! Yesterday?? I didn't quite understand what he was going on about. As I rounded up the boys ... still in their swimsuits after swim lessons, and packed bags, Bryan burst into the house and went straight for the gun safe. We fought for a few minutes over this crazy spur of the moment vacation. Bryan had a wild look in his eyes as he insisted rather vehemently that we drive west. Drive!? AYFKM? Flying with four kindergarteners is bad enough. Driving with them beating the heck out of each other? Really? I demanded an explanation. I asked him if he's on drugs? Yes, I was beside myself at that point. I even questioned if this was his mid-life crisis? Lord knows I'd been expecting it. But no matter what I said, he would not tell me what was going on. The whole time Brody and Brock are crying and Brandon and Bryce are having a food fight I am pacing the kitchen and damn near pulling my hair out trying to figure out what Bryan knows and won't tell me. Grab the Nintendos for the boys is all he was saying. He said it over and over and over. Like a broken record. Uggghhh!! I need a drink.

I was taking things to the van and heard sirens. Lots of sirens! Sounded like they were down by the Charles. Is this a drill? I ask Bryan. He says it's a bigger deal than that. More sirens! Lots of activity on the Mystic Bridge. Bryan said they're probably closing the bridge but won't tell me why he thinks that. Says he can't say in front of the kids and insists we go without finishing our packing. Turns out he was right! I felt like a turd for the first two hundred miles watching people doing exactly what we were doing: running from the unknown. As I write this we are in a little motel with lumpy beds. Big frown! The heated pool is closed. Humongous frown!

The boys have nothing to do but rough house. A hundred channels plus HBO the sign said. Every effin

channel has a frozen image from some governmental agency warning us to stay put and wait for further instructions. Brody and Brock are fighting over the remote as I write this. Great way to start a forced vacation. Only way this gets worse is if Bryan tells me we're going back to Boston to get his Mom. That happens … I'll know he's on drugs!

My world is falling apart.

Calgon, please take me the eff away!

Raven closed the journal and looked up to see her dad hunched over and filling up the back of the van. Looped over one shoulder was a mess of what looked to her like cables. In one hand was a long pole with a lasso on one end. In the other was an overstuffed gym bag that stretched his arm straight as if it weighed a ton. Black grips attached to the red handles of some kind of tool protruded from one end of the bag. As he hopped down from the van to the road, he suddenly pitched to his left and came away favoring his ankle.

Tucking the journal under one leg, Raven pulsed her window down and offered to help.

He waved her off, limped to the truck, heaved everything into the Ford's bed, and then climbed into the cab.

"Your ankle again?" Raven asked.

"It'll never be the same," he answered. "I'll be alright." He regarded her for a beat. "Were you going to tell me about the *crawler* anytime soon?"

Wearing a startled look, Raven checked the mirrors. Lips pursed, she got her knees under her on the seat and surveyed the road all around the truck.

"I don't see it," she said.

"Because there isn't one," replied Cade. "But there could have been. Poked my head out and saw you with *your* head down. You have to—"

"*Stay frosty*, I know. I'm sorry, Dad. I was just reading the first passage in the woman's journal."

37

"Time and place for that. A chain is only as strong as its weakest link," he said. "Do you understand what I mean by that?"

She nodded and apologized a second time.

"What did you learn from the journal entry?"

Raven read the passage aloud.

"They escaped the initial outbreak with all four boys," he said. "Amazing they got all the way here from Cambridge in the first place. The Eastern seaboard was a mess from the get-go. Tens of millions of people packed in like sardines. Plus,"—he started the motor and selected Drive—"Boston is within spitting distance of Cambridge. Across the Charles River if my memory serves."

"Did you and Mom ever go there. See where the Tea Party happened?"

Cade's jaw took a hard set. He said, "Crack the journal and read while I drive."

Raven nodded. "I have one question," she said.

Wheeling the Ford past the van and into the left-hand sweeper, Cade said, "Shoot."

"What's Calgon? Some kind of pill for stress?"

Smiling, Cade said, "Something like that."

Chapter 5

Duncan emerged from the heavily forested stretch of State Route 39 roughly two miles west of the compound and forty minutes after he'd entered its dreary embrace. Whereas it had been quiet as a tomb under the canopy, here out in the open he was experiencing sensory overload. A pair of crows in a distant conifer cawed at each other incessantly. Insects feeding on a twice-dead corpse droned on in the ditch. Its bloated abdomen had been sliced wide open. A failed crisscross attack from the looks of it. Glistening in the morning light, a jumble of unidentifiable organs lay scattered on the grass beside the corpse.

Duncan's eyes tracked from the innards to where the shoulder asphalt began. There he noticed the start of a dark black blood trail stretching from the corpse to the opposite fog line. He wrote it off as the work of a scavenging animal having excised and then dragged away from the corpse a plump, decaying morsel.

Breathing heavy and still suffering mightily from the night of hard drinking, he slung the carbine and worked a water from his cargo pocket. As he stood there twisting the cap from a plastic bottle bereft of most of its rigidity, his own sour breath overpowered the carrion pong.

"Smells like you ate a bag full of assholes, Old Man." As if in response to the self-admonition, the hangover-induced pounding in his head increased in pace and intensity. He closed his eyes and the cacophony rose to that of someone shaping metal against an anvil. He opened his eyes and spun a slow three-sixty. Seeing nothing capable of producing the racket, he closed them again and in his mind's eye saw Daymon's Winnebago. It was rocking to and fro and he saw himself sitting helpless in the folding chair watching the awning undulate snake-like while vertical creases appeared randomly in the RV's thin outer skin. Though the banging in his head was real, the subconscious vision it conjured caused him to throw a visible shudder. *Strange how the human mind works*, he thought, opening his eyes and looking skyward to where he imagined Brook to be.

He took a handful of aspirin from a pocket. Without bothering to count them, he swallowed the whole lot dry. Certainly a dozen of the little bastards wouldn't kill him. Pushing aside the thought of his liver going bad, he took a long pull off the water, the bottle crinkling loudly as its thin plastic walls collapsed.

"You're falling apart, Old Man. Hearing things where there ain't nothing. Having flashbacks when you're supposed to be living in the present." He stowed the bottle, then craned and looked over his left shoulder. He grimaced at the pain the move brought on, but still went ahead and glanced over the opposite shoulder. Absurd as the notion seemed the second it crossed his mind, he still needed to be certain he hadn't been caught talking to himself. Because in his experience, only crazies and senile folks talked to themselves. What did that make a person hearing things that weren't real? Equal parts of the two?

He dragged out his flask. Gave it a good swirl to get an idea of how much forgettin' juice remained inside the slender metal vessel.

Three-quarters, give or take.

That'll do for a start.

He spun the lid off with his thumb and took a long pull. Swirled the contents around again.

Down to half. Eight ounces or so.

Spotting a pair of rotters marching steadily against the wall of fallen trees a hundred yards from where he stood, he spun the lid on and returned the flask to his pocket.

As Duncan resumed his march toward the roadblock, the dead things facing it remained oblivious of his presence. They were fixated solely on a blue-crested bird picking its way through the arboreal tangle to their fore. Only explanation for them not following it was that they had become trapped on protruding branches he and Daymon had sharpened weeks ago. And though he felt empathy for the people the zombies used to be, he was saddened more by the sight of the once stately trees keeled over, most of their branches stripped by weather and time. He'd felt the same way in Nam. The Arc Light strikes conducted by high flying B-52s did a number on the verdant jungle. The trees and bamboo not turned into toothpicks from the seemingly non-stop barrage of thousand-pound bombs were laid out much like these firs. He recalled seeing scores of majestic hopea trees uprooted and flattened by the intense overpressure and shockwaves that came with the shrapnel. He'd stood in steaming bomb craters deep enough to hide a man standing upright. Saw whole colonies of primates unfortunate enough to have been caught up in the strikes. And walked among lifeless enemy bodies, their limbs torn and torsos crushed. The way the blasts caused their eyes to bulge from their skulls always fascinated him.

Six of one, half a dozen of another, was what he was thinking as he strode towards the undead duo. As he slipped the fixed blade from its sheath on his left hip, he couldn't decide which task he dreaded more: getting close enough to these two rank corpses to put them down, or threading his way through wet undergrowth and climbing over fallen trees to reach the bridge at the far end of the roadblock.

Deciding both tasks sucked, the latter a little more on account of the numerous dead things likely awaiting him on the other side, he clucked his tongue to get the rotters' attention. The female zombie nearest to him whipped its head to the right and leaned back as far as its entangled entrails would allow. Locking a lifeless gaze on the approaching meat, the first turn emitted a grating sound that stood Duncan's neck hairs on end.

"What's your hang up, *sweetie?*" He chuckled as the male rotter tore its eyes from the Steller's Jay and thrust its arms in his direction, in the process entangling both bony hands in the lengthening rope of intestine keeping the female rotter at bay.

"Looks like you're playin' cat's cradle with your girlfriend's guts there, *amigo*. I bet she would not approve if she were still of the breathin' variety." Duncan was hit in the face by his own breath, which again reminded him of the previous night's forgettin' session. Taking a hold of the female's greasy, shoulder-length hair, he pulled downward, a move that was met by very little muscular resistance and a mess of neck vertebrae popping. He held his left hand steady and brought the knife in his right hand down hard and fast. Hand-eye coordination a little compromised by the recent slug of Jack having rekindled the past night's drunk, the blade didn't enter dead center on the milky pupil as intended. Instead, the point penetrated at an angle and the serrated edge grated along the outside orbital bone until the zombie went limp and sagged forward, becoming suspended near upright, with the male's hands and forearms still trapped in guts and bending at an unnatural angle.

"Look what Mister Jazz Hands got himself into." Reacting to the quip, the thing craned toward Duncan and hissed. While its teeth clacked out an eerie cadence, its legs pistoned against the damp road and it strained mightily to get close enough to take a bite out of Duncan's face.

Waving a hand in front of the rotter's gaping mouth, Duncan said, "And I thought *I* had bad breath."

In a burst of frantic motion, its wings but a blue blur, the jay took flight.

Duncan ducked as the bird buzzed the air overhead. He watched it wing away to the east, then grabbed hold of the male rotter's hair and buried six inches of his blade into its eye socket. Granted sweet release, the zombie's legs buckled and its arms slid free of the female's slimy intestines.

With the Zs silenced and the noisy bird out of the picture, Duncan picked up on an out of place noise coming from the far end of the roadblock. A soft rushing sound. Like a faucet left on in a service station bathroom prone to echo.

Confident the white noise didn't represent an immediate threat, he cut a length of fabric from the female zombie's shirt and cleaned his blade with it.

Holding the M4 at a low-ready, he parted the ferns bordering 39's eastbound lane and made his way to the beaten path he knew was there. Looking down, he saw a familiar pattern pressed into the soft soil. He followed the imprints west for a couple dozen yards, passing cleanly cut stumps and crushed vegetation along the way.

Well before Duncan reached the end of the trail where the tracks he was following made a hard right turn, he realized the noise he'd been hearing was swift moving water. Pushing aside a clutch of bushes bearing tiny red berries, he saw all the way to the bottom of a thirty- or forty-foot drop. What had recently been a dry creek bed littered with dozens of zombie corpses was now a thirty-foot-wide torrent of turbid water choked with deadfalls and even more zombie corpses. Pale, bloated appendages beat the rocky banks. Whether the rhythmic movements could be attributed to a still-functioning corpse, or just the by-product of the hydraulic energy, Duncan couldn't tell.

He lifted his gaze and studied the bridge crossing the defile. It was blocked on the east end by the chest-high jumble of fallen timbers that ran away a hundred feet or more off his right shoulder. The guardrails bordering 39 leading up to the bridge had taken a beating when Daymon felled the first trees. They were bent and bowed, the once-white paint scratched and bleeding streaks of ochre-red rust.

Where Duncan expected to see dozens of undead pressing against the horizontal timber, he saw what he guessed to be more than a hundred. And they all stood between him and the battered white Land Cruiser left behind after the last trip to Huntsville.

Out of the pan and into the fire.

Duncan scrutinized the swollen creek. No way Glenda climbed down the slick rock face falling away from the edge near his feet. If she had and survived, fording the water would have been a deadlier proposition.

He unslung his rifle and propped it against a stump.

"What would Glenda do?" He sat cross-legged on a pile of sawdust, back against the sap-weeping trunk of a fallen tree, and pulled out the flask.

Drawing a blank on the previous query, he said, "What are *you* going to do now, Old Man?" He didn't answer himself. Instead he spun off the cap and tilted the flask to vertical. Two strong pulls, he gathered, dropped his supply down to just a couple of ounces. "Screw it." He leaned back and froze, arm cocked, narrow mouth of the flask resting on his lower lip.

Barely overriding the noise from below were sounds that caused him to freeze. They were mechanical in nature. A low burble Duncan classified as produced by a chainsaw at idle. A beat later the tinny *braap* of a two-stroke engine rolled across the void from the west. In the ensuing seconds, as Duncan rose slowly from his spot beside the roadblock, a crescendo of moans, rasps, and guttural grunts rose from the undead mass choking the bridge.

Careful to keep his head from rising above the block to his right, he shouldered the M4, swung the 3x magnifier in line by feel, and swung the rifle's muzzle toward the far end of the bridge. At first all he saw was a blur of gray flesh and ratty clothes as the entire throng of dead things about-faced. Adjusting aim upward by a few degrees brought the source of the engine noise into focus. Two people wearing helmets and camouflage uniforms sat atop a pair of idling motorcycles. In the next beat they shouldered stunted rifles and star-shaped licks of flame lanced from both barrels.

The suppressed reports reached Duncan's ears about the same time the rear echelon of rotters crowding the bridge were beginning to fall to precisely aimed fire.

A couple of stray bullets crackled overhead, causing him to duck behind the trees and go back to sitting. The gunfire lasted for a few seconds then petered out to a random shot or two every couple of seconds. Duncan was in the process of draining the flask when the gunfire ceased and the bikes sped away, their exhaust at first mimicking the buzzing of hornets swarming from a disturbed nest, then softening to a purr, then becoming one with the shallow creek's rhythmic rush.

"Now what, Old Man?" He tilted his head back and raised the flask to the sky. He stared through the boughs overhead, deep in thought. Finally he answered his own question with more conviction than he thought was left in him. "What you're going to do is dip the bucket into the well of patience and wait for the deaders to leave." He stuck out his tongue and upended the flask, catching the last few drops of amber liquor on his tongue. Savoring the burn, he twisted the cap on. "That's exactly what you're going to do, Old Man. Wait while the gift horse that just showed up out of the blue draws all the rotters away from your ride. You're going to cool your heels for as long as it takes. Not like you have a job to get to. Or anyone waiting on you to come home." With the little niggling voice in his head reminding him he was out of forgettin' juice, he closed his eyes and pictured the riders. After a few seconds he reopened his eyes, convinced fully that the two were the living counterparts to the undead Chinese PLA Special Forces soldiers he and Cade had stumbled across on their last trip into Huntsville. Same knock-off Multi-Cam camouflage uniforms. Same full-face helmets. Same MOLLE-style chest rigs stuffed with curved magazines. He was also convinced they each carried one of those laminated tri-fold cards plastered with Chinese characters and their corresponding pictograms. A crudely drawn man with hands thrust skyward: *Surrender now!* A rudimentarily rendered forearm complete with missing fingers and circular, red-rimmed bite wound: *Are you infected?* A man placing a gun on the ground: *Surrender your weapons!* A smiling unarmed soldier with both arms outthrust: *We are here to help you.*

My ass, was what he thought regarding that last one. *You mean help yourselves to our country. Never going to happen, fellas.* He shook his head at the thought. Nope. Those two on the bikes were not bearers of any kind of benevolence. Of that he was certain.

He stowed the flask and switched his thinking to Glenda. Figured he would pass the time playing out all the positive scenarios of her getting past the dead things alive. Maybe she was lucky enough to cross over and get off the bridge *before* the dead things had amassed to their current numbers. Maybe she found a way down and across the water and up the other side and was at this very moment breaking brush beside 39 to avoid all of the dead and living that could pose a threat to her.

He'd come up with just those two before his mind wandered and he caught himself obsessing over where he was going to find that next drink.

Regarding the recently acquired Rolex Submariner, he noted the time, then decided to venture forward in twenty minutes to survey the bridge and road for stragglers.

Chapter 6

Leaving the killing grounds and static vehicles behind, Cade pushed the F-650 hard on the straightaways, then braked to walking-speed well before 39 dove into one of the many blind turns between the compound and the junction with 16.

Nearing the upper quarry road, as he slowed the truck once again to negotiate a tight right-to-left hairpin turn, the satellite phone came to life. Nodding to the vibrating, bleating item sitting in the console to his right, Cade said, "You want to answer that?"

Without hesitation Raven scooped up the phone and thumbed a button. All business, she said, "Raven Grayson."

Leaning into the turn and craning right in anticipation of the next straightaway, Cade couldn't help but smile. Because as the Ford came out of the turn, he spotted movement on the road near the upper quarry entrance. As he let off the gas and tapped the brakes, he heard Raven say, "Judge who?"

Cade said, "Pomeroy?" and swung the Ford wide right. Braking more and whipping the wheel hard left, he thrust his hand out, fingers doing the *gimme, gimme* waggle. Finally bringing the Ford to a complete stop perpendicular to the solid yellow bisecting both lanes, he jammed the phone to his ear and barked, "What is it, Judge?"

With Raven staring him in the face, Cade pursed his lips and listened to the man on the other end drone on for a long while. Finished listening, he said, "Understood. Will do," then thumbed the phone off and handed it to Raven.

"What did he want?"

"First things first." Cade fished his Steiner binoculars from the center console, handed them to Raven, then directed her to look out her window.

She pushed the stocking cap up on her head and put the binoculars to her eyes. Stared down the length of 39 for a solid minute. "Deer?"

Though she wasn't looking in his direction, Cade still shook his head. "Nope. Those are elk," he answered.

"Looks like they're coming up from the lower mine operation."

"With the horde recently passing through, these guys are probably stragglers that lost sight of their herd, took a wrong turn, and ended up on one of the many fire or logging roads that crisscross the valley."

Raven lowered the Steiners and shot her dad a look.

Reading it as her *you forgot to be inclusive* look, he said, "Guys *and* gals?"

She set the binoculars on her lap and crossed her arms over her chest. "Gals? What is this, the 1940s?"

Cade shook his head. Most of this was the school's doing, not Brook's, and certainly not his. It was one thing to be polite and cordial. Which he was all for. But it was another to take it to the absurd. Walking on eggshells all the time was *not* his thing. In his day people got their feelings hurt, then built a bridge and got over it.

Sighing, he said, "Bulls and cows … does that work?"

After a slow nod, Raven flicked her gaze back down the road.

Cade picked up the Steiners and glassed the road ahead. Saw an enormous specimen, rack with too many points to tabulate accurately on the fly, standing sentinel as smaller bulls and a number of cows and calves crossed the road right to left. Though the alpha appeared to be stoic and in charge of the herd, his nose twitched and ears swiveled to and fro. *On high alert*, Cade thought. And rightfully so. Taking a cue from the alpha, he looked out his window and checked the nearby curve. Clear.

"They're heading for the upper mine road," Raven said.

Cade said nothing. He killed the engine then stuck a finger vertical to his lips. In the next beat he was shouldering his door open and stepping to the road.

Raven went to her knees on the seat and tracked her dad as he climbed up onto the rear tire and vaulted into the load bed. She watched as he popped open a long black case and went to his knees. Head bowed, he worked furiously at accomplishing some sort of task.

Raven plucked the binoculars from the seat, then turned around and glassed the road ahead. The elk were still crossing, their movements slow and methodical. The biggest one still occupied the center of the road as if he owned it. The way he was standing, statue-still and all regal-looking, reminded her of a commercial touting investing or banking or both in conjunction with one another. Adult stuff she still didn't comprehend. Probably would never have to think about again. Unless she saw another one of these in the wild.

Cade climbed from the truck's bed on the passenger side. He approached Raven without warning, startling her in the process. As she lowered the binoculars, he jabbed a thumb groundward, universal semaphore for *roll the window down*.

And she did.

Brow furrowed, she said, "What are you doing with that?"

He raised the high-tech MSR sniper rifle to her eye level. Held it aloft horizontal to the road. He rolled open the bolt. Pointing to a small metal nub near the trigger guard, he said, "Safety is on."

She repeated her question.

"You're going to bag your first elk with this. That's what."

Her eyes went wide for a beat. "Me?"

He nodded. "Show me your hands."

Raven reached for the sky.

"Don't touch," he said. Keeping the muzzle down range, aimed at the elk, he handed the modular rifle through the window, butt first, the big mirror between him and the rifle's stubby suppressor. "Take it from me. Make sure you practice proper muzzle and trigger discipline."

"I know," she said. "Never point the muzzle at something you don't want to destroy."

"Good. And?"

"Keep my finger off the trigger until I'm ready to destroy it."

"Mom taught you that verbiage?"

She shook her head. "Duncan did."

Cade nodded. Finger to the lips, he looped around front of the Ford and clambered into the cab. He closed his door softly and turned toward Raven. Seeing she already had the rifle resting on the windowsill, and pleased she'd taken the initiative to remove her cap and employed it as a rest under the forestock, he leaned over the console and braced her back with his right shoulder and upper arm. "Chamber is empty," he warned. "And I only left you one round in the magazine."

She rolled the bolt back, paused for a beat, then rolled it forward. Round chambered, she pressed her right cheek to the stock and peered through the Leupold scope.

"Just one bullet?"

"If the first one doesn't do the trick, you won't get a second chance."

"Which one?" she asked, calmly, even as her hand began to tremor slightly.

"The one presenting you a perfect oblique silhouette. Put your crosshairs right behind his front leg. That's where the heart is." He paused a beat. "And remember, this one kicks more than the M4. A *lot* more."

The bank commercial was in Raven's head now as she snugged the buttpad to her shoulder. The majestic beast standing there was a clone of the one in her mind's eye. Though she didn't know its definition, the word *hartford* suddenly came to her. Voice wavering, she said, "Why are they all moving so slowly? Shouldn't they be *running* across the road? In case a car comes, or something?"

50

"One … they're tired from running. Figure they've been Oscar Mike constantly since the dead returned in these larger numbers. To answer your second question: They're getting used to the lack of vehicles."

"Why don't they smell us?"

"Because the wind is at our face," he said. "Means they're smelling stuff from down near Woodruff and Bear River."

"All the way down there?"

Still talking in a soft whisper, Cade said, "Quit stalling."

Raven went quiet and hunched over the rifle.

"Once you have the shot you want, draw in a breath, take up a bit of the trigger pull, then exhale slowly and—"

"And press the trigger as I exhale slowly," she interrupted. "Just like Mom taught me."

"Your mom was a helluva woman. Don't ever forget that."

Cade continued bracing Raven's back. He felt her begin to tremble a bit. Buck fever was what his dad called the mounting anticipation one felt before that first kill.

Cade started just a bit as the rifle discharged.

The suppressed report wasn't as quiet as television and movies made them out to be. It was an abbreviated cracking noise that bounced around the cab before being swallowed up in the roadside clutter and diminishing altogether—a total of maybe two seconds having elapsed. Still, thanks to the suppressor, their ears were spared from the usual ringing indicative of having inflicted any kind of long-term hearing damage.

As if struck dead by a bolt of lightning, the beast dropped straight to the road.

"I got him," she blurted.

Through the Steiners, Cade watched the elk keel over to the left and kick one time at the air. In the next beat, as the bull elk went limp, the tail end of the herd bolted across the state route and melted into the roadside foliage. "Yes you did," said Cade, the pride he was feeling conveyed by the tone. "A perfect kill shot … at that." Which was true. He wasn't pulling her leg.

"Did he suffer?" she asked.

Shaking his head, Cade said, "Not one bit. You pulled your shot right, though. Hit him in the neck. Still did the trick. And all I see is a trickle of blood from the entry wound. Which tells me his heart ceased beating shortly after he was hit."

Raven threw open the bolt and snicked the safety on.

Cade said, "That's not the end of it, though."

Raven looked a question at him.

"Now we have to gut and quarter him." Cade relieved Raven of the rifle and began to break it down.

"Can't we just take him back and have Duncan and Tran do it?"

Shouldering open his door, Cade said, "Your kill. Your responsibility. I'll help you, though. Besides, that old boy looks to be about a thousand pounds. Bigger than I ever bagged. Guts or no guts, there's no way just the two of us would be able to get him into the truck bed whole."

"How do you quarter it?" She gestured at the Gerber. "You going to do it with *that*?"

Cade smiled and shook his head. "I'll show you how. But we're not going to use my dagger. We could if we needed to. I have a set of knives. Let me put this away and we'll get to work." He stepped from the truck with the rifle in hand. With the suppressor threaded off and the stock folded over, it looked more like a close-quarters-battle-rifle than the long-range tack driver that it was.

Raven watched her dad in the side mirror as he circled around back of the Ford. When she returned her gaze to the spot in the road occupied by her kill, her eyes widened and she drew in a sharp breath. Disbelief mounting at what she was seeing, she exhaled and calmly called out to her dad.

Chapter 7

To Duncan, the self-imposed twenty-minute cooling-off period seemed more like half a day. Or like a visit to a DMV manned by sloths on Valium. For the duration, his conscious mind had been engaged in a tug-of-war with Glenda Gladson at one end of the rope and Jack Daniels on the other.

Gathering his rifle, Duncan rose and looked west. Wholly expecting to see the bridge still choked rail-to-rail with dead things, he instead saw only a dozen or so—all of them first turns. Some were stuck fast to sharpened limbs jutting horizontally from the wall of felled trees. A half-dozen badly burned walking corpses caromed blindly off one another, the waist-high guardrails, and anything else that got in their way. They wore forced smiles, the pickets of stark white teeth contrasting mightily with the cracked dermis and shadowy, eyeless sockets. Where patches of blackened, hairless scalp was peeling away, ivory-hued skulls made an unwelcome appearance. Duncan supposed they were victims of the conflagration that all but consumed Huntsville and a good portion of nearby Eden

"You are some ugly mofos," Duncan muttered as he adjusted his Stetson and shouldered the carbine. Eyeing the farthest reaches of 39 through the rifle's optic, he was relieved to see nothing moving save for a single, slow-moving crawler. Missing both legs at the knees and one arm at the shoulder, the thing presented a grotesque sight as it flopped its single functioning arm forward and then dragged itself westward along the centerline, a few hard-earned inches at a time.

He listened hard.

Nothing.

No mechanical sounds.

No muffled exhaust.

And, more importantly—no gunshots.

The riders were gone. That much was clear. And they'd taken the bulk of the rotters along with them.

"Better stay away, Mr. Murphy. 'Cause this old boy don't want to walk one step past that luxo-cruiser over there."

He slung the rifle and swung it around back. With the suppressor tapping against his backside, he scrambled onto the felled tree the rotters were trapped against. As he did so, his boots scuffed the bark and tiny, brittle branches sheared off underfoot.

Alerted to the presence of meat by the new sounds, the nearest rotter—a beefy middle-aged man in life—swiveled its head right, opened its maw, and emitted a long drawn-out rasp.

The big man had died the first time wearing a hunter's get-up: heavy plaid jacket over a pair of tan Carhartt work pants. The suspenders attached to the pants had fallen off the rotter's shoulders and were filthy and tattered from dragging on the ground.

Sharpened branches had pierced through the front of the rotter's blood-spattered thermal shirt and emerged out back to tent the jacket. Canted on the zombie's head was a camouflage hat, the ear flaps in a down position and doing nothing to hide the damage gnashing teeth had done to the cheek and ear facing Duncan.

Clucking his tongue, Duncan rose and heel-toed it along the tree, searching for a spot to lower himself onto the road on the other side. By the time he'd located a suitable area a few feet from the dead hunter, the two rotters on its left were bucking and thrashing and close to freeing themselves from the branches piercing their abdomens.

Peering over an upthrust branch, Duncan watched one of the crispy critters bang into the Toyota and deposit a long black smudge along its already dented and gore-streaked passenger side. The rest of the burned creatures were walking in place against the roadblock twenty feet away and getting nowhere. They had no idea he was perched on the log to their immediate right, and he didn't plan on broadcasting it.

Keeping an eye on the crispy roamers, he went down on his haunches. After choosing a patch of asphalt as his landing spot, he worked the empty flask from his pocket. Under Hunter's rheumy-eyed stare, Duncan spun the cap off and tapped the flask against an upturned palm.

Nothing.

Not one drop.

He spun the cap back on and tossed the flask overhand in the direction of the Land Cruiser. It sailed a dozen yards before coming down nearly dead center on the span. There was a series of metallic clangs as it tumbled end over end. The chain on the cap rattled noisily against the neck as it skittered and bled off speed, finally coming to rest on the solid yellow center lines, just a few feet from the SUV.

"Bruce Jenner, eat your heart out," he crowed under his breath.

Hunter wasn't fooled by the diversion. He continued to march in place and leer at Duncan. The pair to Hunter's left craned around, trying to see what might be attached to the foreign sound. The *Charred Man Group* was a different story. To a man— or woman, there was no real way to tell—the hairless and naked gang bought the ruse hook, line, and sinker. They nearly broke their necks twisting around to triangulate the sound. One lost its balance and went sprawling to the road. Another that had been close to the Toyota did an immediate about-face, running into the rig and bending its breakaway mirror all the way forward.

"Might as well just stop the undead games and gimme the gold medal right now," quipped Duncan.

Hunter hissed at that.

Duncan wanted to go to his stomach and lower himself to the ground, but there were too many upthrust branches in his way. So he bounced on the balls of his feet once, said "Eff it," and pushed off the tree. Though the drop was five feet at best, his stomach rocketed toward his throat. He landed on the bridge with his boots a shoulder width apart and a combination of forward momentum and old age conspiring against him.

The ground rushed at Duncan's face. As his knees reeled in the shock from the sudden deceleration, he pitched forward and slapped both palms against the road. A beat later, eyes widening, he learned he still possessed the upper body strength to keep him from face planting and losing his front teeth. However, there was nothing to stop the rifle slung on his back from completing its downward trajectory.

Take that, Mary Lou Retton was what Duncan was thinking when the M4 cracked him behind the ear and sent his Stetson flying.

Palms abraded, wrists aching, and a new throbbing behind his right ear, he policed up his hat and rose up beside the undead hunter.

At Duncan's back, the metallic sounds returned. He didn't need to look to know the dead had found the flask with their feet and an impromptu game of kick the can was starting up.

"What's your story?" he said to Hunter, his face parked dangerously close to the rotter's face. "Got anything you want to share with me?" He drew his fixed blade from the scabbard on his hip. All the while the Z squirmed and craned and snapped at the air by his face. "Because if you do have something I want," he added, "consider us Even Steven for what I'm about to do for you."

There was a wet squelch when Duncan speared the forgiving spot at the base of its skull with the tip of his double-edged blade. Crunching of bone followed as he forced the blade upward and commenced twisting his wrist back and forth. After a little death-shudder, the thing Duncan had taken to calling Hunter fell limp against the branches supporting him.

Blade still in hand, Duncan stalked over to the other two pinned rotters and dispatched them in the same efficient manner. He searched the female rotter's pockets first, finding only squares of gauze and a crushed pack of menthol-flavored cigarettes, the latter of which went into his pocket.

Strike one.

Rifling through the other rotter's pockets produced a roll of cash secured with a thick rubber band as well as a single, shiny, gold Krugerrand coin. He dropped both items to the road. They were of no use to him and likely wouldn't be valuable to anyone until long after he was feeding the worms.

Strike two.

Moving on to Hunter, Duncan looked sidelong at the crispy critters still chasing the flask from curb to curb on the bridge. Deeming them to be no immediate threat, he turned back to see what was behind door number three.

"Whatcha' holding, Hunter? You have got to be hiding something good in one of those deep pockets of yours."

Kicking the rotter's legs apart like some kind of traffic stop gone wrong, Duncan drove his hand into the first of the Carhartt's many pockets. In the left pocket, clipped to the hem, he found a knife. Just the handle, actually. It was roughly six inches long with a single ridged button near the hilt. No stranger to out-the-front blades, Duncan knew a press of the button would release a double-edged blade from a horizontal slit at the front end of the knurled handle.

"Nice little Benchmade pig sticker you got here," Duncan said as he thumbed the button, causing the blade to deploy out the front of the handle and lock into place with a satisfying *snik*. A second press of the button made the blade snap back into the handle with an audible *click*. "This, my boy, is a step in the right direction. But definitely *not* cigar worthy. I'm beginning to think I may have overpaid on the front end of this transaction. So ... let's see how she performs in a real-world application." He thumbed the button to deploy the blade, stuck the lethal end against Hunter's pasty white temple, and pushed hard. He felt a little resistance at first as the honed tip pierced the thin veneer of bone behind the jaw. The rest was smooth sailing as the blade plunged deeper and found brain tissue.

Not bad, he thought, pulling the blade free. *But I'll stick with my full-tang fixed-blade. Less room for error, thank you very much.*

He tossed the blade into the woods and went to work on the man's other pockets, finding only a half-eaten Twinkie, a balled-up rag soiled with a dried green substance, and a handful of 10 millimeter bullets.

Delving into the coat pockets produced a ring full of keys, a Glock magazine loaded with fifteen 10mm rounds, and a photo of the man with a woman and a grade-school-aged boy. Obviously more prosperous times, as the man in the picture had been carrying some thirty pounds more than he was at the end.

The absence of fast-food drive-thrus when coupled with all the running from the ravenous dead had that kind of an effect on those once used to a sedentary lifestyle. *The Apocalypse Diet.* He'd seen stranger shit hawked on late night infomercials and was certain that if a viewing audience still existed, some asshole would have already copyrighted the name and pitched their product on Shark Tank.

Oh the possibilities, he thought, slipping his hand into the final unsearched jacket pocket. *A combination treadmill and videogame app for your Apple tablet. Cardio is your friend,* the actor on TV would be saying. *Flee the dead in the safety of your own home* he would implore in front of a post-apocalyptic backdrop complete with actors made up as disheveled first turns.

Duncan's whole crazy train-of-thought hit a brick wall as his fingers brushed something smooth and cylindrical tucked deep down in the jacket's inside pocket.

"What do we have here?" His fingers moved over a tapered neck. He felt raised ribs on some kind of cap. When he introduced the item to the light of day and spied the black label and two fingers of straw-colored Canadian whisky at the bottom of the pint bottle, he bellowed, "Who in the hell drinks this *shit* when the world's dying?"

The soccer match on the bridge stopped abruptly and the six zombies turned toward the roadblock in unison. A tick later the raspy hissing was back and six gaunt-faced stares were pointed in Duncan's general direction.

Having inadvertently gained the unwanted attention of the dead, he removed the cap and drew the bottle toward his face. Took a deep breath. As expected, the liquor had a medicinal nose to it.

The rotters were now moving his way. They would take a few steps left and stop to listen. After a second or so they would alter course and take a few more stilted steps and stop to listen.

The span's cement roadway was painted with a colorful mix of blood and bodily fluids. Black smudges marred the far end where the forgotten flask sat. Once shiny and smooth, its surface was now dull and pitted and scuffed.

With a *what the hell* shrug, Duncan leaned back and drained the bottle into his open mouth.

Face screwed up, he leaned forward and planted his hands on his knees. "That is *not* Jack Daniels." In fact, he equated the experience to swallowing a jar full of sewing needles. In his book, imbibing Canadian whisky had always been one notch north of drinking Sterno strained through a heel of bread.

But as the old saying goes: Beggars can't be choosers. So he upended the bottle one final time before throwing it overhand at the approaching rotters.

The bottle bounced off a creature's shoulder, sailed a few more feet, then hit the road, where it shattered into a dozen pieces.

Further confused, the undead troop stopped in place, performed clumsy pirouettes, then traipsed back toward the unattended flask.

With a familiar warmth brought by the belt of whisky reaching his extremities, Duncan made his way to the Land Cruiser, keeping a full lane between him and the blind procession filing away from him.

Reaching into the rear wheel well, he found the fob atop the tire where it was supposed to be. Hinging up, he regarded the dead. They were now a dozen feet away and still unaware of his presence. Hoping to keep it that way, he tiptoed around back of the rig and tested the driver's side door. Finding it locked, he used the key to gain entry, then slid behind the wheel.

First things first. He punched open the glove box and found it empty. Though he remembered pouring out the full bottle of Jack last time he was in this very seat, the compulsion to check and see if it had somehow miraculously returned proved irresistible.

He banged a palm on the steering wheel. "What were you thinking, Old Man? The Jack Daniels fairy stopped by to replenish your supply?"

Wearing a sheepish expression, he crossed his fingers and punched the Start button.

Success.

A wave of elation washed over him as the V8 turned over and commenced a high idle as it warmed up. Filled with hope, he dropped the Toyota into gear and cut a high speed U-turn across the bridge, throwing a pair of the burned zombies against the guardrail in the process.

Ignoring the fate of the dead things, he sped a dozen yards down 39 and ground the SUV to a halt. Reluctant to learn the answer to the question nagging him since finding Glenda had gone outside the wire, he studied the ground-hugging bushes beyond the shoulder. Seeing nothing secreted in the bushes here, he released the brake and let the engine pull the Toyota along the westbound lane. A couple of yards further down the road, a few feet from the shoulder on the right, he detected a glint of light off of chrome. Slowing and pulling over to the right, he spotted the outline of an upthrust rubber handgrip.

The visual confirmation that Glenda's bicycle was still where she had discarded it weeks ago did two things. First it started his heart beating so hard he feared it would burst through his ribcage. Then, as what the bike's presence here represented fully took root in his mind, he craved a belt of Jack Daniels more than he ever thought possible.

Chapter 8

Cade was snugging the parts of the disassembled sniper rifle into their respective foam slots in the Pelican case when he heard Raven call out for him. He was sliding the closed hard case into the bed when she said *Dad* for the second time. He was lifting the tailgate and opening his mouth to answer when he heard her call for him for the third time in the span of roughly ten seconds. Only this time her tone got his undivided attention. Stress was evident and the pitch of her voice rose an octave or two as she begged him to get inside the truck.

"On my way, sweetie."

He threw the tailgate closed and turned and looked east down 39.

What Cade saw momentarily stole his breath. Where he'd expected to see the elk still alive and maybe dragging itself toward the underbrush in a last ditch effort to flee, he instead saw only its antlers rising up from the road. And they were moving. Long exaggerated sweeps back and forth. But not from any kind of resurrection thanks to an incredible will to survive or last-gasp burst of adrenaline. The antlers were moving thanks to the pair of Zs hard at work rending bloody, pot-roast-sized hunks of flesh from its neck. Glistening meat jiggled in one Z's grasp as it shoved the morsel into its mouth whole.

Brush flanking the road on the right parted and more Zs streamed from the lower mine access road. In seconds, the rest of the animal was under assault by probing fingers and gnashing teeth. By the time Cade clambered into the truck and was met by Raven's wide-eyed stare, her kill was mostly hidden from view by the growing scrum of feeding dead.

Cade saw Raven had the M4 lying across her lap. The knuckles on the hand holding the foregrip had gone white. The other encircling the grip was in constant motion, her slim fingers slowly kneading the textured polymer. Stare locked on the gory scene unfolding a few hundred feet off her right shoulder, she whispered, "I haven't seen that many in one place since the first day."

Though a sliver of doubt was worming its way deeper into Cade's mind as he watched the dead continue to pour onto the road, he said, "It's manageable."

"We better go back and tell the others."

"We deal with these first."

"We can't shoot them all," she said. "There must be a hundred or more. And they just keep coming."

The monsters just arriving to the buffet were literally swimming over each other to get a taste of the thousand-pound beast.

Cade looked sidelong at Raven. "They're not on to us yet," he said. "What will happen when I start the engine?"

"They'll realize we're here and start coming our way."

"Exactly. And follow us west and keep hunting us until they reach Daymon's roadblock." He paused for a beat and watched as a dozen or more Zs emerged from the quarry road, the ones on the wings of the surge bending back grabby branches. "These Zs were chasing the herd," he went on. "And that's the reason they were spooked. Also why the alpha didn't seem to care about us before you killed him."

"Lesser of two evils."

"Correct," Cade answered. "I have a bad feeling there's a lot more Zs where these came from."

"I'll call the others." She reached for the radio.

Cade put his hand on hers. "Don't worry," he said. "I have a plan."

"There's too many."

He said, "Take a couple of deep breaths."

She did.

He reached over and punched the button on the glove box.

"Can't you call Lev and have him bring the Humvee with the big machine gun? That should even the odds. Am I right?"

Motioning toward the glove box, he said. "Should be a pair of golf-ball-looking things in there."

Raven's head swiveled right. Gaze fixated solely on the blood-streaked faces rising up from her kill, she reached blindly inside the glove box.

Cade said, "They're bright orange. Real hard to miss … so long as you're actually *using* your eyes."

Reluctantly, Raven peered inside the glove box. "Got one," she said, holding it at eye level in the cab.

"Look for a small panel. Pop it open and you'll see a button. *Do not* push it yet."

"What is this thing and why are you having me mess with it?" She drew in a deep breath and exhaled.

"Good job," he said. "Calmer heads prevail. Don't forget that."

"But I don't know what I'm doing with this—"

"It's called a *Screamer*. It's a diversionary device. And it works as advertised."

Raven took her eyes from the Screamer and looked over her shoulder. Seeing the dead now crowding the road across both lanes and totally shielding the fallen elk from view caused her to gasp. She asked, "Is that considered a mega-horde?"

"Negative," he said. "It takes tens of thousands of dead to be considered mega. This is just a large herd."

"You're having me do this because my fingers are smaller," she stated.

Cade lifted off the seat, craned around, and opened the slider inset into the rear window.

"Am I right?"

"Affirmative." He started the Ford and threw the transmission into gear.

At once a first turn rose up. Both hands clutched an end of a thick length of intestine trapped between its steadily grinding teeth. In a way it reminded Cade of a bovine in a field blissfully working a mouthful of cud.

Goosing the big V10 made several dozen more faces turn in unison. A beat later several dozen sets of dead eyes were locked on the idling truck.

"Got their undivided attention," Cade said. "Push the button and hold it down." He cut the wheel hard right and matted the pedal. Tires chirped and the truck's rear end straightened out parallel to the centerline.

"Won't they stay in one place if I throw it out of the truck?"

Cade nodded. "When I tell you to, lob it through the back window so that it lands among the gear in the bed."

Both brows rising, she said, "Then they'll follow *us*. Mom did something like this. Only Carl was the bait."

"I remember the story. She was driving the bucket truck. Your uncle was suspended in the bucket just out of reach of the dead."

"Yep," she said, a frown forming from the memory.

The first of the Zs were barely a hundred feet off the Ford's grille. "Throw it now and hang on," he said. "The ride is about to get bumpy."

"Dad."

"What?"

The V10 was purring now as the speedometer needle passed thirty.

"I dropped the Screamer in the back seat."

"Unbuckle and get it. It must be in the bed if you ever want to hear Lady Ga Ga again."

I'm over her, thought Raven even as she was clicking out and monkeying over the seatback.

"Five seconds to get it into the bed," Cade said through gritted teeth. *Three until impact*, is what he kept to himself. No sense adding undue pressure on his daughter.

"Got it," she crowed.

Flicking his eyes to the rearview, Cade saw the back of her hand as she lobbed the Screamer through the window. He didn't see her close the slider because he was already looking forward and bracing for the impending collision. "Stay down," is all he had time to blurt before the front row of Zs folded under the F-650's steel bumper like sawgrass in a hurricane.

There was a series of thuds as the truck reared up and the narrow strip of sky peeking between the treetops momentarily filled up the windshield. The multi-ton truck leveled out almost immediately. Then there was a grating noise of something raking the undercarriage as it jounced over the sea of organic matter.

What was that sound? Cade asked himself. Zs having their bones snapped by the weight of the truck? Were they raking the undercarriage with their fingernails as the rig passed over them? Or was he hearing an impressive rack of antlers splintering and shearing off after losing a split-second encounter with the Ford's frame?

Cade hadn't a clue either way. However, knowing that brake lines and electrical wires used the frame as a conduit, he truly hoped for any explanation save for the latter.

Without warning, the Screamer in the load-bed came alive, its life-like female wail drowning out everything as the truck settled into the clutch of dead.

"Almost through," Cade bellowed. On both his left and right, pale palms slapping the window glass registered in his side vision like explosions of old time flashbulbs. Along with the sharp reports from the multiple impacts rattling the windows in their channels, the dry rasps of first turns and hollow moans of the recently changed rose all around them. Then there was the noxious stink of death and decay. It was super concentrated and infiltrating through the heater vents.

Cade breathed through his mouth as the bumper met the dead waist-high, pummeling and casting them aside like so many mannequins. Then a buzzer sounded and his eyes were drawn to an icon flashing yellow on the dashboard. Traction control warning? If so, a little late, he mused as the massive off-road tires spun and the wet pops of skulls imploding rose above the din to give the Screamer a run for its money.

"I hate that sound," Raven called from the back seat.

"You'll *never* get used to it," Cade answered as the truck bucked and shimmied and came down off the drift of mangled corpses, the tires chirping as they made contact with the road. With a flick of the wrist, Cade jinked the truck left to avoid a pair of recent turns. Working to keep the back end from breaking free, he hauled the steering wheel in the other direction, only to narrowly avoid plowing into a knot of dead twenty strong just trooping out of the woods.

"I may have spoken too soon about the number of Zs we're dealing with," Cade admitted. "The elk have gathered quite a following."

Now in the clear of the main body, Cade motored forward another fifty yards or so, then stopped with the tires straddling the dashed yellow line.

Voice muffled, Raven asked, "Why are you stopping?"

"We don't want to get too far ahead of them. As long as they can see us, and the Screamer is doing its thing, they'll follow us lockstep to wherever we want to take them. To the ends of the Earth if need be."

Without warning the Screamer went silent.

With the horde downwind and the engine idling, the silence inside the cab was deafening.

Raven slowly turned to face her dad. "What happened?" she asked, terror creeping into her voice.

"The scream track plays for the better part of a minute, then has to reset," Cade said. "Don't worry. It'll start back up in a few seconds." He regarded his wing mirror. Saw the dead trudging in their direction. At the front of the rotten procession were the fresh turns he had nearly mowed down.

"Do you plan on letting them surround us before moving on?"

Still peering into the mirror, he shook his head and said, "No." Swinging his gaze to Raven, he added, "As soon as the Screamer fires off again, I'll get us back into Pied Piper mode." The idea of the V10 powering the truck for the duration of their

66

slow roll to Woodruff got him thinking about gasoline consumption. And though he knew the large volume tank was near half full when they left the Eden compound, he still was compelled to consult the gauge cluster, where he learned his guestimate of half a tank was spot on. There was also a yellow icon different than the one that had lit up before. It resembled a half full tire and glowed yellow.

As Cade was about to ask Raven to go back into the glove box and haul out the owner's manual—just as the encounter with the undead herd had begun—she said "Dad" to get his attention. Then, pointing at her ear, she added, "Do you hear that hissing? I think a tire is going flat."

Before Cade could answer, the Screamer went live again, belting out its super realistic recording of some anonymous woman suffering a horrific death. Coming to realize what the idiot light in the instrument cluster was telling him, he said, "I'll take your word for it, sweetie," and let his foot off the brake.

Chapter 9

When Duncan first spotted what he guessed to be the tail end of the mini-herd of rotters from the bridge, he was adding items necessary to continue his search for Glenda to the growing list in his head. With the Land Cruiser's gas needle hovering just above the 1/4 mark, fuel for the thirsty rig was on the verge of knocking Jack Daniels from the top spot.

A half-mile west of Daymon's roadblock and coming up on a right-hand curve, he had detected movement in the shadow of a distant roadside picket of trees. Still a couple of hundred feet from the curve, he lifted his foot off the pedal and let the SUV slow on its own. As the distance to the shadows spilling across the two-lane halved, the object in motion took shape. Definitely a bipedal form, its outline still a little fuzzy. However, judging by its stilted movement, this was not Glenda.

Figuring this lone rotter was the rear of the troop he hoped by now was stretched thin along 39, Duncan steered straight for it.

The exhaust note and hiss of tires on blacktop made the rotter stop in place. Like an owl scanning for prey, it panned its head slowly to the right. It had just acquired the Land Cruiser visually and its mouth hung open as Duncan ground the Toyota to a halt broadside to it. As the noise of the window powering down broke the still, the undead female emitted a weak rasp. Pale arms lifted horizontal to the road as the rotter doddered a half-circle across the eastbound lane and set a course for the idling vehicle.

Duncan eyed the emaciated corpse from a dozen feet.

No backpack. No pockets. Only a filthy tattered sundress clinging to a mess of bones wrapped in taut skin crisscrossed with a road map's worth of lacerations, most old and home to fly larva, some new and weeping brackish, black blood.

He stared into its dead eyes as it drew near. They were mostly black with flecks of brown around the edges. The whites were jaundiced and shot through with capillaries gone an angry red.

Strands of raven black hair home to twigs and leaves and who knows what else hung limply on bare shoulders.

Duncan inhaled sharply. He said, "Damn, young lady, you look a little like Brooklyn Grayson on her last good night on Earth." He felt a lump form in his throat. Probably the booze weakening the decades-old wall keeping his emotions at bay. What he really needed was something to numb the feelings. And he sure wasn't going to find it here.

Out came the knife.

He pulsed the window two-thirds of the way up, leaving an opening just wide enough for Brook's doppelganger to worm that once beautiful mug inside. When the thing reached the Toyota, it grabbed for his face with both hands.

Drawing away from the opening, Duncan held the dagger horizontally and face-high to him. He couldn't help but notice his hand shaking. He watched the tip of the blade trace little arcs in space on its own accord.

It wasn't a byproduct of fear. That much was clear. He hadn't experienced the adrenaline dump associated with the classic fight-or-flight impulses that usually sent him on an instant high, only to come crashing down once the action had waned.

The Brook lookalike hooked its twisted fingers over the window's edge, went up on its tiptoes, and mashed its face chin-to-brow into the opening.

"You want to be one of the *grateful dead?*"

Amidst the clacking of teeth against glass, the waxen-skinned woman hissed.

"You do, huh?" Duncan cackled. "It's not what you think it is. I'm not talking about that band out of Haight and Ashbury. No ma'am. No trains and no cocaine. It's all about quid-pro-quo. I help you, and you help me."

Another hiss. Louder and more pronounced.

Hands complete with filthy, chipped nails raked the air inches from Duncan's face. Then the creature's arms retreated and the pallid face was back and filling up his entire left-side vision.

Ignoring the change in scenery, Duncan glanced in the rearview mirror.

Clear.

"OK, missy—listen up." He cleared his throat.

Tracers erupted before Duncan's eyes, the Black Velvet hitting him hard now. Damn if this thing wasn't progressive in nature just as Glenda had warned. Reading about it in the blue book wasn't enough. He'd asked her one time when they were sitting outside by the RV with a fire warming their faces and the night air cold at their backs. Without hesitating she broke it down for him. *Picture your addiction to alcohol as a monster out in the clearing,* she had said, a touch of manufactured menace in her voice. *It's over there in the dark on the dirt airstrip doing pushups. It's getting stronger and waiting for you to fall off the wagon.*

And was it ever waiting for Duncan that night when Cade stepped from the RV, jaw set firm, eyes moist. Duncan had seen that expression more times than he could count since this zombie apocalypse started. And he was not immune. He'd lost his share of loved ones to Omega.

A flurry of movement snapped Duncan back to the present. Those pale hands were again batting the airspace before his face. One finger caught the Stetson's brim, knocking it off his head and onto the passenger seat.

"Hold your pants," he bellowed. "Can't a fella daydream?"

The fingers raked at his wispy gray hair as he straightened his glasses on his face.

In retaliation to the encroachment on his personal space, he motored the seatback to about sixty degrees, so he was just out of reach of those probing fingers.

"Where was I?" he went on. "Oh yeah, *grateful dead*. In many cultures' folklore, when a deceased person isn't given the proper burial they'd arranged with the undertaker, they get pretty ticked off. So ticked off that they wander the back roads looking for a traveler to make it right. So this traveler ... who just so happens to be *me* ... he buries this walking corpse, who, you guessed it, just so happens to be *you*. Now that the wandering dead woman gets her wish fulfilled and she's buried as arranged and finally resting in peace, she's grateful. Get it? *Grateful dead*. Not only is her spirit happy now, it's so effin happy, ecstatic actually, that it bestows benefits on the person who freed it. You following?"

As if the story had triggered something—perhaps a memory buried deep in the undead woman's brain—she canted her head a few degrees and went still for a beat.

Perfect opening.

Though his vision had gone a little blurry around the edges, the knife strike was perfect. It went straight into the eye socket at an upward angle, scrambling brain tissue and releasing a drizzle of yellow pus to sluice over the destroyed eyeball. A perfect "one timer" was what Cade would have called it. And that's exactly how the young Delta operator had described the kill stroke that released Brook's spirit from the infected shell banging around inside the RV that fateful night.

∗∗∗

Duncan carried the corpse to the side of the road where the guardrail ended. She'd been taller than Brook by a few inches. He figured she was five-foot-six and 120 pounds when she was living. Beautiful, too. A dancer's body. He had to avert his eyes when the sundress tore at the sternum and her breasts spilled out.

Now the rotter was prostrate on the shoulder and lined up perfectly with the white fog line. Duncan was no ogre. He covered her up and tugged the hem of her dress down over her nether regions.

When he had initially scooped the body off the ground, it became evident to him how she came to be infected. Up and down both sides of her spine were deep vertical furrows made by fingernails. A two-handed blind-side attack. The bite that did her in was on her right shoulder blade. Deep and ridged around the edges like a crater on the moon, the bite had erased most of the fancy angel tattooed in black across her right shoulder blade.

He found a suitable spot to bury her between clumps of ferns beyond the shallow ditch and started digging. The soft soil yielded readily to the tire iron taken from the Toyota.

"Don't think I'm crazy enough to believe that story I told you," he said, spearing into the dirt with the tool's sharp end. "I just needed someone who would listen to me." He regarded her bare feet, then walked his eyes to her face and met her dead, one-eyed gaze. "Want to know a secret? I'm a closet Grateful Dead fan. Where I grew up, admitting that would get your ass kicked. Texas was no place for a beatnik. Hell, I joined the Army to prove to my father I wasn't one of them. Still, I saw them a few times when I was home on leave. Drove to Frisco one time ..."

A bird alit in a nearby tree and promptly began pounding on the trunk. Rapid-fire, hollow reports that echoed across the road.

"You know the Dobson cover they did in 77 ... Morning Dew?" He paused but kept digging. "That was about the end of the world. The apocalypse. But not due to a little virus like the one that killed you. Killed Brook. And Oliver. And my best friend, Charlie Hammond. Nope, sister, this was about the threat of the day: global thermonuclear war. And it was going to toast us all. Had teachers making kids cower under desks. As if that would have saved them from fryin'."

Back aching, Duncan rose and surveyed his work. Not bad. The grave was a foot deep and five long. He'd have to lay her on her side, but it'd do. Plus, he'd burned some time and got to take a guilt trip down memory lane.

He rolled the corpse into the grave. Began kicking the dirt in with it, starting at the foot and working his way up to her partially upturned face.

"Why am I still here and they're not?"

He stared the corpse in the face.

"Want to know a secret about Cade? It's something he told me after he put Brook down. A regret he's carrying even as I yammer at you."

A blackbird cawed somewhere in the forest.

Duncan brushed the dirt off his pants at the knees. He clapped his hands together and stomped his boots on the ditch's gravel edge.

Peering down at her face, he said, "You probably wouldn't understand if I told you," and nudged the remaining dirt in with his toe, closing her off from her past life forever.

Chapter 10

Raven was climbing from the backseat to the front when Cade put a hand on her shoulder. "Wait," he said, talking loud to be heard over the reactivated Screamer. "We've got a punctured tire. No doubt about it."

The angle the F-650's hood was canted in relation to the horizon showing between the distant trees was all the proof he needed. Suggesting the left rear tire was losing air, in the span of a few seconds the corner of the expansive hood on Raven's side had risen ever so slightly.

Still straddling the seatback, she said, "We have to change it then." She craned to make eye contact. "Don't we?"

"We don't have enough separation from the Zs to do that."

"Drive then. We can stop and fix it somewhere down the road."

"It's not that simple. For one, this rig is so big that driving just a little ways on a flat might throw the tire from the rim. That happens … the tire could get stuck in the wheel well. Then we're really up a creek."

Raven gave him a funny look at the reference. She said, "Why do you have me balancing here on the back of the seat?"

"Get back there and look under the seat. There should be a couple of cans about the size spray paint comes in. They have a clear plastic hose attached to a spray nozzle."

Raven slithered off the seatback and landed on the carpeted floorboard on all fours. A beat later she said, "I can't see anything but speakers under here."

"Do it by feel, then."

While Cade issued instructions, his eyes roamed the mirrors. In the right-side wing mirror things looked under control. So far it was just the handful of new turns overtaking the main body of Zs and fanning out across the two-lane that had him concerned. They looked to be fifty yards back. But when taking into account the *Objects Are Closer Than They Appear* warning etched into the mirror, he cut his initial estimate by half.

"Hurry," he said, palm upturned, fingers waggling. "We've got a minute, tops."

Popping up from the back like a prairie dog, she blurted, "Got 'em!"

He took the cans from her and elbowed his door open. On the way out, he issued orders he expected her to follow to the letter.

Boots hitting the ground, he slammed the door closed. As he ripped the plastic shrink wrap from the first can of FIX-A-FLAT, he detected the satisfying thunk of Raven throwing the door locks.

Weeks ago, while on a foray outside Schriever Air Force Base in Colorado Springs, he had happened upon a boarded-up hardware store in a tiny town named Yoder. It was the same place the Zs had tested him by worming underneath the static F-650.

After doing a little breaking and entering and finding the owner dead from a self-inflicted gunshot wound, Cade had gone ahead and filled up a garbage sack with all of the automotive products on hand. The FIX-A-FLATs were a part of that haul and, until now, had remained out of sight and mind.

Giving the first can a vigorous shaking, Cade inspected the rear tire. Though there was a fair amount of blood and guts coating the wide black sidewall, he didn't see a puncture or tear in the rubber. Using his teeth to remove the cap, he eyed the tire, looking for a shard of bone or antler protruding from the deep-channel tread. Seeing nothing and unable to hear air escaping over the Screamer wailing in the bed above his head, he spun the cap off the valve stem and threaded the hose coupling onto the tire valve. Holding the can upright, he pressed the button. Nothing. The expected rush of air under extreme pressure didn't come immediately. However, after a half-beat he felt some kind of movement in the can and saw the clear tube go white.

Two or three seconds after pressing and holding the button down, Cade saw no movement in the tire itself, while out of the corner of his eye, movement was all he saw.

The dead were coming for them en masse. They were spread across the road, guardrail to guardrail—twenty abreast, Cade guessed. Though the elk was but an appetizer for this crowd, the exposure to fresh meat and hot blood had spurred them on.

The F-650's horn sounded. And though it was an item likely ripped from a semi truck—supersized like everything else on the dead NBA baller's ride—the foghorn-like blare was no match for the Screamer.

As Cade readied another FIX-A-FLAT, the horn sounded a second time. Then a third. And, finally, a fourth. All closely spaced. Manic in nature. Raven's anxiety delivered in spades without a word shared between daughter and father.

The ritual was the same for Cade: Shake the can vigorously, remove the cap, unwind the clear hose.

The first can was still sputtering a bit when he swapped it out for the fresh can.

The Screamer went silent. In its place was a rising din of moans and hisses. Even if the tire was still leaking, there was no way for Cade to tell.

Holding the button atop the FIX-A-FLAT down with the thumb on his left hand, Cade slipped the Glock 17 from its drop-thigh holster. Brandishing the pistol one-handed, he lined up the iron sights on the nearest of the fresh turns and started firing rounds head-high into their midst.

Swinging his arm left-to-right with no discernable pause between shots rendered Cade's initial volley far from accurate. Of the eight Zs he'd engaged across roughly twenty feet of open road, only three went down as a result of accurate head shots. Of the other five, one had taken a round in the chin, another had suffered a through-and-through to the neck, and three caught bullets to the torso. With the Screamer momentarily shut down, sans the suppressor, the three-second fusillade from the Glock had drowned out everything.

As the sharp cracks dissipated and a low ringing started between Cade's ears, seemingly all at once, a bunch of random things happened.

The tube on the FIX-A-FLAT went opaque as the last of the liquid patch left the can.

The F-650's V10 revved high up into the power band, the resulting rush of hot exhaust coming from the nearby pipes warming Cade's face and neck as he rose from the road. Music to his ringing ears, he heard the clunk telling him Raven had dropped the transmission into gear. Finally, with the dead barely a dozen feet away, he hooked an arm and a leg over the top edge of the bed and hammered the Glock against the side of the truck.

Message received.

The truck lurched and shimmied but made no forward progress.

Foot off the brake, Raven.

No sooner had Cade thought it, than the ground began moving in his side vision. He felt the tire brushing his knee and winced at the thought of what was being deposited there, let alone what might happen if his leg somehow got sucked into the wheel well.

Lowering his head and craning around afforded Cade an idea of just how close he'd come to being Z chow. Several of the fresh turns he'd only winged or hit center of mass had avoided tripping over their headshot compatriots, traversed the remaining ten feet under cover of the Screamer, and were already at the spot in the road where he'd been kneeling and trying his best to get the task done without repeatedly checking his six.

As the Ford picked up speed and the ride smoothed out, he watched a male rotter inadvertently kick one of the spent aerosol cans, sending it spinning and bouncing toward the shoulder with the six-inch length of hose whipping the air like a bronco rider's free arm.

After counting to ten in his head with the road scrolling by a few feet from his left cheek, Cade banged on the truck again. Only this time it was two short blows that triggered a preordained action.

The recent turns were maybe a hundred yards back when the Ford came to a stop on the centerline at the apex of a sweeping left-hand turn.

Cade unhooked his leg and went to his knees next to the truck. Feeling a bit nauseous and suffering from vertigo brought on by the road rushing by his face, he bowed his head and continued holding onto the bed rail until the Screamer went silent.

The driver's window whirred down.

"You OK, Dad?"

Meeting her gaze in the wing mirror, Cade said, "I'll live."

"That was a close call," she said. "But they're still coming."

"Good," he said, "That's the plan."

Raven put the transmission into Park. "Get in," she said. "I'll climb over the console."

Cade looked over a shoulder. Determining he had a little window before the dead again reached the truck, he raised an index finger to Raven—universal semaphore for *wait one minute*.

He met Raven's gaze in the mirror, mouthed "It'll be OK," then dropped from the truck, landing cat-like on hands and knees. Still a bit woozy, he rolled over onto his back and drew a deep breath. Senses slowly returning to normal, he grabbed a part of the frame rail near the rear axle that was not thoroughly coated with human detritus and wriggled underneath the lifted 4x4.

The first thing that caught Cade's eye, *was* an eye. And it was huge. Marty Feldman, huge. It was looking down on him from the inner wheel well where some kind of vein or nerve attached to it had become entangled in a component of the truck's long-travel suspension.

Ignoring the accusatory glare of what was clearly one of the dead elk's eyeballs, he gave the tire a more thorough inspection. Thankfully the inner sidewall was not punctured. And in the ten seconds between going to the road and entering into the unexpected staring contest, he hadn't heard any hissing noises save for those coming from the first turns off his left shoulder.

Still not one hundred per cent convinced the puncture sealer was working as advertised, he reached into a pocket and came out with a tactical light. Lying prostrate with two-thirds of his body hanging out on 39 as the Screamer reactivated was unnerving to say the least. Throw in the steadily advancing pack of dead several hundred strong and you had the makings of one hell of a Depends commercial.

Though every fiber in Cade's body was screaming for him to get up and climb into the safety of the truck, he had to be sure. So he thumbed the tactical light on and walked its beam along the tire's top edge. Seeing a length of something slender protruding from the tire, he stowed the flashlight, then snaked both hands into the cramped wheel well.

Acting against instinct, he gripped between thumb and forefinger what he guessed to be a spike broken off the elk's magnificent antlers and slowly worked it loose. He grimaced when the shard of yellowed antler came loose. A cold ball formed in his stomach when he heard the unmistakable sound of air rushing from the hole left behind.

He shimmied out from under the truck with a few precious feet of separation between him and the deceptively fast fresh turns. Knowing Raven was implementing the part of his lengthy orders this scenario warranted, he stayed low and hustled to the driver's door.

Suppressed gunfire sounded from above Cade's head as he hauled the door open. Spent brass arced from above as he planted a boot on the running board and took a firm hold of the A-pillar grab bar.

One component of Cade's hastily concocted plan he hadn't accounted for was how he found the seat when he clambered aboard. To accommodate Raven's small stature, it was now adjusted all the way forward—likely to the furthest extent of its travel. Then there was the power adjustable pedals. They were at the top of their travel—the exact opposite of how the NBA player would have had them set. And Raven was standing in the cab with her head and shoulders through the open moonroof, boot-clad feet straddling the shifter.

As Cade wriggled behind the steering wheel, he also found the horn-ring-mounted airbag nearly touching his chest.

With no time to make all of the necessary ergonomic adjustments, he ran the seat back a bit, dropped the transmission into gear, and bellowed, "Cease fire," as he matted the gas pedal.

The gunshots ended at once, leaving the Screamer and V10 competing with the moans and rasps pushing ahead of the dangerously close mini-horde.

Like she'd had her legs swept from under her, Raven crashed into the cab all knees and elbows. Held two-handed and vertical to her body, the rifle came through the moonroof after.

Cade steered hard left to make the corner. In response, the rear end broke free and drifted toward the right-side shoulder.

Losing her balance, Raven keeled over to the left, nearly ending up on her dad's lap.

Steering counter to the drift, Cade took one hand off the wheel and braced his daughter before she was added to everything else crowding in on him. "Safety on?" he asked as he gently guided her back to her own seat.

"Mom taught me well, remember?" As the Ford straightened out and dove into the nearby curve, she clicked her seatbelt home and regarded her dad. "What about leading them away from the compound? They're going to lose interest if we get too far."

"There's a method to my madness," he said. Then he went on to explain to her how the FIX-A-FLAT was supposed to work. How they had to let the liquid heat up a bit inside the tubeless tire so that it would coat the inside evenly.

She said, "Just like water, the goo in the can finds the path of least resistance, right?"

Cade said, "Precisely." He watched the speedometer needle creep past fifty, then maintained that speed through the short straightaway, through two opposing curves, then into another long straightaway, where he pushed the Ford to seventy before stabbing the brakes a couple of hundred feet short of the looming hairpin.

The Screamer had reactivated during the first straight and was bleating on somewhere in the bed behind them.

Finished swapping magazines, Raven trapped the rifle between her knees, and regarded her dad. "Do you think that worked?"

Cade glanced at the instrument cluster. Saw the tire pressure warning still illuminated. "Hope for the best—" he began.

"And prepare for the worst," she finished.

After getting the truck nosed around with a ragged three-point turn, Cade took it through the paces, getting their speed up to sixty miles per hour for a short stretch, then keeping it above forty until stopping again beyond the opposing curves with a football field's length of road between the truck and strung-out column of walking dead.

"Cover me," Raven said. "I'll get out and check the tire."

Cade had already found the controls for the pedals and was motoring them forward. He nodded. "Take your rifle. And be quick about it."

Raven said nothing. She was free of her belt and already out the door when the Screamer went silent. Three seconds later she was on her back under the right rear of the truck and peering into the gloomy recesses of the wheel well. She listened hard for a long three-count. Hearing nothing but a ticking noise coming from the exhaust pipe routed nearby, she shimmied out and rose up beside the truck.

"Good to go?" Cade called.

Meeting his gaze in the wing mirror, she said, "I think so. But I need to *go*."

Incredulous, he said, "It can't wait?"

The Screamer came alive again as she was shaking her head. "All those curves and then the sudden stops. I *really* gotta go."

He hooked a thumb at the nearby guardrail. Throwing the transmission into Park, he said, "Make it quick." He motored the steering wheel forward as he watched her exit the truck. Finished, he set the E-brake and nudged his door open.

Raven was already climbing over the guardrail by the time Cade reached the back of the truck. He kept her in his sight until she dropped her pants and squatted behind the wooden post supporting the long run of guardrail.

"*Daaad* ... a little privacy *pleeease*," she called, her voice nearly drowned out by the aural trifecta of the Screamer at his back, Ogden River flowing swiftly by barely a dozen feet below her position, and the steadily advancing mini-horde drawing way too close for comfort.

Keeping the blurry form of his squatting daughter in his side vision, he crossed his arms and bellowed, "Hurry it up!"

Chapter 11

Duncan wheeled the Land Cruiser around a blind corner and found himself braking hard and wrenching the steering wheel to the left to keep from plowing into a knot of dead things at least fifty strong.

"Gawd damn it," he bawled as he fought to keep control. A rumble rippled through the frame and rocks pinged off the undercarriage as both wheels on his side tore through the shoulder. A tick later a tremendous bang made his ears ring when the Toyota traded paint with the rust-stippled guardrail.

Equal reactions being what they are, the SUV rebounded off the sturdy barrier, bounced and shimmied as it rode back onto the state route, then juddered violently when a number of walking corpses were sent flying from a very violent impact with the front bumper.

Apparently, Duncan thought, as the jarring impact separated a young girl first turn from her tennis shoes, the time he'd spent spilling his guts to the Brook lookalike, killing her for the second and final time, then burying her in the shallow grave, had given the main group of rotters less of a head start than he'd anticipated. A lot less judging by the vehicular mayhem unfolding before his eyes. And though he hadn't been keeping close watch on the odometer—or much else, obviously—he guessed her grave was barely a mile behind him.

Contributing to the complacency brought on by the low-level buzz softening reality around the edges, during the short drive on the state route, he'd only encountered a handful of rotters. Some were first turns so road-ravaged they shouldn't have been ambulatory in the first place. A couple were burned and blinded just like the ones at the bridge. Then there were the members of the easily distracted crowd. He'd seen their kind before. Prone to standing in a yard and pawing at threadbare wash still pinned to sagging clotheslines. Or stopping to watch a fellow rotter thrashing away in a car and end up drawing an all-encompassing crowd of undead, three deep around the car. Duncan had seen one zombie in Portland standing and gawking at the colorful banners flapping above a used car lot on 82nd Avenue. Hours later, as he returned from a cross-town trip, the single staring corpse had been joined on the sidewalk in front of the lot by three more fresh turns.

The clutch of Zs in question—maybe five total—was stalled out in the shadow of a roadside fir. Heads tilted back, eyes locked on a shiny Mylar balloon trapped high in the upper boughs, they caught Duncan's attention a split-second before he saw the tail end of the herd.

Now, as a waifish first turn was sent cartwheeling over the guardrail and into the gloomy forest, Duncan was in the fight of his life to keep control of the SUV. A fight that was nearly stopped in the opening round when a recently turned male—balding, overweight, and middle-aged—was upended by the bumper, all two-hundred-some-odd pounds of him becoming a pasty blur as he left the road spinning head over heels.

The initial impact with the diminutive first turn left a permanent V in the hood's leading edge.

The portly recent turn crashing face-down atop the hood hammered a man-sized trough down its center.

Because Duncan was still a bit impaired, his reaction time suffered.

The late turn of the wheel and stab to the brake pedal only succeeded in sending the flabby recent turn sliding off the hood and to the road where it hit face first and crumpled like a worn-out accordion. Continuing to haul the steering wheel hand over hand took destroying the guardrail and dying in the ditch out of the equation. The ensuing fishtail, however, sent the Toyota's entire right side slamming into the shambling mass, starting a chain reaction that had a large swath of the column falling away diagonally from the point of impact.

Through the newly cracked windshield, Duncan saw a path opening up. He figured if the rotters continued to halt in place and perform clumsy pirouettes toward the barreling Toyota, he might just get through them all without further damaging the badly battered rig. The shot of adrenaline entering his system as a direct result of this wholly unexpected encounter helped him to focus on his next action. Which was halving his speed and putting the Land Cruiser into *Crawl* mode.

The engine growled and a whine came from the geared-down transmission as the SUV bulled through a sea of slapping hands and leering faces.

Thirty seconds after rounding the corner and being swallowed by the herd, the once white Land Cruiser came out the other end with little more than a few new dents on the panels and a pair of folded back side mirrors.

"Screw you, Murphy," hollered Duncan as the lead element of the herd made clumsy lunges for the rapidly retreating Land Cruiser.

A dozen miles east, on State Route 39, Raven had just completed her roadside business and was cinching her belt when the Screamer abruptly cut out. Instinctively, she regarded the pick-up on the road behind her. She saw her dad standing sentinel by its rear bumper, staring expectantly in her general direction.

After hollering, "I'm coming," across the road, she scooped up her rifle and threw one leg over the guardrail.

Rifle resting across her knees, she paused for a beat atop the wooden post. Off her left shoulder, at the bottom of the gravel and dirt embankment, was the Ogden River. Swollen from recent rains, its surface was frothed and white. To her fore was the mini-horde. It was maybe a hundred feet from her dad and steadily advancing. She threw a shiver at the sight of hundreds of seemingly unstoppable dead things wanting to rip out their throats and strip the meat from their bones. Cursing under her breath at the current state of affairs, she rose, swung her leg over the guardrail, and then stood staring down at the river for a beat. Unlike her, the river was free. It rushed by without a care in the world. It didn't have to constantly watch its back. It wasn't always losing the ones it loved. It had zero worries.

A wave of emotion washed over her. Tears welled in her eyes. Somewhere on the road at her back her dad was hollering for her to get to the truck.

Not wanting to show any weakness, especially now with her mom gone, she remained facing the river and wiped her eyes with a sleeve. Though her vision was a little blurry, she thought the bushes on the far riverbank were beginning to sway back and forth. As she continued to watch, what was at first just a subtle quaking became more pronounced, almost violent. The few leaves not yet claimed by autumn fell from the tremoring branches and fluttered into the racing water. If the trees towering over the river were matching the unexplained movement in the wall of bushes, she would have attributed it all to an earthquake.

Raven was still fixated on the bank of wildly swaying foliage thirty feet to her fore when gnarled hands and pale, welt-covered arms burst through the tangle. Before she could draw a breath and call out a warning, dozens of zombies were spilling through multiple breaks in the bushes. No match for the sheer numbers pouring forth, the grabbing, ground-level branches snapped off, sending loud, gunshot-like cracks rolling up the embankment ahead of the zombies stumbling onto the sandy riverbank.

The first to break through the brush wore no looks of shock or surprise as they were propelled forcefully across the narrow shore and into the turbid water by the crush from behind. They just plunged into the waist-high roil and disappeared from view, unwittingly creating a bridge to the other side for the creatures still pouring from the forest.

All Raven had wanted was a little moment of quiet. A two-second respite from the Screamer. From the calls of the dead. Just her and her thoughts as she caught a breath of fresh air and enjoyed the relaxing murmur of water smoothing river rock.

But the dead couldn't even afford her that one small luxury.

Turning away from the surreal sight below, she said, "Fuck!" at the top of her voice and stalked toward the truck.

Struck speechless, Cade looked a question in his daughter's direction.

Ignoring the expression on her dad's face, she hooked a thumb over her shoulder. "There's more of these *assholes* down there."

Choose your battles, thought Cade as he drew a deep breath. "How many?" he asked matter-of-factly.

Without warning, the Screamer cycled back on.

Raven shot a death glare at the truck bed. She said, "Too many of them to count."

"Dozens?"

She stabbed a thumb at the sky.

"Hundreds?"

"More," she said. She opened the passenger door, then paused and looked the length of the truck. After a moment spent studying the slow-moving procession spread out across both lanes and stretching all the way to the distant bend in the road, she pointed at the mini-horde and added, "About a third as many as that."

"Come here," Cade said, arms outstretched.

"I don't need a hug," she said, sweeping her arm left to right. "I want them *all* dead. Every last one. I'm so damn sick of them."

"Me too," he conceded. "But first I want you to get in back and find that noisy bastard."

Taken aback at her dad's use of a swear word, Raven grabbed the bed rail, pumped her knees once, then jumped and planted both boots on the gore-caked rear tire. She shot another cursory glance at the mini-horde, then hauled her slight frame over the side.

Raven was out of sight for a three-count before popping up in the load bed with the Screamer balanced on her upturned palm.

"Turn it off," Cade mouthed.

Wearing a look of confusion, she popped open the tiny panel on the device and pressed the button to silence it.

"Make up your mind, Dad." She tossed him the device. "You said we were going to lead them all away to the junction with that stupid thing."

Cade reached up and helped her down. "A plan never survives first contact with the enemy." He gestured toward the embankment. "Those newcomers change the dynamic. Exponentially."

"You're afraid there's more of them on the road ahead of us and we might be trapped, right?"

He nodded. "Not so much afraid," he said. "I just need to know. I figure we'll wheel ahead and not stop until we get to the 39/16 junction."

Raven cast a furtive glance at the dead. They had closed to within fifty feet of the F-650. To her right, a zombie was on its stomach and clawing at the road. Its hair and clothes were soaked and coated with sand from the river crossing and subsequent uphill scrabble. Its unblinking eyes never left her as it wormed its way underneath the guardrail.

Cade caught Raven's eye. He gestured at the truck.

"In. Now," he said forcefully.

He made a shooing motion as she passed by in front of him. He waited on the road long enough for her to climb in the already open door, then closed it behind her. As he curled around front of the truck, a trio of Zs crested the embankment. Just the tops of their heads, though. By the time he had made it to the relative safety of the F-650's elevated cab, he was able to see the entire stretch of river. It was teeming with Zs and dozens more were clawing their way up to the road.

A quick estimate of the number of walking dead in the merging columns told him there were enough Zs in one place to jeopardize the Eden compound and maybe even render the surrounding Ogden River Valley uninhabitable. Which meant, he thought glumly, that he not only had to lure them to the junction, but it was also imperative he get them trudging north toward Bear

Lake, where the open terrain would greatly improve the odds of tracking them, and, if Beeson could spare the manpower, eventually eradicating every last one of them.

Scooping up the Motorola, Cade called the compound to report this unfortunate new development.

Chapter 12

As 39 transitioned from a long straightaway into a blind right-hand hairpin, Duncan let his foot off the gas and tapped the brakes. Having learned the hard way a few miles back what kind of trouble a fella with a belly full of booze and a head in the clouds could come up against, he slowed the rig to walking speed and started into the turn as wide left as possible. Nearing the turn, both tires on Duncan's side were riding on the eastbound lane's fog line and he was craning hard to see as much of the unspooling stretch of two-lane as possible.

The approach to the corner was bracketed on both sides by towering old growth. The ever-present guardrail followed the contour of the road on both sides. Beyond the guardrails, the trunks of towering firs and surrounding underbrush were mostly hidden in shadow.

A perfect place to spring an ambush, crossed Duncan's mind as, through the detritus-sullied windshield, the vantage ahead was revealed to him in thin vertical slices.

Thankfully there wasn't a rotter in sight. Nor were there armed foreign soldiers on near-silent motorbikes waiting in ambush.

On the left the forest was rapidly giving way to grass-covered rolling hills cut through by the Ogden River. Here and there copses of trees broke up the monotony.

Duncan saw the landscape to his left for what it was: a perfect place to catch a deer or elk out in the open.

Dead ahead, dark clouds were parked over where he figured Huntsville ought to be. They rose up from the valley floor and seemed to be sucking all of the light from the surrounding landscape.

To the right was a berm of red dirt left behind when the road stretching away into the valley was cut into the soil. As Duncan spurred the Land Cruiser on by giving her a good dose of pedal, the long grass atop the uneven scar in the land seemed to undulate up and down in relation to the level asphalt keeping pace with it. When combined with the effects of the alcohol in his system, the sensation was so unnerving that he used his right hand as a blinder to block it all from view until the slight grade leveled out.

At the bottom of the runout was a flatbed truck with Arizona plates. Its wide, low-to-the-ground front end was facing Duncan. The glint from the sun at his back made seeing inside all but impossible. Both doors were bullet-riddled and standing open. The windows were shattered, the glass remaining in the channels splintered and falling inward. Whatever had happened here was *not* in the favor of the old flatbed Ford's occupants. That much was clear.

He slowed and scrutinized the road on both sides. Just long grass and barbed wire strung between gnarled wood posts for as far as he could see. Not the best place to spring some hate on folks passing through. The concealment component was there. Cover was not. Last he checked, blades of grass did nothing to stop effective return fire.

The closer Duncan got to the scene, the more he learned.

Roughly a hundred feet behind the truck, equidistant to the dashed yellow centerline, two long, narrow stretches of 39 glittered with what looked to be broken window glass. The debris fields were a yard wide, at best, and maybe a dozen feet in length.

This got him to thinking about the tactics the Viet Cong employed against soldiers on leave in Saigon. The city was overrun by rickshaws and mopeds. The former were a convenient and inexpensive way to get from bar to bar in the sprawling city. The latter were sometimes used in hit-and-run attacks on soldiers at open air cafes and markets and those riding in rickshaws. It was more common than reported back home. If Duncan had to put money on what happened here, he'd bet the house that the debris fields and stalled-out truck were direct results of a hit-and-run attack.

Sliding up next to the open driver's side door, he looked through the shot-out window and saw what had become of the occupants. A man had been driving. No way to discern his age. He was shirtless and sprawled across the blood-slickened floorboard. Bullet entry wounds were visible on his left side. Three or four little bloodless holes. A neat line stitched along his ribcage, from hip to armpit. The damage to the other side must have been catastrophic.

The man's pants were bunched down around his knees, with the pockets turned inside out. He died going *commando*—sans underwear—hence the positive gender identification.

"Bunch of shit," Duncan growled. "Assholes left you ass up with your twig and berries showing for all to see."

He let his gaze roam the cab. Saw that the passenger was dead as well. A boy. Maybe twelve. Slouched way down in his seat. No seatbelt. The single gaping exit wound in the temple facing Duncan was impossible to miss. Once blond hair was matted with blood and brain tissue. A big chunk of hair-covered skull was hinged back and resting on the top edge of the low seatback.

No mercy was shown these two. And they hadn't been dead long. Their skin had yet to take on a waxen appearance and there wasn't any apparent bruising due to blood pooling in the downward-facing parts of their corpses—the man's gut and ribcage, specifically.

Rolling forward a few feet allowed for a better look at the flatbed out back. A blue tarp hung off the rear edge, most of it pooled behind the far-side rear tire. Whatever the pair had been hauling was now gone. Most of it, anyway. There was a cooler, lid open and tipped on its side. Nothing in it. Piles of bedding, all of it earth-toned and looking to be of a high thread count, were pushed up against the cab. Duncan could see the plush comforters and sheets gracing the beds in the rooms of the ski resort above Eden. He guessed these two were on a father/son supply run and got caught with their pants down.

Duncan grimaced as he let his foot off the brake, allowing the Toyota to roll forward powered only by the idling engine. Though he hadn't given voice to that last thought, his unintentional choice of words were pretty damn callous.

A quick glance at the rearview showed open road, nothing moving on it.

Once the Toyota was even with the broken glass, Duncan parked between the twin fields and got out.

All it took was a quick walk down the centerline to find what he was looking for. A dozen feet down the road from the glass, in the eastbound lane, was a trail of spent brass. Ten casings in all. Every one of them stamped with the symbol of their Chicom manufacturer.

He turned around and faced the rear of the flatbed. Walking his gaze the length of the westbound lane and shoulder he spotted something throwing the sun. Closer inspection revealed a single identical shell casing that had been partially swallowed up by an unruly tangle of roadside grass. He was sure it was only one of dozens and if he tramped off through the grass he'd eventually find them all.

"Yep," he said as he turned a slow three-sixty in the road, "a couple of *dicks* on motorcycles did this to you. Question is, where are they now?"

Head on a swivel, he stalked back to the SUV, his thoughts divided between the dead, the living, and the sweet temptress bearing a man's first and last name. And damn if the latter wasn't winning the battle for his attention.

Chapter 13

Raising his clenched fist, Wilson stopped in his tracks and dropped to one knee dead center of the weed-choked logging road. Holding his M4 close to his chest, finger beside the trigger guard and suppressor pointing groundward, he slowly pivoted on the knee until he faced Taryn.

A few steps behind and a yard left of the redhead, Taryn froze upon seeing the silent signal, then crouched down in the knee-high grass.

Wilson beckoned her forward, one finger pressed to his lips.

Taryn duck walked to his position. She whispered, "You proposing to me?"

Wilson missed the meaning of her quip. He said, "I see something. A stack of rocks beside the road." He dipped his head for a beat. When he looked up, he added, "Looks like there's a motorcycle parked under a tree near the rocks."

She peered over his shoulder.

"That's how those Chinese soldiers were getting around prior to being bit and turning, right?"

Wilson nodded. "That's what Cade said. I think I better go and check it out."

She put a hand on his shoulder. "So I guess you're *not* going to pop the question."

Wilson shot her a quizzical look. "What?"

"Never mind," she said testily. She flicked the safety off and trained her rifle down the road. "You're not going it alone, Wilson."

Wilson said nothing. He flicked his selector to Fire and moved over to one of the twin ruts long ago etched into the road by the passage of large tonnage vehicles. The grass was knee-high to him here, but he found it easier to keep from wandering off into one of the many clearings purposefully cut from the forest so that ingoing and outgoing log trucks could pull over to allow for passing.

The pair had taken maybe a dozen cautious steps forward when they left the sun-dappled stretch of road behind and entered a pocket of forest where the air was cold and tainted with the faint odor of death. Drops of water falling from the hundred-foot-tall fir trees pattered all around them. As they crept back into the light, where the road widened and the stack of smooth rocks sat, more of the squat vehicle was revealed. It was neon green with splashes of black and white. A short windshield rose up from a pronounced snout. Yamaha was emblazoned on the side facing them.

Breaking noise discipline, Taryn said, "Wilson. Stop."

Somewhere left of them a woodpecker went to work on a tree. Further off a crow cawed.

Wilson halted, went to one knee again, then turned his head slowly in Taryn's direction.

Taryn saw at once the look of surprise on his face. Eyes wide and mouth agape, he lowered his rifle and motioned with his free arm as if to ask *What's up?*

Lowering her M4, Taryn rose and walked toward him.

He made a patting motion at the ground. *Get down.*

"It's a *snowmobile*, Wilson. *Gregory Dregan's* snowmobile. It's not exactly where he said it would be. But then again there *was* a foot of snow covering everything when he rode it in here."

"What about the rocks?"

"Hard to believe inhospitable spirits decided to choose this particular place to leave their warning."

"Music to my ears," Wilson said. "That Blair Witch flick freaked me the eff out."

"How can *anything* freak you *the eff* out at this point, Wilson? We are *living* a frickin' horror flick."

He shrugged, then regarded the road ahead of them. It got real narrow after about a hundred feet or so. There was also some noise coming from that direction. Branches breaking. It sounded as if a grizzly bear might be charging up the road in their direction.

Wilson hustled forward and crouched down by the garishly painted Yamaha's front skis. He made room for Taryn, then braced his rifle on the windshield, its business end trained where he figured the source of the commotion was likely to show its face.

After a few seconds spent kneeling beside the snowmachine, the ground began to vibrate. Something big was coming. And it wasn't alone.

Wilson whispered, "What do you think it is?"

"Not *it*," said Taryn. "More like ... *they*." No sooner had she finished answering, than deer or elk or moose—whatever breed the herd of hooved animals were—blazed by, all coiled muscle and tan fur and mouths frothing white with foam. She saw a huge rack of antlers on one of them. *A buck?* she guessed.

The rest, on account they were much smaller and lacked antlers, she supposed were female. *Does?*

The thud of hooves dissipated first. The sounds of brush breaking lasted a few seconds longer.

Taryn said, "Think those are the ones Cade called in?"

"If so," he replied. "They sure covered a lot of ground in a short amount of time."

She flicked her gun to Safe and rose. Nose scrunched, she said, "You think that smell is the rotters following them?"

"I wouldn't put money on it," he said. "Cade and Raven are supposedly leading the dead *out* of the valley."

"I hate that smell. It gets in your clothes and hair and never leaves."

Wilson looked at her and grimaced. Parroting her, he said, "*We're living a frickin' horror flick*, remember?"

"Yeah, I said that." She sat on the snowmachine and shrugged off her pack. After fishing out a rectangular item in a thin foil wrapper, she said, "Pop Tart?"

"What flavor?"

"Cherry."

Wilson put his hands on his knees and pretended to vomit on the ground between his boots.

"Really?" she said. "End of the frickin' world and you're being picky?"

"Give it here," he said sheepishly. "I was just messing around."

She went to hand him it to him, then abruptly drew it back. "Stop teasing."

She let him have the treat, then took a big bite out of hers. Crumbs falling from her mouth, she asked, "So what's your favorite flavor?"

"S'Mores."

Taryn stopped chewing and stared at him.

"Forgot about those, didn't you?"

She nodded slowly. "Wish you hadn't reminded me." Changing the subject, she said, "If you could teleport anywhere right now—" What sounded like a tree crashing to the forest floor somewhere far away stopped her mid-sentence.

Wilson turned and looked down the fire road in the direction the sound originated.

"Falling tree," she stated confidently. "Go on."

He sat sidesaddle on the seat, his rifle pointed down the road.

She shifted around so that her hip was touching his and looked him in the eye. "Well? Where is Scotty going to beam you?"

Wilson finished the bite of Pop Tart. "I want to be beamed to Central Park."

"Really? In New York? You know how many zombies will be waiting to eat you?"

Wilson bugged his eyes at her and popped the last of the cold toaster pastry into his mouth.

"One point five million people were packed into thirty square miles."

Wilson swallowed but said nothing.

"Seventh grade American history," she said. "I did a four-page report on the 9/11 attacks."

"While I rethink my answer," Wilson said. "Where do *you* want to be beamed?"

"Burbank."

"California?"

Taryn ate the crumbs from the foil, crinkled it up, and stowed it in a pocket. "I didn't stutter."

Closer now, the woodpecker attacked a different tree.

Wilson thought for a spell. Finally he said, "That's close to Los Angeles. You know what Cade said about that city."

"'It's FUBAR,' were his exact words."

Wilson rose off the seat and turned to face her. "Exactly. There are like three or four million people there."

"*Were*," she corrected.

"Why Burbank?"

Something was breaking through the brush down the road. Wilson craned but didn't see anything. Writing it off as an elk straggler trying to catch up to the rest of the herd, he turned his attention back to Taryn.

She said, "The Big Dog Garage has been calling me for years."

He asked, "What the eff is that?"

"It's a huge warehouse where Jay Leno keeps his *ginormous* car and motorcycle collection." She removed her cap and ran a hand through her recently shorn hair. "It's warming up."

Wilson unzipped his camouflage coat to his sternum. "What, you going to drive a Ferrari up the Pacific Coast Highway?"

"A Bugatti Veyron. Electric blue to be exact," she stressed. "If it's hemmed in behind a bunch of cars with dead batteries, I'd settle for an Aston Martin DB10 in silver or a Lambo Huracán in red. I figure to get them all test driven the first year. I'd drive American muscle cars on odd days and hypercars on even. The weekends would be reserved for the classics: Duesenbergs, Bugattis, Jaguars—"

Interrupting her, Wilson said, "You'd be in hog heaven, wouldn't you?"

She bit her lip and nodded. Her eyes teared up.

"Made you think about your dad, huh?"

She looked at the ground by her feet and took a covert swipe at the tears with a sleeve.

Branches were being snapped off real close, now.

The woodpecker went quiet.

When Taryn finally looked up at Wilson, he was no longer facing her. He was standing rigid. Looking down the road. On his face was one of those thousand-yard stares Cade and Duncan talked about. More troubling than the stoic expression was that his M4 was shouldered and trained on whatever he was seeing. As time started to crawl, she heard the *snick* of his safety being thrown and saw his finger slip into the trigger guard. Realizing he was about to open fire and she was directly in the path of the hot brass soon to be spilling from the rifle's ejection port, she rose up off the seat and spun to her left.

Taryn was mid-turn when Wilson shouted a warning. She was tucking her M4 tight to her shoulder and throwing its safety off when his chilling words were drowned out by a chorus of sonorous moans. When Wilson finally did open fire with his suppressed rifle, she was standing and facing the source of the sounds.

The clattering bolt and muffled reports rose over the sounds of the dead as spent brass cut the air a foot in front of Taryn's face. Better than down her collar or front of her shirt, she mused. That had happened one time, the hot shell dispensing a special kind of pain all the way down.

Wondering how in the hell they were going to deal with all of the monsters filing up the road toward them, Taryn picked a target and added her gun to the fight.

Chapter 14

Raven was slouched down in her seat in the F-650, face buried in the leather-bound journal, when the loud trilling of the satellite phone caused her to jump. With the Screamer muted and the hypnotic thrum of the off-road tires infiltrating the cab, she had forgotten all about the recent encounter with the mini-horde her dad estimated was comprised of at least a thousand zombies. Which was perfect. She needed the brief respite from all the awful things that had happened in the span of less than a week. Not a waking moment passed when she wasn't seeing ghosts wearing the faces of all of the people who were dead and gone—her mom first and foremost among them.

Raven was totally oblivious of how far they'd traveled along 39 thanks to a pages-long entry describing how Rose and her family had driven cross country from the Boston area all the way to San Antonio only to end up in a FEMA facility set up outside of Houston, Texas. And they were still in that facility when Brody wandered off briefly and got himself run over by a Texas National Guard Humvee. A tear was tracing her cheek as the sat-phone trilled. She only looked up to learn they were almost to Woodruff when Cade pulled to the shoulder to answer the call.

He answered with a curt, "Cade here."

Wiping the tears on her sleeve, Raven closed the journal and set it aside. Only after dragging the rifle up off the footwell and scanning the road in both directions for threats did she regard her dad and continue to watch him as he listened intently to whoever was on the other end.

Every now and again she could hear the tinny-sounding voice coming from the earpiece, but she couldn't make out any of the words. Which wasn't necessary for her to recognize the cadence and pitch as belonging to Tran.

Cade said, "Why can't Jamie and Lev double back?"

Raven saw him nod and grimace. Interest piqued, she shifted in her seat and shot him a questioning look.

After another thirty seconds spent lips pursed and phone mashed to his ear, Cade said, "The Merlin Drive-In? Nope. I have no idea where that is."

He listened for a beat. "Less than a mile from Bear Lake, huh. They're what … fifteen miles from the airport, then? I agree. Makes no sense having them turn around." He went quiet and stared out his window. Eyes glued to something north of the junction, he added, "I have to deal with a tire issue first. If I can get that sorted, we'll go check it out. Least we can do considering all Dregan and his people have done for us."

Like a typical twelve-year-old dying to be in the loop, Raven pointed at the phone and mouthed, "Put it on speaker so I can listen."

Cade shook his head. He paused for a moment with the phone still pressed to his ear. He tapped the steering wheel as he mulled over how to break more bad news to the already hard hit community of Bear River. Finally, deciding honesty was the best policy, he said, "Tran, this is going to suck, but I need you to call the deputy and tell her I'm going to have to lure the mini-horde south. I'll make sure they're well past Bear River's south gate before I peel away and head back north."

Cade paused again to listen. Finally, feeling Raven's eyes boring into him, he said to Tran, "I'm putting you on speaker." He jabbed a finger at the keypad and held the slim handset in the air between the front seats.

"Hi Raven," Tran said. "How are you?"

"Squash the small talk," Cade said, his tone all business. "When we're finished canvassing Woodruff, I'm going to wait at the intersection for the horde. We'll lead them away when they show up. I figure we have a good hour and a half, maybe two, before the eastbound horde gets to the junction. After we do the

Pied Piper thing, I'll double back and we'll resume our search for Daymon."

Tran said, "East of Woodruff?"

Cade said, "Everywhere else is pretty much covered. Remember to give me a sitrep when you hear from Romeo and Juliet." He paused long enough to take off his hat and worry his freshly cut high-and-tight. "If you hear from Duncan," he added, "have *him* call me." Wearing a look of disgust, he ended the call and jammed the phone into its usual slot in the center console.

Beating Raven to the punch, Cade said, "What you didn't hear before I put him on speaker was that a Deputy MacLeod from Bear River asked if we would keep an eye out for the elder Dregan." He went on to explain how the night before the man borrowed an ice cream truck and led the mega-horde away from the walled community of Bear River. What he didn't say was that he was wondering how the former Soviet-Bloc soldier managed to fit those King-Kong-sized balls of his behind the wheel of the boxy rig he'd spotted from the air that night. It appeared to have broken down, and he feared the worst.

"Why can't *his* people send out a search party?"

"Dregan's brother is damn near on his deathbed with the flu. Hell, the deputy says they have maybe thirty people within the walls who aren't sick with it. Even to check on the welfare of the man who deputized her, she can't spare the manpower."

"What about Gregory?"

"He died last night."

Raven made a face. Then, with a slight tilt of the head, she asked, "How?"

Cade said nothing. He couldn't even hold her gaze.

"Omega?"

Nodding, Cade said, "The antiserum you gave him came from the same batch as the one Mom took."

Raven was quiet for a long ten-count. As she stared out the window, she realized how close they were to the 39/16 junction. The yellow school bus that used to partially block the turn onto 39 was nowhere in sight. The only evidence pointing to its whereabouts was the continuous field of broken glass sitting atop a ten-foot-wide yellow smudge that began on the shoulder near the junction and ran off to the north, diagonally, across both lanes. As her attention was drawn beyond the debris field to where 16 intersected Center Street, she got an eyeful of the destruction wrought on Woodruff by the northbound mega-horde.

"If the same unstoppable mass that did that to Back In The Saddle caught up with Dregan in his ice cream truck—" said Cade, his voice trailing off.

"Then he's toast," Raven stated. "So why bother?"

"Because it's what we do," Cade replied. He shook his head as he surveyed the damage done to the small town. He didn't need binoculars to see that the rehabilitation place from which Duncan had fired down on Adrian's crew was no longer two-stories. The house-turned-business no longer sat on its cement foundation. The remains of the upper story was a jumble of broken timber supporting a barely recognizable roof and had come to rest a dozen yards north of the windowless main floor.

The cannibals' vehicles were no longer lined up facing west on Center street. A 4x4 pickup he recognized was nosed into the rehab place's basement, its load bed upthrust like the bow of a sinking ship. The rest of the cannibals' vehicles had been pushed north by east, ending up a jumble of dented metal and broken glass on the gravel lot behind the business. Zombies were trapped between the mix of cars and trucks and under the debris left behind when the structure collapsed. Some Zs were crushed amongst the vehicles. Others had become mired with the upended 4x4 in Back in the Saddle's exposed basement. Even without the Steiners, Cade detected lots of movement in the shadows.

Across the street from Back in the Saddle, the cinderblock structure housing an auto body shop had fared a bit better. While it remained on its original footing, wide vertical fissures zigged and zagged up the west-facing walls. Some of the cement blocks had been sheared in half. The cars in the lot not pushed against the rollup doors by a previous tangle with a mini-horde were now wedged against the garage, or stacked atop one another. That the thirty-foot-tall structure still stood was a testament to solid design.

"Wow! Look at the telephone poles," Raven said. Once listing west across Main Street, the picket of creosote-stained telephone poles planted on its east side were now down and had been dragged a half-block north by the horde. Likely stimulated by the Ford's exhaust note, a number of dead entangled by the downed wires were looking south and struggling against their bonds.

Cade said, "Those poles may as well have been toothpicks going up against that kind of force."

Voice wavering, Raven said, "I hope Daymon wasn't caught in their path."

"He's a wily survivor," noted Cade. "I'm convinced he held to his word and pushed east after we last saw him."

"What was he doing?"

"He was trying to get a handle on how much looting Adrian's gang did. They pretty much scoured all of the homes and businesses in Woodruff and Randolph. So east is all he really had left."

Raven checked her wing mirror. Seeing nothing, she asked, "Where's Randolph?"

"A few miles north of Woodruff."

Raven nodded but said nothing.

Testing her, Cade pointed at the Bear River range barely visible on the horizon beyond the Ford's hood. "What direction is that?"

"Easy," Raven said. "East."

"How do you know?"

"The sun rises in the east. Sets in the west."

"Good. Then where is Randolph from here?"

Raven pointed left across the hood. "Randolph is that way. A few miles *north* of Woodruff."

Noting that the hood seemed to be dipping more on his side than before, he said, "Then Bear River is where?"

Rolling her eyes, Raven said, "The only remaining direction is south."

"Right direction. Wrong answer. There are more than the four Cardinal points on a compass."

Seeing where he was going with this, Raven pointed out the other four she knew of, beginning with southeast and ending with northeast, a full circle that when completed put a smile on her dad's face.

"Bingo," Cade said. "If you're really getting down to precise waypoints and such, there's three-hundred-and-sixty degrees on the same compass. North is zero. The degrees count up clockwise from there, ending at north, where they started. Strange enough, zero degrees is bordered on the left by three-hundred-and-sixty, which also happens to be north. Are you confused yet?"

She gave him a bored look.

"Okay," he said. "This'll be my last Bushcraft 101 question … for now." He noted the time on his Suunto. "We have a little less than an hour and a half before we need to be parked *where* on 16?" He looked at her.

"South of the intersection and in plain sight of 39." She smiled. "You going to fill me in on what's next … or do I have to keep guessing?"

He waited a beat before answering. "I didn't want to worry you on the way here, so I didn't let on that Black Beauty here isn't steering like she should. I'm pretty sure it's due to air loss prior to me applying the liquid patch."

"We can drive on it, can't we?"

He nodded. "But you shouldn't drive fast with an improperly inflated tire. Especially tires this big. Plus, I'm not certain we don't still have a slow leak. And if we do—"

Interrupting, Raven said, "Please tell me we're not going to be stranded out here after dark."

"I never lie to you, Raven. That being said, anything is possible."

She took her hat off. Put it in her lap and worried the tassel with both hands.

"We won't if I can help it. First things first. We go down to the shop there and see if there's anything useful inside. A foot pump, maybe. A tank of compressed air would be ideal. It's pretty likely there'll be something we can use in there."

She put the hat back on. He noted she wasn't without it since the day they'd buried her mom. He supposed it was her security blanket of sorts. He looked at the bandage wrapping her knuckles. Thanks to Glenda's instruction, Raven was keeping the dressing changed.

"You ought to wear your mom's old gloves from here on out." He fished in the console and pulled out the black leather items.

After watching Raven snug the gloves on, Cade let up off the brake. To conserve fuel, he kept his foot from the accelerator and allowed gravity to drag them downhill toward the 16/39 junction.

Chapter 15

Duncan was a handful of miles removed from his surprise encounter with the herd of dead when he saw a UDOT sign indicating Huntsville lay just eleven miles ahead. For reasons unknown to him, seeing the sign led to him recalling a specific detail of Glenda's flight from Huntsville. One night, shortly after her arrival at the compound, the two had been sitting near a dying campfire. They were watching the star show when, suddenly, she got a faraway look and launched into her story. Fighting back tears, she had recounted how she finally granted her undead husband a second death. She divulged that she'd done it in their shared bed in their home on the hill above the Pineville Reservoir. How she had fashioned makeshift pieces of armor for her arms and legs using gossip magazines and duct tape. Especially harrowing was her escape from Huntsville disguised as the one of the monsters and having to hole up for the night in the garage of a burned-out Shell station. She had related everything in great detail from beginning to end when her journey to Woodruff was cut short by Daymon's roadblock, where she had been forced to abandon the old red Schwinn that had delivered her safely over many miles of state route teeming with walking corpses.

Glenda had liberated the bike from a house once belonging to a friend of hers—an AA teetotaler named Violet who had introduced Glenda to recovery. And if Duncan's memory served, Glenda had said the two-story house with the stoop full of unread newspapers and a Volvo wagon in the driveway was roughly ten miles east of Huntsville. Which meant, if his calculation was correct, he should be seeing the rutted uphill drive any second now.

***

Duncan's "Any second" ended up being a little over two minutes. The house was set back in the trees and partially hidden by shrubs growing out of control.

The drive from the road to the dilapidated two-story affair was fairly steep and rutted by parallel tire tracks. The siding showing through the bushes was a shade of blue, chalky and fading from changing seasons and the steady march of time.

He turned off the state route and motored up the drive at a walking speed. Along the way he sized up the place. The screen on the front door was closed and he could see the pile of Huntsville Times—a week's worth at least—Glenda had mentioned in her telling of the story. Stained glass windows flanked the door. Drawn horizontal blinds backed the windows in front.

Nosed in at an angle on the oil-stained cement parking pad next to the house was the Volvo wagon. On the back tailgate were dozens of stickers. *Glacier National Park*, *Yellowstone*, and *Bryce Canyon* were represented. Mixed in with the stickers attesting to places the car had been were those touting the *Sierra Club*, *Greenpeace* and a slew of other activist groups whose social values fell much farther to the left than Duncan's.

He jockeyed the Land Cruiser around and parked it facing downhill with its rear bumper a foot from the wagon's. As he stared the length of the drive he envisioned Glenda straddling the Schwinn and dodging rotters as she bombed downhill toward the distant two-lane. And in that split second flashback based solely on her exceptional oration skills, he saw her pedaling east with a shit-eating grin on her face. Savoring the first bit of hope she had experienced since deciding to finish her undead husband and leave everything dear to her behind in Huntsville.

Back to reality, Duncan shut down the motor and, using all three mirrors, took quick inventory of his surroundings.

The house was on the right and cast a shadow over the SUV. The fir tree the Schwinn had been leaning against dominated a wide stretch of tilled soil between the house and Volvo. In front of the Volvo, its wood slat doors hanging wide open, was a small swaybacked garage.

Duncan stepped to the drive and locked the Toyota. Head on a swivel, he drew his .45 and made tracks to the garage. A quick turkey-peek around the open door told him, save for the cobwebs strung between the rafters and shadowy corners, a recycling bin full of newspaper, and an old-fashioned push mower leaning against the back wall, the structure was empty.

Turning his attention to the rear of the house, he learned the horizontal blinds in the rear-facing windows were also closed. On the side of the house facing the drive was a small bay window. In the window was a trio of dead houseplants. To the left of the bay window was a rectangular window the size of a pool table. The drapes were parted in the middle. He saw nothing moving in the gloom behind them.

Running behind the fir from the rear corner of the house to the garage was a waist-high fence. The gate was hanging by one hinge. Caught on the failed upper hinge was a foot-long strip of tattered denim.

Duncan squeezed through the gate and quickly surveyed the backyard, finding it as unkempt as the front. Rising up at the rear of the property was a wall of gnarled rhododendrons that looked to have been ignored for many years prior to the dead walking.

The ground beyond the gate was mostly mud. Pressed into the mud were dozens of different prints. Some were made by bare feet. Others were made by shoes and boots in all different sizes and possessing varied sole patterns. So much was going on here that after just a few minutes he gave up searching for the tread pattern specific to Glenda's hikers.

He scaled the short stack of stairs and tried the knob on the back door. Finding it locked gave him a bit of hope. Maybe the familiarity of the place had drawn Glenda here just as the snippet of memory of her story had changed the trajectory of his journey. He looked through the square pane of glass and saw on the back porch a broom with tired bristles, a couple of cold weather coats on a hook, a ratty pair of tennis shoes coated with mud, and, the best clue yet as to who lived here, rain galoshes in two sizes and colors. The size twelve gunboats in black screamed *his*, while the smaller bright green pair had to have belonged to the woman of the house.

Duncan pounded on the door with a closed fist then crouched down out of sight. As he waited to see if the action might draw out any dead roaming freely inside, he thought back to the night Brook turned. Sitting watch on the stairs outside the RV while a woman he'd grown to respect and love like a daughter died slowly inside was a trial he wouldn't wish on anyone. Spending the subsequent hours waiting for Cade to return by a dying fire with the shell of that woman slamming around inside the RV was life changing. In fact, at the time, it had made him question God's very existence. Which started the slide down the slippery slope that deposited him here, alcohol on board, faith shaken, and his chances at maintaining long-term sobriety shattered.

"Glenda! You in there?" He paused and listened hard. During the ensuing seconds of silence, he saw Glenda's face. Only the smile she wore riding the bike to safety was gone. Hopefully not a portent of things to come, he pictured her shark-eyed and slack-jawed. One of *them*. Just like Brook had eventually become.

Duncan waited an additional ten seconds for good measure, then rose and peered inside. Still quiet. Nothing moving that he could hear from outside. So he holstered the .45, grabbed ahold of the stair rails, and delivered a swift kick to the door. His boot heel made contact just below the handle, the ensuing bang shattering the still. There was a vicious tearing sound as wood splintered and the door was driven inward.

Duncan stopped the door midway on its return travel and stepped into the gloomy anteroom. Dust motes and particles of drywall from the hole punched in the wall by the door handle cruised the still air. Straight ahead, Duncan spotted a small galley-style kitchen. On his right was a door blocked by all manner of camping gear. There was a medium-sized cooler with a 24-pack of

Pabst Blue Ribbon beer resting on its lid. A trio of sleeping bags jammed into multicolored stuff sacks sat in a neat row beside the cooler. There was a gas lantern and stove, but no fuel canisters for them. Two empty Rubbermaid bins sat amongst the gear.

After prying a beer from the case, Duncan closed the door behind him and braced it with the broom.

The sound from him cracking open the warm beer echoed in the small kitchen.

As he stood there downing the beer, he took in his surroundings. Aside from the dead plants in the bay window and a light coating of dust on everything, the kitchen was immaculate. No dishes in the sink. Though not running on account of no electricity, the refrigerator was clean and contained only a few condiments gone bad long ago.

It was clear to him whoever was going to go camping had wanted to return to a clean house.

A paper flyer lying on the counter added an important piece to the puzzle. It was an official-looking FEMA document with detailed warnings from the Centers for Disease Control about the Omega Virus and directions to a sanctuary being set up by the state government north of Salt Lake City. The admonishment NO WEAPONS ALLOWED — ALL WILL BE SUBJECT TO SEIZURE was emblazoned in a large bold font across the bottom of the sheet.

No mincing words there, Duncan thought as he turned the notice over. Written in pencil on the flipside was a detailed shopping list complete with milk, eggs, butter, bread and a dozen other items necessary for a long stay in the woods.

Good luck with that. The stores in Portland were empty, or in the process of being picked clean by looters before Z-Day plus two was fully underway.

The only item Duncan found worth keeping during a quick sweep through the rest of the main floor rooms was a full roll of double-ply toilet paper. Apparently they wanted to come home and be able to take a dump, too. The hard to find commodity went into his coat pocket as he approached a door off the living room he guessed to be either a coat closet or stairs going up.

Betting on the latter, he again went through the bang-on-the-door-and-listen routine. Which after a few seconds got results. Not the good kind, though. Instead of silence, a distant scratching noise—like fingernails raking an interior wall—sounded from behind the door. A dry hiss followed. Then, a tick later, the scratching commenced again.

Looking to quell a little of the guilt he carried from leaving Brook to suffer, he drew his .45, worked the doorknob, and dragged the door slowly in his direction.

"Glenda?"

No reply. Just the sounds of restless dead things filtering down the darkened stairway.

Wooden rail in one hand, Colt in the other, he climbed the narrow stairs. All seventeen of them. Halfway up the reek of death was palpable. Another few steps upward and his eyes went level with the floor. Seeing the wide open space in tiny increments between the spindles of a safety rail encircling the top of the well lent him a good impression of the floor's layout. And it was much like that in Glenda's home. Basically a renovated attic with gables on either side and a big window looking out over the front yard. No portico, but there was a king bed pushed against the wall to his left. On the bed was the festering corpse of a woman in her late twenties or early thirties. Her face in death was a mask of peace and contentment. Sticking from the crook of one arm was a syringe with its plunger driven all the way to the stop. Even viewed over a dozen feet of gloom, he couldn't see any obvious signs of infection. Maybe the state of the world had gotten to her and she couldn't take it any longer. Rode the dragon right into the light.

Turning a one-eighty revealed a small bathroom at the rear of the converted attic. Its unfinished wooden pocket-door was open partway. The scratching noises were coming from its general direction.

Business end of his hand-cannon leading the way, he curled right at the top of the staircase, walked straight toward the bathroom and stopped a few feet short of showing himself. To his right was a doorway with no door. All he could see through the sliver afforded by his viewing angle were rows of clothes on plastic hangers. A footstool was lying on its side in the doorway. He took another step forward and, keeping the Colt tucked close to his body, swept its muzzle to the right, cutting the corner by degrees, until he spied the source of the sounds he'd picked up on downstairs. A bearded man, mid-thirties, give or take, was staring at him bug-eyed from a yard away. The man's lips were an angry shade of purple from what Duncan guessed was lack of oxygen prior to death. Both arms were outstretched toward the door header which bore weeks, or maybe even several months' worth of gouges into the wood from scrabbling fingers, the tips of each worn down to splintered bone ringed by blooms of flesh and dermis.

Prior to ending up in this sad state, the man had punched out two holes in the sheetrock overhead, looped a length of yellow climbing rope over an out of sight beam, then jumped off the nearby footstool to hang himself. There was a bite wound on the zombie's left forearm. Fused to the wound with dried blood was one end of the bandage that once covered the near-perfect oval where a mouth-sized hunk of flesh had been excised. The bandage had come unraveled over time and now swayed back and forth pendulum-like as the rotter strained to reach Duncan.

"You know what, Stretch," Duncan drawled. "If you hadn't gone off and got yourself bit before enacting your exit plan"—he holstered his pistol and dragged his knife from its sheath—"your E-Ticket off this planet would have been punched." He pointed the blade at one of the writhing creature's milky eyes. "But you and the missus apparently weren't privy to *all* of the rules. I saw the flyer from FEMA on the counter downstairs. Newsflash, my man. All of the government types were holding their cards close to the vest. Keeping us all in the dark as their failed push for containment ramped up."

A viscous black fluid seeped around the blade as it plunged through the cornea and found brain tissue. A quick little twist of the wrist and the struggle was over.

"You're free now, friend. And all it cost you is that suitcase of camping beer downstairs."

He left the man in the noose and the woman in their bed. Went downstairs and checked all of the cupboards for a suitable alcoholic replacement for the beer. Striking out, he hefted the red, white, and blue box and lugged it to the Land Cruiser.

Chapter 16

With Main impassable from Center Street to the post office several blocks north, Cade had to improvise to get them close enough to the body shop so Raven could stay in the Ford and be his eyes and ears while he went inside to search the place.

After sprinting down 39 to the junction with 16, he cut a left and drove a few hundred feet north until the two-lane was blocked by trampled corpses, downed wires, and debris from the collapsed rehab place. From there he turned left, jumped the curb a half-block short of Center Street, and drove west.

Off of Raven's side was a twenty-foot-wide gully. It looked to be deeper than the Ford was tall and ran straight as an arrow from the series of culverts carved underneath 16 to a gently sloping hillside topped by a copse of juvenile aspens.

Flicking by Cade's window was a nondescript weed-choked expanse of ground that stretched all the way south to the guardrail-topped dirt berm running parallel to State Route 39.

Cade drove off road for twenty yards, said, "Hold on," and dove the truck into the gully. Brush scraped the sides and undercarriage and the rig rocked like a ship at sea as it bounded down what was maybe a thirty-degree decline. Though Raven had the grab bar by her head in a two-handed death grip, she was still thrashed hard against the door and window. The engine growled and small rocks pinged off metal until they hit the flat and entered a twelve-foot expanse of brackish, standing water. For a couple of beats, as the tires fought for traction, twin fans of brown water cut visibility out the side windows. When the Ford left the flat and came up against the much steeper opposing incline, Cade felt the suspension compress and some of the forward momentum bleed away. Halfway to the top, the steering went mushy and the front end started pulling to the left. When the horizon finally reappeared over the Ford's hood, the body shop lay due north across a couple of hundred feet of open field.

Cade looked to his left. Saw a wide expanse of ochre, clay-rich soil dotted with puddles. Farther out, maybe a quarter-mile or so west, a rock-strewn hillside rose steeply to a craggy ridge. Atop the ridge was a picket of firs that rambled off north for as far as the eye could see. And nestled somewhere in those trees was the hide from which Cade and Jamie had sniped at Adrian's people.

As soon as the truck stopped rocking, Raven leaned forward against her shoulder belt, put both hands flat on the dash, and drew in a deep breath.

"What is it?" Cade asked.

There was a moment of dead silence in the cab as they both stared at the blocks of utter destruction filling up the windshield.

Finally, pointing diagonally across the hood, she said, "There's your missing school bus."

Cade looked to where she was pointing. Saw the bus in a side yard on the east side of Main roughly a block north of Center. It was crumpled and windowless and had come to rest with its wheels and undercarriage facing skyward. The streak of yellow paint starting at the 39/16 junction scribed north along Main until its terminus at a shattered length of sidewalk a dozen feet shy of the multi-ton vehicle. It was pretty obvious the horde was responsible for moving it all that distance. And one didn't have to be a rocket scientist to conclude that in transit the bus had somehow contributed to the rehab place's demise.

She made a face. "How'd they do all that damage?"

"Physics, I guess. I know it's got something to do with mass and momentum and inertia. I'm no expert on the matter. But I do know, once a mega-horde gets a full head of steam, they're virtually unstoppable." And though Cade had witnessed a full-blown mega-horde on the move and was well aware of the amount of destruction one could inflict, to keep from further worrying his daughter he didn't let on to her that moving a school

116

bus several city blocks and dumping an old house from its foundation was child's play in comparison.

"How are you going to get inside the garage with all those cars jammed in there like sardines?"

"Improvise," he said and started the Ford rolling forward across the open field.

She fished the Steiners out of the center console and brought them to her face.

Voice wavering, she said, "Dad."

"Yes, sweetie?"

"I count at least fifteen of them caught between the cars."

Having already spied pale hands reaching up from within the warren of glass and steel, he said, "More than twenty, but who's counting?"

Still glassing their destination with the binoculars, she said, "At least the garage is still standing."

Cade glanced sidelong at her. "Don't go jinxing me now, Bird."

A beat later they rolled up and found the lot's main entrance blocked by the crush of vehicles. Chain strung between cement posts served as a barrier to the back lot. So Cade reversed and circled back through the field to an unimproved access road. They bumped along north to a pair of dirt tracks cutting across a strip of grass bordering the rear lot. Along the way they passed a neat assemblage of charred corpses, their faces upturned and heads pointing west.

"Disposing of their dead," stated Cade.

Raven said nothing as the gruesome sight slipped from view.

The chain blocking the drive was fitted with a sign that read NO TRESPASSING. At its centermost point, the chain was, at most, six inches off the drive.

Cade looked to Raven. "Think Black Beauty can drive over it?"

"No problemo," she said.

"Get your head down in case the chain snaps back when it breaks."

Shifting her rifle aside, Raven clicked out of her belt and slumped down in her seat.

Cade let off the brake and allowed the idling engine to pull the Ford ahead. Just when he thought the chain would go taut and stall the rig's forward momentum, there was a sharp *crack* and one end of the chain arced over the right front fender and slammed down on the hood with a resonant *bang*.

Physics, thought Cade as he watched the chain slither snake-like off the hood and disappear from view.

Straight across the lot from them, backed up to the shop's west wall, was a like-new Ford F-350 Super Duty outfitted as a tow truck. Next to the black tow truck was a white pick-up missing most of its windows. Both trucks were dirt covered from sitting in the elements.

Cade drove over the broken chain, started a sweeping right turn, then stopped broadside to the tow truck. Regarding Raven, he said, "That's how Wilson got up onto the roof."

Raven regarded the tow truck then craned to see across the dash. "He climbed up that thingy out back, huh?"

Nodding, he said, "That thingy's called a *boom*."

"Strange name," she said, still gawking at the wall. "Wilson's no ninja," she said skeptically. "And he definitely isn't *Spiderman*."

"Saw it with my own eyes," Cade said, his tone softening. "A few minutes before a whole bunch of Adrian's people went to Hell." He let off the brake and drove south along the west-facing wall. Gravel popped under the tires as mirrored windows bearing alarm company decals and fronted by wire mesh screens scrolled by outside Cade's window. Roughly a truck length from the main lot, he wrenched the steering wheel right and started the Ford on a big counterclockwise U-turn that saw the distant 39/16 junction begin a slow left to right slide across the windshield.

The intersection with Center and Main made a brief appearance over the hood then was quickly replaced by the vehicle- and zombie-choked parking lot fronting the body shop's rollup doors. When it was clear to Cade that Raven would be able to see the entire front of the body shop, its compromised rollup

118

door, and all points of approach save for the blind corner at the shop's east wall on Main, he ground the rig to a halt nosed in diagonally to the shop's southwest corner.

He rolled the transmission to Park, engaged the emergency brake, and shut off the motor.

Raven looked across the cab at him. "Are you used to all of this yet? The death? The violence?" Her nose crinkled. "The *smell*? I'll *never* get used to the effin smell."

Choose your battles, Cade told himself again. Then, remembering all the deployments to the Middle East and the handful to Africa, he said, "I hate to say it, but you will. All of it. That doesn't mean you have to like it, though."

"Do you think it stinks like this in Colorado Springs?"

Cade had told her earlier about the burgeoning walled-in city that had become the United States' new seat of power. However, he had purposefully left out the part about the constant breaches in the wall, outbreaks within the walls, and general hardships faced by all who were making a go of it on the inside.

"I suppose the smell of death is prevalent here, too," he conceded.

She looked out the window. Bit her lip and held the pose for a couple of seconds.

It was obvious to Cade she didn't like his answer.

All business, she said, "What's the plan?"

"I want you to set yourself up just like you did last time. Adjust the pedals, run the steering wheel to the stop, and pick a backpack to sit on."

Looking him square in the face, she said, "I really suck at driving."

"Considering you've had no formal training, your performance under duress back there wasn't so bad."

"How long will you be inside?"

"I hope it'll be a quick in and out. If the Zs come while I'm inside, stay out of sight and try to ignore them."

"You mean, *when* they come." She glanced right. Saw the creatures trapped between the nearby cars already craning and ogling her. And it worried her. Because to the dead, the noise of the truck crawling through the culvert, four-wheeling across the field, and the chain snapping was no different than someone ringing a dinner bell. In her mind's eye she saw Zs perking up for blocks around. Though she didn't let on, she was convinced they were already on the move, the prospect of a meal of fresh meat attracting them like wasps to a picnic.

"Hope for the best," he said.

"Prepare for the worst," she answered.

Nodding his approval, Cade changed the channel on his Motorola, rolled the volume down low, and pocketed it. He pulled the suppressed Glock 19 from his shoulder rig, gave it a quick press check, and set it on the dash. Next, he removed the Glock 17 from the drop-thigh holster and checked it in the same manner.

"Always assume a weapon is loaded," Raven proffered. "Even if you know it isn't."

"Correct. And these both are," he stated, presenting her the Glock 17, grip first, muzzle aimed away from them both. He struck the padded top of the center console with his elbow. "There's a can in there for this one."

Without further instruction, she took the black pistol from him. Keeping her hands away from the trigger, she set the Glock on her lap and retrieved the six-inch suppressor from inside the overflowing compartment. As she threaded the black cylinder onto the barrel, he went on, "When you're done there, change channels on your radio to 10-2. There's bound to be a few Zs inside. No reason to take a chance on Tran or Seth's voice blaring over the radio and getting them all riled up."

Handing back the Glock 17, she said, "You're always preaching to me that the only purpose for a handgun is to fight your way to your rifle."

"Not this time. I can tell just from looking at all the cars jammed into the lot that once I get inside there ... it's going to be hard moving around. No kind of place to be swinging a rifle back and forth."

"It's going to be dark once you get inside." She gestured at the M4. "Your rifle has the light attached to it."

"I have a backup flashlight. Do you?"

She nodded.

"Good girl."

Raven nodded again. "So while you're inside ... I'm to stay low, keep an eye out, and monitor the radio."

"In a nutshell."

"Any other orders? Rules?"

"Just the usual. Keep a round in the chamber ... always. Never forget you have to shoot Zs in the head."

"Mom said with the Breathers you aim for center mass, right?"

Good job, Brook, thought Cade, his throat tightening unexpectedly. *God, I miss you so.* He nodded once and cast a furtive glance at each mirror. Seeing nothing to be worried about for the moment, he said, "I'll radio once I'm inside. While I'm out of sight, I want you to stay low and be still. Only show yourself if the Zs get to be two or three deep outside the truck. Use the Glock to clear the driver's side so I can get back in when I return. If it looks like the Zs are on to me and a whole bunch of them start heading for the rollup door while I'm still inside—"

One brow arched, she said, "Define *a whole bunch.*"

He shrugged. "Fifteen ... or more."

She screwed up her face.

He said, "Are you finished interrupting me?"

She nodded and crossed her arms.

"If you're sure they are coming for me—"

"Honk?"

He shook his head vigorously.

"Never, ever honk."

She smirked. "I was joking."

"This is not the time or the place for that, Bird."

"Mom said humor is my coping mechanism."

Cade pinched the bridge of his nose and looked toward the moon roof. "Understood," he said in a near whisper. "While I'm happy she diagnosed it, and I'm really, really happy you're astute enough to recognize and embrace it, there *is* an appropriate time and place for humor." He paused to check the mirrors. "The time for joking is when I'm back inside here safe and sound and we're driving off."

Nodding in agreement, she asked, "What if there are fifteen or fewer?"

He mulled it over for a second. While ammo needed to be rationed from here on out, Raven hadn't done much "real world" shooting with the M4. Deciding that expending a few rounds would be worth the benefit reaped, he said, "Use your best judgment. If you think the Zs may pose a threat, you have the rifle. Warn me first, then deploy the three-power magnifier and take out as many as you can from *here*."

Brow furrowed, she said, "You'll be downrange, Dad. I don't want to accidentally shoot *you*."

"The shop is constructed from cement blocks." He paused for effect. "The walls are a foot thick."

She shot him a doubtful look. Said, "You're assuming you'll be able to get in. Can't we just change the tire here?"

Cade shook his head. "The wheel and tire and all the gore on it probably weighs upwards of two hundred pounds. Even if I could get the thing jacked up and the lug nuts off and drop the wheel … getting the full-size spare in place by myself is probably not going to happen."

Raven said nothing. She was busy worrying the sling on her M4.

"There has to be a way in," he said. "You won't accidentally shoot your dad. I promise." He paused, then added, "I'll radio you a heads up before I come out. Two clicks of the talk button." He demonstrated with his radio. "Does that set you at ease?"

She made a face he found difficult to interpret. "Be careful," she said, putting her hand atop his. "It's just you and me now."

Cade leaned in and kissed her forehead, then drew back and stuck his right hand in the air, palm out. Keeping three fingers pressed together and extended, he trapped his pinky finger with the pad of his thumb.

Raven smiled because she knew what was coming next.

Suppressing a grin of his own, he shot her a quick salute. "I will be *very* careful … *Scout's honor.*"

Though she wanted to remind her dad of his *time and place* rule pertaining to humor, she refrained from doing so.

Without another word or backward glance, Cade was out the door and padding away from the Ford, Glock in hand and head on a swivel.

Chapter 17

The suitcase of Pabst was three beers lighter when the familiar red and yellow *SHELL* sign pierced the horizon.

Duncan cracked beer number four one-handed and was lapping at the overflowing foam with his tongue when the Land Cruiser began to shimmy. Coming even with the driveway to the burned-out gas station, the engine stalled out, causing the steering to get difficult as the power steering pump stopped doing its job.

"Gawdammit," he bawled as the warm beer spewing from the can wet his crotch. He looked to the gauge cluster and pored over the lit-up symbols. A crudely rendered engine that looked more like a pregnant prop airplane than what it was supposed to represent was yellow. A red rectangle sprouting a pair of posts he took to be the check battery warning was also ablaze. Most troubling of all was the admonishment spelled out in plain English on the computerized display nestled between the tach and speedometer. It was telling him in red letters that he was OUT OF FUEL. And the big cosmic "eff you" was that the luxury off-road rig was giving up the ghost in front of a filling station that no doubt had been bone dry since the day the first wave of desperate folks fleeing Salt Lake and Ogden surged through here.

Cursing under his breath, he jammed the half-full can into the center console cup holder. To conserve the diminishing forward momentum, he slammed the shifter into neutral and began hauling the steering wheel hand over hand hard to the right. Getting the Land Cruiser to yield to the input was a chore. He felt the burn starting in his forearms as the SUV rode over the sidewalk and coasted onto the expansive asphalt parking lot. He muscled the front tires straight and pulled sharply alongside the fueling station as if he were stopping for a fill up and to scrape the bugs from his windows. Those days were long gone. Only thing needed scraping off the windshield was the film of mystery liquid he couldn't identify and, frankly, didn't really wish to.

He set the selector to Park and pulled the e-brake.

After downing the half can of beer with one solid pull, he tossed the empty to the floor and pulled the suitcase of beer onto the seat next to him. He loaded a can into every available pocket, ten total. He stepped out onto the pad, closed the door, and set the locks.

Though lacking several inches of freshly fallen snow, the place was just as he remembered it. Same bowed-in rollup door. Same decaying corpses lying in a jumble at its base.

Approaching the burned-out shell of what used to be the convenience store component of the station, he spotted the interior door leading into the garage. Scrawled in the soot near the top of the fire-proof metal door was the word DEAD. The elements had scoured the word INSIDE from Glenda's hastily scrawled warning.

Behind the building were the same dozen or so cars and trucks. All had been torched by whoever started the fire that claimed the store.

"Might as well be a sign says last gas for a million miles," Duncan muttered. "Looks like you gotta walk now, Old Man." He chuckled softly to himself as he worked a beer from a pocket, pulled the tab, and took a long slug. Holding the near empty can at his side, he looked west in the direction of Huntsville. After about a half-mile, 39 reared up into a pretty steep grade that seemed to go on forever. Out of sight on the far side of the rise was the failed National Guard roadblock. Barely visible over the hill's apex was the Wasatch Range. At the moment the rambling band of upthrust rock was just a horizontal gray smudge due to distance and clouds hugging its flanks. Closer in were Mount Ogden's forested foothills. Home to Snowbasin ski resort, the 9,569-foot peak separated Huntsville from Ogden, a fifteen-mile drive north through the canyon.

With the picket of trees behind the gas station blocking Duncan from seeing Eden and Huntsville and the mountains he knew rose up behind the small towns, he inexplicably recalled a place he'd been that lay a short distance beyond the trees. A place out of sight and mind to most. He let his eyes roam the trees from right to left and caught a glimpse of where a short run of gray feeder road dodged north off of 39. It was unmarked and roughly equidistant from the station and where 39 started to rise. He put it at a quarter-mile, maybe less.

Duncan knew from past experience where the feeder road ended. And he knew it was unmarked because the facility at its terminus was of no concern to the general public. He set out walking toward the trees, west by north across the lot. Trudged through an expanse of knee-high grass and continued on the diagonal tangent taking him to the point in the distance where the secondary road disappeared into the trees.

Before Duncan reached the trees, beer number five was in his gut, the can crushed under his heel, and the evidence stuffed into his jacket pocket. *No sense in leaving a trail of crumbs for someone to follow*, he mused, as he opened another beer, wholly intent on lightening his load while doing a little much needed forgettin' on the way to his destination.

Two birds, one stone.

***

On the unmarked logging road, roughly two miles northeast of the Eden compound, Taryn and Wilson's fight for survival was in full swing.

Taryn was standing as Brook had taught her: wide aggressive stance to absorb recoil, a slight bend to her knees in case she had to rapidly fall back or dive to evade incoming fire, shoulders generally squared to the target to allow a natural pocket in which to snug the M4's buttstock.

She was firing and reloading with the snowmachine as a buffer between her and the dead streaming up the road. One male zombie was sprawled across the padded seat, twice-dead, its back bent at an unnatural angle in relation to its hips. A bullet fired

126

from either her or Wilson's M4 had caught it in the face, erasing its nose and right cheek, stopping it mid-stride, the vicious blow sending it windmilling away. To add insult to injury, a follow-on shot had opened up its guts, spilling a morass of putrid organs on the ground beside the Yamaha's rear track. A second rotter on the ground by the first had caught a two-round tap from Taryn's rifle. A face already beat upon by some kind of blunt weapon collapsed in on itself like an empty potato chip bag. Rear of its head opened up like an overripe melon, brain tissue dribbled to the forest floor from a flesh-ringed exit wound that may have once been an ear.

Advance stalled by another ferocious volley fired from Taryn's first magazine, another pair of undead had come to rest tangled together in a verdant bed of ferns growing beside the road a few feet beyond the first two to fall to her accurate fire.

A dozen feet to Taryn's left, standing roughly where one of the parallel tire ruts would be, stood Wilson. The floppy brim on his boonie hat partially obscured the sneer on his face as shell casings arced from his rifle.

"These are not stragglers," he stated emphatically.

Slamming a fresh magazine into her rifle, Taryn answered, "We can't hold them off here." She was searching her memory for the exact verbiage Cade had taught them when Wilson voiced it, saying, "*Break contact ...* we'll regroup a few yards west and cull some more."

"The uneven ground," called Taryn, exasperation in her tone. "They're weaving and bobbing." She fired a dozen rounds, dropping only two of the ten or so rotters coming at her. Breathing hard, she backpedaled from the Yamaha. "Makes it near impossible to get a head shot."

"Keep it up," Wilson bellowed as he dropped a fast-moving fresh turn angling for Taryn.

Down on one knee in the center of the road and shooting head-high into the advancing column, Taryn called, "Can our stray bullets reach the compound?"

"Too far," Wilson said, leapfrogging a fallen rotter. "Wrong direction, too." Seeing Taryn raise her rifle and turn to run, he pumped a few rounds into her pursuers, scoring only a single headshot for his efforts.

Already a number of paces ahead of Wilson, Taryn slowed and said, "Aren't we leading them toward the compound if we stick to the road?"

Wilson heard her but didn't answer. A radio was pressed to his ear and he was focused on his footing as he broke through the gun smoke haze.

Taryn shouldered her rifle after he passed by her. She estimated the magazine was half empty. Maybe even down to ten rounds or so. Definitely a no-no in Cade's book. Any chance he got he stressed the importance of practicing solid situational awareness—the amount of ammo in a mag at any given time being a major component to the edict. She steadied her breathing and settled the holographic sight on the closest zombie. Head high. The bridge of its nose, specifically. Less bone mass to contend with. Which lessened the chance of the speeding 5.56 hardball round to be deflected into the woods. Ineffective. Thus a waste of a hard to come by commodity.

The thing's face imploded and she blinked as the contents of its brainpan tumbled out mostly intact. She had already shifted aim and was engaging the next zombie in line. Thanks to the flurry of suppressed gunshots, she was spared from hearing the wet thud the three-pound organ made when it struck the ground and broke apart.

Wilson waited for the tell-tale sound of Taryn's bolt locking open to reach forward and grab her arm.

"This way," he called, pulling her off the road and into the woods. Parting bushes with one hand, he rolled the M4 to his back with the other. Ducking under a low branch, the boonie hat was ripped from his head. But he didn't lose his only good luck charm. Cutting a horizontal abrasion across his Adam's apple, the hat's long, leather chin strap arrested its fall and sent it spinning around to his chest, where it bounced and swung back and forth as he broke brush for Taryn.

Sticking close, they pushed deeper into the forest. Once the noise of branches breaking and guttural moans and raspy calls of the dead were almost out of earshot, Wilson stopped and plucked the radio from a pocket with trembling hands. His chest heaved as he tried to catch his breath.

In the trees above some kind of bird squawked. A high-pitched sound that was promptly answered by a similar call from somewhere higher up in an adjacent tree.

Fielding a questioning look from Taryn, Wilson rolled the volume up and hailed the compound.

Tran came back at once. "What's up?" he asked.

Wilson gave a quick rundown of their situation then asked if one or more of the group could meet them by the road with a machete or two and spare magazines for their M4s.

"If Seth wants to take over for me," Tran answered, "I'll head out as soon as possible. If not … you know how he's been talking about pulling his weight around here. Especially after Daymon—"

Cutting him off, Wilson said, "I don't care if SpongeBob and Patrick the frickin' starfish meet us on 39 holding machineguns. Just make it happen." Tran's reply was a bit garbled, because Wilson was already putting the Motorola away. He figured it had begun with a query about the two fictional characters he'd just referenced. Tran knew a lot; however, he knew very little when it came to pop culture. The guy hadn't even seen a Star Wars movie, for crying out loud.

"They're coming," Taryn said. Save for big red splotches on her cheeks, her face was ashen. Gulping air, she turned and looked the way they'd come. "Are you sure about this?"

"Got any better ideas?"

Taryn bit her lip and shook her head.

The noise of twigs and branches breaking was getting louder. As the reek of carrion became evident, the birds went deathly quiet.

"Let's go," she called.

Hat in hand, Wilson dragged a sleeve across his brow. Shaped by the boonie hat, his shock of red hair looked a bit like a pencil eraser.

A sight that would normally conjure a half smile or draw a quip from Taryn, did nothing. She took a few steps deeper into the woods and looked over her shoulder.

"They *have* to see us for this to work," Wilson explained.

She shook her head slowly side to side. She hadn't felt this exposed since the daring rescue by Cade on the tarmac at Grand Junction Regional, surrounded by dead things and with bullets flying.

Cupping his hands around his mouth, Wilson faced where he guessed the rotters would soon reappear. In a voice he didn't know he possessed—a booming baritone rivaling James Earl Jones'—he bellowed, "Come and get it pusbags. Dinner is served." Then, much higher in tone, added some sound effects. "Ding, ding, ding ..." Still imitating the dinner bell, he looked right just in time to see branches fold around Taryn as she stole away in the general direction of the nearby state route.

When the first slack face emerged from the woods a few feet to Wilson's fore, he waited until the dead eyes acquired him, then set off after Taryn, his throat burning from a combination of the noxious odor preceding the dead and vocal cords getting a workout they hadn't seen since the early days when screams came early and often at the sight of just one of these dead things.

Chapter 18

Cade covered the distance from the F-650 to the westernmost edge of the body shop's car-choked lot in four long strides. Wedged in tight against a half-dozen similar vehicles in front of him was a four-door sedan. As he planted a Danner on its rust-pitted bumper and scrabbled onto its trunk, he was reminded of the Washington D.C. mission.

Hard as it was to believe, it'd been less than a week since he was with the Pale Riders and clomping across the sea of cars clogging the six-lane boulevard fronting the National Archives building. *First time for everything* had occurred to him at the time. *Boot, roof, bonnet,* was Axe's unique way of describing the method they'd all employed to reach the target building unscathed. *Trunk, roof, hood,* was how Cade described it to Duncan as they sat in camp chairs in front of the dying fire talking about anything and everything *but* his experience inside the nearby Winnebago.

Stuffing the thoughts of that awful night back down where they belonged, he picked his way carefully from car to car. Along the way he came across Zs trapped *between* the cars. He batted their grabby hands away using the Glock's stubby suppressor. Two-thirds of the way across the lot, a Z in a closed-up car made a play for him. The sound of teeth splintering against the partially open window was still with him as he reached the final car, ran up the Chevy Nova's gently sloped trunk, and vaulted over its expansive rear window.

A hollow *pop* and sharp *crack* sounded back to back when his hundred and eighty pounds came down hard on the roof, causing it to buckle and the grimy windshield to spider in a hundred different directions.

He slid down the cratered windshield and sat on the hood, staying there only long enough to survey the damage.

From the ground to about the top of the Nova's hood the rollup door was out of its tracks. If the car's left front fender hadn't hit the cement block wall, the point on the hood where Cade was sitting would be inside the garage. As it was, the angle the car had come to rest left only a triangular opening at ground level that looked barely big enough for him to squeeze his body through.

He banged on the metal door three times then waited ten seconds. Time crawled, but nothing rammed against the door from inside. However, he did hear what sounded to him like a barber running a straight razor back and forth along a leather strop. It lasted for a few seconds then was gone.

Satisfied an attack on the door from inside was not imminent, he slid off the hood and stood on a tiny triangle of cement bordered by the car at his back, the rollup door to his fore, and, bumping out a couple of feet on his right, the thirty-foot-tall cement block column rising up between the two rollup doors.

A quick peek around the column confirmed there was no getting to the rollup door through the vehicles stacked up against it.

There's got to be a way in. Resigned to the fact the jagged hole by his feet was it, he fished out his tactical flashlight and thumbed it on. Flashlight clamped between his teeth, he went to his stomach, crawled forward, and stuck his head and arm through the opening. Playing the harsh white beam from left to right only revealed to him a tiny percentage of all that was in there. And while he wasn't bothered by enclosed spaces, what little he did see led him to believe he was about to venture into a claustrophobe's worst nightmare.

With the flashlight back in his mouth and the beam tracing crazy patterns on the ceiling, he wriggled the rest of the way into the garage bay flat on his back. Once the toes of his boots were clear of the bottom edge of the rollup door, he immediately transitioned to his stomach and drew the Glock from the thigh holster. Quickly rising to one knee, he snatched the tac-light from his mouth with his left hand, leveled the Glock's suppressor across his left wrist, and swept the room visually for threats.

Unable to see much more from this elevation than he had from the worm's eye view, he braced the hand with the flashlight on the car to his left and rose up off the cool cement floor. Caught in the light spill beyond the car was a windowless door. On the center of the door at eye level was a sign that read OFFICE - NO ADMITTANCE. Seemingly yanked from an episode of *Hoarders*, twin towers of newspapers and magazines stacked haphazardly to the header bracketed the office door. The shelves on the wall to the right of the office door held dozens of automotive repair manuals and parts catalogs.

Painting the rear wall and ceiling with the beam explained the reason for the garage's unusually inky interior. The four rectangular windows running along the back wall were papered over on the inside. That the sheets of newsprint had yet to go yellow and turn brittle told him the papering job was recent and likely done to guard against the prying eyes of the dead. Overhead, the glass in the skylights was coated with leaves, their irregular edges overlapping to create a near impenetrable veil against the weak sun.

Lighting up the car to his left revealed it as some kind of American classic—an early model Buick Riviera according to the emblem on the trunk lid. It was white and low to the ground and wide at the hips. The rear sheet metal was formed into a V that started wide at the roof and culminated in a rounded hump where the trunk met the W-shaped bumper.

Someone had definitely planned on restoring the aerodynamic beauty—*had* being the operative word.

Sandwiched between the Riviera's bumper and bowed-in rollup door was an impassible jumble of fenders and doors. Wedged in there with the loose parts was an old motorcycle. The wide sweeping handlebars and teardrop tank suggested to Cade it was a Norton Indian or early model Harley Davidson. The cracking paint and rusting chrome told him a restoration had also likely been in its future. *Best laid plans.* Then the world went to shit and survival trumped the long-term aspirations so prevalent to that old way of life. And just like the tiling job and honey-dos he was poised to tackle back in Portland the weekend Omega reared its ugly head, these projects had lost all relevance.

With every nook and cranny in the garage filled with one thing or another, the Buick's roof had become a place to store yellowed cardboard boxes brimming with trim pieces and upholstery parts. A number of the boxes, their sides split open to reveal more chrome trim pieces and shiny emblems, had slid down the windshield and come to rest in a heap on the Buick's massive hood.

Rising a few feet over the hood was an enormous upright tool box. Like the motorcycle and parts behind the Buick, the multi-shelved tool box was pinched between the Riviera's front bumper and a waist-high workbench running the length of the garage's entire back wall.

Cade illuminated the right-side bay. Saw more of the same. Nearly touching the rear wall, its black paint and matching convertible top wearing a thick coating of dust, was a two-door Chevrolet Impala. A second car with black badging identifying it as a Triumph TR-7 was perched precariously on a four-corner lift, its undercarriage visible and hovering just a handful of feet above the Impala's vinyl top. The lift was leaning forward and listing in the direction of the left-side bay. Somehow the red sports car had ridden part way off the lift, ending up with its angular nose touching the back wall, its left front fender resting on one of the building's two cement support columns, and both driver's side tires hanging off the lift.

Scattered about the floor under the Triumph's nose were dozens of paint cans and the lengths of fiberboard shelving on which they used to reside.

Taking up most of the dead space between the Riviera and pair of support columns was a tire balancing machine and a second piece of equipment fitted with wires and hoses. Opposite the equipment was the female first turn responsible for the razor on leather rasp. Trapped between bays, it made lazy laps between the pillars while dragging in its wake a splinted and bandaged left leg.

As the tac-light beam spilled over into the far bay, there came the all too familiar nerve-jangling screech of fingernails on metal. A middle-aged male Z had somehow become trapped between the Impala and workbench. Now fully aware of its proximity to fresh meat, the thing thrashed around and continued to drag its fingernails across the Impala's severely scored hood.

Amid the dry rasps and keen of nails on metal, Cade detected movement in the shadows on the floor between columns. *Rats?* Not likely considering the company he was already keeping. It was his experience that, big or small, animals wanted nothing to do with the undead.

Illuminating the floor revealed another Z. It was pinned face down and mostly hidden from view by the pair of toppled welding tanks lying across its upper back. Naked from the waist up, crisscross welts oozing pus and brackish blood covered its pale, hairless back. He saw that all of the muscle and flesh had been surgically excised from its legs. Neat rectangles a few inches deep were carved out of its neck on both sides. Whether the damage to its back was from branches in the wild or a sadist with a whip, he hadn't a clue. The missing flesh pointed to Adrian and her gang, which lent credence to the whip and sadist theory.

As soon as the circle of light made its way to the oil-stained cement near the butchered rotter's head, the thing arched its back, lolled its nearly detached head to the right, and stared side-eyed into the beam. Near simultaneously, the sound of its bare feet and hands slapping the floor echoed around the room. Down to the wanting look on its features, the thing appeared to be in the throes of the mother of all temper tantrums.

If the stakes behind his foray into the garage weren't so high, Cade might have found a bit of humor in the sight.

Trying his best to ignore the macabre symphony being put on by the trio of trapped dead things, he played the light left to right along the workbench at the back wall. Shelves on the wall above the work surface held what looked like cans of body putty and paint primer. Several specialized paint nozzles hung on hooks above the shelving. Which made him think that where there were nozzles, there was likely a tank of compressed air.

He walked the beam along the leading edge of the workbench but couldn't see past the boxes and parts littering the Riviera's sloped hood. To cut the angle so he could determine what was underneath the workbench, he was going to have to pick his way through the middle of the junk-filled shop and dispatch the Zs along the way.

The former was easier said than done for a guy his size wearing a plate carrier and MOLLE rig stuffed with spare magazines.

The latter would just take a bit of patience and planning to safely execute.

Chapter 19

Cade made his way to the right-side bay, stopped next to the Impala, and illuminated the female roamer already taking stilted steps in his direction. Adopting a shooter's stance, he met the monster's soulless gaze and tracked it all the way to the nearest column where its path was blocked by some king of machinery used to shape metal. *An English wheel?*

The piece of equipment was head-high to the Z and heavy enough to halt its forward march. Undeterred, the thing continued to shuffle its feet on the dusty floor and reach for him. The knee brace clanked against the tool and the tool banged into the near pillar as the Z hissed and craned its neck, trying to get to the meat.

Taking advantage of the waifish Z's ambulatory misfortune, Cade made his way to the first pillar, where he paused and lit up its sneering face with the blue-white circle thrown from his tactical light. Enjoying a six-inch reach over the grabby monster, he threaded the Glock past the machine's vertical arm. Fighting the tug of the Z's kneading fingers, he pressed the suppressor firmly against its milky left eye and caressed the trigger.

There was a wet squelch and the creature's right eye bugged out under pressure. While the 9mm round was touring the inside of its cranium, the metallic rattle-clatter of the slide ejecting spent brass was touring the garage. Most of the report and all of the muzzle flash was absorbed by brain tissue.

Cade pushed aside the metal-shaping machine and stepped over the twice-dead corpse. Coming around the backside of the first column, he sidestepped a wheeled welding rig and then stopped and illuminated the second Z. As he steadied the Glock over the hand holding the flashlight, his eyes flicked from the hissing monster to the tanks pinning it to the floor. Quick to conclude one or both contained enough flammable gas to ruin his day, he holstered the pistol.

Clamping the light between his teeth, he drew the Gerber and took a knee beside the Z. Holding its head firm to the ground with one hand, he positioned the Gerber's razor-sharp tip at the base of the writhing monster's skull. A little pressure applied to the pommel started the blade on its journey through the tiny gap separating medulla and vertebra. A quick twist of the wrist severed the spinal cord and scrambled the brain, stilling the rancid-smelling beast instantly. It was the same highly effective and silent one-two punch he had employed on the living dead many more times than he cared to count. And in hindsight, he should have done the same to silence the female Z.

With the zombie to his right still assaulting the Impala's hood, Cade cleaned the sullied blade on the fallen Z's shirt. As he snugged the Gerber into its scabbard, a drawn-out groan joined the trapped Z's ongoing solo performance. Looking up to where the sound of what he guessed was metal shifting under stress had emanated, he received a face full of white powder. It was real fine and smelled faintly of chemicals. *Cement dust? Plaster?*

While he couldn't quite place the odor and had no idea what the white stuff still drifting to the floor was, its presence told him the place was in no way as structurally sound as it had appeared from the outside. His admonishment to Raven echoed in his head. *Don't go jinxing me now, Bird.* And though he knew her words had zero impact on what happened in the real world, Mister Murphy was always present, cracking his knuckles, eager to throw a monkey wrench into his plans.

Prepare for the worst. Hope for the best.

Aiming the flashlight at the back half of the garage, he rose and stepped over the leaking corpse. Wary of the sports car looming over his right shoulder, he ducked under a piece of automotive trim curling off its driver's side door and waded through the paint cans littering the floor.

Cade was still envisioning the red car sliding off the lift and doing to him what the welding tanks had done to the Z when the second support column was caught up in the bouncing beam of his tac-light. It was clear to him straight away the column was compromised structurally. Some of the cement blocks on the right side and a good deal around back had come loose. Broken blocks and strips of mortar from the side and rear of the column had settled in one large pile that filled up the space from the Impala's left front fender to the partially crushed workbench. And though the debris field was blocking his path to the workbench and whatever was being stored underneath it, if he could find the angle, the flashlight's beam would get in there and tell him all he needed to know.

With the zombie continuing to rake on the Chevy on his right, and the listing car overhead impossible to forget, Cade ducked under the forward edge of the lift supporting it and clambered up the unstable mound.

Stretched out atop the pile with the sharp edges of masonry stabbing into his thighs, stomach, and elbows, he took the flashlight from his mouth, craned his neck, and aimed it at the infinite darkness in front of the Buick. Beginning at the floor by the car's front fender, he walked the beam forward slowly all the way to the upright tool box. Only thing he saw was more cobwebs, dust bunnies, and tiny conical piles of the same white stuff that had dusted his face and chest rig. On the return pass he made sure the beam infiltrated the deep shelving underneath the workbench. About the point on the Buick's bumper where a license plate would be, pushed in deep on the lowest shelf, was what appeared to be an air compressor. It was oblong with wheels on one end and a stubby handle on the other. Wrapped around the U-shaped handle was an orange power cord. Next to the wheeled item was a plastic milk crate brimming with hoses and various attachments. As Cade resumed the sweep, the light revealed a red cylindrical item pushed all the way to the rear of the same shelf that held the crate and compressor. Compared to the tank affixed to the compressor, the red tank was smaller by half. And though it looked to be slimmer and taller, Cade figured, viewed side-by-side, it could easily be confused with one of the propane tanks that fired Tran's outdoor grill. A black hose snaking off the side of the tank was fitted with a nickel-plated nozzle that reflected the beam back at him. Attached to the tank was a gauge roughly the circumference of a baseball. Noting where the smaller tank sat in relation to the items on the wall directly above the workbench, he returned the beam to the sliver of ground below the Buick's bumper. While Cade would have rather crawled under the bench to get to the items stowed there, it was clear to him he was going to have to navigate the foot-wide gap between the Buick's front end and workbench. And to make matters worse, the gap narrowed exponentially where the car's hood and front bumper came to a point.

Seeing no other viable option, he again clamped the light between his teeth, then removed the bulky MOLLE rig and dumped it atop the workbench. Grateful he didn't share Daymon's fear of dark, cramped spaces, he turned sideways and slipped by the pillar, then continued on, scraping his butt against the land yacht's right-side headlight housing as he positioned himself to try something that would cause a man Tran's size to think twice. With the beam from the flashlight skipping wildly across the shelves to his fore, and the irregular edges of car parts and stiffened flaps of split-open cardboard boxes caressing his back, he began a slow shimmy to his left. Protruding a few inches over the grille, the hood followed the bumper's contour. And though the gap between the hood and workbench widened after he pushed past the headlight stack, it narrowed almost immediately and was damn near crushing his pelvis.

From the distant recon, he knew the out of sight tank was nestled under the workbench near here with the compressor and attachments crowding in on it. Viewed from a weird angle and nearly twenty feet distant, gauging its exact location in relation to the car was a guessing game at best. Seeing as how the wall was, give or take a few inches, a yard back from the front edge of the workbench, he was certain the tank he needed to get his hands on lay somewhere between eighteen and twenty-four inches from the front edge. Hoping for the former, he tried a couple of stunted kicks to the out of sight airspace, wracking his shin on something sharp in the process.

Cade's attempt at a side bend didn't fare better. And he guessed it looked just as awkward, because his upper body didn't get past forty-five degrees before the workbench came into play, grinding into the plate carrier strapped over his Crye Precision shirt. With a sizable group of dead heading east on 39, and who knew how many congregating outside the garage, the last thing he needed was to become trapped in here and have to call his daughter for an extraction. So instead of forcing the issue, literally and figuratively, he hinged up and thought things through.

Short of cleaning out the mess behind the Riviera and rolling it backward—a laborious and time-consuming task for one person—there was only one way he could think of to access the lower shelves. Liberating a piece of chrome door trim from a box on the hood behind him, and fully aware of the ball busting he'd endure if any of the Pale Riders were here to see what he was about to do, he drew in a deep breath and put his arms down by his sides. Keeping the air trapped in his lungs and his stomach muscles tensed, he attempted a ballet move he'd seen Raven perform but whose name he didn't remember. Feeling his cheeks go hot from the lack of oxygen, he pronated both feet until his heels were touching and his toes pointed in opposite directions. Finally, in one fluid motion—as if he'd been taking notes at Raven's dance recital—he bent his knees and dipped his hips, all the while keeping his back ramrod straight. Slow and steady, he let gravity drag him down until his chin was nearly resting on the dusty workbench. Holding the pose, he maneuvered the piece of trim underneath the workbench and swept it blindly left to right on a level plane.

At first all he felt was the feathery kiss on the backs of his hands of what he imagined was an intricate network of cobwebs being destroyed. Then he heard a hollow *clang* as his makeshift probe struck metal. Gripping the piece of auto trim two-handed, he exerted pressure on the object, trying to get it to move, and failing, because the length of sixties-era metal gave first, bending at a right angle before snapping off completely.

Left holding a worthless six-inch piece of broken trim, Cade rose and exhaled sharply.

Seeing nothing on the bench to his fore to employ in place of the auto trim, he dragged the Glock from the drop thigh holster and put the light beam on it. Gauging its length from grip to suppressor at a little over a foot, he decided it might do the trick. But first, to extend his reach, he shuffled his feet forward—heel, toe, heel, toe—gaining ground on the out of sight tank in tiny increments.

Again he drew in a breath and repeated the yet to be named ballet move.

Feeling the burn work its way through his shoulders and down both arms, he strained hard against the bench top and probed the dark under the workbench with the Glock. He worked the pistol left to right until he heard a hollow *thunk* and felt the suppressor skip over top of something solid.

The milk crate?

He repeated the move, Glock sweeping right to left on the same flat plane, and felt the contact again. Firming his wrists and applying a hard forward press got the item moving on a diagonal path toward his knees. There was a scraping noise and the item continued its forward march until the suppressor lost purchase and he rapped his knuckles on something hard.

All in all he guessed the item moved about six inches.

Close, but no cigar.

Feeling his heartbeat in his temple, he took another swipe at the out of sight object. There was another *thunk*, followed by a grating noise, then the Glock was unexpectedly light in his hands and the item he'd struck with it was on its way to the floor. The *bang* the item made when it hit was followed at once by a clatter as something else landed on the floor near his feet.

While Cade's first instinct was to eyeball the fruits of his labor, he was literally in no position to do so. Instead, he rose and again purged the air trapped in his lungs.

A quick turkey peek told him he'd knocked the crate from the shelf. It was on its side, the items it once contained now on the floor by his boots.

As Cade drew another deep breath and dropped back into the ballet pose, the trapped Z to his right ramped up its attack on American sheet metal.

Remembering the crate had been sitting to the right of the tank, he tightened his grip on the Glock and moved his hands slowly right to left until the suppressor once again struck something solid.

This time there was a soft *clang* instead of a *thunk*.

Bingo.

Attacking the item in the same manner as he had the crate brought mostly the same result. Only the item didn't end up on the floor by his feet; instead it fell over and rolled forward, coming to rest against his right knee.

Still holding his breath, Cade placed the Glock gently on the workbench. Then, hoping he wasn't going to throw away all of his hard work, render the contorting and oxygen deprivation moot by fumbling the tank and send it rolling on a one-way trip off the shelf and under the Buick, he felt around gingerly until his fingers found what had to be a handle of sorts. Saying a silent prayer, he threaded his fingers into the handle and rose, bringing the item along with him. The tank he placed upright on the workbench. Pointing his light at it, he saw the attached hose was fitted with a trigger-actuated air gun. Holding his breath solely as a precaution against failure, he picked up the handle and gave the trigger a gentle squeeze. The burst of air that shot from the nozzle was rivaled only by the whoosh of air leaving his lungs. Relief washed over him as the stale smelling air started a tsunami of particles roiling through the flashlight beam.

Grateful that the tank contained air, he shoved the crate aside with a nudge from his boot and looked sidelong at the items on the floor. Due to the viewing angle and that he could only train his right eye on the jumble of hoses and couplings and air tools, he wasn't certain the item specific to his needs was even there. So he placed the flashlight on the workbench and again performed the ballet move— hopefully for the final time. In fact, if he never had to contort his body like this again, he would die a happy man.

Coming up with a fistful of hoses, he dumped the items on the workbench. Spreading them out with both hands, he spotted the gas-station-style tire inflation gun he needed. And it came complete with the same rudimentary pop-out pressure gauge as the ones he was familiar with. The cherry on the sundae was the three-foot length of hose and quick-connect coupling attached to it.

The inflation gun went in the pocket with the radio. He didn't have the energy to do anything with the hose, so he let it dangle down by the side of his leg.

Abs and lower back a bit sore from holding the most uncomfortable position in the world, he made a mental note to ask Raven if she remembered what the nightmare pose was called.

Something French, no doubt.

Consulting the Suunto's glowing green display, he learned he'd been inside the garage three full minutes and away from the truck less than five. Wanting to spend no more time than necessary near the compromised column and ton or so of British steel resting against it, he clamped the flashlight between his teeth, threw the MOLLE rig on, holstered the Glock, and slid the tank off the workbench. Holding the hard-won prize one-handed in front of him, he shimmied back the way he'd come.

Pausing at the column to switch the tank to his left hand, the beam inadvertently swung right and put the trapped Z in the spotlight. As the thing stopped attacking the hood and craned in Cade's direction, he spotted on the thing's neck a near-perfect rectangle where skin, flesh, and a substantial piece of trachea had been excised.

Adrian's doing.

As Cade slipped past the column, he saw that the Z's constant movement had just about finished the job the Impala's front bumper had started. The skin around its waist was rubbed raw. Where the muscles meant to keep internal organs in place were failing, greasy ropes of intestine had snaked out. Another day or so spent writhing and scratching paint off the hood and this guy would be freed of his lower extremities.

"Can't help you, buddy," Cade said, his words a little garbled thanks to the flashlight in his mouth. In a rare moment, he let his guard down and began to feel sorry for whoever the middle-aged man once was. For the people he once loved, and likely lost to the same thing that had him here rotting away in a garage instead of looking for something to assuage the crisis that inevitably struck people his age. Maybe a red Corvette. A chromed-out motorcycle. Or a woman fifteen years his junior.

None of it was going to happen.

Though Cade contemplated taking the time to release the poor guy from his worldly bonds, the unstoppable forward march of time trumped pausing to grant the mercy kill. After one last glance and a mumbled, "I'm sorry," he ducked under the bent trim piece, hustled past the menacing Triumph, and crabbed around the welding gear.

Four minutes after entering the garage, Cade was kneeling before the rollup and shoving the air tank into daylight. Ignoring the sounds of another dead thing slamming into the nearby office door, he broke squelch two times on the Motorola and stuffed it back into his pocket.

Promise to Raven fulfilled, he laid flat on his back on the cement floor and wriggled headfirst into daylight. And as he lay there squinting against the watery sun, the radio hissed static and Raven delivered a one-word order that was wholly unexpected.

Chapter 20

Raven had watched her dad intently from the moment he closed the door behind him until he was safely inside the garage. Seeing him bound from car to car to get to the rollup doors made her think of a frog using lily pads to cross a pond. When he slid down the last car and disappeared from view, the realization she was truly alone outside the wire started within her the first stirrings of an anxiety attack. Having no way of self-diagnosing the sudden rapid rise in heartbeat and inability to draw a normal breath, she rose up from the seat and checked her surroundings.

North, along the body shop's west-facing wall, the view was unobstructed. *Nothing moving there.* To the west was just the empty field and distant tree-lined ridge to look at. A quick glance in the rearview told her the route they had taken to get here was zombie-free all the way to the 39/16 junction.

The knowledge that her blind sides were clear for now helped to calm the caged animal trying to claw its way out of her chest. Which in turn allowed her to draw a few deep, calming breaths.

Confident *her* six was clear, she scooped up the Steiners so she could watch her dad's six. She glassed the corner of the garage farthest from her position. It was adjacent to the sidewalk and just a few feet removed from the right-side rollup door. If any dead things were coming down Main from the north, this was where she would see them first. It was the most dangerous of all the approaches, because if the dead somehow managed to navigate the downed poles and power lines and get to the blind corner, she would have little time to warn her dad, and even less time to react.

The second approach was where her dad said the Zs were most likely to appear. *The path of least resistance* was what he called it. It just looked like a block-long stretch of Center Street to her. But she knew what he meant.

Beginning at the body shop's blind corner, she slowly panned right to the intersection of Main and Center, maybe a hundred feet total. From there she walked her gaze slowly eastbound, all the way to the next intersection, which was bracketed on two sides by medium-sized trees. Unable to see the road through the trees, she began the return sweep, pausing here and there for closer looks at the bullet-riddled vehicles sitting on Center beside what was left of *Back In The Saddle Rehabilitation.* Seeing nothing moving inside the pair of pickups along the building's south wall and unable to see inside the lone SUV listing precariously over the partially exposed basement, she gave the gravel lot behind the compromised structure a quick onceover.

Determining the lot to be free of dead things, Raven turned her attention to the tiny house across the street from the destroyed vehicles. Behind windows mostly devoid of glass, tattered curtains hung limply from bent rods. Moving on to the door, she saw it was dotted with jagged-edged holes created by what she figured was a large volume of incoming gunfire. The door had taken so many hits in the center that the white X Adrian's people had scribed there was barely recognizable as a letter, let alone a sign the house had already been cleaned out of anything useful to surviving the zombie apocalypse.

Seeing nothing to worry her inside the house, or roaming about its expansive side yards, Raven reversed the sweep, dragging the binoculars west down Center, then north along Main and, after a seconds-long pause at the blind corner, started the process all over again.

On Raven's second pass with the Steiners along Main and Center, barely thirty seconds into her first ever overwatch, as Duncan liked to say about any and every situation involving the dead things: *The shit hit the fan.*

Drawing a deep breath, she settled the binoculars on the first Z to emerge from the lot behind the rehab place. It was definitely a first turn. Affected by time and the elements, its skin had gone tight all over and turned a light shade of gray. As one jaundiced eye roamed the road ahead, the other, suspended by something thin and stringy and about a foot long, jerked to and fro with each stilted step. The only stitch of clothing on its shriveled body were the torn and blood-spattered dress pants. Held up by a wide leather belt buried deeply into decaying flesh and muscle, the pants did little to conceal a penis that looked *nothing* like the pictures she'd seen in Mom's nursing books.

As the first turn performed a low-speed step to the left to get past the inert SUV blocking its path, more dead things spilled from the lot behind it. As the rapidly forming group rounded the SUV, she saw it was made up of five road-worn first turns and six recent turns, the skin on the latter still somewhat pliable and pale as freshly fallen snow. While the new arrivals straightened into a ragged line in the middle of Center Street, another three recent turns surged into view from behind the rehab place.

In seconds, all of the hungering corpses had threaded between the pair of abandoned pickups and coalesced into a pack fifteen strong.

Finished counting heads, Raven brought the binoculars to bear on the male Z leading the procession. And though she had dutifully followed her dad's orders, keeping down in the cab and her movements economical, inexplicably the zombie's unblinking eyes were locked with hers. There was no emotion relayed, only the insatiable hunger that caused her to throw a hard shiver. Feeling the hair on her arms prick, she moved the binoculars along the line, from sneering face to sneering face, and came to believe they were *all* staring at her.

As Raven watched their advance, trying to decide when and where to engage them, she noticed the leader's eyes tracking left of her. The shift from her to the garage came in barely discernable increments; however, the closer the Z got to Main, the more its gaze moved to the latter.

Walking the Steiners up the line, Raven learned they were all following the same pattern.

They weren't focused on me, she thought. *They're hunting Dad.*

The revelation hit her like a gut punch.

How the monsters knew he was in there was beyond her. Maybe the *pop-thunk-pop-thunk-pop* of car roofs buckling as he traversed the lot had drawn their attention. Did he make noise getting into the garage that she wasn't able to hear from inside the cab? Maybe. *Every* little sound carried great distances now that there were no cars driving the state routes, no jet airplanes overhead, and no distant trains blowing their horns.

The only scenario that she could think of was they had spotted him from beyond the blind corner, gotten diverted by the junk blocking the road, and then worked their way around back of the rehab place.

Path of least resistance.

None of that mattered right now. What did was that her dad was exposed and all alone inside the place. And to make things worse, a pack made up of that many first turns, a pack that *should* be moving painfully slow, was now in *hunt* mode with the much faster fresh turns setting the pace. And much to her chagrin, the older specimens were, for the most part, keeping up with them.

Screw you, Murphy.

At the speed the pack was moving, Raven figured she had less than a minute to decide what to do and act on it before they made it to the garage.

She couldn't let that happen. No way. If the pack reached the cars straddling the sidewalk, there was no doubt in her mind some of them would find a way to get to the last meat they set their eyes on—her dad.

Chapter 21

Heart rate ramping up, Raven set the radio aside and hauled the M4 into her lap. She burned a few seconds going through the motions of readying the rifle. Finished locking the 3x magnifier in place, she grabbed the radio and reached up and hit the rocker switch to start the power moon roof rolling back in its tracks. Once the pane of smoked glass hit the stops, she rose up through the opening. After planting her boots a shoulder width apart on the center console's padded top, she rested her elbows on the flat expanse of sheet metal between the moon roof's lip and the passenger-door rain channel.

She ripped her stocking hat off her head, positioned it on the roof to lay the M4's forestock across, then returned her attention to the fast-moving pack, learning straightaway it was about to flow onto Main.

Use your best judgment.

Having made her mind up on a course of action, she was going for the radio when two distinct clicks emanated from its speaker.

You can't come out yet, Dad.

She snatched up the radio and thumbed the talk key. "Wait," she blurted. Definitely not how she heard the grownups begin a conversation, but it got her point across. "There's a pack of rotters heading right for your position."

"Copy that. How many?"

While the agreed-upon signal assuring Raven her dad was OK and on his way out of the garage had quelled the rising panic attack, hearing his voice coming out of that speaker bolstered her confidence a thousand-fold.

"Fifteen or so," she said in a voice firm and full of confidence.

"First turns ... or?"

"A mix," she replied. "I got this."

"Can you do them with one magazine?"

"I'll hope for the best." She set the radio on the roof beside her, snugged the buttstock to her shoulder, and framed the front of the pack with the optics. While the dead looked close enough to touch thanks to the magnification, they came across a bit jittery.

You got this.

She threw the safety off. Put her finger in the well and touched the cool, smooth trigger.

Breathe in.

Draw up some trigger pull.

Smooth on the follow through.

As she went through the checklist in her head, it was her mom's reassuring voice she was hearing. When she finally tensed her finger on the trigger, she heard her dad in her head.

Work smarter, not harder.

The Zs were two abreast up front and about to round the corner when she let the crosshairs slip from the targeted Z's face to its crotch and let loose the first 5.56 hardball round.

The report sounded like a textbook slamming shut. The metallic *tink* of the spent brass striking the closed tailgate was reaching her ears when the rotter went down, its right leg hinged strangely away from its body, and on its ashen face no comprehension whatsoever of what had just happened to it.

In one fluid move, Raven altered her aim right by a few degrees and put another recent turn in her crosshairs. Oblivious of the half-dozen undead falling domino-like to the pavement in its wake, the male fresh turn began making the slight course correction that would see it to the garage.

Ignoring the cluster of Zs writhing on the ground not thirty feet from where her dad was holed up, Raven squeezed off shots two and three. Striking a few inches south of her aim, the first bullet split the new leader's breastbone and splintered into three smaller pieces of hurtling lead that came tumbling out its back.

Trajectory altered by muzzle climb, the next bullet tracked high and right and carved a fist-sized wedge of flesh and dermis from the creature's neck, sending it spinning into the trailing first turns that had avoided the initial pileup.

Only three rounds expended and she was looking at half the pack sprawled out on the road and another three or four in the process of joining them there.

Not bad at all was what she was thinking as she set the rifle on its side and scooped up the radio.

The satisfaction Cade felt after realizing he'd likely never do another ballet pose was squashed by Raven's unexpected situation report. Hearing her describe her situation and how many Zs were coming his way, even delivered calmly and in a cadence reminiscent of her mom, did nothing to make Cade feel good about the situation. The distant reports of a suppressed carbine and familiar *snap-crackle* sound of rounds cutting the air nearby was no kind of comfort, either.

Sure, Raven was trained to use her weapons and possessed a rudimentary knowledge of tactics, but none of that changed the fact she was twelve years old. No amount of time spent surviving in the current environment could ready a person in her position to bear the weight of the responsibility she had just taken on.

Now, as he lay on his back with the Glock clutched to his chest and counting Raven's rounds, it was all he could do to keep from popping up for a quick recon. Nothing worse to someone like him who was used to having an eye in the sky and a team of highly trained and very lethal men on his side when facing a threat than to be left completely in the dark where situational awareness was concerned.

Three rounds? That's it?

The shooting had lasted all of ten seconds and Cade couldn't imagine a good reason why. He did, however, think of a hundred bad reasons why a shroud of silence now hung over the lot. He was fishing out the Motorola to see what was the matter when Raven radioed to tell him in a calm, somewhat smug-sounding voice that the threat was neutralized.

Thumbing the Talk key, he said, "Thunder," which was preordained code to assure her he was not compromised.

She replied at once saying, "Lightning." Then added, "The Zs are starting to get back on their feet. You have to go *now!*"

Cade didn't need to be told twice. He sprang up and all in one motion holstered the Glock, dumped the radio in a pocket, and clean-jerked the air tank off the ground.

Raven didn't need the Steiners to watch her dad's progress as he bounded from roof to trunk to roof. Though she hadn't asked if his foray into the garage was successful, the red tank swinging wildly from one of his hands was a good sign.

She watched him until he was safely down from the nearest car before tossing her backpack into the rear seat and popping the locks. Having already swapped out magazines, she double-checked the safety and stowed her M4, suppressor first, into the footwell.

Cade sprinted past the truck's grille then disappeared from sight by the left front fender.

As Raven sat there in the cab watching the pack of dead scrabbling over each other to get into the lot, she noticed a subtle movement in the truck and thought she detected the horizon out over the hood shifting slightly.

A minute passed and there was a clang in the load box and the door across from her hinged open. Her dad climbed in, bringing with him the visceral stink of rotten meat.

Nodding at the hood that was now level with the horizon, she said, "Tire's all the way full?"

"Mostly," he answered.

"You did good," she said. "And I did, too."

He said, "With only three rounds?"

She nodded. Smile forming, she said, "Work smarter, not harder."

He fiddled with his radio then put it back in his pocket. Starting the motor, he said, "After you switch your radio back to 10-1, I want you to tell me *all* about it."

Raven switched frequencies, then rolled the volume up.

The F-650 was already reversing away from the cement block wall as she dove into the story.

Chapter 22

Duncan stopped walking and put his hands on his hips. He was a bit winded as he stood there in the middle of the gravel access road with nothing to see but gray sky overhead and the reaching boughs of tall firs flanking him on both sides. Long, fuzzy shadows from the trees fell across the road, adding to the gloom, which invoked within him a strong feeling of foreboding he couldn't explain.

"Trudging the *happy* road of destiny, my sagging, lily-white ass," he drawled as he dropped the empty PBR can at his feet. He stomped it flat, leaned over with a bit of difficulty, and plucked it up with two fingers. In doing so, the M4 cascaded off his shoulder and hit the road with a clatter. This started a string of curse words directed at God as Duncan rose up and adjusted the sling so the rifle fell across his body in front. He was only muttering halfheartedly by the time he was stuffing the hockey-puck-sized chunk of aluminum in his pocket along with the other similarly flattened cans.

Hauling another beer from his coat pocket, his hand brushed paper. The *Dear John* letter from Glenda. His mood instantly turned as dark as the stretch of road he stood on. Darker, even. He hadn't felt like this in a long time. Back in the late '70s, when a doctor at the Portland V.A. hospital prescribed him Naltrexone and Antabuse and urged him to attend Alcoholics Anonymous meetings, was the last time he could remember having slipped this far down the *give a fuck* scale.

Taking the Antabuse didn't deter him from drinking. It only caused his heart to race and made him puke.

The Naltrexone he poured in the toilet on account of a fella in a bar he didn't even know telling him how it had turned him into an emotionless zombie and stole all the lead from his pencil. Last thing his much younger self wanted to hear at the time. He was still a hit with the ladies at Earthquake Ethel's and didn't want to lose his *moves* on or off the dance floor.

His stance at the time was that Alcoholics Anonymous was full of losers, people with no willpower, and those lacking discipline. That didn't describe him. He was a decorated helicopter pilot. He had no problem waiting until after five to drink. And he sure as hell knew discipline. The Army had pounded it into his every fiber starting on that bus ride to basic.

He never did set foot inside a dank church basement to drink the prescribed Kool-Aid, and as a consequence of that stubbornness, he had paid the price dearly for almost three decades.

Ignoring the letter, he zipped the pocket and got back to walking.

Duncan had covered maybe a quarter-mile and was nearing the bend in the road ahead when he popped the top on beer number six. The can was empty seconds later when he made it to the bend. Two or three long gulps and the forgettin' juice was in his gullet. But who was counting? Who even gives a shit about Old Man, now?

He was firmly seated on his pity pot and had already crushed the empty underfoot when he looked up to discover the dense woods had given way to mostly open range. The road ahead was flanked by pickets of juvenile trees and ran away die straight for a hundred yards or so to a razor-wire-topped gate. The gate was closed. Or so he thought. Everything was a bit fuzzy around the edges.

So he removed his glasses and cleaned them with a kerchief. When he put them back on, nothing had changed.

***

Three minutes after downing beer number six and one long pull into beer number seven, he was standing before the gate. It was indeed topped with coiled razor wire. And it was closed. But it wasn't locked. It was secured with a length of chain. The same one Cade had cut the lock from last time they were here.

The air was heavy with the odor of death. Like he had walked into a stagnant pocket of carrion-rich air. Only he couldn't see the source. The fence stretching away left and right was clear. No wavering rotters grasping the links with gnarled fingers. A quick glance at the ditch and tree line on either side of the road didn't identify the source. So he turned his attention to his destination.

Save for the lack of snow, everything about the Utah Department of Transportation facility was as he remembered it.

Situated diagonally from the entrance on the far right corner of the neatly graded plot of land were two outbuildings the size of double-car garages. Fronting the two outbuildings was a thirty-foot-tall structure with a shallow pitched roof that was open to the air on all four sides. Sheltered from the elements was an immense poured-concrete pad. The pad still bore a thin layer of gravel and tire marks from the loader Daymon used to fill the spreaders on the plow trucks the group liberated from here. A pair of the trucks now sat on shot-out tires in the Ogden Canyon pass, shoring up the cargo containers placed there to hold back the hordes migrating east from Ogden and points beyond. So far the block seemed to be holding. The dead were only showing up at Daymon's tree roadblock by the dozens, not hundreds.

The sturdy twelve-foot-tall hurricane fence had cost taxpayers a pretty penny. Signs warning that the premises were monitored 24/7 by closed circuit television cameras were attached to the fence chest-high about every thirty feet. And displayed prominently on the front gate was another sign featuring a crude caricature of a dog. Underneath the cartoon-like dog, in big red font, were the words GUARD DOG ON DUTY.

Duncan chuckled. "More like Benji on duty," he muttered as he stood looking at the sign. Because of the warning, or the rabid dog caricature, last time Duncan stood here, Daymon had been the most apprehensive of the group. *No way in hell*, were his exact words as he balked at cutting the lock and going in first.

Duncan studied the ground by his boots. Saw chevrons pressed into the gravel. The tire tracks continued on under the gate and faded a dozen yards inside the facility where the gravel looked to be a bit deeper. While the tires responsible for the patterns were wide enough to have been made by one of the UDOT trucks, the narrower wheelbase suggested they were left here by another type of vehicle. Or perhaps many similar vehicles traveling single file.

The gate rolled on a pair of steel wheels shod with rubber. A heavy-duty chain was looped twice around the gate's vertical pole, both ends left to dangle outside the fence.

Duncan threaded the chain ends back through the fence then let gravity take the entire length to the ground. The noise it made falling at his feet echoed across the facility. He took hold of the fence two-handed, leaned to his right, and rolled the door open just wide enough to admit his beer-bloated carcass.

As he closed himself in and looped the chain as he'd found it, his mind went back to the topic of conversation the last time he'd crossed this threshold. Daymon had been needling him about quitting drinking. Haranguing him about Glenda's part in the whole affair.

It's none of your dang business, he'd told the younger man. Then he'd admitted to Daymon that he had in fact been sober since hearing Glenda's story.

As Duncan trudged toward the prefab buildings, he remembered Daymon calling him a "liar" and busting balls for drinking while the rest of the group were busy clearing the undead from the bridge fronting the downed tree roadblock. That had been a watershed moment of sorts. He even went so far as to evoke God as his witness and swear to anyone within earshot that he was sober. Affirmed then and there how he had poured out all of his Jack Daniels.

God damn if he wasn't so far removed from that day now. Then, suddenly, as if he was one of Pavlov's damn dogs, the mere thought of his favorite whiskey induced an actual physical response from his salivary glands.

Duncan was still on the move and equidistant to the entry and prefab building when he heard the distinct sound of someone, or, more likely than not, something—a zombie, or ten—rattling the chain-link fencing somewhere off to his right. He stopped walking and made a visual sweep of the facility.

The rectangular area inside the fence was roughly the size of two football fields laid end-to-end. His ultimate destination, the boxy building to his left, was about half as big as a single mobile home. The door was closed. Horizontal blinds behind the windows flanking the door were drawn tight.

He returned his gaze north. To a long row of heavy machinery. There were snowplows and graders parked side by side. A pair of bucket trucks with wood chippers hooked to them were parked nose to tail along the north fence. The discordant metallic rattle was coming from behind a row of trucks hitched to flatbed trailers carrying huge spools of wire, line-painting equipment, and steamrollers of different sizes. Every piece of equipment on the lot was painted the same safety-orange and was dirt-streaked from sitting in the elements unused since that Saturday in July when road improvements and public works projects took a permanent back seat to surviving the dead.

He looked sidelong at the trailer as he drained the last of his current PBR into his open mouth. Then the chain-link jangled again, far away to the north. *Whatever is making the noise is outside the wire and can wait,* was his thinking as he diverted to the trailer.

Stopping at the base of the short stack of steps, he chucked the can amongst the weeds growing by the foundation and let the M4 fall off his shoulder and into his waiting hands.

He listened hard but heard nothing. No voices drifted from within the structure. Most importantly, when he banged on the door a tick later, he didn't get the same result from within as he had from the Winnebago a few nights ago.

He gave it a few more seconds before trying the knob. *Unlocked.*

He pushed the door inward with a nudge from the suppressor. His finger slid into the trigger guard and he tracked left to right, following the door sweep with the M4's business end.

The interior was revealed in small segments. To the left were a trio of chairs pushed up to a small table. Atop the table was an old television. Next was a garbage can overflowing with beer cans.

"My kind of folks," he joked.

Mounted to the wall above the garbage can was a whiteboard. Once filled with maintenance chores, it was now covered with squiggles and geometric shapes. There were mythical creatures and monsters that looked to have leaped straight off the pages of a Tolkien novel. There was no rhyme or reason to the placement. No kind of symmetry or balance. And it was all done in red, yellow, and black.

"Guess the county didn't spring for the rainbow pack of dry erase pens." Duncan chuckled. The graffiti reminded him of a Beatles album jacket. The one with the yellow submarine bobbing in a sea resembling a beatnik's worst acid trip.

Pressed up to the wall facing him was a low-slung love seat wrapped in tan fabric. On the far right, at the end of the building, was a trio of sleeping bags. All were Dijon-mustard-yellow and spread out on the floor. The narrow ends where a person's feet should go were all aimed at Duncan. A trio of pillows were propped against the wall before each bag.

"Somebody has been lying in my bed," Duncan said in his best big-bad-bear voice.

He looked behind the door. *No backpacks or cooking gear. And no food.* Which led him to conclude that whoever had been squatting here was long gone now. He figured they'd been eaten by the dead or killed by a desperate breather. At any rate, the place was his for the plucking.

And pluck he did. He took a handful of keys off the pegboard on the wall behind the door.

The little niggling voice was back and whispering a reminder about the beers still secreted in his coat pockets.

He started the door closing and the love seat drew his attention. *Just five minutes,* he told himself. *Put your feet up. Hell, Old Man, you walked a mile. You deserve to take a load off. Have a beer. Or three.*

He threw the lock and propped the M4 beside the jamb. Plucking another beer from his coat, he sat down hard on the love seat. As he popped the top, his eyes roamed the wood paneling. There was a calendar on the wall beside the window left of the door. It was a freebie plastered with photos of heavy equipment and still turned to July 2011.

Which told him the first people who stayed here hadn't lasted very long before abandoning the place. It also indicated that whoever was here last, likely the owners of the sleeping bags, didn't give a rat's ass what day it was. Maybe they were taking it one day at a time like Glenda urged him to before he went and screwed it all up.

Duncan stuck a hand into his pocket. He ran his fingers over the smooth surface of the Dear John letter.

A sour look settling on his face, he destroyed the beer in one long drink and hurled the empty at the calendar. He closed his eyes and listened to the noise it made as it caromed off the floor and came to rest somewhere off to his right. With one hand clutching the note in his pocket, the other wrapped around one of the remaining beers in another pocket, he transitioned from just *forgettin'* to the warm embrace of sweet oblivion.

Chapter 23

The driver steered the jacked-up 4x4 left off of 39 and coasted to a full stop a hundred feet west of the burned-out Shell station. Leaving the V8 idling, he looked past the twenty-year-old blonde to his right and addressed the scruffy-looking teenager riding shotgun. "Good eye, Nate Dog. You got 20/20 vision or some shit?"

The passenger shrugged his narrow shoulders. "Far as I know," he said, tugging nervously on the wispy beginnings of a mustache. "Haven't had 'em checked since I was twelve. Been about six years, I guess." He regarded the young woman to his left. "How often did you go to the ornithologist?"

"Ophthalmologist," she said, snapping her gum. "*Ornithologist* is a faggot who studies birds."

The driver shot her a sidelong glance. Speaking slowly, he said, "Homosexual. A fag is a cigarette. Speaking of …" He reached across the seat, brushing the young woman's breasts in the process. He smiled and wiggled his fingers before Nate's face. *Gimme.*

Without protest, Nate relinquished his last cigarette. He made a show of crumpling the empty box before chucking it into the back seat.

The young woman looked to the driver first. She let her gaze linger for a second then regarded Nate with a coquettish smile.

"If I would have asked you for a cigarette, too, who would you have given it to … me or Otto?"

"I'm pleading the fifth," Nate replied.

Otto laughed at that. It was the kind of drawn-out bray that usually preceded him committing violence. He said, "You and

162

Holly *drank* the fifth, dumbass." In a sing-song voice he added, "And you didn't save any for good ol' Otto."

With the tension she'd just created taking on a palpable air, Holly excused herself to go take a pee.

Nate scanned the lot on his side before elbowing his door open.

"If you want some privacy, you better make it quick," Otto called as he watched her shimmy her way onto Nate's lap.

Flashing the same smile at Otto she'd just covertly hit Nate with, she ground her ass against the younger man's crotch and then hopped down from the truck, along the way raking her nails across the front of Nate's stiff new Levi's.

The second the door thudded shut, Nate faced Otto. Again worrying his sparse facial hair, he said, "She's been asking questions."

Otto took a drag on the cigarette and exhaled through his nose. Wisps of smoke curled through his beard and around his head. With the tendrils drifting lazily toward the open door, he said, "What's she saying?"

"She saw the bump on Tyrone's head."

"Who gives a fuck," Otto spat. "Just tell her the same story *I* told her."

Nate looked questioningly across the cab.

"The dumbfuck was drunk and high. He probably fell against one of the rocks in the fire pit. That'll make a motherfucker dizzy as fuck. Then he wandered off in a daze and next thing you know … voilà, he's getting ate by a Mortimer."

"She doesn't buy it." Nate checked over his right shoulder. Saw that Holly was almost to the SUV. Turning back, he leaned in close, saying, "She told me your tattoos are prison tats. She saw the SS thing and the WP and the swastikas the first night you—"

"I didn't *rape* her. She wanted it. She even said so in front of you and Kerry."

"The black eye?"

Otto laughed. "She fell against a rock by the fire pit." Then he got real serious and fixed Nate with a menacing glare. "That fucker *Tyrone* and her met *after* the shit hit the fan. They were *not* an item. That was a union of convenience. Just so happens that the Otto Train is *more* convenient. She gets to *live* with us. Besides, Tyrone's nonstop beatboxing and rapping was going to get us all killed."

After a long moment of strained silence, in a conspiratorial tone, Nate said, "Can I have her first tonight?"

Otto nodded. "But you have to ask her in front of me. And at the end of your query, I want you to add *pretty please with cream and sugar on it.*"

Nate peered out his window and watched Holly drop her jeans and pink thong and squat beside the banged-up white SUV. As if a formed thought was about to spill forth, his lips parted.

"You were about to agree, weren't you?"

Nate's jaw took on a hard set. He continued to watch Holly but said nothing.

"Don't you *ever* fucking beg for pussy," bellowed Otto. "Do *not* stoop that low. You fucking embarrass me sometimes, Nate Dog. And just for that personal display of your own lack of self-respect, I'm going to have to reverse the Fifth Circuit Court of Otto's decision and say *negatory* to your request. Now gun up and get out. Grab the can and hose while you're out there."

Halfway out the door, Nate turned back to face Otto. "We already have all the gas we're going to need."

Otto gestured at the Toyota with his cigarette. Glaring at Nate, he said, "But we don't have *that* gas." He held the stony expression even as he took a long dramatic drag off the Kent and stubbed the butt out in the ashtray.

After blowing the stale-smelling smoke into the younger man's face, Otto snatched up his rifle and piled out of the truck.

The trio stood shoulder to shoulder next to the battered Land Cruiser, the roof over the filling islands casting a shadow over them all. By chance they had lined up by size, with Nate at five-foot-five and the smallest of the three, on their left flank.

At six-foot-three, shoring up the right, Otto towered over Holly, who fell somewhere in stature between the two men.

Strangely enough, the arrangement also mirrored their ages, from youngest to oldest. Nate had hit voting age the weekend the calamity happened. Before the dead began to walk, Holly had been anticipating her first legal drink on Thanksgiving Day. And though Otto claimed to be thirty-one to anyone who asked, his ruddy complexion and receding hairline was that of someone knocking hard on the door to forty.

Nate slung his AK-47 over a shoulder and stepped to the dented door. He cupped his hands on the glass and looked inside. "Dumbass left behind the better part of a case of Pabst Blue Ribbon *and* a roll of toilet paper. It's two-ply, too." He did a little hip thrust followed by some kind of leg kick to show his delight at their good fortune. Whether it was the beer or asswipe that precipitated it, he didn't let on.

Holly smiled at the Michael-Jackson-esque dance move. "A little late for the latter," she said. "I already let the gy-gy drip dry."

Nate tried the driver's side door handle. "Figures … it's locked."

"Not for long," Otto said as he delivered a solid shot to the glass with his AR-15's collapsed buttstock.

Both Holly and Nate flinched and their hands went up to ward off the ensuing shower of pebble-sized pieces of lightly tinted glass.

Brushing remnants of the window from her shoulder-length hair, Holly said, "Could have warned us first, *Otto*."

Nate spit out a tiny shard of glass but added nothing to Holly's stern admonishment.

"Fore," Otto bawled, ahead of another fit of laughter. "At least the glass didn't blacken your other eye."

Holly stuck out her lower lip and jammed her hands into her coat pockets.

After reaching under the dash and popping the fuel flap, Nate walked around to the right quarter and set up his siphoning operation.

Otto snatched up the PBR suitcase. He ripped into the box and laid the beers out on the hood. "Ten left," he said. "That means five for me. You two can fight over the rest."

Cheeks sunken and with the length of hose snaking from his mouth, Nate rose up and shot a glare through the glass. If Otto saw, he didn't let on.

"Not cool," Holly said as she grabbed three off the hood and promptly opened the top on one. "Why do you get the lion's share?"

"Consider it *Dad* tax," said Otto as he returned his beers to the box.

Nate rounded the back of the SUV, shaking his head.

Otto opened a second beer. Regarding Nate, he asked, "Tank empty?"

Nodding, Nate said, "Gas station is a hell of a funny place to go dry."

"Ironic," Holly corrected.

Otto looked west toward Huntsville. "Sure is," he said agreeably. "On both accounts." He grabbed a beer off the hood, then paused and looked queerly at Nate.

"What? Why are you looking at me like that?"

Otto placed a palm on the Land Cruiser's hood. "The beer is warm and this dented-ass hood is cold. Means this thing's been parked here for a while."

"Who cares?" said Holly, finishing with her first beer. She did a little dance, complete with a few provocative gyrations and toe touches. "We got their beer. Let's get our haul home and parrrr-tee."

Nate shot Otto a knowing look. Then, with Holly still facing the Land Cruiser, he mouthed, "We need a stripper pole."

"Mount up," Otto said, a sly grin materializing. "Our party pad awaits."

Chapter 24

Wilson burst onto 39, arms following his body as it spun counterclockwise and his feet lost contact with the dirt path. Before he could recover from the hockey check just delivered to his left shoulder by the weathered corner fence post, he was flat on his back, legs and arms akimbo, the M4 lying across his neck.

"You just lost your shit, Wilson," called Sasha, her voice carrying across the desolate two-lane. "I wish I would have gotten that on video." As soon as she said that last part, her smile disappeared.

Breathing hard from running his first ever sub-eight-minute mile in boots and parka while carrying a ten-pound weapon, he gasped, "What are *you* doing here?"

Already walking west down the center of 39, Sasha patted the little Ruger 10-22 rifle and pointed its muzzle at the pair of twice-dead corpses stretched out side-by-side on the nearby shoulder. "I'm pitching in," she said. "That's what."

Rising up off his haunches, an M4 cradled in the crooks of his folded arms, Tran said, "I gave her permission."

Having arrived a few seconds before Wilson, also unaware she'd just run her first sub-seven-minute mile in boots, parka, and carrying a weighty rifle, Taryn said, "Surprised the hell out of me, too." Unlike Wilson, Taryn was standing upright on the fog line a few feet from the fencepost, breathing normally and still in possession of her rifle.

Wilson picked himself up off the road. Rubbing his shoulder, he shot a perturbed look at Tran and said, "Who died and made you guardian?"

Wearing a thoughtful expression, Tran said, "Cade asked me to keep an eye on the girls while he was away. Sasha falls under that category. The situation, I would think, falls under those orders."

"I'm her *brother*," Wilson said. His hands went to his hips. "She could have gotten killed by those things."

Taryn was standing by the fencepost, one ear cocked toward the foliage-choked fire lane Wilson had just erupted from.

"I know that," Tran replied calmly. "Cade also asked that I watch Sasha when you're not around. As a courtesy. I definitely wasn't trying to step on your toes."

"No worries," Wilson shot. "I'm just pissed at the fencepost. That's all."

Holding the M4 at a low-ready, Tran approached Wilson. He said, "No affront taken. Seth isn't ready to come out here. And someone had to drive."

Shooting a look of incredulity at Tran, Taryn said, "You don't know how to drive?"

"I'm just rusty," Tran admitted.

"It's no big deal," Sasha interjected. She zipped her parka to her neck, then pulled the fur-trimmed hood over her shock of red hair. Looking skyward, she added, "It's about to rain."

Taryn said, "I can hear them coming now."

Tran asked, "How many?"

"Dozens," replied Wilson as he went through the motions of checking the M4's magazine and confirming a round was chambered. Looking up from the task, he added, "That we know of. I have a bad feeling the mega herd ... or horde, whatever they're calling it, has split up."

"Makes sense," Tran conceded. "There's a big herd chasing Cade and Raven. Bear River called with word of a second smaller horde that surged north on 16 last night."

Brow furrowed, Wilson asked, "When?"

Tran said, "Real early. Between two and three in the morning."

"I've heard Cade call that time of the morning zero dark thirty," Taryn added. "Did you inform him? How about Lev and Jamie ... they're up north. Did you tell them?"

"I called them both on their satellite phones. Lev and Jamie were real close to Bear Lake and hadn't seen the actual horde yet. There's a lot of damage from their passing, though." Tran cocked an ear towards the fire lane. "And these ones are getting close."

Wilson was standing over the corpses. Addressing Sasha, he asked, "You did both of these?" He squatted and examined the male first turn. Cause of second death was obvious: one eye was reduced to a pool of milky sludge ringed by tiny black dots. The last outfit it had shrugged on as a breather consisted of gray sweatpants and an oversized Pittsburgh Steelers jersey. The sweatpants were black in places where blood had soaked in and dried. The jersey appeared to have taken a ride through a wood chipper. And from the looks of the ashen, welt-addled dermis showing from underneath, the middle-aged rotter had been wearing the jersey for the ride.

The female first turn wore tightly laced leather hiking boots and was dressed in expensive outdoor gear, most of it new looking. Blood trickled from a pencil-eraser-sized entry wound an inch in front of its left ear. The powder burns to the temple were identical to those around the male's eye.

Both kills had been of the up close and personal variety.

Sasha nodded. "I watered my balls, Bro. Two bullets … two rotters down. Good ROI if I don't say so myself."

Head tilted at an angle, Tran said, "ROI?"

"Return on investment," answered Sasha. "Cade wants us to conserve ammo."

Tran nodded and smiled.

The loud *crack* of a substantial-sized branch breaking sounded from within the forest somewhere beyond the corner fence post.

Wilson rose and stared off to where the sound had come from. "How fast do you think the rotters move?" he said to

nobody in particular. "A mile … maybe a mile and a half per hour?"

"Not these ones," Taryn said. "I think you're being real conservative with your estimate."

Wilson asked, "Well, what do you think then?"

With the others looking on, Taryn made her way to the fence on the far side of 39. She leaned against the weathered post. It was sunk deep into the ground and didn't budge. Next, she reached over and tugged on the barbed wire. Some of the strands were firm. Others showed some give. She walked her gaze up the gently sloped clearing. The graves of her friends were up there somewhere, but that wasn't what was on her mind.

"They'll be here in less than fifteen minutes," she said, her face a mask of concern. "We shouldn't be out in the open like this."

Sasha shot the young woman an inquisitive look.

"Those things in the woods are in full-on hunt mode," Taryn said. "Hell, they were already all spooled up by the deer or elk or whatever those things were when they spotted me and Wilson."

Wilson said, "Those were elk."

All business, Tran said, "They were following the elk. Maybe we can draw them away with the truck. Honk the horn and drive real slow. That'll keep them following."

"I don't think we should split up," Taryn said soberly. "No disrespect, Tran. But there's just me and Wilson here who can drive." She paused to return Sasha's sour look. "Besides," she went on, "with Duncan and Glenda AWOL there's already too many of us scattered to the wind."

"Speaking of Old Man," said Wilson. "Any word from him or Glenda?"

Tran shook his head. "Neither of them answered last time I radioed."

"He's a big boy," Wilson said. "At least that's what he always says when Daymon goes off—"

"Newsflash, bro," Sasha interrupted. "Daymon isn't just missing. I get the feeling from what Cade saw the other night … Heidi getting killed and all, that Daymon would fall into the presumed dead category."

Tran looked to Wilson. He drew a deep breath and exhaled. "I hate to say that I agree with your sister. But I do. When Cade said he was going outside the wire with Raven, I got the sense that searching for Daymon was a thing, just not *the* thing. Then when I called to relay the message from the new sheriff at Bear River, he seemed to be more interested in what he had going on than fulfilling the sheriff's request."

Wilson said, "The writing's on the wall. Captain America is on a mission to toughen her up."

Sasha made a face. She said, "Like make her kill a deer and eat its heart and drink its blood kind of tough?"

Taryn said, "That's some Red Dawn shit right there."

Head taking a strange tilt, Wilson shot Taryn a questioning look that went unanswered on account of Tran saying, "Cade asked if he and Raven could watch me next time I dress a deer. I gather it's mostly for her benefit."

"With no Daymon to kill said deer," Wilson noted. "It may be a long while before that happens."

"Enough jawing," Taryn said as she slowly backpedaled away from the fire lane. "The dead are coming and we're standing around and doing nothing." She looked to Tran. "You're the oldest here. Do you have any ideas other than fracturing our already fractured group?"

Tran was shaking his head the moment she looked to him. By the time she finished her thought, he was pointing at Wilson and staring her in the face. "You and Wilson," he said. "You've seen and done way more than me."

Taryn shrugged and put a hand on Wilson's shoulder. "Sasha. Tran." She beckoned them over. "Bring it in close. I have an idea."

Chapter 25

Jamie and Lev were in a place familiar to them. Less than a
week ago, Tran had broken in to the home via the dog door inset
into the garage rollup. Five minutes ago, after having employed
the usual knock and wait protocol, the pair had waltzed in
through the unlocked front door. With Adrian and her gang
disposed of, neither Lev or Jamie expected the place to be
occupied by anything living or dead. In fact, they found the
brown two-story affair perched on the southern edge of Bear
Lake just as they'd left it. Situated in a row of homes of similar
style and earth-tone hue, the only thing that made the nondescript
home they were in stand out from the others was the white Ford
Raptor nosed in against the street-facing two-car garage.

Standing on the upstairs wraparound porch and being
buffeted by an onshore breeze, Jamie was busy steadying the
tripod with one hand as she rotated the humongous spotting
scope a few degrees left. After giving the locking nut a quick
twist, she smoothed out the bandage covering the wound on her
neck and cheek, then positioned her face above the ocular lens.
Holding that pose, she stared one-eyed into the eyepiece and
applied downward pressure on the aiming handle until the top
third of the three-story house she was surveilling filled up the
lens. A quick twist of the focus knob and everything snapped
crisp and clear.

The cul-de-sac the house sat on was the makeshift town
square of what had been a satellite outpost established and
manned by the gang of cannibals led by Adrian. The red-roofed
home was one of three that had not been occupied by Adrian and
her ilk the last time the Eden group tangled with them here.

Acting on Duncan's orders, Daymon and Lev had torched the other houses around the cul-de-sac.

Now, Jamie was focused only on a tiny porch she thought was called a Juliet balcony. It was a small outdoor space at the front of the home. A white railing supported by a picket of vertical wood balusters surrounded the porch on three sides. Three adults, two men and a woman, were crouched down behind the rail, just the tops of their heads visible.

Behind the people, in the shadow of a two-foot overhang, was a pair of French doors. They were both hinged open, the full-length drapes framing them blowing in the wind. Though she couldn't see inside what she assumed to be a top floor master suite commanding a stellar view of Bear Lake's stunningly blue water, she knew from the short twenty-minute recon she and Lev had put on the place that there were three grade-school-aged children upstairs with the adults. And judging from the size of the home, the space behind the gloom likely wasn't suitable to accommodate a group that size for very long.

Nose crinkling at the thought of the stench produced by that many unwashed bodies in such close proximity, she said, "You think they were already calling the place home? Or did one of the hordes come in so fast last night that they were forced to flee from somewhere else and got to the lake and had nowhere to go but up?"

Hands on his hips and staring off to the west, Lev said, "My money is on the former. The courtyard is pretty chewed up. Lots of foot prints made by the passing horde. But those patches by the house. They're too symmetrical. I think those were going to be gardens at some point. Soil is much darker than the rest. And I don't remember that chain-link fence being here before. Last time we were up this way the place was ringed by cement panels. I see the holes where they used to stand."

"But no panels," said Jamie.

"I could see Adrian returning to her airport compound up north and ordering her gang to come back for the panels."

Yeah," Jamie said agreeably. "I don't remember the chain-link either. And the dirt sticking to the bottom of the fence posts looks pretty fresh."

"This all happened hours ago," Lev said. "The horde probably caught them sleeping."

"Or caught their only guard sleeping."

Lev ran a hand through his chin stubble. He rested his elbows on the porch railing, squinted, and watched the ant-like figures roaming the cul-de-sac and trampled landscaping encircling it. Saw a single rotter stagger from the house's broken front door and tumble down the porch stairs. Though he couldn't see it without the telescope, Lev still shuddered at the thought of the corpse he'd spotted on the ground by the toppled stocks. The same stocks Duncan had left Adrian to die in. From collarbone to toes, the human remains had been stripped of every last scrap of flesh. Not that there were any toes left. Or fingers for that matter. Where there had been feet and hands, only bloody nubs of bone, cartilage, and severed tendon remained. Adding to the nightmarish vision, the Omega-infected body had turned. Aside from the wisps of black hair clinging to its skull, only its jaw moved. It was barely perceptible. Just a slow chewing motion. Millions of years of instinct still being relayed from its intact brain to the last vestiges of temporalis and masseter muscle making the movement possible.

"How sure are you those are the same men?"

Lev met her gaze. He said, "One thousand percent."

"And what do you base that on?" she asked, a trace of skepticism evident in the tone.

"Me and Daymon freed them from the basement of one of the houses we burned. I'll *never* forget the look on their faces when we opened the door to the combination laundry room/pantry they were being kept prisoner in. As you may have already guessed, the shelves were bare. Not a can or bag of food. Just knives and saws."

She looked up at him. Making a face, she said, "Rendering tools?"

Lev nodded. "The men were trussed up on the floor." He paused and looked toward the distant compound. "And the floor was slick with blood. So much that it had run across the room to the floor drain and was backing up."

She threw a shudder and went back to watching.

Lev tapped Jamie on the shoulder, causing her to hinge up and shoot him a questioning look.

"Keep an eye out for their hands. They're both missing some fingers."

"Ewww." She put her eye back to the lens. "Seeing Oliver's leg on the grill was enough to make me puke."

"You and me both," admitted Lev. "The smell of his flesh cooking *did* make me puke. I still haven't forgotten it. Sometimes I find it damn hard to eat Tran's venison without thinking about that charbroiled leg."

Jamie put her hands on her thighs. She said, "My back is beginning to ache. One of you dudes needs to do something."

As if they had been listening, both men rose up until their chests were level with the rail. The younger man on the right grabbed the handrail with both hands and stood up straight. It was clear he was missing at least one digit on each hand. The man on the left with the narrow face and deep-set eyes began talking. While Jamie couldn't hear what he was saying or read his lips to any degree that would be useful, she did see his hands when he began gesturing at the nearby foothills. And sure enough, he was missing two fingers on each hand. The two fingers bookended by the pointer and pinky. The person responsible must have thought themselves a comedian, because as his mouth moved both hands were constantly flashing the universal *rock on* sign, or, depending on what generation you came up in, *devil's horns*.

"We have confirmation," she said, her voice rising an octave. "Guy with the hat is short a couple of fingers. Narrow-face beardy guy next to him has a total of six fingers. That is if you're allowing thumbs into the finger category."

"They'd fit right in at a high school shop teachers' convention," quipped Lev, cracking a joke for the first time in a long time. He caressed Jamie's shoulder. "I want to take another look. Just to be sure we won't be rolling into a trap."

"They're the ones who are trapped," she said, stepping aside and resting her hand on the war tomahawk strapped to her right hip. "And they're going to die up there if nothing distracts the deaders and draws them away."

Lev stared at the house through the scope for a few seconds, his lips moving as he counted heads.

"How many Zs, you think?"

"I stopped counting at thirty."

"We need to talk to those people," she said. "See if they saw Daymon recently."

"He does stick out in a crowd," Lev said. "And logic tells me, if he was following whoever took Heidi, he'd have to pass within sight of our fingerless friends in the compound."

"How do we go about making contact without ending up trapped up there with them?"

"Let's go," he said, already heading for the glass slider. "I'll tell you my plan once we're underway."

She picked up the telescope and put it inside where she'd found it. As she followed him down the stairs, she said, "I'm driving."

Looking up at her over his shoulder, Lev said, "I wouldn't have it any other way."

Chapter 26

Avoiding the stretch of Main demolished by the passing horde, Cade canvassed Woodruff without seeing anything to point to Daymon's whereabouts. No spent shell casings speaking to a skirmish. Not a single dead breather. No piles of decapitated rotters being watched over by their own neatly arranged severed heads.

Nothing.

Not even a scrap of fabric from a ghillie suit, which was what Daymon had been wearing when Cade saw him last.

As they were making a final northbound pass on 100 Street, the satellite phone in the center console bleated its annoying electronic trill.

"You get it," Cade said. He was busy scanning empty fields bearing for sale signs and straining to see inside the smattering of one- and two-story pre-war houses bordering them.

"It's that woman, *Nash*," Raven said, venom dripping from the words.

"She's a Major," Cade replied. "Gonna answer it?"

Raven's expression said *no*. Her actions contradicted the narrowed eyes and set of her jaw.

She thumbed the talk key and then fiddled with the slim Thuraya until she found what she was looking for. All in all she had left Nash hanging for less than ten seconds when she finally said, "You're on speaker. This is Raven Grayson. My dad is next to me. He's *busy* driving."

"So good to hear your voice, Raven." If Nash had detected the animosity in Raven's tone, she didn't let on. "Your dad says you're blossoming into a fine young lady."

Raven brought the phone closer to her mouth and said, "The word *blossoming* has never passed my father's lips." She looked sidelong across the cab and saw that her dad was not smiling.

"*Raven,*" Cade said. And that's *all* he needed to say. No matter what she was feeling at the time, that was no way to talk to an adult, and she knew better.

Raven faced him. In a low voice, she said, "Sorry, Dad." After pausing and looking out the window as the F-650 swung left onto Woodruff's northernmost street, she added, "My apologies, Major."

"No offense taken," replied Nash. "You've been under immense pressure. I get it. I really do."

Nudging the subject in a different direction, Cade said, "What's the news?"

"Still on speaker?"

"Affirmative."

Nash said, "What I have to tell you is not PG-13."

Still smarting from the blowback he had received as a result of his decision to have Glenda sedate Raven the night Brook died, he said, "Raven can listen in. I'm all about transparency from here on out."

"Understood," Nash replied. She described in great detail the interrogations applied to the prisoners taken in the raid on the Bear Lake airport compound. "They started out as garden-variety lowlifes. Lack of authority emboldened them. Hell, emboldened is an understatement. The quick evolution brought on by our current circumstances has twisted their idea of behavior that's acceptable in normal society."

"I was there. I saw what they're capable of. And I made their leader pay for it," Cade said. "Did they make contact with my friend?"

There was a long pause.

Glancing at the satellite phone, Cade said, "The one with the dreadlocks? Daymon Bush is his name."

"Negative," said Nash. She sounded tired. "And I can't send any help from Bastion at the moment. Chinese PLA activity is ramping up. They're like roaches. Stomp on one and three more appear. We've even caught a couple of them infiltrating Springs."

"Can you divert a drone? Have it take one or two passes over Bear Lake? You'll get intel on the hordes. We kill two birds with one stone."

Voice full of surprise, Nash said, "Hordes? Plural?"

Cade told her all about the situation at Bear River and how in the early morning hours they'd spotted a second horde moving north. Then, as he wheeled a slow right turn at an intersection on the north edge of town where he could see down Main Street, he described the destruction laid to Woodruff in painstaking detail. After informing Nash he would likely have more intel on the state of things from Randolph on up north to Bear Lake once two of their own who were in the vicinity reported back with their findings, he dropped the bomb that at once rendered Nash speechless and caused Raven to lean forward and fix him with a probing stare.

Open fields blipped by outside the truck. By the time Nash recovered enough to say, "And when is this happening?" they had bypassed nearly a quarter-mile of barbed wire fencing uprooted from churned up fields bordering the two-lane.

"I want to make it happen before winter," Cade replied.

Raven had rotated her upper body to face her dad. The probing stare had morphed into a look of bewilderment.

"I've got to go," said Cade. "I'll call when I know more."

"I'll do the same if we get anything actionable out of the prisoners," Nash said.

Cade nodded to Raven. "You can end the call. Don't want to burn up all our minutes."

She ended the call. "Time and place, Dad. *Remember*?" She dumped the phone into the console and slammed it shut. "When were you going to tell me? Better yet ... when were you going to ask for my opinion?"

"It just came to me a minute ago," he admitted. "With the Chinese growing more emboldened and now two hordes roaming the area ... just makes sense tactically."

She said, "Colorado Springs?"

"I said we'll be pulling up stakes and moving on before winter gets rolling. I didn't specify Colorado Springs or Bastion."

"Are we going home? To Portland?"

Cade shook his head. "Not yet, sweetie. Maybe one day we will. Or, perhaps, you will by yourself. Right now it's too dangerous to go back."

"My vote is for Springs," she said. "That is, if I have a say in the matter."

"First things first," he said. "We need to check out the ice cream truck. See if Dregan made it out or not."

Raven made a face as the caged animal in her chest stirred. She asked, "What about the zombies on 39? Aren't we going back with the Screamer?"

Cade said, "No. I think they're set pretty firmly on the hook. We've got about forty-five minutes to an hour until they get to the junction. If we aren't there in time, they could turn and head north. If they do that, then Lev and Jamie will have to face them."

Feeling the calm returning, she said, "Fingers crossed Lady Luck is looking out for us."

"Copy that," Cade said as he jinked the wheel right to avoid driving over a six-inch-tall mound of organic sludge. From a distance it had looked like clay-rich soil that had sloughed off the side hill paralleling the road. Once he'd drawn to within two truck lengths, the scraps of clothing and human bones jutting skyward told him the true story.

"First time I've seen rotter paste," said Raven, her right hand instinctively going for the grab bar by her head.

"Not for me," Cade said. "The mega horde me and Desantos—"

"Nuked to kingdom come," Raven said. "That's what you did, right?"

"It was a group effort," Cade conceded. Then, hoping to steer the conversation in a different direction, he asked Raven if she remembered much from her ballet lessons.

After shooting him a quizzical look, she said, "I was, like, eight or nine. I remember a little. First position is when your feet are like this." She put her feet up on the dash in front of her seat and demonstrated.

Cade glanced sidelong at her boots. Shifting his attention back to the road, he said, "What's the one where your toes are pointing away from one another and you bend your knees and almost break your back and get a double hernia as you lower yourself to the floor?"

Raven regarded him. On her face was a *Who stole my dad and replaced him with a space alien?* expression.

"I think you mean plié. If you bend down it's a plié squat," she answered. "What the heck does that have to do with the price of tea in China?"

Cade did a double-take and said, "Where'd you learn that ... Duncan?"

"Grandma," she said. "When we got to Myrtle Beach to visit them ... before all of this happened, I asked her why she was picking us up by herself. And that's when she looked at me and said, 'Raven, dear, what the heck does that have to do with the price of tea in China?'"

"Grandma was a bit of a feminist. She probably thought you were insinuating Grandpa should be driving. That to her came across as you insinuating a woman's place is in the passenger seat. She didn't mean it."

"It's a funny saying, though. Isn't it?"

Not if you knew what I know about China, is what Cade was thinking. He said, "Your grandma and grandpa had more funny sayings than Duncan." His mood turned sour at the thought of what had happened to Brook's parents. Then he started to wonder where Glenda had gone off to. Which led to him worrying about the mess Old Man was in. The drinking roaring back. The talk of the good old days. All the maudlin behavior that started when he learned of Heidi's killing and Daymon's subsequent disappearance.

"Stay frosty," Cade said. "We're nearing the mile marker Lev mentioned."

In a flash Raven scooped up her M4, sat upright in her seat, and started to scan the fields, head moving slowly left to right—*on a swivel*, was how her dad would describe it.

Eyes roaming a swath of field on his side, Cade dropped the F-650's speed and slalomed the big rig right to avoid a long length of tangled wire still attached to a trio of weathered fence posts.

Two minutes after leaving Randolph in the rearview, Raven was again rising off her seat. Only this time words spoken by her dad weren't the cause of her concern, it was the large, boxy vehicle resting on its side behind a two-foot-tall wall of mud in the distant field.

"I think I see the truck," she said.

Cade lifted his foot from the accelerator and followed her gaze. "That's got to be it," he said. "Use the binoculars. See if you can pick up anything moving in or around the truck."

He steered the truck to the right side of the road on a slight rise and stopped on the shoulder where Raven had a commanding view of the field and the Bear River Range backstopping it. A mass of trees began a few hundred yards behind the ice cream truck and rolled on to a thin line of ochre-colored hills far off in the distance.

Closer in, the fencing on both sides of the road was flattened or had been yanked from the ground altogether. The fields bordering the road had been trampled by the passage of thousands of feet. The first dozen yards or so of field were churned to mud. The next thirty or forty feet of field beyond the mud, the grass was trampled and pointing north.

Raven powered her window down. A blast of cool wind infiltrated the cab, bringing with it the heady scent of pine and earthen notes of freshly tilled soil. She braced on the windowsill and trained the Steiners on the distant vehicle. She remained stock still for a full minute before pulling her head back inside the truck.

Cade had been glassing the vehicle through the M4's 3x optic. Putting the rifle down, he regarded his daughter.

He asked, "See anything?"

Biting her lip, Raven nodded. "Something *is* moving. Looks like on the driver's side."

"You sure? Because I didn't see anything using the EOTech." Gesturing for the Steiners, he said, "But that's not saying much, considering the distance."

Cade spent a few seconds glassing the vehicle and came away agreeing with Raven. "Could be a seatbelt blowing in the wind. Could be the belt on Dregan's duster. Only way to give Peter some closure is to go and check it out. Buckle up," he said. "We're going to do a little off-roading."

Complying with the order, Raven asked, "You sure we're not going to get stuck?"

"In life, sweetie, nothing is guaranteed."

"We can drive closer, park parallel to the truck, and leave Black Beauty on the road." She picked up the binoculars and panned the field from the road all the way to the ice cream truck. Dropping the binoculars to her lap, she said, "Walking in wouldn't take very long."

Cade shook his head as he put the highly modified Ford into *4x4 Hi* mode. "I don't want to take the chance of us getting caught out there in the open. Kind of like oil and water … *running* and *mud* do not go together."

Raven didn't acknowledge her dad. She was busy surveying the two-lane behind the Ford. Swiveling back around, she stared out over the hood for a beat before finally saying, "There's a mile or so of open road in both directions. Even if someone did come along while we're out there, we would hear them well before we saw them. That'd give us enough time to run back to the truck, wouldn't it?"

Steering off the blacktop, he said, "You must not have been listening to me. Have you ever tried running in ankle-deep mud?"

She shook her head.

"It's nearly impossible ... especially for someone with a bum ankle like mine." He paused as the truck rolled into the soupy morass. Looking sidelong at her, he added, "Last chance to call it off."

Without pause, Raven said, "We promised. And like you always say: A person is only as good as their word."

"Final answer?"

Nodding at the vehicle at their twelve o'clock, she said, "It's the right thing to do. Drive, Dad."

That's my girl.

Chapter 27

As per Taryn's plan, when the dead finally began to spill from the overgrown fire lane and spread out on SR-39, all four of the Eden survivors were crouched down in deep grass behind the run of barbed wire fence on the opposite side of the two-lane. Tran's position was directly across from the compound's hidden entrance and the farthest from the fire lane. Sasha and Wilson were prostrate in the grass less than twenty feet from the dead things and enveloped by the stink of death hanging over the road. Thirty feet to Wilson's right, nearly equidistant to Tran's hiding place, Taryn was making herself small and hoping her woodland camouflage wasn't standing out from the grass rising up all around her.

The ditch running the length of 39 separated the fence from the road's gravel-strewn shoulder. It was deep and wide and held several inches of standing water. Hidden by the brackish water was a bed of boot-sucking mud—also inches deep. Behind the hunkered-down survivors was a wide open field of knee-high grass sloping gently uphill to a stand of firs. Near the tree line was the nondescript row of graves where several fallen members of the Eden group were buried.

Seeing the dead congregating on the road to his fore, Wilson brought the radio to his lips, thumbed the talk key, then whispered, "Now."

Twenty yards east, Tran heard the order and showed himself to the dead. Shorter than the others, the grass rose to mid-thigh on him. In his hands was an uprooted sapling five feet in length and nearly as big around as his wrists. Both ends of his makeshift staff were stark white where he had whittled them to sharp points.

While calling out at the top of his voice, "I'm right here, demons! Are you hungry?" he jumped up and down and waved the staff back and forth over his head.

Attracted by Tran's sudden appearance, a female first turn locked her hungry stare on the slight man and began a steady march east, bringing with her the entire group of rotters now spreading across both lanes and growing exponentially.

Relieved the Zs hadn't struck off west when they first emerged onto the road, Wilson put a hand on Sasha's shoulder and said, "You're doing great. Just a little bit longer." He could feel her shaking but couldn't blame her. The rasps and moans of the dead had the hair on his arms standing on end. In just a couple of seconds the sound of feet scuffing the road rose to a din and the herd was on the move.

Through a part in the grass Wilson saw all ages represented in the mix of fresh kills and first turns trundling from the woods behind their leader. Wilson and Sasha kept quiet and remained out of sight until the head of the column reached Tran's position. Then, whispering into the radio, Wilson said, "Your turn, Taryn."

Also brandishing a long branch sharpened to a point with her Tanto blade, Taryn rose up from the grass, pumping the crude weapon up and down like a drill major and hurling insults at the Zs directly in front of her. This caught them by surprise, freezing a number of them in their tracks. The sudden halt by the Zs in the lead slowed down the ones following, which started an undead pileup along 39's eastbound lane.

Taking the bait, a male rotter, arms outstretched and a guttural moan rumbling deep in its chest, locked eyes with Taryn and staggered across the shoulder and into the ditch where it became mired in the diarrhea-like morass.

As soon as Wilson saw the conga line of dead on the road before him come to a lurching, slow-motion halt, he tapped Sasha on the shoulder and popped up from the crushed grass. Waving his sharpened length of wood overhead, he screamed at the dead and jumped up and down.

Feeling the silent signal, Sasha sprang up beside Wilson, reached out with her sharpened sapling and began beating it against the top strand of barbed wire.

Like lemmings near a cliff's edge, three separate groups of dead marched off 39's shoulder and into the ditch. Muddy water was kicked up and bodies were trampled as the mass of dead flesh scrambled to get to the meat. However, the first into the ditch weren't necessarily the first out. A handful of dead among the second wave bridged the gap on the backs of the first in and started stomping postholes into the crumbling hillside.

Seeing Tran and Taryn engaging the dead and holding their own, Wilson stepped to the fence and buried one end of his staff in a rotter's eye. He pulled the weapon free, aimed it at the sky, and ran behind Sasha. Coming to a sliding halt a couple of yards beyond his sister, he knelt before an undead boy busy worming his way underneath the fence and christened the other end of his staff with the snarling Z's brackish blood.

In just a few seconds the dead already on the road were amassed in four loose knots separated by twenty or thirty feet. The group near the fire lane was still swelling with new arrivals. Crowded from behind, the first Zs to navigate the ditch and reach the length of fence where Sasha was scrambling brains were beginning to lose digits and chunks of putrid flesh to the taut barbed wire. Meanwhile, a dozen yards east, the two groups in the middle were coalescing into one and under attack on two flanks by Wilson and Taryn. The ditch to the pair's fore was thick with Zs struggling to extricate themselves from the mud. A dozen yards east, Tran was felling Zs like dominos. His staff was a blur and blood and brain tissue traced gory arcs over the fence as he stabbed repeatedly into the milling throng.

Wilson sent another creature to its second death, yanked his staff free, and slipped behind Taryn. Bellowing, "Spread them out!" at Tran, he sprinted back to where Sasha was engaging the Zs hung up on a sagging length of barbed wire. Along the way, he discarded the staff, dragged the M4 around on its sling and thumbed its selector from Safe to Fire.

Skidding to a halt beside Sasha, Wilson hooked a thumb over his shoulder. "Fall back!" he ordered, making chopping motions toward the spot uphill where he wanted her to go.

Feet planted a foot apart on the spongy ground, Sasha turned to run but got nowhere. Instead, as the muck refused to release her boots, the unused momentum was redirected groundward and her body followed suit.

Sasha sat down hard, then pitched over onto her back. As a result, one boot tore free from the mud and her leg followed through. Mud sent airborne from her freed boot traced a lazy parabola above her body before plopping to the ground about her head and shoulders. As she went to roll to her stomach so she could rise and run, cold fingers wrapped around her ankle and she was being dragged toward the fence.

Seeing all of this happening in her side vision, Taryn left the clutch of rotters to her fore and followed in Wilson's footsteps.

Thrusting blindly at the dead with her staff, Sasha screamed to Wilson for help.

A yard from Sasha's prostrate form, Wilson summoned the Todd Helton in him and went to ground, sliding on one hip, feet first toward Sasha as if she was home plate. Coming to a grinding halt, with more grass and mud pelting Sasha, Wilson thrust his M4 through the fence at the dead. Unable to discern which of the creatures in the pile owned the hand attached to his sister, he poked the suppressor into a random face and triggered a round. He continued firing into the scrum, three or four seconds in all, until the fingers gripping Sasha's ankle went slack.

"The fence is failing," cried Taryn as she grabbed some of Sasha's jacket and helped Wilson get the teen to her feet.

If Sasha was grateful, she didn't voice it. Instead, she tossed her staff to the ground and in a flash the Ruger rifle was off her shoulder and in her hands. In the next beat she was stepping to the listing fence and firing into the dead, to no great effect.

"Cease fire, Sash," Wilson screamed. "Uphill, now!"

As he raised his rifle to acquire a new target, he heard a groan off his right shoulder. Swinging his gaze toward the sound, he witnessed the wooden fence post jerk once and then lean hard over in his direction.

Reacting quickly to Wilson's command, Sasha lowered her rifle and started backing away from the fence, uphill, her boots finding purchase this time.

With the post working its way out of the ground before his eyes, Wilson looked away long enough to get Taryn's attention and motioned for her to follow Sasha. Then, as Taryn was turning and taking her first steps toward their agreed-upon fallback position, Wilson looked across the field at the rapidly approaching Tran. Directing the sprinting man uphill with the same chopping motion as he had his sister, Wilson bellowed, "Fall back and ready your rifle."

When Wilson finally reacquired Sasha, she was already a good distance uphill and nearly to the row of graves, where everyone was to regroup.

Chapter 28

Ten seconds after Wilson rejoined the others at the top of the hill where the ground was mostly level, the fence opposing the fire lane where the dead had emerged finally failed. Initially the top two strands of wire snapped, sending a row of rotters five abreast face first into the trampled grass where Sasha was nearly lost. Then, under great stress from the two dozen dead things scrabbling out of the ditch, the remaining shin-high strand of wire snapped and brought the pair of gnarled fence posts down with it. As the sharp *cracks* echoed around the clearing like a pair of high-caliber gunshots, a third post was uprooted and an additional ten-foot-wide gap of fence east of the first was breached.

Wilson flopped down onto his stomach next to Heidi's grave. He was breathing hard and the sweat beading on his brow and upper lip was migrating south. To his left, near Helen and Ray's freshly filled graves, Taryn was comforting Sasha. Off his right shoulder, lying between the twin rectangles of bare soil holding Brook and Foley's remains, Tran was fumbling with his weapon.

"Pull the charging handle all the way back," said Wilson. "It's the T-shaped thing below the rear sight. Then you throw the safety … it's on the left side near the trigger guard." He paused while Tran followed the directions. As the man snugged the rifle to his shoulder and peered through the EOTech optics, Wilson went on, "Go for the newer turns first. Head shots if you can. If they get too close, go for the legs to disable them. Then finish them while they're down."

"I know the basics," Tran said. "It's just that guns are still Greek to me."

Sasha's little Ruger came to life. Three shots. Back-to-back-to-back. The crackling reports rolled across the tiny group and swiftly dissipated.

"I'm still learning," Wilson admitted. "And I'm not sure if it'll ever be second nature to me." Through his M4's optics, starting east and slowly panning west, he surveyed the gently arcing length of 39. The roadside ditch where Tran had been looked as if it held a dozen or more twice-dead Zs. Tracking left a couple of degrees revealed the Zs he and Taryn had culled. He figured there to be maybe eighteen kills between the two of them—most of them belonging to her. Continuing on, he glassed the ditch and road adjacent to the failed run of fence. His dozen kills there had been trampled into the ditch as the two dozen dead currently clambering uphill toward him poured through the breach.

Arms and legs bent in unnatural angles jutted from the ditch. A slack face atop the pile stared up at him. The male Z's lifeless eyes wore a sheen of mud. Grass and dirt caked the shock of blond hair. Mud had found its way into its ears and spilled from its gaping mouth.

Finished with his split-second assessment, Wilson aimed his M4 at the approaching pack and selected a target. With the holographic pip centered on a female Z's nose, he threw the safety off and pressed the trigger. The suppressed report was nothing like the noise made by the failing fence post. It also paled in comparison to Sasha's rifle. The abbreviated pop of the round leaving the M4 was swallowed up by the trees at Wilson's back.

The speeding 62-grain hunk of lead was traveling close to 3,000 feet per second when it struck the rotter between the eyes with a wet smack. Instantly the Z's head snapped back like a broken Pez dispenser and its body jerked up straight. As the corpse continued its one-way trip to the soft ground, back arched at a crazy angle, a rooster tail of brain matter spewed from the mortal wound.

To Wilson's left, Sasha's little weapon reentered the fray. Her shots were coming slow and steady now. *Little Sis is listening to*

Taryn, he thought to himself as petite shell casings trailing wisps of gun smoke skittered across Ray's grave.

On Sasha's left side, Taryn was making her shots count. With each bark of her suppressed M4, a rotter would fall and begin a slow motion downhill tumble, steamrolling the long grass flat along the way.

Wilson glanced to his right and saw Tran heeding his words by targeting the speedier Zs. For every three or four shots fired from the man's rifle, one Z would convulse and crash vertically and get swallowed up by the long grass.

Seeing the last of the dead summit the ditch and begin the long uphill trudge, Wilson rose up to one knee and started targeting the more mobile specimens among the twenty or so spread out before him on the lower half of the hill. In a matter of seconds he had burned through an entire magazine but had only thirteen kills to show for thirty spent rounds. Not a good ratio by any stretch.

To Wilson's left, all firing ceased. Simultaneously, Sasha and Taryn aimed their rifles at the sky and commenced changing magazines. Off his right shoulder, Tran's rifle went silent. In the next beat the older man was leaning over his rifle and tugging on the slightly curved magazine.

"Right side of the rifle," Wilson called over. "The button above the mag well dumps the spent magazine."

He did a hasty head count of the dead still moving uphill toward them.

Seven.

Mostly first turns.

Wilson looked over his shoulder at Sasha. He said, "Check your fire. You too, Taryn." He cupped a hand by his mouth and told Tran to pull the charging handle, engage the safety, and stand by.

Gun smoke drifted west from Tran's position as Wilson rose, moved the M4 around to his back, and picked his staff up off the ground.

Wilson looked to Taryn. "I'm going to get these," he said. "Keep them in your sights in case it's too much for me."

"You sure you want to do it like this?" Taryn asked.

"Got to save the ammo," answered Wilson. He regarded Sasha. "You did good. Make sure you keep one eye on the woods to our left. Though it's overgrown, the fire lane continues on somewhere back there. I figure there's an outside chance some of the deadheads could have picked it up on this side of the state route."

Sasha shot him a look that could only be construed as *No effin duh*. She had already been jumped by a deadhead real close to where she was right now. She sure as hell wasn't going to make that same mistake twice.

Taryn rose up to one knee and snugged her rifle tight to her shoulder.

Wilson looked each person in the face. Without another word, he started waking downhill, on a collision course with the remaining monsters.

***

A minute after switching weapons, Wilson had released seven more souls from their hell on earth. It made him feel good. He hoped if his mother had turned, someone got to her early. Set her free, too.

Savoring the thought of Mom being in a good spot instead of shuffling around some airport somewhere, he looked at his small group's contribution to the cause. Twice-dead Zs littered the lower two-thirds of the hill. Here and there amongst the unmoving corpses, gravely injured Zs struggled to stand. Near the breach in the fence, a pair of first turns looked pathetic as they tried to claw their way from the roadside ditch. From one end to the other, State Route 39 was rotter free.

Blood still dripped from Wilson's staff when he returned from his own personal crucible.

Taryn and Sasha were huddled together on the ground next to Heidi's grave. Their rifles and staffs sat in a jumble beside them.

Tran was standing nearby but wouldn't look Wilson in the eye.

"What's up?" Wilson asked. "I finished the job without wasting any more bullets."

Lifting her gaze to meet his, Taryn said, "It's Sasha. You need to take a look at her leg."

Face blanched white, Wilson dropped his staff and ran to his sister's side.

Chapter 29

Cade pulled the F-650 close to the ice cream truck's crumpled rear end. On the passenger side, upside down and flanked by waffle cones heaping with colorful scoops of ice cream, were the words, *Brady's Treats*. The truck's dirt-caked grille faced north by east. The doors out back hung open—the passenger's side door connected by a single hinge. The ground in the truck's shadow had been tilled up by the passing hordes. In the mud just off the truck's fender were numerous prints made by bare feet. Nearby were imprints left by tennis shoes with intricate-patterned soles, boots with lug soles, and, seemingly, everything in between. Every single one of the thousands of individual prints in the vast mud plain were facing north; the direction of the horde's march.

Stilling the motor, Cade said, "While I take a look inside the truck, why don't you climb in the bed and see if you can find the Screamer."

Shaking her head, Raven said, "I'm going with. I'll look for that noisy piece of junk when we get back."

As if saying *Suit yourself*, Cade shrugged and scooped up his M4.

Raven lifted her rifle from the floorboard and elbowed her door open. Jumping from the truck, she found the ground on her side pretty firm. It was dotted with patches of grass and showed very little evidence of the zombies' passage. Swinging her gaze forward, she saw a ten-foot-wide swath of smooth ground mostly devoid of grass. It was the starting of an uninterrupted path that ran diagonally south by west from the ice cream truck, all the way to the state route. Though she was no great judge of distance measured in feet or yards or miles, like her dad, as she traced the path from the road back to the truck, she knew it had to equal at least a full city block. The footprints dotting the compressed dirt were nowhere close to being as deep as the ones marring the soil flanking it.

Cade slammed his door and looped around front of the Ford. He was nearly to the ice cream truck's open sliding door when Raven sidled up next to him.

She said, "Do you see anything moving?"

He nodded. "Still belted into the driver's seat. I think it's big enough to be Dregan. And I'm pretty sure he's no longer one of us." He regarded Raven, "You want to check it out?" He was testing her. However, when she said yes, he had a hard time concealing his amazement. "You sure? I totally understand if you don't want to see him as a zombie."

Raven said nothing. She strode around front of the truck with purpose, crouched down by the open driver's side door, then craned her neck and looked inside.

Cade followed but kept his distance as she moved aside what looked to him like a misplaced curtain.

Raven said, "Dad … you need to see this."

After checking his six and their flanks, he made his way to the open door and crouched next to her. Seeing that the fabric hanging down where window glass should be was tenting in places, he said, "What's up with the curtain?"

"That's no curtain," she said unemotionally. "It's Alexander Dregan's long cowboy coat."

"It's called a duster," Cade said as he tugged aside the stiff canvas-like fabric to expose the pale hand and scrabbling fingers that had been causing it to bulge and ripple. From wrist to elbow the appendage was stripped of its skin and most of the underlying flesh. The inside of the duster was coated with dried blood. Stiff scraps of flesh and skin clung to the fabric.

Cade crouched, craned like Raven, and peered into the gloom. Sure enough, the elder Dregan was in there. And he was upside down and still buckled to his seat. He had suffered greatly at the hands and teeth of the dead. Also, based on Cade's initial glimpse, it appeared he had suffered greatly at his own hand before the ravenous dead got to him.

Pointing to the latter was the fact that his face was peeled away from the nub of cartilage that used to be his nose to the rear of his skull. Powder burns stippled the ashen lump of flesh dangling where an ear should have been. Starting a couple of inches above the powder burns and directly in line with what Cade presumed to be the man's ear canal was a shallow, two-inch-wide furrow. The damage, likely caused by a glancing blow from a large caliber bullet, ended at the crown of Dregan's head where the round all but scalped him before careening off on its altered trajectory. While Cade was no kind of ballistics expert, he figured if he looked long and hard he would find a thumb-sized bullet hole somewhere in the ice cream truck's roof. Likely directly above the passenger seat.

That wasn't going to happen. This wasn't an episode of CSI. Dregan was done now. That much was clear. Cade hoped the man hadn't suffered before he died the first time. Hell, if the reports were accurate, Dregan had single-handedly saved Bear River from falling to the mega-horde.

The man deserved a monument erected in his honor, not the second-guessing sure to come should the obvious failure of his last mortal act come to light.

Cade looked to the pistol in Raven's hand. It was black with knurled walnut grips, its slide locked open. Even though undead Dregan's flesh was beginning to spoil, Cade smelled the gunpowder clinging to the recently discharged weapon over the sickly sweet odor coming off the body.

"I found this on the roof," she said, offering it to him butt first. "Which is now basically the floor."

Nodding, Cade took the pistol. "Dregan knew his job was done. He got the horde this far and tried to end his own life before they could get to him. He used the last bullet in the magazine, too." Keeping his fingers clear of undead Dregan's snapping teeth, Cade pointed to the burn marks he'd spotted. Then, using the pistol's muzzle, he traced the channel the errant bullet had carved into the man's skull. "He must have jerked his hand at the last moment."

"Maybe the horde hit the truck and *made* him miss. There's a bunch of dents in back. Like it got rear-ended by a dump truck, or something."

"That's a possibility. At any rate, the damage caused from the bullet entering and then immediately exiting at the crown of his head was catastrophic. I'd be willing to bet he lost consciousness instantly."

Raven made a face. "He still suffered," she said with a certainty only a twelve-year-old could convey. "And in a way, he still is suffering."

As if the thing hanging upside down and batting futilely at the duster in the way of a possible meal understood that its previous life and current predicament was under scrutiny, a wet guttural growl rolled over its bloated tongue.

Cade removed his cap, bowed his head, and wagged it slowly side-to-side.

He went still and regarded the Colt Model 1911 clutched in his fist. "You want the honors?"

Nodding, Raven said, "Should I use *his* gun?"

"I think you should. That way we can say he died by his own hand."

"But he didn't the first time."

"Maybe he bled out from the wounds and did die. We don't know either way. I think it's best if we finish what Dregan started and let his kin build their own version of what happened here."

"It might make it a little easier on Peter if he thought his dad shot himself, then died and stayed dead. I wish I didn't know Mom turned," she said, her voice cracking. "Makes it harder to remember her as she was." Tears welled in her eyes. "I wish I would have been there at the end, though. So I could have held her. Told her how much I loved her."

Cade said, "I did that for the both of us." He reached out and wiped the tears from his daughter's cheeks. "You sure you're up to it?"

She nodded.

He thumbed the Colt's slide release, sending the slide home with a loud *snick*. He de-cocked the hammer, then dumped the mag and pocketed it.

"Hold tight," he said, then ran back to the Ford where he fished a single .45 caliber shell from the small stockpile of different caliber rounds that, over time, had collected at the bottom of the center console. On the way back to where Raven was waiting for him, he loaded the single bullet into the magazine, inserted the mag back into the Colt, and smartly chambered the round.

Showing the pistol to Raven, he said, "There's *one* in the pipe." He pointed to the lever on the pistol's backstrap. "It's a bit different from your Glock. That's your safety here on the back of the grip." Next, he indicated the hammer behind the slide. It was in the down position, yet still stuck out a half-inch or so. "Since a round is chambered, all you have to do is get a solid hold on your pistol, aim it at what you're going to shoot, and thumb back this hammer."

Raven had been listening intently and nodding during the entire demonstration.

Handing the pistol to her butt first, he added, "She kicks like a mule. Hold her real tight. And to make sure you don't wear any of the Z's brains, stand back a few feet." That he had not called the creature Dregan was by design. No reason to chill her this far into the exercise.

Gun at her side, Raven regarded her dad with red-rimmed eyes.

"Go on," he said. "I'll get a tarp from the truck."

She looked a question at him.

"We're going to take him home."

She shook her head ever so slightly.

"I'll take him out," Cade promised. "I'm a big boy. Pretty sure I can get him into the truck solo, too."

She turned and they parted ways.

Cade was jumping down from the open tailgate when the single report sounded. He met Raven in front of the ice cream truck with the tarp in one hand and Screamer in the other. He said, "Is it done?"

She nodded as she handed the gun over. She said, "Mister Dregan is no longer suffering."

Trading the Screamer for the Colt, Cade said, "Get in the truck and dig out the sat-phone. I have a call to make."

Chapter 30

Jamie tried to mimic Taryn in the way she drove the race-tuned Raptor, using as much of the 6.2 liter engine's 411 horsepower as she dared while transporting her and Lev from the house on the southern tip of Bear Lake to the once walled-in subdivision roughly a mile or so north by west. Showing zero concern that the noise of their approach might reach the people trapped in the home on the cul-de-sac, she threw the off-road beast into each corner, powering through them with enough zeal to cause the rear tires to chirp and tattoo the road with chevron-patterned skid marks.

Crouched down in the bed, back against the tailgate, Lev held on for dear life. He was armed with Jamie's war tomahawk and sitting on what was to be his primary mode of communication with the people he and Jamie hoped to spirit to safety.

When Jamie wheeled the Raptor onto an unnamed and unfinished access road running north into the heart of the cul-de-sac, it was clear to Lev that the dozens of undead were well aware of the rapidly approaching vehicle. He also saw the three adult breathers on the upstairs portico rise up and gesticulate wildly to draw attention to themselves.

The noisy approach was supposed to check two boxes at once: distract the dead and gain the undivided attention of the breathers. By the time the entire cul-de-sac was visible to the occupants of the Raptor, it was clear they had accomplished both tasks in spades.

Jamie braked hard, causing the Raptor to judder to a halt half a block from where a gate once prevented access to the cul-de-sac. Previously ringed by a patchwork wall comprised of cement freeway barriers and a myriad of other fencing components, the homes still standing and facing the turnaround were now entirely exposed. Which was a good thing. Because it gave Jamie room to maneuver the white pickup. It also provided three or four viable egress points, versus the two available when the fortifications still stood. Since the Raptor was designed to drive at high speeds over rolling desert terrain, possessed nearly a foot of ground clearance and a stance much wider than a stock F-150, driving over bodies and debris to keep from becoming trapped was a viable option should things go sideways on them.

Taking a page out of Duncan's playbook, Lev had written a message for the survivors on a 12x24-inch piece of cardboard he found in the lake house garage. WE ARE FRIENDLY was printed across the top in black Sharpie. Below that were succinct instructions he feared the survivors would balk at following—the woman, especially.

He moved forward to the cab and stripped off his coat. He spread the coat out on the bed floor. Sign in hand, he rose and displayed it for the survivors to see.

The woman's mouth fell open and her head began a slow side-to-side wag.

Lev didn't need binoculars to see she didn't like his written proposal.

As the men spoke to the woman, apparently trying to reason with her, the head wag grew so pronounced that her shoulder-length brown hair was slapping her in the face.

In the next beat three little faces appeared from behind the adults and the woman seemed to calm down.

Lev leaned down and spoke to Jamie through the sliding rear window. He said, "I think they talked some sense into her."

Before Jamie could respond, a group of rotters eight strong staggered into the open and started a slow, steady advance along the left side of the access road.

Lev sat, snaked an arm through the slider and took hold of the back seat headrest. Bracing one boot against the wheel arch, he banged the tomahawk on the bed floor and told Jamie to drive.

As the truck accelerated and Jamie swerved right to avoid the dead, Lev's sign was caught in the slipstream and fluttered away. In the next beat Jamie was driving the Raptor over the recently added chain-link fencing and he was being thrown back and forth like a ragdoll in a clothes dryer. Just when Lev thought the ride couldn't get any rougher, the off road tires rolled overtop a post studded with steel mailboxes and without warning he was weightless. The sensation lasted a microsecond. When the truck came back to earth, his tailbone paid the price.

The lightning bolt of pain running up his spine was like nothing he'd experienced before. It was ten times worse than the headache caused by the vast overpressure following the detonation of the one and only roadside bomb he'd had the displeasure of tangling with in Tikrit, Iraq. If given the choice between a swift kick to the balls or the sphincter-clenching sensation he was suffering now, he'd gladly go for two rounds of the former.

The Raptor striking the front stairs broadside and coming to a sudden halt helped to clear the fog from Lev's head. Jamie's hollering at the top of her voice brought him to his feet.

The first thing to occur to Lev was that the truck was seconds from being surrounded on three sides. The second thing he saw was a familiar face looking down on him from above. The man's expression was one of resignation. *Out of the pan and into the fire.* He disappeared for a second then came back into view holding a young girl by the wrists. She was kicking and screaming as the bearded man lifted her over the rail and thrust his arms out over space.

Adding a bit of bend to his knees, Lev nodded, reached to the sky, and mouthed, "Drop her."

He was hit across the arms and chest by fifty-some-odd pounds of squealing girl. Tensing every muscle in his torso and lower body saved him from punishing his tailbone for a second time. Instead, the girl's weight pulled him forward and a resonant gong-like sound rang out as both of his knees struck the ribbed metal floor.

Pointing to the jacket by his feet, Lev told the girl to cover up and keep her head down. As he was issuing the instructions, a pair of rotters hit the rear bumper with a bang and draped their pustule-riddled arms over top of the tailgate. That was all the girl needed to see. She turned ostrich and buried her head deep in the rumpled camouflage coat.

The second kid was already being dangled overhead when Lev rose up. More rotters were arriving at the truck to his left, the hollow thuds of their bodies colliding with the sheet metal making the girl by his feet flinch and cry out for her mom. As the growls and hisses of the dead rose in volume, the girl curled up into a fetal position and the words trailed off.

"It'll be OK," Lev said, stretching and tensing to accept the next kid.

The shock from catching the falling weight wasn't as bad the second time around. Having his feet a shoulder width apart and knees bent a little less helped to distribute the weight and soak up the momentum. That the boy was several years younger and a dozen pounds lighter spared his knees. However, it did nothing to alleviate the nonstop throbbing near his butthole. In a way it felt like he had to crap, but he was pretty sure he didn't. Or maybe he already had and wasn't aware of it.

Lev set the little blond boy down next to the girl. Forgoing the instructions on account of the pale arms swiping the air near the huddled kids, he held a finger up to hold off another falling kid and snatched up the tomahawk. Feeling the eyes of the hungry dead boring into him from two flanks and the frantic gaze of the living cast on him from above, he shuffled to the driver's side, grabbed one of the arms reaching over the box bed, and brought the tomahawk down hard atop its owner's head. The skull came apart like an overripe melon, oozing brains and releasing one eye from its socket. Lev kept hold of the arm as the rotter it was attached to went limp. Supported by the creatures pushing in from behind, the twice-dead corpse added an extra eight-inch buffer between the kids and newly arriving monsters.

Lev lashed out two more times, the vicious downward blows from the razor-sharp weapon sending bone and hair and brain tissue into the gathering crowd.

With the carrion barrier stretching from the rear of the cab to the tailgate, maybe five feet total, Lev returned his attention to catching the third kid, who to his horror was half the size of the second. A toddler at best. Maybe even younger. He was no expert on these things. In fact, he was an only child who'd rarely been around small children prior to deploying to Iraq. After coming home, he'd avoided them like the plague.

Problem here wasn't catching the girl. It was detaining her *after* that had him worried. Judging from the videos of relatives' kids he'd seen on social media before the zompoc, the little buggers were slipperier than greased pigs when they wanted to be.

Catching the girl proved to be the easy part. She actually seemed to enjoy the freefall. Like it was a game. However, her body went limp and folded in two when she hit his arms. Breath stolen from her lungs, the girl stared at him questioningly, tears forming in her blue eyes. No time for consoling. Thankful she hadn't tried to rabbit, Lev nudged her under the jacket with the other kids.

"Hold on to her real good," he whispered before rising and looking up at the balcony.

Lev saw the bearded man and his clean shaven friend helping the woman over the rail. She looked to be somewhere between thirty and forty, likely closer to the former. And thin as a scarecrow. But real tall. The men each had one of her wrists in a two-handed grip as she planted her tennis-shoe-clad feet on the steeply pitched porch roof.

"Jump," one of them urged.

She shook her head.

Lev felt fingers brushing the seat of his pants. Every little tug and tap on the fabric sent fresh bolts of white hot pain up his spine.

Ignoring the grabby dead, he stretched his arms wide and beckoned to the lady.

I'm not catching you was what he was thinking when she committed. It was a slow motion type of thing. Like a person jumping off a quarry wall into deep black water for the first time. First the knee bend. Then the hip bounce as nerves were steeled. Then the head wag as body language still said *no* even as gravity was in control.

Miraculously, she landed feet first. While her knees soaked up some of the momentum gained from the fifteen or so foot drop, they still suffered the same fate as Lev's.

The woman was rolling around on the floor of the box bed and clutching both knees when the clean shaven man alit ninja-like next to her. It almost looked like one of those parkour moves making the rounds on Facebook before things went to shit. Lev always wondered how that would help a person in times like these. Maybe he'd just found the answer to that question.

The man with the beard was carrying a little more weight than the other—most around his hips and belly. He landed feet first and off axis. Knees buckling, he rolled sideways, bowling over both Lev and Parkour Guy in the process.

The third loud thud told Jamie all of the adults were in the box bed. With the truck still spasming on its springs from the impact from above, she threw an arm over the seatback and craned her neck to see out the slider. One, two, three, and, most importantly, Lev. He was on his back, head to the tailgate and staring at her. He was mouthing "Go" even as ashen, stick-thin arms were hooking over the tailgate and bony hands grabbed at his shirt.

Accelerating and wheeling left to escape the dead spilling from the home's destroyed front door, Jamie flicked her eyes back to the mirror and saw Lev batting at the hands hauling him over the tailgate's top edge.

In the next beat, as Jamie watched helplessly, Bearded Guy and Parkour Guy, propelled backward by the sudden acceleration, slammed hard into Lev, causing him to cry out and the dead hands to lose their purchase on him.

Dead things caromed off the truck's bumper and a couple were sucked underneath as Jamie laid twin stripes of smoking rubber down on the cul-de-sac's asphalt. She fought the fishtailing truck for control, spinning the steering wheel in the opposite direction the rear end was drifting. A dozen feet before she reached the spot they'd entered, she reined the Raptor in by letting up on the gas and braking hard.

The equal and opposite reaction part of Newton's Law kicked in and Lev, Bearded Guy, and Parkour Guy shot forward and piled into the others. Sparing the occupants in back the same fate that had befallen Lev's tailbone, Jamie let off the brake and allowed the idling motor to pull the truck up and over the partially crushed bank of mailboxes at a walking speed.

In seconds Jamie had wheeled the Raptor over the fallen chain-link, through the debris field, and was speeding down the short access road. At the T she swung wide around a clutch of rotters and pointed the grille east towards Bear Lake's southernmost shore.

Chapter 31

Getting Dregan's body into the back of the truck all by himself took much more out of Cade than he would be willing to divulge to anyone other than Brook or Duncan. If he was still on the teams in the old world and a peer had witnessed him struggle like he had with the near three-hundred-pound corpse, it could have led to him being bumped to a secondary role on the teams. If you couldn't pick up a wounded comrade in a fireman's carry and get them to cover or a waiting helo, what good were you? It all boiled down to the weakest link in the chain theory. As it was, he had damn near pulled his groin getting the top half of the man's torso onto the tailgate. Heaving Dregan's tree-trunk-like legs after and folding them so he'd fit in with the other stuff in back of the F-650 hadn't been much easier.

Catching his breath, Cade thumbed the Thuraya to life and placed a call to the Bear River sheriff whose name escaped him. The call was picked up after two rings and a female voice said, "Sherriff MacLeod here. To whom am I speaking?"

"Cade Grayson. I'm one of the—"

"Eden gang," MacLeod interrupted. "I use the term *gang* affectionately. I know of you. You've earned yourself one hell of a reputation at Bear River."

At Bear River, Cade thought. Not, *here in* Bear River. Wondering where this MacLeod was at the moment, he said, "I'm relieved we got all of that out of the way." Without any pleasantries or words of condolence, he added, "We found the ice cream truck with Alexander still at the wheel." He paused.

As silence descended, Raven looked sidelong across the cab.

The sheriff spoke first, saying, "He didn't make it, did he?"

"I'm afraid not," Cade conceded. "But we're bringing him home. His body is in back of our rig."

"Oh good," she said. "That'll bring his son, Peter, a little closure."

"That's what my daughter and I were thinking."

"We'll bury him inside the walls. Someplace prominent. A place worthy of what he did for all of us," MacLeod stated solemnly.

"We're a few minutes from making the 39/16 junction," Cade said. "I think we still have a bit of a wait before the herd makes the junction."

"Understood," said MacLeod. "See you in a bit."

Cade said nothing. Heavy of heart, he ended the call. He put the phone down and started the motor. Stared out over the front of the truck and compared where the horizon sat in relation to the left front edge of the hood. He panned right and found that the distant break in the trees was still lined up perfectly with the crease in the hood. Satisfied the truck was sitting the same on all four tires as it had been when he pulled up behind the ice cream truck, he applied pedal and started into a wide-ranging one-eighty turn that would put them back on the two-lane and see them heading south.

Finally Raven broke her silence. "At least you didn't have to lie to her."

"Thank God for that," Cade replied as the Ford tackled the incline paralleling the state route. At the apex, all four wheels working in conjunction pulled the oversized F-650 onto the blacktop where Cade stopped to shift out of four-wheel drive.

"I'm glad that's over," Raven said.

"The hunt for Dregan? Or the four wheelin'?"

"Both."

"Bad news," Cade said. "To get to the junction, we're going to have to go back around behind the garage, across the field, and through the culvert."

Raven made a face and sank into her seat. Nonplussed at the thought of riding a bucking and wallowing Black Beauty through that thing again, she crossed her arms over her chest, closed her eyes, and let the thrum of the tires on smooth asphalt serenade her.

***

Twenty minutes after leaving the ice cream truck in the rearview mirror, Cade was nosing the Ford off the access road running behind the auto body shop. He slowed considerably to navigate the field north to south. Pulling parallel to the culvert, he braked and threw the transmission to Park.

Raven opened her eyes, saw the culvert, and her hands shot for the grab bar by her head. Realizing her dad was waiting to commit, she asked, "Why are we stopping here?"

"To conduct a quick recon," Cade said. "You see anything?"

She leaned over the dash, pointed south, and said, "There's a white truck parked at the 39/16 junction."

"Good eye," Cade said. "Binoculars, please."

The Steiners hit his upturned palm and Raven stated, "I can tell without using those that it's not Jamie and Lev in the Raptor."

Though the pickup was parked where the school bus used to be, just south of 39 on a flat parcel of ground, it was smaller and mostly obscured by the gently sloping westbound stretch of 39.

Cade was glassing the truck when the Thuraya emitted its shrill electronic trill.

He said, "Answer and put it on speaker."

As soon as Raven had complied with her dad's order, she let her eyes roam the mirrors, then rose up off her seat and checked all points of the compass. Seeing no threats to report to her dad, she settled her gaze on the distant pickup.

The same female voice as before said, "We see you, Grayson. We're in the white Tundra at your eleven o'clock. We already drove 39," she said. "The herd is still a half-mile out. What are you waiting for, the Second Coming of Christ?" The sheriff laughed at her own funny.

A real comedienne, Cade thought. Steiners still aimed at the truck, he said, "There's a drainage culvert we need to negotiate first. Wait one. We'll get there."

As Cade set the binoculars aside, Raven's hands went back to the grab bar. "Make it quick, " she begged. "Just power through it. Down and up."

"And buck Dregan out?"

"Fine," she said, her lower lip jutting out. "You're bound and determined to get your daughter her very own *puker patch*, aren't you?"

"Nothing could be further from the truth," he said. "The tire is holding air. No sense in inviting Murphy to deal us more vehicular issues."

Raven stared at her dad side-eyed as he maneuvered the Ford down one side of the culvert and up the other. The whole way she was swinging from the grab bar like a monkey at the zoo.

As the truck leveled out, Cade said, "You survived. How 'bout that."

"I'm about to hurl," she said. "How 'bout that."

"Like the last time you rode the Mad Mouse rollercoaster?"

The lip came out again. "I miss Oak's Park," she declared. "Think they'll ever get the rides going again?"

"Lots more important things on the government's plate than getting our old amusement park up and running." In his mind he was wondering how far inland the PLA had pushed in Oregon and Washington. Reports out of California suggested their landing had been thwarted. Or at least repulsed. What he feared was the West Coast invasion had just been delayed and that their major landfall would now occur north of San Francisco, or, worst case scenario, Astoria, Oregon, or Long Beach, Washington. If that came to fruition, going home would not happen anytime soon. Which nixed the possibility of setting eyes on the Mad Mouse, let alone riding the thing.

"You know what I miss about Oak's Park?"

Raven said nothing. Just stared at him as he wheeled the truck along the edge of the culvert heading toward the state route.

"Winning those goldfish for you. They didn't live long, but you really squealed when the ping pong ball landed in the cup."

"Remember how I stopped naming them until they lived at least a week."

He nodded.

"You named the last one *Connie*. It lived a year or so."

She made a face as the truck eased back onto the two-lane. As Cade stopped on the road facing south, she said, "Why did I do that again? It wasn't because Connie is a girl's name. Mom said something and I misinterpreted it."

"You hadn't mentioned the fish in a few days and me and Mom figured it had died. So she grabbed the net and went to your room. I remember her calling you up from downstairs. When you got there thinking the worst, Mom said, 'Wow, Raven. This one's got a heck of a constitution'."

"That's it ... *Constitution*."

Cade chuckled. "Since it was the day before the 4th of July, you thought it *had* to have something to do with *the* Constitution. You named the fish Connie right then and there. First goldfish of yours to get a name."

Smiling at the memory, Raven released the grab handle and put the binoculars to her eyes.

"What do you see?"

"Two people. Driver is older than Mom and younger than Glenda."

"That's more than a twenty-year gap," he said, "So you think our sheriff is about fifty?" Which, incidentally, was the age he'd assigned her when he glassed the pickup earlier.

Raven said, "Yes. Around fifty. She has the gray hair to support it."

"Good," he said. "How about the passenger?"

"He's a guy your age. Mid-thirties. Blond hair. Soft face. He hasn't seen and done all the things you have. Before all of this ... I bet he was a fast food worker like Wilson. They both have long guns. I see the muzzles sticking up over the seatback."

"Good eye," Cade said. He drove in silence as they crossed the short, flat bridge spanning the culvert. Once they were on the south end and the angle on the pickup was better, he said, "Glass them again. You missed one important detail."

She left the binoculars alone. She said, "I saw him. Blond hair. Blue eyes. Maybe my age."

"Think it's Peter?"

She nodded. "Why in the hell would they bring him here?"

Language, Cade thought to himself. Then, in his head he heard Brook say: *Choose your battles wisely, Cade Grayson.*

He said, "Maybe they didn't know we were bringing the body back with us."

"Probably thought you wouldn't find him alive or dead."

She's channeling Brook, thought Cade. *And she's wise beyond her years.*

"Maybe he's training as a junior deputy, or something."

He said, "Let's go find out," and accelerated southbound on 16.

***

In less than a minute Cade was steering off of 16 and onto the grass infield. He parked the larger F-650 broadside to the Tundra and buzzed his window down.

The sheriff's window was already down and she'd removed her ball cap.

From his elevated perch in the F-650, Cade saw the bespectacled sheriff wore a tan uniform. The pants bore sharp creases. The breast pockets on the blouse were trimmed with dark brown flaps, both ironed flat. *MacLeod* was stitched in red on the tan fabric strip curling over her left breast. Though the uniform wasn't standard issue, it said the woman meant business. That she was taking the new position seriously. Cade introduced Raven, then himself. Afterward, acting purely out of habit, he scanned the road all around for threats. All was clear. Just the thrum of the big V-10 keeping them company.

"We're clear," MacLeod declared. "Me and Deputy Hunt cleared the roamers off of Main and Center before I called you."

Cade said, "The hordes sure did a number on Woodruff."

The sheriff nodded. Grabbing her hat, she said, "Let's take a walk."

Cade looked to Raven. Mouthed, "Stay frosty," as he grabbed his rifle. He pulled his hat down tight on his head and zipped his jacket to his chin.

He met MacLeod on the infield. They were standing on the parcel of ground where the school bus used to reside. Virtually on the same spot where his wife was bitten by the crawler weeks ago.

Now wearing a powder-blue medical mask, MacLeod spoke first. Voice a bit muffled, she said, "Thanks for bringing Dregan back with you."

"It's what we do," Cade said. "He was a friend to us."

"He spoke very highly of you. Of *all* of you there at Eden. That's why I met you here instead of letting you lead the procession of dead south and doing the handoff at Bear River."

Though Cade had a hunch where this conversation was heading, he looked a question at the sheriff.

Chin upthrust and staring him directly in the eye, she said, "Gregory Dregan has a posthumous request."

Cade arched a brow.

MacLeod said, "He just asks that you honor his father's wishes and take his brother, Peter, back to Eden with you."

Cade said nothing. Shifted his weight and stared out at the Bear River Range.

"He's just turned thirteen. He *needs* to be around kids his age," the sheriff pleaded. "Bear River is made up of childless young people and people my age. Most of them drink to pass the time. Nearly all of them are sick with the flu right now."

Looking to the Tundra, Cade asked, "Is he sick?"

She shook her head. "He isn't running a temp. And he's been isolated from the population. Alexander made sure of that. Then Gregory stayed away once he got really sick."

"Gregory turned last night?"

MacLeod nodded.

Cade clasped his hands behind his neck. Staring at the gray sky, he spun a slow three-sixty.

"I'll get him," MacLeod said.

"Help me with the body first. It's going to take the three of us." Cade paused and stared her in the eye. "The boy can't view the body." Whispering, he added, "Dregan tried to end it himself and failed. The Zs ate most of the left side of his body before he turned. It's going to give me nightmares. I'm sure of it."

"We'll have Peter stay in the truck, then."

Looking the sheriff in the eye, Cade said, "Nobody but us needs to know how Dregan went out. Understood?"

She nodded solemnly.

It took Cade, MacLeod, and her deputy, Hunt, working together, to transfer the limp, dead weight from the Ford to the Toyota.

Finished, Deputy Hunt walked Peter to the Ford. In the officer's hands were two bulging sports bags. Halfway to the Ford, Peter broke away and ran back to the Tundra. He threw down the tailgate, crawled into the load bed, and wrapped his arms around his father's tarp-shrouded corpse.

MacLeod allowed Peter a couple of minutes to mourn. Then she gave him a medical mask and escorted him to the Ford.

Cade and Raven had already mounted up, Peter's bags were in back, and the passenger's side rear door was hanging open.

Before buzzing his window up, Cade said, "Oh yeah. I almost forgot." He reached across the space between the trucks and handed MacLeod the safety-orange Screamer. He gave her a quick primer on how to activate and deactivate the compact device.

"Just like the Pied Piper, eh?"

"Keeps them locked on you," Cade promised. "It's loud as hell though. If you don't have a pair already, I'd fashion some earplugs out of something."

MacLeod flashed him a thumbs-up. She pulled the mask to her chin. "Thank you," she said and started the Tundra rolling toward 16.

Cade watched the pickup turn left at the juncture and drive slowly up the gently sloping stretch of 39. Once the Tundra was out of sight, he wheeled the Ford in a big sweeping one-eighty, bounced onto 16, and drove north toward Woodruff.

Chapter 32

State Route 39

The hidden gate to the Eden compound's feeder road was hinged open and Wilson was working the 4Runner through a stilted three-point turn.

Stopping with the bumper pointing down the feeder road, he threw the transmission to Park, set the brake, and leaped from the cab.

Wilson started spouting orders at once. "Tran, grab a leg. Taryn, you get the other." Hooking his fingers under Sasha's armpits, Wilson stared down into her green eyes. A cold ball forming in his gut, he said, "Hang in there. You're going to be fine."

"Don't lie to me, Wilson. You don't know that. You're not a nurse. All of the nurses are dead or gone," she reminded him. "So I'm pretty much effed."

Tran said, "Best to be positive, Miss Sasha."

Taryn said, "On one," and began counting down from three.

They lifted Sasha onto a tarp spread out in the cargo area. Wilson climbed in and pulled the tarp until Sasha was clear of the rear-hatch door.

"Close it up," he said to Taryn. "Tran ... radio Seth and have him meet us at the RV. Have him bring water and blankets."

Three minutes later, after closing the gate to 39 and negotiating the middle gate, the SUV was parked beside the RV with the motor stilled.

Wilson slid from behind the wheel and alit on the soft ground. He looked all around. "Where's Seth?"

Taryn shrugged.

As Tran was plucking the radio from a pocket to hail Seth, Max came roaring across the clearing. He was bounding through the tall grass, showing above the bent stalks and then disappearing momentarily. As he drew near, it became obvious his white muzzle was stained red.

Blood, Wilson thought as all hell broke loose across the clearing.

***

Forty-five miles north of the 16/39 junction, Jamie was pulling the Raptor onto the cement pad fronting the brown house on Bear Lake's southern shore. She stopped a foot shy of the garage and shut the truck down.

In the Raptor's load bed, Lev was sitting between the passenger's side wheel well hump and tailgate. His back was pressed to the sheet metal and his M4 rested across his extended legs. On his face was a pained expression. He wiped away beaded sweat with a sleeve, only to feel more appear seconds later.

"What is this place?" asked the woman who called herself Fiona. The three kids were huddled around her. Clinging to her, actually. Strangely, during the short ride from the cul-de-sac to the lakeside house, they hadn't gravitated toward either of the male survivors. As Lev expected, they had stayed as far away from him as possible and avoided eye contact—until now.

Now the kids were wide-eyed and staring at him. They seemed eager to hear what the man with the big gun had to say.

"It's a safe place," Lev answered. "The owners were either moving in or out when the crap started. The garage is full of boxes and some furniture. Carpet upstairs is plush. You'll have great visibility. And there's a rowboat lashed to the dock out back."

The woman listened but didn't reply.

"I'm Michael," said Parkour Guy. He stuck out his hand.

In too much pain to move, let alone reach across the load bed, Lev shot the man an abbreviated salute. "I'm Lev. Jamie is our chauffeur."

Bearded Guy had been staring at Lev for the duration of the ride. All of a sudden, when Lev introduced himself, the man perked up and wagged a finger in the air. "I know you. You set me free from Adrian's people." Forgoing the handshake, he added, "I'm Payton. My dad was a big Colt's fan. Owned a diner Archie used to frequent occasionally."

Lev nodded. He grimaced as the slight head bob resulted in a fresh explosion of pain at the base of his spine. Through clenched teeth, he asked, "Do you remember my friend? The tall guy?" He was being vague about the details on purpose.

Eyes misting over, Payton said, "Rasta-looking black dude. I'll never forget him."

Jamie was standing beside the truck and playing peek-a-boo with the youngest of the three kids. Hearing this, she looked to Payton. "Have you seen him since?"

Payton grabbed at his beard as he shook his head. "Nope," he said, "After he freed me, I took off to find Fiona and the kids. I was worried sick about them."

Remembering how the kids had seemed a bit aloof toward the men, Lev asked, "So they're your kids?"

Hands up in mock surrender, Payton said, "No, sir. Michael and I were thinking about adopting before all this happened. Now … I wouldn't wish that on anybody. This world is no place to raise a kid."

"I took it upon myself to raise them," Fiona said. "The littlest, Sabrina, is mine." She patted the other kids on the head one at a time, saying, "Harley … he's six. Quinn here is nine. They're siblings."

Michael said, "She's the bravest woman I know. Killed one of Adrian's watchers and spirited the kids away. We all met up at this little drive-in not too far from here. Some of Adrian's people caught me and Payton there." He pointed to Fiona. "She shot her way out and made it back to the kids. When me and Payton came back to the cul-de-sac to look for food, Fiona was already there with the kids."

Lev asked, "Adrian was already gone?"

Nodding, Payton said, "Her people must have come and took her down minutes after you and the others left."

"Daymon wanted to kill her," stated Lev. "He was overridden because another of our people wanted her to get bit and turn. So she could spend a little Hell on Earth time."

"And we all know how that ended up," Jamie interjected.

"Adrian always referred to the cul-de-sac as her *Satellite Outpost*," Fiona said. "It was unfinished when you attacked. I bet they just decided to abandon it and go back north and lick their wounds."

"That's not all they were licking up north," said Michael, the disgust evident in his tone.

Lev said, "I heard the crap that was going on at the airport compound. Sickens me someone could do that to a child."

"Speaking of the airport," Jamie said. "Daylight's burning. We need to get going." She looked to Fiona. "Be careful ... you have two hordes of rotters north of here. Thanks to the lake being so close, you're probably safe here."

"I'm going nowhere," Fiona stated. Jaw set, she regarded her male friends. "You two can stay if you want. With Jim gone, I could use the help."

While Jamie helped lower the kids from the truck to the driveway, Lev asked Fiona, "Was that Jim by the stocks?"

Fiona nodded. "He tried to shore the fence. He went down when the first wave of roamers surged into the development. He didn't live long enough to learn there was nothing he could have done to stop the dead. Hell, a semi-truck would have been swatted aside like a toy. The surge was immense."

"Overwhelming," Michael added.

Payton shook his head. "We barely made it upstairs before the door folded in. Our only gun was in the kitchen. We're just lucky the upper floors were well furnished. It all went into the stairwell to keep the zombies from climbing 'em."

Lev said nothing. He'd seen it all before. Firsthand, unfortunately.

Jamie climbed behind the wheel and closed the door. She beckoned Fiona over and covertly slipped her a Beretta pistol and one fully loaded spare magazine for it.

"You sure?" said Fiona.

Jamie nodded.

"I'll give it to the guys," said Fiona. "Thank you. I'll never forget your act of kindness." She leaned closer. "You two be careful up north. We saw some soldiers on motorcycles and more riding in some trucks."

"Ours?"

Fiona shook her head. "They're all the same."

"What do you mean?"

Voice hushed, Fiona said, "They're Japanese … or Korean or something. All of them."

The Chinese, thought Jamie. Glancing at the rearview, she called, "Cut your story short, Lev. We have to go."

Arms outstretched, Lev looked to the men, then nodded toward the cab. "I'm hurtin' here. A little help, fellas?"

Chapter 33

The access road to Daymon's burned-to-the-ground chalet-style home slipped by on the right. Cade didn't slow or let on he knew anything about where the southbound drive led. There was no visible smoke, yet he could have sworn there was a detectable gray smudge lingering in the general vicinity.

Nobody spoke for another five minutes. During that time the road jogged north then back east and they passed a number of farmhouses, some of them with barns and outbuildings—all of which bore big white Xs on their front-facing doors. Victim to the elements and relentless march of time, farm implements and old cars wasted away in yards and fields. Signs at the ends of overgrown drives offering *Fresh Eggs by the Dozen, Cords of Seasoned Fire Wood,* and other rural goods flitted by on both sides of the Ford in blurs of garish color.

Along the way Cade consulted the rearview three times. The first two stolen glances revealed Peter lying on his side on the back seat, legs drawn up to his chest, arms wrapped tightly around his knees. On the third furtive glance Cade found himself staring into the boy's ice-blue eyes. Though they were red-rimmed and swollen, the irises pierced like twin lasers. "Thirsty?" he asked.

Without blinking, Peter nodded.

Cade nodded to Raven. Pointed to a water stuffed in the door pocket. Looking back at Peter, he said, "It's clear you're not spiking a fever. You can lose the mask."

Peter peeled off the mask and took the water from Raven.

Raven waited for him to finish drinking, then said, "Your dad didn't suffer."

Nothing from Peter. He was directing the thousand-yard stare out the passenger window.

Changing the subject, Raven turned to her dad and said, "Isn't the place Daymon and Heidi were staying around here somewhere? We're east on Center. And I figure we've gone well over two miles."

"We passed it. Back before the jog in the road. I'm pretty sure we're on a state route, now."

"Why did you pass it? Wouldn't that be the logical place to start?"

Cade shook his head.

She asked, "Why not?"

He said, "Because if we find him there, he's dead. I want to find him alive. I'll revisit that house when I've exhausted all other possibilities."

Raven nodded, then looked out her window.

The satellite phone emitted its usual electronic trill.

Cade fished it from the center console, looked at the screen, then thumbed the Talk button.

"Cade here."

He listened intently for a few seconds. Jaw taking on a granite set, he said, "Understood," and ended the call.

Sensing the abrupt change in her dad's demeanor and tone, Raven said, "What is it?"

"This thing is nearly dead, that's what. Plug it in, please." He tapped the console lid with his right elbow. "Charger's in there somewhere."

Raven double-checked the display. Sure enough, the battery was nearly depleted. She found the end of the cord that fit the phone, plugged it in, and replaced the phone in the console. Closing the lid, she said, "Well ... what's up? Why the stony face?"

Eyes narrowing, Cade said, "Wilson and Taryn were ambushed on the fire lane by a second herd of Zs. Either the Zs or the elk they were hunting breached the wire somewhere near the compound. They drew the dead to the road and were met by

Sasha and Tran. Sasha was injured somehow. They took her to the compound where they found Seth in a bad way—"

Raven shifted in her seat. "Sasha was outside the wire?" She made a face. "And Seth went out by himself, too?"

"It was just him and Max left inside," Cade said. "He had to go out to deliver a first aid kit. Looks like a Z was lingering near the compound blind and caught him as he came out."

Words coming real slow, Raven said, "Did ... they ... *both* get bit?"

"Tran said they were both injured. Only thing he's certain of, is that Seth *was* bitten."

"Shouldn't we go back?"

Cade glanced over his shoulder. The boy was still lost in thought. Or mourning in his own way. That two more people may be lost to the Omega virus didn't seem to register. Swinging his gaze forward, Cade indicated they would drive until they came to a point in the road where at least two homes with no Xs on the door were visible. His plan was to search both for clues, then start back toward the compound, stopping at Daymon's final residence if they found nothing in the homes or immediate vicinity to suggest the man was still alive.

Coming up on a slight rise where twin pickets of firs bookended the two-lane, the first of Cade's boxes got checked. The house on the left was a solitary two-story clapboard affair set back from the road. There was no X on the front door. The windows were boarded over but appeared to be intact. Parked on the drive was a small RV. It was maybe twenty feet in length and leaning slightly to the left. Grass growing beside the drive rose to the lower edge of the Itasca's side windows. Victim to rust and rot, dozens of old cars sitting on flat tires dotted the landscape all around the house and RV.

As the Ford motored onto the spot in the road where the incline transitioned to a short run of level road even with the drive harboring the RV, the second box was checked when a sprawling operation came into view on the left at the bottom of a long runout.

"What's that?" Raven asked even as she was grabbing up the Steiners to see for herself.

Squinting at the boxy red object hogging the road a few hundred yards beyond the fenced-in parcel of land dotted with a house, barn, silo, and numerous outbuildings, Cade said, "Looks like a car hauler."

Cade put the distance from the front of the trailer abutting the cab to the tail end currently facing away from them at seventy feet or more. The trailer sat on twelve wheels distributed evenly, two to a side, between three axles. The axles were positioned close enough together at the rear of the trailer to lend the impression the massive tires were touching. At first blush, he guessed maybe twenty feet separated the trailer's glossy red roof from the road's pale gray surface.

"A what?" Raven asked.

"Exactly what the name implies," Peter said.

Raven lowered the binoculars and spun in her seat to face him. Her expression said *Elaborate already*.

Taking the cue, Peter said, "We had one back home. Dad bought it at auction. Said he was going to use it to transport a racecar to Bonneville Salt Flats one day. He was always dreaming up a new adventure. That trailer was much smaller than the one here and would have held only four cars. That one looks to be twice the size."

Raven asked, "How do you fit *eight* cars in there?"

"The trailer is divided horizontally," Cade said. "I'd guess there is a hydraulic ramp that allows access to the upper loft."

"I'm not sure," Peter admitted. "I never went inside it. Dad frowned on me messing around on the trucks. He was afraid I'd let some gas out or something."

"Well, yeah," Raven said. "I'm afraid to go anywhere near the tank thingy your dad's friend delivered. And Tran cooks on a grill not too far from the big shiny *bomb on wheels*."

"Like I told you," Cade said. "It's perfectly safe."

Raven didn't respond to that. Instead, she drew in a breath and said, "There's a body on the road by the right front wheel."

Cade said, "On the shoulder?"

"Yep," she said. "Almost buried in the grass. It's not moving. Which means it's probably not a rotter."

"I agree," Cade said. "We're close enough now, if it was one of them, it would probably be up and looking for us already."

Peter was hanging over the front seats now, elbows braced on the seatbacks. His long blond hair spilled over his forearms as he rested his chin on his stacked fists.

"Looks like it has no head," Peter noted.

"He's right," Raven said. It wasn't the first decapitated body she'd seen since that awful Saturday in July. And it surely wouldn't be the last. This one, however, was special. Because if it was a clean cut and if the head was arranged on the road or shoulder somewhere nearby, they just might have found a clue to Daymon's whereabouts.

"Gun up," Cade ordered.

Raven swapped the binoculars for her M4.

Peter said, "What about me?"

Simultaneously, Cade and Raven shook their heads.

Cade said, "We'll revisit you and guns later." He left it at that and focused solely on his driving.

At the bottom of the decline, with still a hundred of feet to go before reaching the semi-tractor hitched to the trailer, he brought the truck from forty miles per hour to a walking-speed— three miles per hour or so. Once the distance to the auto hauler was halved, Cade saw the decapitated head. It was on the road behind the trailer. He also saw that a ramp was deployed behind the trailer. The two lengths of perforated metal looked to be a couple of feet wide. Black strips of traction tape ran horizontally across them.

As the F-650 came even with the semi-tractor, which took up most of the westbound lane, it became clear to Cade the severed head was facing his way, the eyes tracking his approach.

Cade was out of the truck first. Calling over his shoulder, he told Peter to stay put. He approached the rear of the trailer, M4 held at a low-ready, his own eyes mimicking the movements of those in the head on the road before him.

Materializing from around the front of the Ford, Raven immediately voiced her displeasure at the sight and feigned as if she was about to kick it into the ditch where a sleek red sports car wallowed in the tall grass.

"Wait," Cade said, extending an arm to slow her approach.

"Joking," she said as she crouched next to the head. Wisps of gray hair encircled a balding crown. Wrinkles, crow's feet was what she'd heard them called, swept from the corners of each roving eye. The man looked to have been about Duncan's age. The gnashing of its yellowed teeth produced a faint grinding noise that caused the hair on her neck to prick.

"Looks like Duncan," observed Cade.

He had Raven back away, then snatched the head off the road by its hair. It had the trademark look of a first turn: gray-green dermis gone mostly dry and stretched tight over atrophying muscles. The whites of its eyes were jaundiced, the pupils twin pinpricks framed by irises the color of fine opal. He held the weighty item at eye level and saw the decapitation was real clean. No jagged edges on the ashen skin to suggest anything other than the blade had been razor-sharp and lot of force went into the single swipe that did this.

"Kindness?"

"No doubt." Cade looked west. "Daymon did this." He peered into the trailer. Saw a half-dozen car-sized shapes in the gloom. There were four vehicles parked nose to tail on the top loft. All were wrapped with lots of chrome and bore fancy lines. Classics bound for auction, no doubt. Parked in the front two spaces on the lower level were a pair of ground-scraping wedge-shaped Le-Mans-style race cars. The two spaces closest to the ramp were empty. One of the missing vehicles was in the ditch. It was red and bore a prancing horse logo on the front fender facing the road. At once something clicked and Cade heard a familiar theme song start up in his head. For a split second he was transported back to his childhood home in Portland. It was 1986 and he was Raven's age and sitting on his beanbag chair on the floor. Dad and Mom had the couch. On the television was a show that transported him to a tropical island where for an hour he lived vicariously through a swarthy private investigator named Thomas Magnum and a brash helicopter pilot called T.C. If there had been another vehicle in the trailer, it was long gone.

Raven said, "Think Daymon took the missing car?"

Cade shook his head. "Not one hundred percent." He drew the Gerber and thrust it into one of the head's wandering eyes. Brain sufficiently scrambled, he tossed the decapitated head to the ground under the truck's rear wheels. It bounced once, then rolled out of sight. He regarded the truck, then locked eyes with Raven and went on. "This truck has been parked here a long time. There's a fine coat of dust on the cars inside. And the windows on the tractor are coated with grime. For all I know, Adrian's people could have done this. Daymon's not the only one with a machete and whet stone."

"The head was left the way we found it on purpose, right?"

Cade looked to the F-650. Saw Peter staring back at him from between the front seatbacks. He worked the equation for a second.

"Adrian's people *were* pretty methodical. But I don't think this is their doing."

Raven's lips curled into a wide smile. First real one Cade remembered seeing grace her face in some time.

"Let's go," he said. "We're heading back to the farmhouse without an X on its door."

"To look for supplies?"

"That, and—"

"And what?"

"You'll see," Cade said cryptically.

Chapter 34

Coming out of the shallow sweeper, Otto jammed the brakes. The pickup juddered on the washboard gravel and then came to a complete stop a couple of hundred feet from the UDOT lot.

"Fuck, Nate. You had one motherfuckin' job." Otto shoved Holly's upper body hard into the seatback with his extended right arm and fixed the younger man with a look cold enough to freeze water.

Palms upturned, Nate said, "I was gonna get around to it."

"You were supposed to get *around* to it be-*fuckin*-fore the meat sacks got all the way around the motherfuckin' fence."

The veins on the sides of Otto's neck were standing out. His suddenly tensed neck muscles rippled and distorted the spider webs tattooed there. Saliva launched from his mouth as he spit the damning words had landed on Holly's cheek. Nonetheless, she remained motionless between the two men, every muscle in her body primed with adrenaline. Amazingly, her eyes had remained forward, locked on the assemblage of dead things gathered before the gate.

Nate swallowed hard but said nothing.

"I spent twenty minutes of my morning luring those shabby motherfuckers to the back fence so you could take care of them," Otto bellowed. "I. Am. Not. Pleased."

Stammering slightly, Nate said, "I'll take care of them." Lips moving subtly, he jabbed a finger at the zombies. "There's eight of them. That's half of a magazine. We can afford that."

The truck's motor idled down a bit as a fan under the hood kicked on. The added noise caused the zombies not already aware of the truck to turn their heads in unison.

Otto was shaking his head as he said, "You don't get that luxury, Nate. You fucked up. Better get that blade of yours out now and get busy before they spread out on the road. Wouldn't want you to get surrounded and get bit." Finished with his diatribe, he turned to Holly and gently wiped his saliva from her cheek.

Nate elbowed his way out the door.

Otto called after him, "I've watched people go through the *change*. It ain't pretty."

Dispatching the first three zombies went well for Nate. Grab the neck, stick the eye or temple, let it fall where it had stood. From the safety of the truck it looked easy. Otto regarded Holly as Nate seemed to struggle with a real big meat sack. He said, "Might just be you and me tonight."

Holly exhaled as Nate lashed out with a wild overhand right and the Ka-Bar in his hand speared the big zombie in the temple. She drew in a deep breath and held it as Nate backed across the road, leaving two more bodies in his wake. As the last of the dead things fell to the blood-soaked blade, she released the trapped breath and sank into her seat.

"You didn't want to be alone with me," Otto stated. "I get it. *I* don't like being alone with me." He let loose a wild throaty howl and leaned forward and plucked three beers off the floor. He cracked one and drained it down as Nate unchained and hauled the gate open. Otto reached across Holly and placed a beer meant for Nate on the passenger seat.

Holly received her beer unopened. She promptly trapped it between her legs and turned in time to see Nate backing away from the gate.

Otto dropped the truck into gear and steered for the gate. Once the truck was inside the UDOT facility and the gate was closed behind them, Nate climbed back in for the short drive to the trailer. He was breathing hard. Despite the fall-like temperature outside, he was also sweating profusely.

Otto wheeled the truck to within a truck length of the trailer and parked it there with the grille aimed for the door. After killing the engine, he turned and fixed a hard stare on Nate. "You didn't say if the chain was how you left it."

With a dumb look parked on his face, Nate said, "Nothing looked out of place."

Otto grabbed his rifle off the floorboard. He looked to Nate. Asked, "Was it, or wasn't it, as you left it?"

Swallowing hard, Nate said, "*Exactly* as I left it." It was a lie. And a poor one at that. Because he honestly wasn't paying attention when Otto told him to make note of how he'd left the chain in the first place. Besides, if someone had come and opened the gate, why hadn't they culled the meat sacks first? Experience told him it was always harder to leave a closed perimeter through a gathered crowd of the things.

Holly nullified the need for a second admission of incompetence on Nate's part by noting exactly what he'd been thinking. She said, "The deaders probably came back around this morning when he opened the gate to let us out. That was *way* more than twenty minutes ago. Plenty of time for them to shuffle back here to wait for us to return."

"Or wait for more meat to exit the place," Nate added. He cracked the beer, thanked Otto with a tip of the can, and took a long pull.

"Keep your eyes open," Otto growled. Stepping from the truck, he wagged a finger at Holly. "You stay put until I'm sure *doofus* here didn't drop the ball completely."

Always someone else's fault, Holly thought as the doors thunked shut on either side of her.

"That chain was looped twice around the bars and pulled through the fence, just as I left it," Nate said assuredly. He skirted a mud puddle in the trailer's shadow then stopped long enough to drink the beer down. He crushed the can between his palms and tossed it to the ground beside the short stack of steps. In the next beat, as his foot landed on the first tread, his breath was knocked from him when Otto's right arm came out of nowhere, swinging on a chest-high horizontal plane, the spider-web-tattooed elbow catching him square on the solar plexus.

As Nate wheezed and doubled over, the can he had just tossed onto the ground entered his line of sight. Though his eyes were clouded by fresh tears, he still saw why Otto had abruptly stopped him from climbing the steps. It wasn't a trip wire attached to a grenade like in the movies. There was no rattlesnake waiting to strike from the gloom under the step. It was the second identical beer can already there that had spurred the spontaneous reaction. Which in turn had led to Nate hinging at the waist and avoiding receiving a face full of lead. Instead, his forehead and eyes became pin cushions for the wood splinters exploding from the hollow core door half a yard from his face.

The pair of ear-splitting booms preceding Nate nearly going blind were followed by the *snap-crackle* of a single bullet cleaving the air a foot over his head.

Otto wasn't so lucky. One bullet struck him in nearly the same place on his body that his surprise elbow had connected on Nate's. Only Otto hadn't doubled over forward. The first millisecond, as the bullet reduced his sternum to a thousand tiny splinters of bone, his body went rigid and the kinetic energy from the mule kick to the chest stood him up straight. In the next beat another bullet struck home and his upper body was limp and bending over backward, both feet leaving the ground.

While Otto's head was impacting the ground a few feet from the trailer steps, Nate was bringing his AK-47 on line with the door and pressing the trigger.

The first five rounds fired on full-auto stitched the door right-to-left in a neat diagonal line with maybe three inches separating each jagged bullet hole. The AK's muzzle rise, when combined with the fact that Nate was seeing everything through the veil of crimson blood cascading off his brow, caused the next twenty rounds to walk a near vertical path from the doorknob to the top of the door. With the doorknob left dangling by a single bent bolt and the jamb beside it utterly destroyed, the door swung inward freely through a swirling gun smoke haze.

There was a keening of metal as three more bullets leaving the AK pierced the aluminum door header. The only sound that followed the final two AK rounds sailing harmlessly toward the pewter sky was the clack of the Kalashnikov's bolt slamming closed on an empty chamber.

Clutching his chest, face up to the sky, Otto was in the process of dying. And he wasn't going without a fight. One hand was clutching a gushing neck wound and he kicked at the ground, his boot heels carving deep furrows into the moist gravel as he tried to get ahold of the rifle that had landed just outside of his reach.

Dazed by the loss of blood and ears ringing from discharging an entire thirty-round magazine in just under three seconds, Nate fumbled to drag his Glock from the holster on his hip. As he fought to pull the long tail of the parka over the pistol's polymer grip, he heard a man groan. Close on the heels of that disconcerting noise, a horn resounded behind him. Not a single toot. This was Holly laying on the thing as if she was trying to relay something urgent.

As the horn went silent, the blare was replaced by Holly yelling for him to step aside.

What's she going to do, Nate thought, *start the rig up and drive the shooter over?*

Having finally wrenched his pistol free of the holster, Nate swung it up and aimed for the destroyed door. By now the dust and blue-gray smoke had mostly cleared, allowing him to get a good look at the damage done by his sustained burst.

It was impressive.

The wood paneling on the back wall of the trailer had a fault line running vertical from the back of the love seat all the way to the ceiling. The love seat was a mess of protruding springs. Cotton-like stuffing spilled from holes where the bullets had punched through it.

A body lay flat and still on the floor in front of the love seat. Next to the body was a shot-up cowboy hat and pair of glasses. The only details of the body Nate could make out from his viewing angle outside the trailer were the worn soles of the man's leather boots and wisps of gray hair rising up over the neck of a rumpled camouflage jacket.

"I got you covered," Holly called from the truck. She was aiming a long rifle at the trailer, the blued barrel wavering in the void of her open window.

Nate crowed, "I got the fucker."

Holly asked, "What about Otto?"

Nate looked over his shoulder at the prostrate body. Otto's arms were outstretched in a position of surrender. A crimson puddle had formed on his left side. Nate thought, *Otto's done*. He said, "First things first. I want to see what I inherited from *Cowboy* here. Otto will be just fine." He smirked at the last part as he turned back toward the yawning door.

Chapter 35

Eden Compound

Sasha was sitting on a folding chair under the RV's metal awning. Nearby, stretched out on the ground, Max was resting his head on his paws and eyeing her every move.

Draped across Sasha's lap was a colorful blanket with a host of Navajo-inspired patterns running its length. Her bare legs were propped up on the Coleman camp cooler on the ground before her chair. The wound on the teen's ankle stood out starkly against the pale skin around it.

"I wish Glenda was here," Tran said. "I know many things, but unfortunately, first aid is not one of them." He wore purple surgical gloves and held a bottle of hydrogen peroxide in one hand. He poured a liberal amount of the clear liquid on the abraded skin above Sasha's ankle bone. Watched it bubble and froth in the wound for a few seconds. "This is supposed to make the bad stuff come out."

Crouched next to the cooler, voice wavering as he spoke, Wilson said to Tran, "Do you think it's a bite?"

Standing under the awning, her shoulders slumped, Taryn sighed and wiped a stray tear from her cheek. Without a word, she turned and walked the dozen feet or so to the front of the RV, raised the tarp covering Seth's outstretched corpse, and lifted his limp arm off the ground.

"These defensive wounds were made by nails and teeth," she called. "Mostly nails, though. He was fighting it off at first. The one to the neck did him in. Severed the main vein or artery there."

"The *bullet* to his head did him in," mumbled Sasha.

"He was turning," Wilson whispered. "I had no choice." Hand shaking, he pinched the bridge of his nose and looked toward the sky.

Taryn's head started a slow side-to-side wag. Voice exuding a measure of optimism, she said, "I don't think that's a bite on Sash's ankle."

Tran began, "Since we can't be sure until—"

"We're sure she isn't infected," finished Wilson. "I get it. She'll need to be quarantined until we know she's out of the woods." He rose and regarded his sister. "Don't worry, Sash. This is no different than what happened to you in Castle Rock when the undead butcher got ahold of your ankle."

"I remember," Sasha said, her voice cracking. "I'm thirsty." She drew in a deep breath and coughed before accepting the offered canteen from her brother. "And Wilson ... I know you had no choice. Don't beat yourself up. You just happened to get to him first."

Wilson said nothing. The tears carving tracks in the grime on his face did all the talking.

Without warning, Tran probed Sasha's wound with a finger.

Gasping, she said, "Can you just bandage it up now?"

"As you wish." Tran fished items from the kit and went to work wrapping the wound in gauze and taping it in place.

"I'll get you some books," Taryn said.

"I already read them all," Sasha replied. She made a face and the tears started to flow. "It's not fair," she said between sobs. "Seth died because of me. Because I slipped and fell and this happened, he was forced to leave the compound without backup. I'm soooo stupid."

"When it's a person's time to go, it's their time to go," Tran said. He nodded. "That's my belief. Seth fulfilled his purpose on Earth. He's off on another adventure now."

The others said nothing.

Wilson took the canteen from Sasha. "This is yours until we know for sure. I'll fill it and bring it back to you."

"What?" said Sasha, a hint of a smile ghosting across her lips. "You afraid to swap spit with your sister?"

"Better to be safe than sorry," he said. "That's all. Glass is still half full where I'm concerned."

Taryn and Wilson helped Sasha to stand.

Tran said, "I'll go and check the area around the compound entrance for rotters. Then I'll check the sat-phones to see if we missed anything." He paused to face the trio. "You stay strong, Sasha. It'll be all right. And you two ... be careful out here when you're coming and going. Our numbers are small. We have to use the utmost caution from here on out."

Wilson nodded and opened the RV door. Ushering the girls in, he said, "I'm really worried about Glenda and Duncan. Radio me if you hear from them."

"Will do," Tran answered. He turned and nearly tripped over Max as the shepherd formed up next to him. Black rifle in hand, he strode across the clearing toward the compound's camouflaged entrance, the dog matching his every step and stealing furtive glances toward the RV every few feet.

***

Six miles east of Woodruff, Cade was pulling the F-650 off the two-lane and onto a short gravel drive leading to a two-story farmhouse surrounded by too many outbuildings to count. He told the kids to hold on as he goosed the engine and guided the truck through a series of wide channels carved into the drive by runoff from the two weeks' worth of heavy rains bookending the recent out-of-the-blue early-season snow event.

By the time they had motored halfway through the rutted section of the narrow drive, the zombies Cade had spotted from the road on the eastbound pass were turned away from the house and taking their first steps in the direction of the vehicle angling toward them. While initially Cade had counted only three shamblers, now there were four. Standing head-high to the female Z's waist, the fourth rotter looked to have been six or seven when she died the first time. What at one time had been blonde ponytails sprouting from each side of the girl's head were now two unruly tufts of hair that bobbed to and fro in concert with the lolling of her head. The pom-pom-looking things were home to twigs and leaves and streaked black by what Cade guessed was dry blood from a recent meal.

The surprise appearance of the undead girl started Cade thinking he was again witness to a phenomenon he and Raven had discussed earlier. When viewed together with the adult male, adult female, and portly, pock-faced, teenaged male Z, the girl Z rounded out the nuclear family. All that was missing from this decaying lot was the ubiquitous family pet.

Both Brook and Raven had sworn up and down that Max had seemed to be attached to a trio of undead they'd culled outside the Schriever perimeter back in August. That *family unit* had been a man, woman, and young boy. All seemed to have suffered the same rate of decay, which suggested they had all turned at roughly the same time. And adding to the mystery, all three of them had been moving in the same direction, never straying far from one another.

Cade stopped the Ford a fair distance from the shamblers. Gaze roaming the property, he plucked his Nomex combat gloves from the voluminous center console.

"Why are we here?" asked Peter.

Working his left hand into the glove, Cade answered, "You know we're looking for our friend, Daymon, right?"

The boy nodded.

"We're multitasking on this little trip outside the wire. Raven, here, has already bagged her first elk." He looked in her direction, momentarily taking his eyes off the approaching Zs. "Sadly, she didn't learn how to gut it."

Peter said, "Roamers got to it first?"

Cade adjusted the glove so the thermoplastic rubber knuckle guards were in place. He snugged the hook-and-loop closures tight around his wrist. Slipping on the other glove, he added, "Then she drove this big ol' truck for the first time." Glancing in the rearview mirror, he saw Peter's eyes bug.

The kid said, "How did you reach the pedals?"

Raven said, "It's complicated."

Cade smiled at that. He added, "My baby Bird also stayed by herself outside the wire for the first time. Five whole minutes without anyone around. We're planning on doubling that, though." He bumped the knuckles on both gloved hands together and winked at her. "But with an added wrinkle."

With Raven shifting uneasily in her seat, Cade urged the truck forward, steering clear of Father Z's reach. He then drove another hundred feet with the Z family in pursuit before finally parking the pickup broadside to a small shed a little bigger than an outhouse. The boards were weathered to a light shade of gray. A rack of eight-point antlers off a white tail buck, still rooted in a saucer-sized oval of the beast's skull, graced the header above the narrow door.

Raven looked to Peter. "I was in the truck for five whole minutes. I had the keys, a number of guns, and plenty of ammo. So no big deal, really."

Cade said, "*In the truck* is where I want both of you to stay until I come back."

Raven nodded as her dad picked his M4 off the floorboard. As he exited the truck, she said, "I won't honk. Don't worry."

Flashing a half smile, Cade closed the door and stalked off toward the rear of the truck. He had the M4 slung over his back and the suppressed Glock 19 drawn and aimed at Father Z before the door locks thunked home behind him.

In the truck, Raven had scooted to the edge of the seat and was peering over the steering wheel and wondering what her dad was up to when a puff of reddish-black mist erupted around the nearest zombie's head. As the monster was crashing vertically to the ground, her dad was turning back to the truck. For reasons known only to him, he climbed onto the rear tire on her side. Craning around to the right to see through the rear sliding window, Raven watched him vault into the bed, the Glock already holstered.

"What is he doing?" Peter asked.

"Your guess is as good as mine," she conceded.

In the load bed, Cade took hold of the dog catcher's tool he'd liberated from the A-Team van. After acquainting himself with how to lock and unlock the mechanism that allowed the plastic-coated cable at the far end to tighten and loosen, he aimed the collapsible aluminum pole at the sky and practiced running the cable out and drawing it taut without watching the hand doing the work. He did this until he was proficient at making a semi-flexible noose large enough—in theory—to slip over a human head. With the three remaining Zs nearly to the truck, he rapped on the sliding window.

Peter looked away from Cade and regarded Raven. On the teen's face was an expression that was one part confusion, and one part horror.

"The latches in the middle," she said, pointing to them. "Open the slider and see what he wants."

When Peter parted the two halves of the rear window, Cade said, "Duct tape," and thrust his gloved hand into the cab. "Saw it last in the door pocket."

Raven dug out the roll of tape and passed it to Peter, who, in turn, put it in Cade's upturned hand.

Pom-Pom Z made it to the truck before Mother Z and Zit Face Z. Remarkably, the undead girl was shorter than Raven, the top of her head barely reaching the *FORD* emblem centered on the F-650's tailgate. Cade slipped the noose over her head, wriggling the pole side-to-side and yanking down on it rather violently to get the cable to slide over the twin tufts of hair.

Fish on.

He ran the cable in and cinched it tightly around her neck. With two hands gripping the pole, he clean jerked the writhing Z off the ground, lifted the sixty-some-odd pounds up and over the bed rail, and dumped it in the rear of the load bed.

Thrusting the end of the pole nearest his hands through the slider, Cade looked Peter in the eye and said, "Hold this. Pretend it's a trophy bass. *Do not* let it get away from you."

When Cade turned back toward Pom-Pom Z, Mother Z had made it to the truck and was already swiping the air near his right hip. Batting away the pale hands snaking over the bed rail, he tugged a few inches of leader off the roll of tape, clamped it between his teeth, and cautiously approached Pom-Pom Z.

Planting one boot on the rotter's narrow chest, Cade leaned forward and pinned the snarling beast to the load bed's metal floor. Feeling vibrations course his leg from the thing's nails raking his Danners, he ran out a foot of tape, held it horizontal to the Z's face, and slapped it firmly over its open maw. He grabbed one tuft of hair and started the roll of tape in a clockwise orbit around the Z's head. When all was said and done, Pom-Pom Z was silenced by eight layers of silver tape wrapped so tightly over its mouth that the other features had the droopy look of a plastic surgery gone bad. Since one tuft of hair was caught up in his hasty tape job, Cade grabbed the other with one hand and worked the noose from its neck. Being none too gentle, he firmed his grip on the lone dirty pom-pom, took hold of a pistoning leg, and heaved the Z over the tailgate.

Zit Face Z was now next to Mom Z at the bed rail. Trying to find purchase on the meat to their fore, both Zs moaned and strained and banged their bodies against the truck.

Holding the pole horizontal to the ground, Cade looked to Peter. "Same as before," he said with a nod. Then, addressing Raven, he said, "I need you to get the younger Z's attention and keep him occupied."

She asked, "How?"

He called back, "Put your window down a couple of inches and lure him over with the red tassel on your stocking cap. Then try to keep him occupied."

Cade didn't wait to see if his suggestion was being acted upon. Instead, he noosed Mother Z and guided her away from Zit Face Z, all the way around to the tailgate, where he dragged it hard to the sheet metal and again passed his end off to Peter's waiting hands.

"Hold her," he said. Seeing that Pom-Pom Z was up from the spill and ambling toward the tailgate, he scooped up the cables and padlocks he'd taken from the A-Team van and slithered over the passenger side bed rail.

He stood just outside Mother Z's reach and waited for the girl to get close enough to grab. As she ambled past the detained Z, Cade saw she was dragging one leg. He guessed the injury had resulted from the long fall from the truck.

Avoiding Pom-Pom Z's clumsy chest-high swipe, he grabbed the nape of her neck and led her to the farmhouse, where he mounted the steps and went through the motions he always employed prior to entering a structure.

He delivered three sharp raps to the door. Then waited the customary minute, during which he heard nothing moving inside.

Still holding the struggling Z at arm's length, he glanced at the Ford. The top of Mother Z's head was barely visible over the tailgate. Just nose, eyes, and the top of her head. The way the Z had ahold of the edge of the tailgate made him think of the *Kilroy Was Here* sticker a cousin who followed the Grateful Dead around had placed prominently on the back of her VW van.

Beside the driver's side door, the teenaged Z was lunging for the bobbing tassel. He watched Raven drag it back inside the truck and grimaced when the Z mashed its face into the window.

Another fish on.

A game of cat and mouse being conducted perfectly.

Chapter 36

As Duncan lay there semi spread-eagled on the floor, ears ringing mightily, face pressed to the filthy all-weather carpet, he revisited the events that had gotten him here.

Two distinct male voices, muffled and faraway sounding, was what he first heard as he came to. For a split second, as the drink-induced cobwebs began to lift away and consciousness returned, he had no idea where he was. What he did know, however, was that he still had not found Glenda, and he was sitting on a small couch all alone inside a cramped building, *not* a bleach-smelling RV or the semi-damp environs of the subterranean Eden compound. Those two certainties, when put together with the realization that the unfamiliar voices were drawing steadily nearer and growing louder by the second had started the adrenalin dump to his system that shocked him awake and had his hand going for the pistol on his hip.

The sound of a boot striking the stair tread outside the door dictated his first move. With one in the pipe, so to speak, all he had to do was thumb back the .45's hammer and aim for where he thought center of mass to the person mounting the stairs would be. His second move came as a result of one of the voices dropping off mid-sentence.

Without hesitation, he had fired two rounds at the door. They struck a few inches below the midpoint and did a great deal of damage. Two distinct bars of daylight snapped through the ragged holes. And though the back-to-back gunshots had momentarily drowned out voices and the like, the familiar report of a Kalashnikov rifle being fired on full auto had not been lost on him.

Training dormant for decades kicked in and fast twitch muscles used little in the last few months propelled him up and off the low-slung love seat. But before he could adjust aim and return the incoming fire, gravity and a pair of arthritic knees had him crashing to the floor, blood pouring into his eyes, and armed with the knowledge that he hadn't survived the abrupt encounter wholly unscathed.

Now, as Duncan lay on the floor, he became aware of several new developments.

First, as trivial as it might be, he was fairly certain the already bullet-riddled Stetson sitting an arm's reach from his face had taken a round or two, likely when he had lifted his decrepit carcass off the love seat. More troubling was the wetness spreading around his midsection. It was warm and his parka and jeans were thoroughly soaked by it. He was pretty sure he hadn't pissed himself, but couldn't rule it out. There was also the numbness spreading throughout his midsection. As best he could recall, the injury had happened when his forward momentum was bleeding off and his body was on the return trip to where he was now. And though he had been focused entirely on avoiding being struck by the bullets shredding the door before his very eyes, he vaguely recalled one of them punching him hard in the gut, somewhere between his navel and right hip bone. Precisely where the numbness was beginning to subside.

Strange, he thought. *Where's the insurmountable pain that comes with being gut shot?*

Is the alcohol keeping it at bay?

Is shock setting in?

This was no time to obsess over it. Because he heard a young-sounding female say, "I got you covered."

One of the male voices he recognized from before the bullets started to fly said, "I got the fucker." The owner of the voice sounded real pleased with his shooting. *Spray and pray* would be a more apt description.

The female asked, "What about Otto?"

244

The shooter said, "First things first. I want to see what I inherited from *Cowboy* here. Otto will be just fine."

Not likely, thought Duncan as he dragged his right knee slowly along the floor. The movement was subtle. Just a couple of inches on a gradual arc that saw his kneecap relocate to a point to the right and four inches up from where it originated.

The same hollow *clomp* of a boot striking wood sounded inside the trailer. It was barely audible to Duncan, but he heard it, nonetheless. Save for the sound of an AK magazine being swapped out, the clomp and follow-on creaking of the wooden tread was exactly what he'd been waiting to hear.

Lifting his pelvis off the floor created enough separation for him to covertly raise the Colt's barrel to an angle he guessed was center of the void where the door used to be. Praying he wasn't about to blow a hole in his thigh and sever an important artery or three, he let loose two quick shots.

The shrill scream that followed was extremely satisfying. The single shot crackling over his prone body as he began a slow roll onto his back was not.

With the man's screams intensifying, Duncan found himself on his back, ears ringing anew, and unable to see more than a big purple blur filling up the door frame. The person responsible for the screams was out of sight near the bottom of the steps. The owner of the other male voice, likely the guy called Otto, was unaccounted for. Since Duncan hadn't heard the voice since he'd fired those first shots through the door, he suspected Otto was now the proud owner of a pair of mashed-up hollow point slugs. Or maybe a pair of through and through wounds that, given the size of the bullets and their incredible velocity, was likely sufficient to put him down for good.

Senses returning, Duncan picked up on the sour nose of stale beer on his breath. Detected the heavy acrid stink of gunpowder riding the air. The only thing missing was the copper smell of freshly spilled blood.

"Surrender and I promise I will not kill you," he bellowed. Though it was a lie, he thought it sounded damn convincing.

Award me the Oscar now, crossed Duncan's mind as he let loose four shots rapid-fire at the truck. He'd been aiming along the length of his body, the bullets cutting the air somewhere between the pointed tips of his fancy ostrich skin boots.

There was a sonorous bang as at least one of the slugs found automotive sheet metal. A woman's wails immediately joined the dissonance.

As soon as the woman went silent, the man's animalistic wailing morphed to plaintive calls for someone named Holly to help him. The man pleaded and cussed for a few seconds, then called for his mother.

"Nobody is coming," Duncan hollered.

"I know," said the female. She sounded tired, her voice wavering.

Duncan detected defeat in the tone. Maybe it was a lifelong thing finally coming to a head for this one.

He said, "Drop the gun."

"It's empty," she said.

"Throw it down, then."

A clatter of metal was followed by the distinctive sound of gravel being displaced.

Duncan groped to his left and found his aviator glasses by feel. Keeping the .45 trained on the purple blob, he hinged up to a sitting position and slipped the glasses on one-handed. At once the purple blob became a full-size pickup. A Dodge dually 4x4, no less.

A young woman, arms upthrust in the classic *reach for the sky* pose, was hanging partway out the driver's side window.

Chapter 37

Cade stood on the farmhouse porch a foot from the screen door. There was no WELCOME mat. A good thing, because he was well past the point of caring what anyone thought.

Though the door to his fore was situated on the left side of the wraparound porch, and the big picture window to the right of it, he figured the floorplan inside would be similar to that of the Thagons' home—where there had been a WELCOME mat. *Little good that did them,* he thought glumly. Ray and Helen were six feet under. Same as Brook and countless others who'd been struck down well before their time.

Finding the door locked, Cade resorted to the Danner-to-the-jamb method of entry.

The aging wood housing the striker plate disintegrated on the initial kick. There was an immediate explosion of sound and puff of plaster dust as the door blasted inward. Finding the foyer booby-trap-free, he stepped through the roiling dust cloud, the M4's stubby suppressor leading the way.

"Hello," he called out.

A tomb-like silence greeted him.

He pushed Pom-Pom Z in ahead of him and toggled on the tactical light attached to his M4. At once he learned that the boarded-up windows were papered over on the inside. It looked as if an entire week's worth of the local newspaper was used to cover the large picture window to his right.

To his left, after a short three-stair run to a small landing, were the stairs to the second floor. From the landing they shot off to the right, the darkened well quickly swallowing them up.

Same as the Thagon home, splitting the main floor in two, a narrow hall ran from the front living area to a kitchen in back.

Figuring the stairs to a basement—if there was one—would be found somewhere off the kitchen, he struck out down the hall, steering the staggering Z ahead of him one-handed.

In the Ford, both literally and figuratively, Raven was tiring of the one-sided game of keep away. She had already switched hands twice. Her shoulder and upper arm muscles were beginning to burn. She was elated to see her dad exit the house alone and angle for the truck. Conversely, she was crestfallen when he skirted her side and snatched the dog catcher's tool from Peter's hands.

Letting the teenaged Z get a taste of the tassel, she watched her dad guide Mom Z into the home through the front door. Once they were both inside, she swiveled in her seat and asked Peter what was in the two duffel bags.

After casting a quick glance at the two-lane, then scrutinizing the drive and gravel expanse the Ford was parked atop, he said, "One has some clothes, a laptop, and a sword handed down to me by my father. The other bag," he added, "has my three video game systems. I have lots of different games for each one, too."

Brow rising an inch, Raven said, "Do you have extra game controllers for all of them? Maybe me and Sasha—" Abruptly she went quiet and buried her face in her hands.

"What is it?" he asked, voice full of concern.

"My friend may have been bitten," she said through her fingers. Looking up at Peter, she added, "For a split second there, I forgot it even happened."

"My brother was bit, too," Peter said morosely.

"I was there," Raven said. "He got a shot from the same bad batch of the supposed *cure* that my mom did. She died almost a week ago."

"I'm sorry to hear that," Peter said. "Gregory … he died this morning. He was fine when my dad went on his mission. Next thing I knew he was down with what we hoped was the flu."

"Who did *it*?"

"My father's friend, Cleo. He has the flu, too. But he still came home with us after my father left. I think they both knew and didn't want to tell me the truth. Probably didn't think I could handle it, what with my father going out among thousands of roamers in an old ice cream truck."

"I'm sorry for your loss," Raven said, as her gaze skipped from mirror to mirror. "Sounds like they were both brave men."

Peter said nothing. He was busy thumbing tears from his eyes.

"Here comes the man of mystery," Raven said.

"You really don't know what your dad's been doing inside there?" said Peter. He wasn't looking at Raven. His eyes were following the dog catcher's tool Cade was slowly lowering over the teenaged Z's head. "He hasn't come out with any supplies yet."

"It's part of my training," she said. "Dad calls it *Bushcraft one-oh-one.*"

All of a sudden the teenaged Z was backpedaling, the noose tight around its neck as it fell hard to the ground.

Raven and Peter watched in silence as her dad manhandled the Z to its feet and propelled it toward the farmhouse.

Once the two were gone from sight and the front door had again swung shut, Peter said, "You're not scared of whatever your dad has planned for you?"

Parroting her dad, she said, "A healthy dose of fear helps to keep a person sharp."

"Makes me want to crawl under the covers," Peter admitted.

***

Cade was inside less than five minutes. When he returned to the truck and the door sucked open, first off he said, "Anything moving out here?"

Both kids shook their heads as he displaced Raven from the driver's seat.

"Good," he said, looking mostly to Raven. "Because I have a story to tell you. Either of you heard of Operation Slapshot?"

Again both kids shook their heads.

"Good," he said. "Because it's still classified." He began retelling the story of the cobbled-together mission to rescue a handful of scientists from Canada's counterpart to the Centers for Disease Control and Prevention. Keeping details to a minimum, he told the part in which he and his Delta Team were inserted onto the National Microbiology Laboratory's sloped roof. He briefly mentioned how they'd cleared the Zs from the floor with the cube farm where the scientists and a dozen or so survivors were located. Finally, when he started in on the part of the rescue mission during which he was on point and leading the terrified civilians down a darkened stairwell full of hungry Zs, he switched gears and made sure to add every gory detail.

He recounted the gut-wrenching horror of seeing through the night vision goggles the snarling faces of the dead up close and rendered in dozens of shades of green. He made sure to make clear how the smells and sounds had been amplified tenfold in the dark and humid stairwell. The kids were both wide-eyed and hanging on his every word when he finished by saying, "To date ... *that* was the scariest thing I have ever faced."

Screwing up her face, Raven said, "What about Mom? Uncle Mike? Iraq? Afghanistan?"

"Those first two were the *saddest* tasks I've ever faced. All of the instances you just mentioned were actions I followed through on because I was duty bound. I made promises to both your mom and Mike Desantos. And I followed through on those. As for the Sandbox ... save for missing you and Mom terribly while there, I loved every second I spent in-country."

"So you want me to go inside and cull the rotter family?"

Peter's arms were draped over the seatback. He was following the conversation with rapt attention.

"Best you face the stuff of your nightmares under semi-controlled conditions."

She looked to the farmhouse and noted that the windows were all boarded over. She swallowed hard then said, "It'll be real dark in there."

Swiveling around in his seat, Cade said to Peter, "Hand me the plastic case that's back there. I think my ruck is sitting on it."

"Ruck?"

Raven smiled.

"My camo backpack," Cade answered. "Sorry for spouting Army lingo at you."

"I play first person shooters," Peter said, as he hefted the sturdy case over the seatback.

Cade chuckled softly. "Not exactly the same experience." He set the attaché-sized case on the center console, rotated it clockwise until the word PELICAN emblazoned across the top lid was upright and the carrying handle faced him. He disengaged the half-dozen double-throw latches one at a time, each making a sharp *click* as he did so. Carefully, he worked the item inside from the charcoal-gray foam it had been snugged down in.

"Night vision goggles," Raven said matter-of-factly.

Peter was hanging over the seatback, obviously intrigued by the contents of the box.

Holding the device up for all to see, Cade said, "See anything different about these and the ones in the footlocker back home?"

Raven handled them for a second. She said, "Four tubes instead of two. The controls seem mostly the same."

"Correct," Cade answered. He adjusted the flexible head strap to the smallest possible extent. "Try them on."

Raven slipped them over her head, finding them a little loose.

Cade took her hat from the dash and handed it to her.

Shooing it away, she said, "There's rotter spit on the tassel. Cut it off."

Cade complied. Tossed the slimy ball of yarn out the window.

After snugging her black cap on, the NVGs fit perfectly. With the ocular lenses hovering close to her eyes and the four front-facing tubes sprouting from her head, each at a slightly different angle, she looked like some kind of futuristic robot.

Nearly in the front seat by now, Peter twisted his near-horizontal upper body to face Raven. "Turn them on," he urged.

Finding the power switch by feel, Raven tilted her head forward and turned the devices on. Instantly she saw everything in the shadowy footwell clear as day. The black carpet on the floorboard, her black boots, and the black rifle trapped between her knees was rendered in a hundred tones of gray. Compared to the green display of the NVGs she'd had the opportunity to use, the phosphor white display of these goggles lent much more definition to what she was looking at. And though she had only used the other devices on a couple of occasions, she still noticed that these vastly improved her depth perception.

Craning around toward Cade, Peter said, "Can I try?"

Cade shook his head. "Got to save the batteries."

On cue, Raven powered the goggles down and went to remove them.

Putting a hand on the goggles, Cade said, "Leave them on. Take your rifle, the Glock 19, and a radio. Turn the radio up in case I need to contact you."

Now Peter was gawking at Raven. His jaw was hinged open and it was apparent he was going green with envy.

Goggles tilted into the up position, Raven shot a nervous glance at the farmhouse. "I'm going in there with ... *them*?"

"You don't have to," Cade said. "I'd be happy if you did." He paused. "They can't bite you. I made sure of that by using the whole roll of tape. They can get ahold of you if you get too close. Shouldn't happen, though. You'll have the upper hand wearing those."

She said nothing.

"Better to do this the first time under controlled circumstances," urged Cade. "I'll be out here if you need me."

"You mean *when* she needs you, right?"

Cade said nothing. He was waiting with rapt attention for his daughter's response. And it came fast, catching Peter by surprise.

Twisting in her seat, Raven leaned in real close. So close her nose was nearly touching Peter's. Brown eyes locked with his baby blues and lips drawn tight, she snarled, "Don't patronize me." And though she didn't know the exact meaning of the words she'd heard the strong women in her life employ in situations such as these, it sure felt good to use them.

Leaning back in his seat, Cade threw his hands in the air. "You're on your own, Peter."

As Raven gathered up her gear, Peter disappeared into the back seat.

Cade said, "I want you to put down each Z using a different weapon."

Raven said nothing. She seemed to be lost in thought.

"Toothpick, Glock, Rifle," prompted Cade.

Making a face, Peter said, "Toothpick?"

Raven showed off the slim blade.

"Ahhh," exclaimed Peter.

Cade looked to Raven. "Your mom did it. So can you."

She nodded. After a second's hesitation, she leaned across the console and wrapped her arms around her dad's neck. "Your stubble is coming in," she said, running a finger over the five o'clock shadow come early. "It feels weird. Why'd you shave?"

"I just felt like a change." Navigating past the NVGs, Cade kissed her on the cheek. "You have five minutes. I put one on each level."

"There's a basement?"

He nodded.

"Sounds like a video game," Peter said to nobody in particular.

"Nothing like it," Cade said to Peter. Regarding Raven, he added, "Go get 'em, Bird."

She exited the truck and they watched her mount the steps and form up before the door.

Cade drew his radio to his lips. Thumbing the Talk button, he said, "Comms check."

After a short burst of squelch, Raven's voice emanated from the speaker. "Good copy," she said and disappeared through the gloomy doorway.

Chapter 38

Duncan had just gotten to his knees and spotted the dead men on the ground near the trailer stairs when blood spilling from a wound somewhere on his scalp began the slow steady march down his already bloodied forehead, nose, and cheeks. Ignoring the warm sticky tendrils working their way into his collar, he eyed the corpses.

The older of the two, a wiry man with wild hair, full beard, and sporting crude prison tats on his arms and neck lay to the left of the steps. He was closer to forty than thirty. His body had absorbed the two bullets fired from the .45. One had struck the man's sternum, blowing apart his tee shirt and opening up a fist-sized hole in his chest. The other entered a few inches higher, near the man's Adam's apple, rendering him mute and excising a substantial chunk of his neck on the way out. A soon-to-be-fatal through-and-through from the looks of it. The amount of blood present was the first clue to the chronology of events. After the man had fallen where he lay, his heart had continued to beat long enough to purge an ample amount of blood from the neck wound, through one curled hand, and onto the ground around his head and upper torso.

Though the other corpse's face had been peppered by what looked to be splinters from the door, he had died from a massive gunshot wound to the upper chest. The traces of acne and wisp of a beard told Duncan the *man* was new to the title. He put his age at eighteen or nineteen. Mouth agape in a final silent scream, the man had curled up and died in a fetal position. Blood was pooled around his midsection. Already beginning to glaze over, the brown eyes stared accusingly in Duncan's direction.

With his .45 still aimed at the woman seated in the purple Dodge, Duncan unzipped his parka and conducted a one-handed examination of his aching midsection.

At the spot near his navel where numbness was quickly giving over to shooting pains, he felt nothing pointing to the fact he had caught a bullet. There was no bloody hole waiting to accept his probing fingers. He detected no rips in the shirt and no furrows underneath the wet fabric where he may have been grazed by a bullet, or fragment thereof.

"My arms are getting tired," called the woman. "I can't hold this pose much longer."

"Your best thinking got you there," Duncan sneered. "Suck it up, *buttercup*. I'll get to you in two shakes."

Tentatively, Duncan brought his hand up in front of his face. He examined his fingers, then looked at his palm. His hand was all wet, but there wasn't a spot of red on it.

He brought his fingers to his nose and sniffed.

Beer.

Saved by the very thing that's slowly killing me. He said, "Damn it all to hell! Your AK-wielding friend blew a hole clean through my Blue Ribbon."

Favoring his right side, he rose to his feet and unzipped his parka pocket. Dragged the exploded can into daylight, gave it a cursory look, then tossed it out the door. It bounced off the bottom stair and came to rest next to two other cans bearing the same red and blue *Pabst* logo.

He left his ruined Stetson in the trailer. Bracing himself on the jamb, he took the steps one at a time. With the .45 never wavering, he skirted the bodies and blood and made his way to the truck. Reaching the driver's side door, he kicked the bolt-action rifle aside and looked the woman in the face. Up close, she looked much younger than his initial impression. A youthful face like that with no emotional wear and tear told him she was either just getting her feet wet in the nightclub scene before the dead began to walk, or the experience had been just around the corner.

Voice devoid of emotion, he said, "Do you have another gun on you?"

She shook her head.

"Any in the truck?"

She nodded. "One in the glove box."

"OK, then," he said, all business. "Keeping your hands where I can see them, pop the door with the outside handle and push it open with your knee."

She did as she was told, then shot him a *What now?* look.

Face a bloody mess, Duncan stalked to his right and peered inside the cab. Seeing she was indeed unarmed, he ordered her out of the truck.

She stepped to the ground and immediately heaping platitudes on Duncan. Thanking him for "rescuing" her from the rapists.

Waving her out of his way, he craned and gave the cab a longer visual inspection. Saw the near empty Pabst suitcase. The cardboard was torn, a couple of full beers spilling out on the seat.

"You found my rig at the Shell station, I see."

"You broke into our place," she said.

"Those aren't the words of a captive," he noted. "What's your name?"

She was shifting from foot to foot now. She said, "Holly."

A hint of skepticism in his tone, he asked, "How old are you, Holly?"

"Twenty-one on the fifteenth," she said.

"Of this month?"

She nodded.

"Then you're old enough to know better." Nodding toward the trailer, he added, "I saw your sleeping arrangements in there. You three were thick as thieves, weren't you? You were on those boys like a shorthaired hound on a wounded duck. Or was it the other way around?" He paused and clucked his tongue. "You were playing a little good cop, bad cop with them, weren't you?"

After a few seconds, she nodded. She said, "It was exciting. All the looting and shooting. I come from a family of bankers and accountants. I was set to go to an Ivy League school in the fall before all of this derailed that."

"In all your galavantin' around, did you see a woman? Name's Glenda. She's a little younger than me. Mid-fifties. Graying reddish-brown hair. Prettiest green eyes you'll ever see." He held his hand up to his nose. Blood was still dripping from the tip. "She's about this tall to me."

The young woman just stared.

"Well?" he asked. "Did you, or didn't you?"

"I'm thinking."

He pulled his left arm inside his parka sleeve. Being careful to not dislodge his glasses, he dabbed the blood from his face.

Finally she said, "We haven't come across anyone who fits that description."

Gun unwavering, he demanded, "Who have you come across?"

"Couple of soldiers on motorcycles. A few more in those square military trucks."

"Humvees?"

She nodded.

"Were the soldiers ours?"

"How would I know?" She crossed her arms across her chest.

"What did Frick and Frack here think?"

"Didn't say one way or the other. We stayed at the ski resort night before last and spotted them going through the burned-out town. And like we always did, we just stayed out of sight and watched."

"You mean if they were stronger than you three desperados, you just watched. Am I right?"

She said nothing.

"Actions speak louder than words," said Duncan. "And oftentimes they beget consequences." As he motioned with the gun for her to walk the length of the Dodge's load bed, he saw Adrian in his mind's eye. She was captive in the stocks at the cul-de-sac compound. And she seemed to be smirking at him. Then she winked and mouthed, *No more loose ends.*

Shaking her head, Holly said, "I have a feeling I know what you have in mind for me, Mister. I'll just go ahead and make it easy for you." She unzipped her fleece jacket and turned toward him. Her right hand went to her left breast and she cupped it and squeezed the erect nipple between thumb and forefinger.

"Put your damn teat away," he growled. "That's the furthest thing from my mind. Just turn around and walk."

Lower lip sticking out, she pulled down her shirt, zipped up her fleece, and turned away.

Duncan's gun hand was beginning to shake. He swiped at the blood on his nose and then pressed the trigger. The boom was tremendous, even out of doors. It rolled away and crashed around the UDOT yard, scattering birds from a nearby tree.

The young woman pitched forward violently and her feet lifted off the gravel. For the first half beat she seemed to be imitating Superman in flight. In the latter half of that beat, gravity brought her back to the ground, where she hit face first, arms bent at unnatural angles, and plowed the patch of gravel with her face into the neat little pillow her head eventually came to rest on.

Duncan exhaled the breath he'd been holding. He removed his glasses and gave his face a thorough wiping.

He didn't look at his grim work. No reason to have that as visual fodder for the nightmares already visiting him regularly. If last night was any indication, drinking excessively to keep them at bay was no longer an option.

After holstering his pistol, Duncan retrieved the keys for the Dodge from the tattooed man's pocket, policed up the weapons, and then slow-walked back to the pickup. As he pulled back the tarp to place the rifles in the load bed, he noted the rest of the stuff scattered about the floor. It appeared the crew had just returned from a scavenging trip. And a fruitful one, at that. Judging by the items near the tailgate, they had recently relieved an automotive parts concern of all the things necessary to keep the Dodge running. He saw a case of motor oil, gas additives, windshield cleaner, several cans of instant flat tire repair, a couple of gallons of severe weather anti-freeze, and a host of other items. Clothing and bedding was also represented.

A plastic bin near the cab held hundreds of rounds of ammunition for the rifles—some already loaded into a half-dozen magazines for each.

"You kids were busy little beavers," he said, pulling the tarp to cover the loot.

He patted his pockets, then muttered an expletive. "Left my Dear John in the trailer."

He trudged back to the trailer, the gash on his head bleeding the entire way. As he mounted the steps, he looked down at the Pabst cans. "Nearly a fatal mistake you made there, Old Man. Might have cut out the middleman, though. Saved you the trouble of doing it yourself one day."

The folded-up letter was on the floor beside the love seat. He scooped it up and stood amongst the debris from the door, staring down at it while turning it over and over in his hands.

He stuffed the letter in a pocket not soaked with beer.

He made his way to the small bathroom at the end of the trailer opposite the sleeping bags. Examined the wound in the mirror. There was no water, so he dabbed at the wound with his coat sleeve. Revealed an inches-long furrow maybe a half-inch wide at the start. Where there should have been an exit wound, there was a lump, the jagged gray edges of what was likely a bullet fragment pressing through his scalp.

"Another quarter-inch south and you'd be dead, muchacho."

To staunch the blood flow, he cut a few strips of liner from one of the sleeping bags and, using some of the fill, made a crude bandage.

After a little reshaping, he jammed the Stetson down on his misshapen head.

Walking back to the Dodge, he kept his gaze level.

The truck started on the first try. No reason it shouldn't, it was barely broken in. He supposed it was three years old, max.

He didn't bother reclosing the gate after rolling the Dodge through. Just continued down the feeder road to the junction with 39, where he turned right and tromped the gas, a whole host of problems in the rearview and many more on the cloud-choked horizon.

Chapter 39

Eyes already sweeping the dark interior, Raven reached behind her and closed the door to the farmhouse. M4 aimed forward, she stood in the entry to the two-story affair for thirty seconds, to let her eyes adjust.

They did not.

Save for the stairs to her left being partially illuminated by the sliver of light coming in from where a piece of door jamb was missing, a veil of inky darkness enshrouded the entire main floor.

What would Dad do? she thought. *He'd achieve tactical advantage at once*, she told herself, sliding the night vision goggles down in front of her eyes. With an economy of movement, she powered the device on and raised her rifle, its stubby suppressor pointed toward her right flank, the likely place for a rotter to be lying in wait.

Once the NVGs powered on—the cycle taking a second at most—she saw the entire room rendered in shades of white, gray, and black. Phosphor white was what her dad called it. Like looking at old timey television, *I Love Lucy* or *The Three Stooges*, is how she saw it. And she saw it all. In crystal clear clarity.

To her right, a long hallway led off to the back of the house. She was standing in what looked like a living room. Only there was no furniture to speak of. She guessed it had all been broken apart and used to board up the window on the outside. Inside, the windows were all covered with newspapers. Headlines on some of them jumped out at her like the credits at a 3D feature film. *The Dead Have Come Back To Life. President Odero says: Shelter In Place. Governor Silcox Calls Up Utah National Guard. Government Is Collapsing Across the Nation.* All of this she already knew. But God how she missed going to the movie theater. The buttered popcorn. Sour Patch Kids. All of it.

To her right lay what she guessed to be a formal dining room. There were built-in shelves on two walls. A partition chest-high to her separated the two rooms.

Though their stink was hanging in the air, there were no zombies in sight. She put herself in her dad's place. If he wanted to test her to the fullest, he would spread the rotters out and make her hunt for them.

Three rotters.

Three floors, counting the basement.

Speaking softly, she asked herself, "Where would *you* start, Dad?"

Brook had taken great pains to impart all of her recently learned survival skills on the girl. The tactics she was pulling out of her head were learned from listening to her dad talk to her mom and the other adults. Some had been gleaned from watching how her dad approached each new obstacle the zombie apocalypse threw at him and others.

Though it was her thoughts, she still heard her dad's voice in her head.

Take out the nearest threat, then look for a secondary exit.

Raven started for the hallway, the worn wood floor creaking under her boots. Cutting the corner and moving down the hall, she heard an out-of-place noise. It reminded her of Max scratching on the metal door to her quarters back home. Since her mom's passing, begging to be let out into the clearing was a regular occurrence. The going theory was that Max was waiting for Brook to return. Only this wasn't Max. This was the sound made by Test Number One.

After a twenty-foot walk down the hall, during which she passed the open door to an empty powder room, she ended up in the kitchen. It was twice the size of the one in her old home back in Portland. Save for the oversized gas range and undersized single-door refrigerator—both gleaming white in the NVGs—this kitchen contained none of the countertop appliances she was used to seeing. No toaster. No coffee maker. And worst of all, no waffle iron—a must have, in her opinion.

The cupboard doors were open, the shelves empty. Attached to one cupboard was a hand-cranked tool with opposing gears that she didn't recognize. The metal arms of an empty paper towel holder opposite the mystery tool reached out at her from the dark like a robotic praying mantis.

As she stood still, surveying the kitchen, the noise came again, off her right shoulder, near the end of the kitchen where she saw three closed doors. She dropped her gaze to the floor by her feet and saw evidence that something had been dragged half the length of the kitchen. The swath of liquid left behind shone brilliant white, thanks to the NVGs. Resembling a reversed J, the mess on the floor curled out from the hallway and continued on in a straight line all the way to the door with the key. Her best guess was that she was looking at bodily fluid belonging to one of the rotters. Which led her to believe her dad had dragged one of them through here. However, the slick trail ended *in front* of all three doors. Determining which of them Rotter Number One was behind was going to take a bit of detective work.

M4 held at a low-ready, she turned right and approached the trio of doors. The door on the left, beyond the range, most likely led to outside. It was fitted with a formidable-looking deadbolt. Like the rest of the windows on this floor, the one inset on this door was papered over.

Raven turned her attention to the door ahead of her. It was two-thirds the width of the door to outside.

Suddenly the sound was back. A metronomic *scritch, scritch, scritch* definitely emanating from behind the door to her fore.

To her right, opposite the door to outside, was a similarly sized item she guessed led to the basement. The rounded end of a skeleton key protruded from the keyhole below the doorknob.

For some reason, as she stood there contemplating which door to try first, she recalled advice her dad had offered up during an impromptu bushcraft session held under the awning next to the RV, at the edge of the heat zone radiating off one of

Daymon's famous camp fires. He had been stressing situational awareness. He had said: *"Always know your location on the map and where you'll go if you're forced to retreat."*

With this advice in mind, she unsheathed the Arkansas Toothpick and scribed a porthole out of the newspaper covering the window on the door to her left. Peering through the makeshift peephole told her the house abutted a picket of trees identical to the ones ringing the clearing back at the compound. She also saw that the door opened onto a small elevated porch. A pair of handrails bracketed a short run of stairs leading down to an unkempt strip of lawn bordering the forest's edge.

Again the sound from the door ahead of her. *Scritch, scritch, scritch.* On the heels of that came a muffled *bang* from behind the door to her right. Not just behind, though. The sound had filtered up from somewhere below the kitchen.

Three rotters.

Three floors, counting the basement.

The new noise all but affirmed to her the other interior door led to the basement, where Rotter Number Two lay in wait.

While tempted to go *eeny, meeny, miny, moe* to choose which door of the two obvious candidates to open first, she sheathed her blade and brought the M4 on line with the interior door in front of her.

She tested the knob.

Unlocked.

She drew a breath, held it in, then pulled the door open. It swung freely toward her on well-oiled hinges.

The door had just cleared the jamb when the female adult rotter sprang out of what looked to be a pantry lined with bare shelves. Its eyes were white and wild and roving crazily as it searched for prey in the dark. Raven saw that its mouth was thoroughly sealed shut with a copious amount of duct tape. Her dad had also bound the fingers and thumbs on both of its hands together.

The rotter didn't moan or rasp as it lunged and craned its head all around.

The way the thing moved reminded Raven of the T-Rex from *Jurassic Park.*

Breath still trapped in her lungs, she noticed her heart hammering against her chest. Exhaling slowly—as she'd been taught—she sighted down the rifle and triggered two rounds.

The first bullet struck the Z dead center on its face, driving its upturned nose inward and drawing those crazy eyes together. The weight of the suppressor helped keep the muzzle rise to a minimum. Conversely, the follow-on 5.56 hardball entered the gaping wound behind the first. With most of its kinetic energy intact, upon exiting, the second round split the thing's skull out back. There was a sound like hail pelting a tin roof as brain tissue and hair and bone fragments peppered the bare shelves behind the Z.

The whiplash effect from the double-tap slapped the Z to the floor where it came to rest supine on a bed of its own gray matter.

Without thought, Raven slammed the door and about-faced right.

The skeleton key in the second interior door turned freely and there was a click as the lock disengaged. She removed the key and looked through the keyhole. There were no crazy roving eyes peering back. All she saw was a flat white surface sloping gently downward. *The ceiling to a stairwell.*

The door opened as easily as the first. Unlike the first, nothing lunged at her from within. However, the noise of something moving around down there meant she still had work to do.

Work smarter, not harder.

To keep from having to set foot in the basement, Raven crouched by the top of the stairs and hollered, "Here rotter, rotter. Here rotter, rotter."

She found it strange nothing showed its face at the bottom of the stairs. Theorizing her dad may have somehow added another one of his *wrinkles* by deafening the zombie moving around down there with a few stabs of his combat dagger, or maybe a couple of layers of duct tape, she entered the stairwell and jumped up and down on the top tread. Though she didn't weigh much, the old staircase shimmied underneath her boots. Dust and accumulated dirt was dislodged from where the treads and stringers came together. It rained down and settled on the cement floor with soft little patters.

While Raven's shouting had had no immediate effect, the vibrations from her footfalls instantly drew the attention of the source of the noises. She heard a shuffling and then another loud bang as a long-handled push broom fell across the bottom of the stairs. As she took a seat on the top stair, the teenaged rotter appeared at the bottom of the stairwell. It looked up, white eyes probing the dark in search of meat. It was restrained from reaching further than the lower step by the cables her dad had removed from the gaudy van. Duct tape wound around its head vertically covered both ears and prevented its jaw from opening.

Raven's breathing had returned to normal, her heart beating only mildly now.

She shouldered the rifle and settled the EOTech's holographic pip atop the rotter's head. Instead of red, thanks to the NVGs, the glowing circle was showing up gunmetal gray against the creature's pale dermis.

Finger tensing on the trigger, she heard her dad's instructions in her head: *Toothpick, Glock, rifle.*

"Guess I'm working in reverse," she mumbled as she threw the M4 around to hang at her back and dragged out the Glock.

To conserve ammo, she discharged just one round from the Glock. One round was enough. The entry hole was minuscule. The internal damage was catastrophic.

Like a marionette with snipped strings, the rotter crashed vertically to the cement where it settled face-down, arms outstretched, unmoving.

Raven rose from the stair, turned around, and closed the door on Rotter Number Two.

Two down, one to go was what she was thinking as the radio in her pocket emitted a burst of white noise and her dad came on, barking orders at her, his tone all business.

Chapter 40

In the F-650, Cade and Peter were embroiled in a spirited conversation initiated by the boy.

Cade had opened Pandora's Box upon agreeing with Peter that Marvel superheroes held his attention more than those of the D.C. Universe.

After gushing about Thor and the Avengers, Peter said, "Cap or Iron Man?"

Cade grimaced. Said, "Captain America, hands down."

Wearing a look of amazement, Peter said, "Cap's gadgets *suck*. Iron Man is *the bomb*."

Thinking, *That saying survived all this?* Cade said, "But Cap spans decades. My dad had some of his comics from the forties." He paused and scanned the road in both directions. Nothing moving. He went on, saying, "He got those comics from *his* dad … who was *my* grandfather."

"I know how the family tree works," quipped Peter. "I still like Tony Stark over Steve Rogers."

Cade made no reply. He was looking at his Suunto. Seeing that Raven had been inside going on three minutes, he began to grow a bit nervous. Though he'd taken great care to render the Zs mostly harmless, Mr. Murphy was always out there, willing and eager to muck things up.

"OK, then," said Peter, "Deadpool or Wolverine?"

Wringing a hand on his M4's forestock, Cade said, "No contest."

With a tilt to the head, Peter looked side-eye at Cade. "Wolverine?"

Cade smiled and nodded. "Star Trek or Star Wars?"

Peter didn't respond. He was craning and looking over his right shoulder, his attention on something down the road to the west.

Cade pulsed down his window. "What is it?"

After running his window all the way down, Peter said, "I hear an engine."

"Get your head down," Cade barked. Then he poked the M4 out his window and threw the safety off. He fired the Ford's motor and dropped his right hand to the console, coming up with the radio.

The exhaust note grew louder. Ten seconds after Peter pointed out the distant engine noise, a motorcycle entered the picture, moving fast, right to left on the nearby two-lane.

Cade slumped low in his seat and did two things simultaneously. He set the emergency brake and lifted his foot off the brake pedal so that the red flare of the lights wouldn't advertise their presence. While he was doing that, he drew the Motorola to his lips and hailed Raven.

Hearing her dad's voice coming from the radio in her pocket, Raven dragged it out and listened to the instructions being relayed to her. Thinking that this might be part of the exercise, she said, "What? Are you sure?"

He radioed back. "Just do it."

The radio went quiet.

Raven was still expecting him to come back on and reel her back in to reality when she heard the gunfire. Six or seven shots, total. Because the reports were muffled somewhat at first and the echoes never came, she was confident she was hearing an M4 discharging not too far from the front of the house. From the direction Black Beauty was parked, to be exact.

Cade breathed a sigh of relief when the motorcycle passed the end of the drive without slowing. His gut clenched when a second motorcycle appeared, moving the same direction and roughly the same speed. It was nearly identical to the first. A motocross number with knobby tires, long-travel suspension, and clad with plastic body parts painted in earth tones.

When the second motorcycle slowed, Cade noted that the rider wore camouflage fatigues vaguely familiar to him. The rider also wore a sidearm in a drop-thigh holster. A bullpup-style carbine was slung across his back.

Cade snugged the carbine to his shoulder and sighted on the end of the drive. Waiting for the rider to prove he'd seen the big Ford by committing to the drive, he slipped his finger into the trigger guard and took up some of the pull.

The second bike stopped at the T where the drive met the two-lane. A beat later, the first bike returned and formed up next to the second.

The riders flipped up smoked visors and held a brief conversation.

Hoping the truck's wide A-pillar would work to break up his outline, Cade remained stock still in his seat. Out of the corner of his mouth, he said to Peter, "Get out and close your door quietly. Keep this truck and the outbuildings between you and the road. Get to the woods as fast as you can. Find a good place to hide and stay there."

"They're bad guys, aren't they?"

"Go," Cade growled. "I'll tell Raven you're coming."

As the passenger's side rear door opened and Peter crawled out, the dome light lit up. Though first twilight was still a couple of hours away, the possibility the riders had picked up on the brief light flare against the dark winter sky couldn't be ignored.

Once Cade saw the boy disappear from view, he regarded the bikes. They were facing opposite each other. Both riders' heads were turned, their eyes locked on the Ford.

"Damn it," Cade spat. "I was hoping it wouldn't come to this." He steadied his breathing and pressed the trigger. The action sent three rounds downrange at the rider on the left. Blooms of red walked up the rider's body from hip to armpit. The ejected brass pinged off the inside of the windshield. The gun smoke drifting inside the truck's cab was strangely reassuring to Cade.

One of those should do it, he thought as he shifted his aim a few degrees right and repeated the process with virtually the same result. However, sometime between the fifth and sixth discharge, two pickup trucks entered his field of vision from the right. They were moving fast. Which meant the riders had likely reported their findings before he'd engaged them.

Time began to crawl. Everything in front of Cade snapped into sharp focus. Before the remaining rider had absorbed the entire three-round salvo, Cade had conducted a rough headcount of the new arrivals. *Ten camo-clad soldiers. Save for the drivers, all of them brandished bullpup-style rifles.*

Moments Ago

Raven hadn't immediately followed her dad's barked instructions as he had ordered. Instead, she had sprinted to the front of the house, toward the sound of gunfire. With the Arkansas Toothpick, she had cut away a long, wide swath of the newspaper covering the window. She had flipped the goggles away from her eyes and, peering through a gap between the boards nailed to the outside of the window, viewed a scene that caused a cold ball to form in her gut and sent her heart rate rocketing.

Chapter 41

The sight of the charred bodies at the failed National Guard roadblock added to the sorrow already weighing heavy on Duncan's heart. He saluted as he navigated the Jersey barriers and the black smudge of the impromptu funeral pyre slid by in his side vision. He held the crisp salute as he wheeled past the cars in the ditch. Kept his hand to his bloodied brow until the familiar scene was small in the rearview mirror.

Between the Shell station and turnoff to the street running up to Glenda's painted lady on the hill, Duncan saw no evidence of her passing. No leaking twice-dead corpses. No dead breathers. Not even a discarded water bottle or cereal bar wrapper to give him hope she had made it beyond the rotters amassed this side of Daymon's roadblock.

As he slowed to avoid the burned-out shell of a small compact, he thought about Daymon. Wondered if he had burned to death in his shot-up Chevy pickup outside the McMansion he and Heidi had claimed as their own. A place where she could be free of her Jackson Hole demons, and him no longer a prisoner to the crippling claustrophobia triggered by the Eden compound's cramped quarters. What a short-lived stint that had been. Days, at most. Duncan shook his head at the terrible hand fate seemed to have dealt them both. He truly hoped they'd made the most of those last few days together.

The colorful multi-story house suddenly appeared over the Dodge's hood. The lower branches of the trees flanking it were home to dozens of birds, their black forms rippling as the engine growl reached them.

Seeing the birds as an omen, a portent of bad things to come, he said, "Go away, or I'll make you."

271

As if privy to the muttered threat, the birds took to the air en masse, cawing and squawking to show their displeasure at being disturbed.

Duncan pulled the rig to the curb in front of the house and shut off the engine. He pulsed down his window and regarded the scenery to his left. Far off to the west, just its snow-dotted lower flanks visible, was the Wasatch Range. Closer in was the rambling secondary Ogden Range which consisted of several smaller mountains, only the tallest of which wore dustings of white on their peaks.

Sandwiched between the base of the nearest mountain in the Ogden Range and downtown Huntsville was the black and foreboding waters of the Pineville Reservoir.

The small flotilla of sailboats and powered watercraft once moored offshore was now scattered across the reservoir. A few still lolled at anchor. Others were white specks adrift on the vast expanse of water. Most had become beached on the south shore bordered by a long stretch of greenspace dotted with tents and vehicles and twisted corpses. Though he'd seen the breakdown of society ripple across Portland early on, he couldn't imagine being among this first wave of thousands upon thousands of desperate people fleeing Salt Lake City and dozens of other zombie-choked towns and burgs along the Wasatch Range's western flanks.

Pressing the binoculars he'd brought from the truck to his blood-caked face, Duncan glassed the burned-out city, left to right.

He scoured the cemetery first. Seeing nothing of interest moving amongst the headstones rising up from the grass- and weed-choked expanse abutting the reservoir, he panned a few degrees right and focused on the handful of buildings still standing in downtown Huntsville. It was as if he was looking down on a ghost town. Only shadows occupied the trash-filled doorways and once-bustling business concerns now fronted by windowless frames.

On Huntsville's north side, where the road leading to Eden shot off north by west along the reservoir's jagged shore, a small herd of rotters loped into town.

"Where are you, Glenda?"

He walked the binoculars back and forth, lifting them away from his face only when he was sure nothing moved close-in on the charred ground between the soot-blackened cement foundations of the houses once dotting Huntsville's east side.

"Gone. That's where," he whispered, his hand absentmindedly going to the Dear John letter in his breast pocket.

The fifth of whiskey Duncan found in the looted supplies went in the Pabst case with the remaining beers. He grabbed his rifle, plucked the case off the seat by its cardboard handle, and stepped to the road.

The driveway climbing along the right side of Glenda's former home was a narrow, sixty-foot run of moss-covered cement. Cracked and frost-heaved in places, it stretched from the street to a swaybacked garage sitting on the southeast corner of the lot.

Forgoing two steep runs of stairs leading up to the front porch, Duncan set out for the back of the house to enter through the same door he and Cade had breached weeks ago.

The gate to the fence bordering the drive between the house and garage was hanging open. He saw at once the mound of dirt he knew to be Glenda's husband's grave. On the muddy ground next to the grave, scattered along its entire length, were several articles of clothing he recognized as belonging to Glenda. He saw numerous footprints presenting the same pattern he'd seen near the roadblock on 39.

She was here.

But where'd she go?

Duncan stirred the clothing with the M4's suppressor. Knelt and looked closely at the stains and detritus soiling the pants. Some of it was blood and still tacky to the touch. Scraps of flesh and what looked to be intestine clung to the fabric that used to be her shirt. On the ground near the clothing was more flesh and clumps of blood-matted hair. His skin went cold and his stomach twisted into a knot. He hung his head and cursed God. Hand shaking, he dragged the bottle from the case sitting near his knee and spun the cap off with a practiced flick of the thumb. He drank down a big swallow, making bubbles in the neck and feeling the burn that always preceded the all-encompassing warmth he craved.

"Fuck you!" he bellowed, shaking his fist at the air. "Why her and not me?"

The sky quickly darkened and big fat raindrops pelted the ground. Soon the sporadic drops were replaced by a furious downpour.

Rainwater overflowing the brim of Duncan's tattered Stetson cut paths through the blood on his face. As he rose with his rifle in one hand and the box of booze in the other, a rivulet of salty water wet his lips.

Walking achingly slow, he made his way to the back door. Found it unlocked, just as he'd left it last time he was in Huntsville.

The mudroom was still home to cobwebs and not much else. The kitchen was as they'd left it.

Forgoing a side trip to the dining and sitting rooms in the front of the home, he turned right at the first hall and began the long climb to the second floor. He stopped at the landing to catch his breath. Finding the break a perfect excuse to drink down a beer, he fished a Pabst from the box and cracked the top. He downed the beer in two quick pulls and dropped the can at his boots.

Beginning to scale the remaining run of stairs, he chuckled and said, "Onward and upward, Old Man."

Reaching the top of the stairs, Duncan saw that the master bedroom was in disarray. The acrid stench from the flash bang grenade Cade had deployed to stun Glenda's son, Oliver, still lingered. The dark shape of a queen-size bed dominated the room. The bed was bare and flanked by a pair of Edwardian-era nightstands. To his left, pushed up against the stairway rail, was an ornate vanity and padded chair, the latter stuffed into the vanity's kneehole.

Beyond the bed was a set of French doors. The doors opened up to a medium-sized deck overlooking Huntsville and the reservoir and mountains to the west, all of which were visible now due to the passing of the fast-moving storm.

Duncan set the box of booze on the bed and laid his rifle next to it. He stood at the end of the bed and planted his hands on his hips. Staring out at the darkening sky, he said, "Take a load off, why dontcha?"

Heeding his own advice, he grabbed the chair and booze and made his way to the second-story porch.

On the porch, he arranged the chair near the low wall overlooking the front yard and purple Dodge on the street below. Slipping another beer from the case, he sat down hard on the chair and put his boots on the rail. He popped the top and tilted his head back, can in hand. From this angle he caught sight of the alcove jutting out over the French doors. It was bullet-pocked, the wood scarred by multiple craters ringed by splinters and chipped orange paint. It was the perch from where Oliver wielded a precision sniper rifle against him and the others who were hunkered down in the snow on the streets of Huntsville. Purposefully inflicting zero casualties, Oliver had only wanted to keep their heads down long enough so he could rabbit under cover of darkness. However, due to Cade's quick thinking and sound planning, the youngest of the Gladson boys was taken down without a shot being fired in anger.

Though only a couple of weeks had passed since that day in October, it seemed so long ago. And thanks to Adrian, Oliver was dead now. As was Heidi and, presumably, Daymon.

So much senseless loss in such a short span of time, he thought. *And now all that is left of Glenda is a pile of her bloodied clothes and tufts of her hair.*

Duncan finished the beer and set the empty on the rail. He drank two more beers, slipping generous slugs of whiskey in between. When he had a neat little can pyramid on the rail before him and a healthy buzz raging in his head, out came the Colt 1911. He dumped the partial magazine and slapped a full one home. *Seven rounds plus one in the pipe.*

What to do?

In answer to his own question, he racked the slide on his pistol and aimed for the can atop the pyramid.

The single discharge set his ears ringing. The bullet obliterated the can, the follow-on kinetic energy sending the jagged pieces spiraling down toward the yard and street below.

"Nice shootin', Tex."

He blew away the gossamer strand of gun smoke curling off the muzzle, then set the pistol on his lap. In one motion, he hefted the fifth bottle with his left hand, and took the Dear John letter from his breast pocket with his right.

"Now that's multitasking," he said with a sad chuckle as he spun the cap off.

After flipping a coin in his head and seeing it come up *Heads*, he said, "Stayed, for now, Old Man," and brought the bottle to his lips.

Wearing a sad half smile and shedding tears for the recently departed, he took a long, hard pull off the upturned bottle.

Chapter 42

In the farmhouse east of Woodruff, Raven was backing away from the papered-over living room window when the radio in her pocket came alive with a burst of static. The white noise was followed at once by her dad's harried voice. "I want you to just listen," he said, right off the bat. "I just engaged enemy soldiers on the road. I took all of them out ... but it was only their lead element. Two pickups carrying more soldiers just arrived. I'm afraid I have no choice but to hit them first and try to draw them away from you and Peter. I just sent Peter into the woods to join you. I want you two to stay together and move west. Find a safe place outdoors to lay up. Wait there until either darkness falls or you are certain there are no soldiers looking for you. Then I want you to get to the 39/16 junction where you'll be on the outer edge of your radio's range. Use the emergency channel and hail the compound. Talk to Lev or Duncan ... they'll know exactly what to do." He paused to catch his breath. Then, all the edge gone from his voice, he added, "I love you to the moon and back, Raven." There was a click and the radio went silent.

Tears cascaded down Raven's cheeks as she reached into her pocket and depressed the Talk key two times to let him know she understood. What she really wanted to do was drag the radio out and spew a whole bunch of syrupy stuff to him, but she didn't. She knew in her heart of hearts all of it had already been conveyed by her in action and deed since Mom died. In fact, standing by the rear door with the real possibility she was about to lose him too weighing down hard on her, it suddenly occurred to her they had never been closer to one another than they had been since Brook's passing. In response to the emotion welling within her, she heard her dad's voice in her head: *What's the most important thing, Bird?*

"Family," she said aloud to herself as she threw the locks and shoved open the door. Rifle in one hand, the other bracing the NVGs on her head, she launched herself off the back porch. As she landed cat-like on the grass beyond the short run of stairs, she registered peripherally to her left a blurry snippet of someone dressed in camouflage clothing entering the tree line.

With the sounds of a major gun battle just breaking out somewhere behind her, Raven sprinted into the woods to her fore. As she took a left and batted branches and ferns from her face, she caught sight of Peter and called out softly for him to join her.

Panting hard, Peter emerged from a clutch of ferns. On his face was a confused expression that seemed to ask *What now?*

Raven said nothing. She grabbed his coat sleeve and dragged him along, moving west and plunging deeper into the woods with each forward step.

Moments Ago

Cade dropped the radio on his lap and regarded the scene on the road. Maybe the riders hadn't given the soldiers a heads up after all. It looked as if the drivers were still trying to figure out what had befallen the bikes and their riders. If Cade hadn't been the one responsible for them ending up dead and tangled atop their bikes, he might have presumed they collided or simply took a spill on the straightaway and were momentarily stunned. If that had been true initially, the jig was up now.

The driver of the first pickup, who was dismounted and looking down on the fallen riders, abruptly hinged up and turned toward the farmhouse. In the next beat he was drawing a sidearm and pointing a finger at Black Beauty, which happened to be a relatively shiny sore thumb sticking out against the group of structures in their sad state of disrepair.

Seeing the driver level his pistol and begin to drag it on line with the Ford, Cade drew the Glock 17 from the holster on his thigh and performed a quick press check. *One in the pipe. Good to go.*

He quickly tucked the pistol under his left thigh, scooped the M4 from off the passenger seat, and collapsed the buttstock all the way to its final stop. He flicked the selector from Safe to Full Auto and was pulsing down the passenger window when the sonic signature of poorly aimed shots reached his ears. Sounding like a downed powerline dancing somewhere just outside the passenger door, the bullets crackled and popped as they cut the air and kept on moving.

While the driver was snapping off shots and the other soldiers were readying their weapons, Cade released the brake, matted the pedal, and steered for the two-lane.

"Twenty-four rounds, Wyatt. Let's see whatcha got."

Working the wheel left-handed and clutching the M4 tightly in the other, Cade extended his right arm across the cab and rested the rifle's suppressor on the far window channel.

Nearing the T at the end of the drive, the Ford began to buck and jounce like an angry stallion.

Just as the bikes and dead riders were blocked from view by the F-650's front end, star-shaped muzzle flashes erupted from the soldiers' weapons. As the truck transitioned from gravel to smooth blacktop, the tires caught and chirped. With the sudden din of incoming gunfire rising over the roar of the V10 and protest of tire rubber, Cade pressed the M4's trigger and held it down. Spent shell casings bounced off the rear of the passenger seat and clattered into the narrow space where the dash and windshield met. *What would Desantos say if he saw me spraying and praying like this?* Cade fought the steering wheel and pressed the brakes hard to keep the wildly slewing rig from entering the ditch opposite the gravel drive. *Desantos would say nothing at all,* he told himself. *Because he's the one who taught me how to improvise.* And improvising was exactly what Cade was doing. He wasn't expecting to rack up a big body count by blindly firing two dozen rounds at the soldiers and their vehicles. His only aim was to make them duck and cover long enough for him to get a little bit of a lead on them.

In the next beat, as the F-650 regained traction and tore off to the east, Peter's bags were ejected into the ditch and a flurry of bullets found their mark. The pinging on the tailgate and load bed wall behind him lasted only a couple of seconds. During the first second under fire, the sliding window imploded and pebbles of glass peppered the inside of the cab like a shotgun blast.

The car hauler and Ferrari blurred by on the left, just a flash of red, and then its bulk was blocking Cade's view of the pursuers in the wing mirror. Unable to see out of his dominant right eye, he dumped the empty M4 on the seat next to him and snatched the Glock from under his thigh. Pulling the trigger as fast as humanly possible, he blindly fired sixteen rounds back at his pursuers through the very window they'd just destroyed.

Cade didn't take the time to see the response his poking the hornet's nest generated. Instead, blinking away tears and blood, he reached into the center console and, by feel alone, found the cord to the sat-phone. Tugging hard, he dragged the Thuraya into the open only to see the end of the cord he was holding had not been plugged into the auxiliary power port.

"No, no, no," he chanted. Getting the phone oriented in his palm, he brought it above the steering wheel so he could keep his good eye on both the road and the tiny screen as he thumbed the green talk button.

Cade saw nothing come of the action. Where he would have seen a flare of color and the *Thuraya* logo splash across the screen, he saw only a solid field of dead pixels. He tossed the phone on the seat beside him and tore a thirty-round magazine for the M4 from his MOLLE rig. Still driving one-handed, he picked up the M4 and dumped the spent mag.

A quick glance to the driver's side wing mirror told him he was being pursued by both trucks. The number of soldiers in said trucks, a mystery.

After jamming the fresh magazine into the well and getting the rifle charged one-handed, he swung his right arm wide around and rested the suppressor on the scraps of jagged glass remaining in she slider channel behind him.

Multiple split-second taps on the trigger sent the entire contents of the magazine at the pursuers in the form of several volleys consisting of four to six rounds apiece.

Cade peeked at the mirror in time to see the pickups swerving and falling back.

With no way to alert the others he was being hunted, he pressed the pedal to the floor in hopes of outrunning the hunters.

Seeing a distant road coming in from the left forced him to make a choice: go left there and possibly draw the bad guys back around to Woodruff, or keep running flat out on the straight and draw them up into the Bear River Range growing larger in the windshield with each passing second.

In the end the decision was made for him when a pair of southbound traveling motorcycles appeared at the end of the merging road and stopped just short of the juncture. They were followed by a single flatbed truck that slid past them and blocked the two-lane from fog line to fog line.

Displaying military-like precision, the riders dismounted and brought rifles to bear.

Cade glanced at the speedometer and saw the needle edging past seventy. Lifting his gaze, he judged the distance to the flatbed at half a mile and quickly learned that all of his options were off the table when the driver of the flatbed revealed the gaping muzzle of some kind of heavy machine gun.

Between a rock and a hard place, was how Duncan would have described the developing situation.

Total goat fuck, would be Desantos' interpretation of what Cade had just gotten himself into.

Live to fight another day was what Cade was thinking *and* hoping when he jammed on the brakes and held the steering wheel firm as the tires grabbed and began to belch blue-white smoke.

The sound of bullets smacking the slowing truck were loud in Cade's left ear. The impact from them striking him center mass punched him back into the seat and caused his hands and feet to come off the controls.

Without any kind of input, and still moving nearly twenty miles per hour, the F-650 slewed left, drove itself into the shallow roadside ditch, up the other side, through a barbed wire fence, and into a murky pond where it came to a full stop in half a foot of black water.

The gunfire had ceased the moment Cade lost control of the truck. It was now replaced by doors slamming and voices calling out in Chinese from somewhere near the two-lane. What dialect of Chinese they were speaking, he hadn't a clue.

He wiped at the blood on his face. Peered between the seats, looking for the Motorola. Saw that it was out of reach on the passenger floor. Nearing the dark edge of unconsciousness, he reached out to the passenger seat and came back with the Thuraya. He turned the sat-phone over in his blood-slickened hands until he found the SIM card port. He sighed and slumped in his seat upon learning a special tool was needed to access the card.

In his head, overriding the constant ringing caused by all the gunfire in the truck's cab, he heard Desantos say, *Improvise, Wyatt.*

The sound of splashing water filtered in through the blown-out sliding window. Steam was drifting up through the seams where the hood met the fenders. Amazingly, the airbags hadn't deployed. Maybe the NBA baller had them disengaged. Cade figured he'd never learn the answer to that.

Using all the strength at his disposal, Cade slammed the phone hard against the dash, causing it to break in two and the guts to be exposed. He located the SIM card just as the barrel of a gun was being thrust in through the passenger window.

Orders delivered in Chinese were being barked at him as he pried the card loose and palmed it. Still fighting the circle of darkness closing in, he transferred the card to his left hand and surreptitiously dropped it out his window.

Cade didn't hear evidence the card made it into the pond water. There was no audible splash. No soldier letting on that he had witnessed the deed. All he heard was the ringing between his ears as the circle of darkness tightened before his eyes and the sensation of floating weightless enveloped him.

Chapter 43

Raven had led Peter through the thickening woods, moving fast and silent, carrying the positive knowledge that the distinctive sound of Black Beauty's engine had indeed been retreating east prior to the sounds of the soldiers opening fire and then speeding off in hot pursuit.

By the time the noises and their echoes had dissipated, less than two minutes had passed and Peter was beginning to tire. "Can we stop now?" he asked.

It was very dark within the stand of old-growth firs. But not so dark that using the NVGs made sense. Raven steadied the constantly shifting goggles with one hand and slowed for a tick to answer. "Two more minutes," she demanded. "By then we'll have put close to half a mile between us and them."

"What then?" he asked.

Batting a branch heavy with wispy lichen from her path, Raven said, "We find a place to hide and wait for my dad to radio us."

"What if he doesn't?"

"What if a purple dinosaur jumps out of the woods in front of us?"

"Point taken," said Peter between labored breaths.

"First person shooters didn't prepare you for this, did they?"

"Can I have a gun?"

Raven didn't respond to the plea. She was focused solely on their surroundings, head on a swivel. As they exited the stand of firs, facing a twenty-yard stretch of open field to get to an awaiting grove of aspen, she whispered, "Move fast, stay close, and keep a low profile."

"The gun?"

She shot him a glare her mom would have been proud of. It silenced him instantly and brought him in close.

Without a word, Raven struck out west at a fast lope. During the short stint in the open, she spotted the two-lane. It was at roughly their eleven o'clock, maybe a quarter-mile off, and curled left to right in front of the single house she'd seen from the Ford. The house sat in the shadow of tall firs and was surrounded on three sides by at least two dozen broken-down vehicles and a broken-down-looking RV. She'd seen the rusting hulks from her seat in the truck on the way in and given them no mind. However, seeing them up close gave her an idea.

Just as Peter made it to the aspens, a fork of lightning lanced toward the ground far off to the south.

He counted, "One Mississippi … two Mississ—"

The bass-heavy clap of thunder rolled over the countryside off their left shoulder and seemed to dissipate as it hit the picket of trees sheltering them.

"That struck less than two miles out," proffered Raven. "We should find shelter."

Peter slowed, then stopped altogether. Placing his hands on his knees, he said, "The house? Maybe that old RV?"

Curling back around a tree, Raven stopped beside him. She was breathing about the same as always.

Back arching with each deep breath, Pater said, "How is it you're not winded?"

"My dad is a slave driver. At least that's what Mom used to say." She paused. Stared off in the direction of the field and house beyond. "He's been getting me ready for this."

"You don't think he's coming back for us?"

Fixing him with a hard stare, she said, "Hope for the best, prepare for the worst."

Lightning struck again, somewhere out of sight. A beat later they felt the rumble of thunder in their chests.

"Is that a family motto?" asked Peter.

Raven chuckled and slowly shook her head. "Just one of my dad's many sayings."

Peter stood up straight. Eyes gleaming with newly formed tears, he said, "My dad was the same. He was a very smart man."

Turning back toward the aspens, nose crinkled, Raven asked, "Do you smell that?"

Nodding, Peter said, "Roamers. We better go."

"We can't," she said. "Those things will follow us to where I want to go. They'll be a dead giveaway."

"Bad pun," Peter said.

If the observation registered, she didn't let it show. "Stay here," she ordered.

"Can I have the pistol?"

Back turned toward him, she took the pistol from the holster, dropped the magazine from the well, and jacked the live round from the chamber. Slipping the bullet and mag into a pocket, she passed the pistol back to him over her shoulder.

Grabbing the Glock, Peter turned it over and stared into the empty mag well.

"It's not loaded."

"You passed your first test," she said. "This isn't a game." She raised her M4 a few degrees and faced Peter. "Stay down and keep your eyes open. I'll be back in a bit."

He said nothing. Just went to one knee, useless pistol in hand, and watched her go.

Ten paces into the aspen grove, Raven's nose told her the dead thing, or things, were somewhere up ahead. Two more paces and she caught sight of a flash of color. Amongst the mostly white trees, finding a bearing toward the owner, or owners, was easy. However, instead of moving laterally and intercepting the interlopers face-to-face, she ranged left in a wide circle to come at them from behind.

Thirty seconds after leaving Peter alone, Raven was twenty yards northwest of him and coming up on the dead. There were three. On account on their varied sizes, she labeled them in her head: Small, Medium, and Large. All were adults. All were first turns and so badly decomposed, determining sex or age was impossible. But that didn't matter. The only thing that mattered was disposing of them without having to use the suppressed weapon. Contrary to popular belief—as her dad would say—suppressed weapons aren't silent, they're only easier on the ears, and harder for the enemy to pinpoint in a firefight.

She came upon Small from its blind side. It was half a head taller than her and missing so much muscle mass that its arms and head bounced around as if connected to the torso with overused rubber bands. Achieving a killing blow with the Toothpick took two tries. On the first roundhouse strike, her blade carved a chunk of putrid flesh from the rotter's neck.

For the fatal stroke, she rose up to her tiptoes at the moment she started the blade moving on a right to left arc toward the Z's temple.

There was an audible crunch as the Toothpick pierced skull. Simultaneously, there was a soft squelch of its brain accepting the blade and all movement and sound ceased.

As the Z collapsed and the others became aware of her presence, she slipped deftly into the trees, continuing on the clockwise circle to further separate the remaining two Zs from each other.

Once Raven had achieved a lead on the Zs and Medium and Large were a good twelve feet apart, she stopped in her tracks and whipped around to face the latter of the two. As the big Z stumbled forward, arms reaching for her, she vacated the airspace with a quick hop to her left. Following through with her plan, she ducked the arms and stuck out her right foot, tripping the creature up. She waited for the hollow thud of it striking the ground, then put a knee in its back and jabbed the Toothpick into its right ear.

Sickened by the stink of the liquid weeping from the lethal puncture wound, she leaped up and continued in the same direction as before; a full-circle tack that would see her back to the edge of the clearing where Peter was waiting.

Before exiting the trees, Raven slipped behind a pair of conjoined aspens and called, "Marco."

When Medium doddered past the aspens and swung its gaze toward the sound it associated with fresh meat, Raven had already flanked it on the left and was approaching from behind. "Dumbass," she said, adding a swift kick to the back of one stick-thin leg and watching it lose its balance and sprawl forward.

The way Medium had landed, face planted in the dirt, arms in front and twisted across one another, made pouncing and pinning it in place unnecessary. It was having problems lifting its own diminished body weight off its trapped arms.

Never look a gift horse in the mouth, popped into Raven's head. It was one of Duncan's sayings she didn't quite understand, but seemed appropriate for the moment. She had always associated it with wasted opportunity. And this was one opportunity she was not going to waste.

Work smarter, not harder.

Keeping her body low to the ground, she edged around so the Z's head was between her boots and leaned out over its upper back. From this position, dispatching Medium was as simple as slipping the Toothpick into the tiny opening where its mostly hairless skull connected to its spine. Though she didn't know the names of the bones that came together there, she knew the channel would allow access to the brain and stilling the thing forever required but a quick flick of the wrist. Which she did. *Mission accomplished*, she thought as the struggling ceased and another soul was released to go wherever it was supposed to.

Raven rejoined Peter two minutes after leaving him and just when another lightning bolt arced to the ground. Before she could think her way to *One Mississippi*, the clap of deafening thunder stole her breath.

Sizing Peter up and determining the only thing standing out sorely on him was his near white shock of hair, she removed the NVGs and stocking hat and commanded him to wear the latter.

"You got *all* of the roamers?" he asked, pulling the hat down low.

She nodded. "All *three* of them." Pointing to his hair, she added, "Tuck it all under the cap. Then let's go before a stray bolt finds us."

As Peter worked his hair under the cap, he said, "Isn't thunder and lightning mainly a spring and summer thing?"

Finished tightening the NVGs to the smallest setting, Raven swung the M4 around in front of her. Locking her gaze on the field and house before them, she said, "One of our people, Glenda, has been going on about the early snowstorm and that golf-ball-sized hail we had a while back. She's lived here a long time and says these kind of weather fluctuations are a direct result of global warming."

Peter scoffed at that. "I'm only thirteen and I still know the news people couldn't predict the weather in Salt Lake ten days out. That's why I don't believe we'll all be under water in a hundred years."

"You're just repeating what you hear people around you say, right?"

Peter said nothing.

"Well," said Raven, "That's how Duncan thinks, too. Doesn't matter now. Doubt if there will be anyone left in a hundred years to find out."

Near their position in the trees, a pair of dirt strips packed hard from the passage of tires cut through the field, passed close by a burn pile, and then curled around the east side of the house. Nearly a dozen cars dotted the field left of the worn tracks. There were no fences anywhere. Not even the short ones people around here liked to erect to keep the deer from eating their plants and flowers.

"What do you think?" Raven asked. "Fifteen yards or so to cover?"

"To the house?" he said. "No way. That's a hundred feet, easy."

"If they came looking—"

"When they come looking," he interrupted.

She nodded. Eyes on the distant road, she said, "When they come. They'll search the house for sure. Then the RV."

A low rumble lasting a few seconds made her pause.

Looking skyward, he said, "You're thinking of hiding in one of the cars?"

She said, "The trunk, if we can find one open."

"That's like begging to be electrocuted."

"I've heard that rubber grounds electricity. They might be flat, but those tires on the cars are still rubber."

"I think you're mistaken," said Peter. "I don't like it."

"It's got to be safer than standing out here in the open." A no-nonsense look on her face, she motioned for him to follow, then set off jogging toward the cars parked on the left periphery of the makeshift junkyard.

The trunks of the first two cars they came to were closed and locked. The third car in a jagged row of six was facing them. On all four doors, weeds and grass grew up nearly to the bottom of the windows. The hood was wide and long and shaped like a pair of opposing waves rearing up and touching in the middle. The chrome grille and bumpers matched the curvature of the front edge of the hood, At first glance it looked as if the car was frowning. A round, red enamel emblem bore the words HUDSON HORNET.

Looping around back, Raven said, "It's open." She ushered him in first.

Lightning lit up the clouds. Thunder followed. Next came the rain. Big fat drops slapped the flat metal surfaces with a slow steady cadence.

Peter showed a little reluctance, but clambered in at her insistence.

To the sound of approaching engines, Raven rolled over the knee-high bumper, lifted her boots over the bumper over riders, and pulled the trunk down on their heads, careful to leave it open a smidge. Inside it smelled of must and rust and death.

Peter did his best to keep from spooning Raven too hard. He sniffed the air once and said, "You smell like one of them."

Craning her neck, she said, "It's the hat you're wearing. Same one the rotter was French kissing back at the boarded-up house."

Peter threw a shiver. He couldn't raise his arms above his head without disturbing the trunk, so the hat remained on his head and he breathed through his mouth.

Though Raven strained to hear over the rain pummeling the car, she couldn't pick up anything else. No gravel popping under approaching tires. No exhaust notes. No slamming of vehicle doors.

Chapter 44

The ear-splitting explosions came back-to-back-to-back with no end in sight. In fact, there were so many detonations in so short a time, they eventually became one continuous rumble that went on for several seconds—or minutes, now that he thought about it. For some reason Duncan's sense of time was skewed. It was as if his mind was a tapestry and someone had a hold of the edges and was pulling it this way and that, with no apparent rhyme or reason to the movements.

As he watched the barrage responsible for the cacophony from a vantage whose origin he couldn't explain, he noted the individual shockwaves moving from the epicenter of each explosion. He caught himself marveling at the eruptions of flame roaring vertically through the voids created thanks to the immense overpressure. It all reminded him of watching a flower's bloom in time-lapse photography. Only on a grander scale. And to his horror, the dozens of concussions appeared to be on a collision course with him.

Duncan jerked awake with a start. He was still at Glenda's house on the hill. Which came as a great relief. Because in his unconscious state he'd been back in the jungles of Vietnam, in the direct path of an Arc Light strike, with dozens of 1000-pound bombs walking their way toward him. It had been so vivid, he'd even detected the whistling of lethal lead shrapnel seeking his flesh. Felt the overpressure crushing down on him and causing his ears to ring.

It took him the better part of ten seconds to fully come to.

As the first half of those seconds slipped into the past, he became aware he was still reclining in the padded chair, on the outside deck, with his boot heels parked on the rail. At the end of those ten seconds, he was in a somewhat coherent state when distant lightning lit up the night sky and he caught sight of Glenda's Dear John letter resting on his chest. It was soaked; the writing on the outside, once legible, now just a spider web of black ink running from the center. It also occurred to him as darkness crowded back in that he was as wet as the paper on his chest, and still all alone.

The drawn-out rumble of thunder helped him to understand why he'd just been in the path of a B-52 bombing run. But it sure didn't explain his seeing his long dead friend Thigpen during the horror movie in his mind. Maybe the helicopter door gunner was expecting him soon, and this was his way of communicating the fact.

Pushing the thoughts aside, Duncan found the fifth bottle by feel. Gazing out at the darkened town and reservoir beyond, with not so much as a distinguishing silhouette to orient west from, he spun the cap off with a flick of his thumb and chucked it out over the rail.

"If I can't see where I am," he drawled, "I won't know where I'm going." He chuckled, then tilted the bottom of the bottle to the sky.

After pouring half of the remaining whiskey down his throat, he set the bottle on the floor by the chair legs, picked the .45 off his lap, and thumbed back the hammer.

Aiming at the row of cans on the rail, he swept his arm real slowly toward the one right. "Don't need you," he said and blew the can to pieces.

With the ringing between his ears rising over everything, he flipped the make-believe coin in his head.

Tails it is.

The side of the coin he'd selected.

"Time to shuffle off this mortal coil, Old Man. Here I come, Mom … Dad, Logan."

He pressed the muzzle to his temple. Let it linger there and burn his skin as blood seeping around the splinters ran down his face. He tasted its saltiness on his lips as he mouthed a simple and sorrowful "I'm sorry" for the people close to him he felt he'd let down. For all of the young soldiers bleeding out in his Huey over Vietnam that never went home. For the little girl gutted by the big biker at the I-84 roadblock in Oregon. For Leo and Rawley, whom he'd known fleetingly and had died horrible deaths on the road near Boise. For Oliver and all of those who died or suffered at the hands of a murdering cannibal because, he, Duncan Winters, had inadvertently let her live to see another day.

With the ghostly faces of dead acquaintances and loved ones long gone jittering through his mind like an old timey newsreel, he pulled the trigger.

While he'd expected to at least see a blinding light and hear an ear-splitting boom prior to his brains becoming a gory Rorschach test on the deck wall to his left, he instead heard a woman's scream and the pistol was ripped out of his hand. And though his hearing was greatly affected from shooting empty cans, he knew the owner of the voice was close. *Danger close.* The hot breath on his neck told him so.

The scream morphed into a string of curse words, each one altered by a letter or two so that they'd get by a government censor—or pass scrutiny of a Higher Power.

Duncan heard only half of what was said. And of that half he recognized enough of the words to believe he knew the person who had just postponed his inevitable meeting with the Grim Reaper.

"Glenda? That you?" Though he didn't know it, he was yelling. As he waited for an answer slow in coming, he turned his head in the direction of travel he thought his pistol had taken.

In the next beat he was blinded by three tiny, blue-white orbs. They were above his reach and sending separate beams lancing down to converge on his upturned face. His pupils shrank to pinpoints and he squinted and instinctively turned his head.

"Help me," she said, her hands coming into the picture. He saw the silhouette of his .45. For some reason it was cradled between her hands, muzzle aimed at the night sky.

The light beam wavered and her hands started to shake. She was in great pain. That much was clear.

Drawing her hands close to his face, he saw that the pinky finger on her right hand was trapped under the hammer and sear. Suddenly it dawned on him she had chopped down on the pistol. Her intervention couldn't have been timed better. The hammer was just coming down when the tip of her pinky got in its way, stopping the chambered .45 ACP round from discharging and saving his life.

Tails didn't win today, he thought as he thumbed the hammer back and panned the muzzle away from them both. After de-cocking the Colt, he slipped it into its holster. Moving her hand into the light, he saw the damage to the pinky. It was somewhat flattened at the end, the nail there already showing the beginnings of a subungual hematoma.

She yanked her hand away. "I'm fine," she snapped. "It's just a blood blister. What the heck were you thinking, Duncan Winters? Why were you putting a gun to your head?"

"Because if I didn't," he conceded, "eventually I was going to read this Dear John letter you left me. Then I'd go out knowing way more than I need to. More than this old fella's heart can handle."

"You think *that* is a *Dear John letter?*" She spat the final three words as if they were poison. Tone softening, she added, "I may be from that generation, but that's not me. Not my style. I confront my problems. Tell my truths in person and to the face."

"Am I your problem?"

"Of course you are, Duncan Winters." She held up the soggy square of paper. "This, sir, was my way of telling you something without making you waste your time trying to change my mind. If you would have gotten off your high horse long enough to get over yourself and read it"—She planted her hands on her hips— "You would have learned I was coming here to see if my oldest, Pete, finally made it here with his family. I lost Oliver over a week ago. Now Pete is all I have left."

"Now that I know this isn't one of *those* kinds of letters," grumbled Duncan as he turned the harmless message over in his calloused hands, "it would appear to everyone present that you still have *me*."

She lifted the bottle from the floor. "Not if you can't put the plug in the jug and leave it there. Ever heard of Rule 62?"

He thought about it for a second, then shot a questioning look her way. "If I've ever heard of it, I've forgotten in my old age."

"Stop taking yourself so damn seriously, Duncan. Stop using humor to hide your feelings. Stop using this"—she tossed the bottle over the railing—"to make everything you don't want to face go away."

He tried to speak.

She put a finger on his lips. "I'm not finished yet. But I can't let you bleed out while you *listen*. And *listen*, you most certainly will. I'll be right back. Don't do anything stupid while I'm gone."

He said nothing. Watched the beam from her headlamp wash the bedroom walls as she pushed through the French doors and disappeared into the bedroom.

Glenda returned two minutes later carrying a few items in her hands. She snugged on a pair of rubber gloves, then illuminated his scalp with the headlamp beams. As she began to probe the wound with a pair of tweezers, a wind gust kicked off the reservoir. As a result, the rain came in at a shallow angle, stinging their exposed skin and prompting Glenda to insist they move inside.

Duncan rose and followed her inside and then closed the doors behind them. The quiet made him aware of the damage he'd done to his hearing. Though not as intense as the job Steppenwolf stage-right for two hours had done to him at Shreveport Auditorium in 1978, the ringing was going nowhere soon. He supposed it would be with him for a day or two. Even a week after Steppenwolf, the low-level buzzing was still there.

Glenda sat him down on a chair taken from her sewing table. She said, "I've come to the conclusion, Peter is gone. Even did a quick 10th Step over it." He looked at her queerly. Ignoring him, she went on, "Aside from you heathens, nobody has been here since I left for Woodruff weeks ago. The note I hid specifically for Peter to find was still in his old room downstairs. Now, with Oliver gone and Louie buried out back"—she went quiet for a beat and locked eyes with him—"all I have is you."

He said, "And that ain't saying much, these days. Lord knows I've tried to put it down."

A thoughtful look on her face, she said, "You need to start living life on life's terms. You've been good at it for short stretches. And during those runs you've put it down. But now it's time to settle in for the long haul." She paused, lifted her chin so the light painted the wall behind his head. Eyes boring into him, she added, "I'm with you for the long haul if you can follow those simple suggestions."

"I can follow direction," he said. "Feelings are a whole 'nother animal. I've *never* been good about telling people the truth about how I feel. '*OK*' has always sufficed for me."

She shook her head, the movement causing the beams to walk back and forth across the wall. "You have got to open up. If you don't … that stuff will eat you up from inside. Like hydrochloric acid."

"Or that little bastard from Alien," he quipped while pretending his hand was a monster clawing its way out of him through his ribcage.

"Get serious with someone, DW. Then you can get on with living."

"Hell," he replied, his eyes following her hands as she got ready to dig into his scalp again. "I'd rather do the worm buck naked across a floor full of rat traps than tell a woman my true feelings."

Again the light followed the side-to-side motion of Glenda wagging her head.

Feeling uncomfortable awash in the spotlight thrown from her headlamp, he shifted in the chair and said, "I'm curious about a couple of things. Why didn't you ride the bike? And those bloody clothes out back, where'd they come from? They weren't here before."

Answering the last question first, she said, "Like before, I smeared blood and guts on my clothes to blend in with the rotters."

Duncan nodded. "The bike?"

She tugged at the wound.

He grimaced and gripped the chair arms.

She dropped a mangled piece of lead onto the table top. "I didn't think I could reach the bike and mount it or push it away without drawing deadly attention to myself. There were just too many deaders packing the bridge to even try it."

He went cross-eyed as he watched her plucking wood splinters from his forehead. "I concur on that part," he said. "I came across the biters down the road a spell from the bridge. Did you see any men on motorcycles?"

She shook her head. "Nope. Didn't hear any, either. Probably because I was up at the ski lodge most of today. Figured I might find my boy up there. Maybe staying in a nice room with his family. It was a longshot. Did it out of desperation. Yep ... denial runs deep in Glenda. However, I did see what looked like a family taking bedding and the like out of some ground-floor rooms."

He mentioned the truck and dead bodies. "I saw the bedding. Left it there." Pointing to the bag on the floor, he asked, "What's in there?"

"Long range radios. There's wall chargers as well as the automotive lighter plug-in type for them. I stumbled upon them in the guest services office. Believe it or not, they were still in the box and sitting atop the ski patrol's filing cabinet."

"Break them out. We'll call the compound." He looked up at her. "I'll come clean to them all. Tell 'em everything I've done."

She dabbed at the wounds with a towel. "They don't have a charge. Besides, it would probably be better to wait until you get there to tell Cade and the others what you've been up to and the reason you left. You do it in person, face to face, there's no wiggle room. You do that, you're practicing rigorous honesty."

"I suppose that's a reasonable request I cannot refuse."

"That's the Duncan Winters we all know and love." She smiled and finished bandaging the wounds that warranted it.

"My gunplay is probably going to draw a crowd." He rose with the bag of radios in hand. "We better get a move on."

She put a hand on his shoulder. "I'll take the keys and go start one charging. By the way ... where did you find the purple Dodge?"

Sounding real tired, he said, "It's a long story."

"I suppose in the telling of said story I'll also learn how you nearly got scalped."

"That's an affirmative." He handed her the keys, paused, then unholstered his pistol. "You better take this, too."

"You're past that ... aren't you?"

He smiled, the pain brought on from doing so causing him to wince. "It's to use on any rotters you may come across."

She took the pistol. "Okay ... if it'll make you happy."

"That it will."

A couple of minutes after leaving, Glenda returned, spun a chair around, and sat with her face a foot from Duncan's. "Spill," she said. And he did, beginning the story at Daymon's roadblock, intent on sparing her none of the grisly details.

Chapter 45

The Hudson Hornet's trunk lid had settled down on Raven and Peter just as the pickup full of soldiers passed by the end of the drive. Raven knew this only because she'd quickly pressed her face to the inside of the trunk and peered through a quarter-size hole she presumed used to house the trunk lock. At any rate, due to the angle of the car in relation to the house and two-lane beyond, she saw most of the road running left to right in front of the house as well as the solitary dwelling's entire east elevation. All of which meant she would be privy to anyone coming or going through either door, front or back.

She'd chosen to get in the trunk after Peter and settle in facing the rear of the car for two reasons. First, she'd wanted to be able to keep watch through the makeshift peephole. Second, facing the rear of the car, where anyone opening the trunk would be fully exposed, gave her an enormous tactical advantage. In the event the soldiers decided to wade into the sea of cars and open the Hornet's trunk lid—*BANG*, you're dead.

At least that's how she imagined it going down.

Raven divulging to Peter her reason for choosing the car trunk over the house had brought an unwanted barrage of questions her way.

"How are you going to take out more than one soldier before we're both shot dead?" he'd asked. "This isn't *Modern Warfare*."

Touché, she'd thought at the time. "You have a better idea?" was how she'd replied to the stinging barb. It was at that very moment when she came to realize how much she really didn't know about surviving outside the wire. There were so many variables. It was also when she realized just how much she missed her mom and, now, though he'd been gone less than an hour, her only surviving parent.

While Raven silently cursed Murphy for the soldiers' initial arrival, Peter had asked, "What if some roamers saw us climb inside here and surround us?"

She had repeated her dad's nugget of wisdom. "Hope for the best, prepare for the worst." Then, after a perfectly timed comedic pause, she'd added, "Or I'll trip you so they have something to eat while I get away. I won't have much of a head start, though."

"Why is that?" he'd asked.

"Because there's not much meat on your bones," had been her instantaneous response. The second the quip left her mouth, she'd wished she could take it back. After all, the Zs *had* fed on the kid's father. Figuring, *What he doesn't know, won't hurt him*, she had wisely kept that detail to herself. The fact she had put the bullet in the elder Dregan's head would also forever remain her own dark secret.

"Not funny," had been Peter's curt reply.

As Raven chided herself for again resorting to humor to ease her own anxiety, she could almost hear the gears turning inside Peter's head. Despite their close proximity, it seemed as if a mile-wide gulf had just opened between them. She had a hunch he wanted to ask those very questions concerning the hows and whys of his father's demise, but was afraid to.

As it grew hot inside the trunk from their combined body heat, they both began to sweat. To add insult to injury, Peter took to repeating the same two words every couple of minutes until the soldiers returned in their truck nearly half an hour after they'd motored west.

Raven and Peter were both holding their breath in the dark, tomb-like trunk when the approaching engine noise and hollow pops of tires on gravel overrode the patter of raindrops on the Hornet's thin sheet metal.

They had remained hidden as the soldiers ransacked the house and RV. Then, Raven had watched wide-eyed through her peephole as a pair of stony-faced Asian soldiers moved from car to car, searching trunks and interiors, beginning with a big rusting Cadillac near the back of the house. After thirty minutes or so, with the pair of soldiers yet to search any of the cars near where the Hornet languished, a small man who seemed to be in charge bellowed something in a foreign language. Seeming eager to leave, the subordinate soldiers piled into the pickup, which promptly started up and drove away east, toward the darkening sky.

The moment the truck was out of earshot, Raven and Peter had scrambled from the trunk and sprinted for the perceived safety of the aspen grove.

During their first hour on the move, the kids had remained inside the tree line. However, the closer they got to Woodruff, the more zombies they began to encounter within the rapidly thinning forest. Aside from the herd hunting the elk in the woods near the quarry, this kind of behavior was new to Raven.

After coming close to being surrounded by a number of rotters hanging out behind a partially burned Itasca travel trailer hidden just inside the tree line, Raven had led them from the woods to the road, where they endured a ten-minute barrage of stinging rain being driven hard in front of a prevailing west wind.

Over the course of the second hour, the pair had covered the three miles to the outskirts of Woodruff, walking single file down the center of the road. Along the way, attracted by the sound of their boots striking blacktop, slowly but surely the kids had attracted an entourage of undead.

Now, two hours after slipping from the trunk and melting into the aspens, Raven and Peter stood amid jumbled squares of city sidewalk, underneath a massive oak tree looming tall over a sign that read: **Entering Woodruff - Pop. 180**. The night was moonless. High cloud cover completely blotted out the stars and planets normally dominant overhead. To the naked eye, everything spread out before Peter was black and indistinguishable.

Viewed through the four-tube NVGs, everything spread out before Raven from where she stood to the debris-strewn intersection of Center and Main was rendered in tones of white, gray, and black.

As she looked over her shoulder to relay to Peter what she was seeing, she spotted the undead posse that had been hunting them for the better part of the last hour. They were still a couple of minutes back, maybe five long country blocks. And though she was certain the two-dozen-strong clutch of recently turned zombies couldn't see a thing in the dark, judging by the way they panned their heads back and forth, eyes roving wildly in their skulls, it was obvious they were still hunting her and Peter by sound.

Raven watched Peter react to the distant moans. Saw his face go slack and his body snap rigid. If this was what abject terror did to a person, she knew what she had looked like that day when she saw her undead grandfather after he'd been feeding on Nana.

Willing the vision away, she swung her head in the opposite direction. Focused her attention two blocks west where Center crossed Main. She saw the same static vehicles from earlier, only from a different perspective. Facing her were tailgates and bumpers and shot-out rear windows. A dozen zombies, likely the ones from earlier, milled about the intersection. More were mired in the vehicles on the auto body shop's lot. Viewed in phosphor white, the glass littering the street beside the pickups sparkled like the Milky Way. Walking her gaze back, following the sidewalk on their side of Center, she spotted a number of corpses. Skeletons was more like it. These were the cannibals her dad and the others had killed. After the short and violent encounter, her dad told her he guessed their own people returned and butchered them for their meat, leaving behind a bunch of bloody bones and grinning skulls and decaying piles of guts.

Raven threw a shudder at the sight. She nearly gagged from the stench.

"Do they see us?" whispered Peter.

The skeletons or the zombies? she thought to herself.

Confidence in her tone, she said, "No, they can't. But they know we're here. Main and Center is crawling with them, too. I think that's because me and my dad were here earlier. Didn't help matters that I shot a couple of them. We all know gunfire drives them nuts."

"Maybe they're leftovers from the herd you guys came up against."

All business, Raven said, "Whatever the case, we're going to have to either creep past them in the dark, or shoot a few in the middle of the pack and charge on through."

Voice void of all emotion, Peter said, "Red Rover, Red Rover, send some *meat* right over."

Stealing Peter's line, she said, "Not funny. And that's the *only* time you're going to hear me say it." She grabbed his hand and started walking him slowly down the sidewalk, along the way, saying, "You're going to want to stay left. Far left."

Stammering a bit, Peter asked, "Can they reach us?"

She stepped up onto the curb, then helped him to avoid tripping as he followed.

"Who's *they*?" she asked.

"Whoever will be on our right, up ahead."

"Nope," she said. "They're all dead. Real, honest to gosh, cold-corpse-type of *dead*." No reason to tell him the truth, she reasoned. That'd only spook him further.

As they slipped by Skeleton Row, Raven picked up on movement to their right and instinctively looked in that direction.

Sensing the subtle tug of her hand on his from her panning her head, Peter demanded, "What now?"

"More rotters coming at us from the parking lot behind the rehab place."

"Back in the Saddle?"

"Yes." She squeezed his hand tighter. "Keep walking."

"They're surrounding us," he whispered, a rising panic evident in his tone. "There's a little house across from the rehab place. Can't we go around it and through the field across from where 39 and 16 meet?"

Again Peter felt the slight tug on his hand. Only to the left this time.

"Negative," she said. "We'd have to go through a bunch of brambles. No telling how many rotters got themselves tangled up in there. Better we stick to the plan."

She put her head down and picked up the pace, leaving behind the slack-jawed skeletons and hoping to build their lead on the shambling crowd of undead.

A minute after setting out from the distant intersection, Raven and Peter were nearing the west side of the small house. Though they were keeping to the sidewalk and away from the field of broken glass, Peter was having a hard time moving without making noise. A few feet back he had inadvertently kicked a brass shell casing out into the street. Reacting to the noise, the Zs behind Back in the Saddle began a steady march across Center Street, their bearing taking them on a collision course with the exact spot on the sidewalk the kids were currently traversing.

"How much further?" Peter asked as a kernel of glass popped underneath his boot.

The weight of the NVGs was beginning to take a toll on Raven's neck muscles. Panning her head right, she said, "We're going to make it, Peter. We will be just fine. Hold it together for a few more minutes."

In reality, she doubted her own words, because she was looking a small throng of Zs in the face from less than a dozen paces. They were off her right shoulder and picking up speed in reaction to Peter's latest transgression in noise discipline.

"I don't believe you," he said. "I can smell them. They're real close."

All at once, Raven said, "Get behind me," and helped him comply to the whispered order with a sweep of her right arm. In the next beat, there was a rustle of clothing and light rattle of metal against metal as she shouldered the rifle.

A sharp metallic *click* came next.

Peter jumped as the first report from Raven's M4 shattered the still. He was blinded momentarily by the orange-yellow flash leaving the rifle's suppressor a yard to his fore. In that split second of time, as his pupils were collapsing to needle points, he saw silhouettes of roamers. There was a whole bunch of them. And they were reaching for him, their twisted faces and claw-like hands illuminated by the strobe effect of the recurring muzzle flashes. Their throaty moans rose to a crescendo just as he lost the ability to see.

Rising over the tinkle of spent brass and calls of the dead were two distinct exhaust notes. They were coming from somewhere behind the auto body shop, more than two blocks west. Hearing this, Raven stopped firing into the dead and set off toward Main, dragging Peter along by the hand, and telling him to "Keep quiet."

The far-off exhaust burble was soon supplanted by the sound of two different engines seemingly working hard and under load.

One engine was foreign to Raven's ear. It seemed to be chugging along. Though the engine sounded powerful, the exhaust seemed restricted.

The second engine, its growl low and menacing, was familiar to Raven. She felt the heavy thrum deep down in her chest as a pair of blue-white headlight beams lanced up from the viaduct at their ten o'clock. The shafts of light painted the low clouds for a moment, then leveled out and fell across the field. After spinning its tires at about the same place the F-650 had trouble finding traction earlier, the truck turned east and lit up a long swath of Center with the spill from its headlights.

"That's Taryn's truck," Raven gasped. "But she's not driving. Lev is." She scrutinized the passenger. Noted the feminine features partially masked by a white bandage.

Jamie!

Feeling a sense of calm come over her, Raven raised the M4 and emptied the magazine into the dead coming for them from across Center. Swinging the M4 to her back, she grabbed Peter's

306

hand and set off west, for the intersection with Main. As she angled into the street and the first pebble-sized pieces of glass crunched under her boots, she saw the second vehicle come out of the viaduct across Main. Witnessed the same movement of the headlight beams. The upward tilt to the night sky. The beams leveling to reveal the field behind the first vehicle.

When the second vehicle finally cut around to face Raven, she noted the close spacing of the weak yellow headlights, and realized she was looking at a vehicle she'd never seen before. It was boxy and much smaller than the Raptor. But that didn't matter. Because the man driving *was* known to her. He was wide of shoulder and filled up the squared-off windshield. Even taking into account the scarf riding high on his neck and obscuring the lower half of his face, there was no mistaking those spiked dreadlocks bouncing and swaying to a rhythm all their own.

Daymon!

Running now, Peter still in tow, the Glock taking the place of the empty rifle banging against her backside, Raven said, "I know these people," and opened up with the pistol on the dead things blocking their path.

Sneering faces revealed to Peter by the muzzle flashes passed by on either side as he stumbled and almost fell. But her grip was tight on his hand. He felt her determination leaching into his skin. It invigorated him. Made him step higher and pump his free arm that much harder.

Once they were clear of the grabbing hands and on the west side of Main, Raven cut a hard left and led Peter along the stretch of 39 spanning the viaduct. After running another dozen yards, she took a knee next to a sign identical to the one east of town— **Entering Woodruff - Pop. 180**.

Wasting no time or words, she dragged the Motorola from a pocket, cycled the channel to 10-1, thumbed the Talk key, and said, "This is Raven Grayson ... how copy?"

She waited, thumb off the button for a long three-count, listening to Peter breathing hard, before the reply came.

"Good copy," said a voice she recognized as belonging to Lev. Incredulous, he asked, "Where's Cade?"

Tears welling in her eyes, Raven radioed back. "He's gone."

Chapter 46

Immediately after reuniting with the trio of Eden survivors, while Daymon and Lev were stalking off to dispatch the Zs still in hot pursuit, Raven and Peter were plopping down in the light spilling from the Raptor's headlights, cracking the tops on bottled waters and tearing into MRE poundcake.

Once Daymon and Lev returned, Raven sat on the Raptor's tailgate and detailed what had happened between the time she'd entered the farmhouse five miles east, Cade getting into the gunfight with unknown hostiles, and their journey to the 16/39 junction. Finished, she assessed the faces of the adults standing in a ragged circle a yard to her fore. "Well?" she said. "Shouldn't we all be gunning up and heading east?"

As her gaze settled on Lev, he inexplicably said four words to her that she couldn't bear hearing. In fact, she couldn't comprehend how he and the other adults could make a decision whose consequences, should the worst case scenario come to fruition, leave her an orphan.

Looking Raven in the eye, Lev had said: "We're not going now."

Only Raven had heard: "We're not going *ever.*" And she went supernova, leaping from the tailgate, sprinting past Daymon, and heading north down 16, toward the intersection of Main and Center, where a number of newly arrived zombies owned the blacktop from curb to curb.

In the end, Daymon's history as a cross-country runner, coupled with his long reach, proved to be Raven's undoing. He had caught her before she made the north end of the viaduct bridge.

After the dust had settled, Peter climbed willingly into Daymon's new rig. Though the boxy SUV was a two-door model, he was still able to squeeze into the back seat without moving the passenger seat forward on its tracks.

Raven, on the other hand, after a forced-upon ride over Daymon's shoulder, was placed in the passenger seat and strapped in while still kicking and screaming.

Now, sitting in the passenger seat with the soft hum of the heater filling the cab, Raven looked to Daymon. The dome light was on and cast the lower part of his face in shadow. He looked calm and rested even after having run a half block to catch up with her and then a country block's worth of circles on the viaduct bridge to snare her.

"We *have* to go and find him," Raven demanded.

Daymon sighed. "We can't. Your dad's orders. *Not* our lack of willingness."

Face flushed with fury, she said, "Why didn't you tell me he called? What did he do, call Lev's sat-phone?"

Daymon shook his head. Illuminated by the beams of his rig's headlights, he watched Lev take the driver's seat in the Raptor. "No," he finally said, "Only person who called on that phone to deliver good news was Tran."

Eyes red with emotion, Raven said, "Sasha is going to be OK?"

Peter inched his head between the seats. Interrupting, he said, "Looks like your friends are leaving."

Sure enough, the Raptor's brake lights flared once, settled back to a muted shade of red, then the truck started rolling west onto 39.

Daymon shook his head. "I don't know about Sasha."

Raven wiped her eyes on her sleeve. She said, "So ... Duncan found Glenda?"

"Other way around," said Daymon. "Glenda found *his* sorry butt. They're on their way back now. Glenda is going to see to Sash. She'll be in good hands."

"And my dad?"

"He left a sealed envelope with Tran. It contained specific instructions we're to follow to the letter in case something like this happened."

The fury was gone from Raven's face. Brow knitted, she said, "What were those instructions?"

He said, "Don't worry," as he worked a long-handled stick shift and pumped a pedal on the floor. After a gnashing of gears and the truck was finally moving, he looked across the cab at her and added, "Captain America protocol has been enacted."

A knowing look settling on his face, Peter whispered to himself, "Captain America," and settled in for the ride.

Having calmed down a bit, Raven said, "Me and my dad saw your message. The head you left looking west on the road by the car hauler."

Daymon said nothing. He was busy working the wheel and goosing the throttle to catch up with the retreating tail lights.

"That where you got this old ... whatever it is?"

"Bronco," he said. "When I opened the trailer it called to me." He shrugged. "It's not Lu Lu. But close enough."

Raven asked, "Where'd you go after that?"

"West and then north. And if you're wondering, *no*, I didn't find what I was looking for." He paused and looked out his window. "Instead I found Lev and Jamie trying to pick their way through Fish Haven. What a noisy pair those two are."

"Do you know about—"

"Heidi? Yeah. Sore subject." And those were the last words spoken by anyone inside the cab of the booger-green 1968 Ford Bronco during the somber, hour-long drive west to the Eden compound.

Epilogue

Cade came to a few seconds after his initial blackout. His firefight with the advancing Chinese PLA soldiers had lasted all of about thirty seconds. After dumping an entire magazine into their midst, and dropping three of the six soldiers on the field beside the Ford's passenger side, he had rolled out the door and splashed through the pond, every nerve in his body seemingly on fire. He had nearly reached cover in a nearby grove of trees and was feeling confident his three weeks of escape and evasion training at the John F. Kennedy Special Warfare Center were about to pay off when the grenade exploded nearby. Last thing he remembered was leaving his feet, wheeling around in mid-air, and coming back down with little use of his extremities and the cold realization dawning that in addition to the shrapnel his body had just absorbed, he'd also taken a number of rounds to his back and right arm.

He'd already been shot in the chest before crashing the big Ford into the pond, so this was just mortal insult to what he had initially suspected—thanks to the ballistic plate carrier he was wearing—might be a survivable injury.

Cade came to again after the soldiers had stripped him of his weapons. Pain occupied every fiber in his body as they carted him across the field, past the shot-up F-650, through the ditch, and placed him roughly into an idling Humvee, on the side of which *Utah National Guard* was stenciled. He was losing a lot of blood and sliding in and out of consciousness as the driver navigated a combination of smooth and rough roads. As a result of his inability to remain lucid, keeping track of time or guessing an average speed to establish distance travelled didn't happen.

Therefore, when he regained consciousness tied to a chair with the stink of pesticides in the air all around him, he had no clue at all where he was being held.

Now, willing his swollen eyes to open, Cade learned he was wearing only his boxers. And he saw the pathetic example of a battlefield dressing that had been taped to his abdomen. It was blood-soaked and beginning to unravel. He looked at his forearms. Once bronzed by the last vestiges of tan acquired over long summer months spent outside running and gunning, they were now blanched white due to all the blood he'd lost. Except for the ends of his fingers. They were an angry shade of purple and swollen and they throbbed crazily with each labored breath. The nails missing from the bloody nailbeds, he saw, had been arranged in a neat row on the floor where they wouldn't go unnoticed.

He wanted to curse the men on the sofa playing video games a dozen feet to his fore, but he couldn't. His tongue had swollen to double its original size and it was stuck like Velcro to the roof of his bone-dry mouth.

Just the act of opening his eyes and dropping his chin to his chest had been strain enough to start a sky show behind his partially open lids.

***

Cade came to for the fourth time thinking he was dead and languishing somewhere between Heaven and Hell. There was a deep throbbing in his head and chest. It was caused from something external and seemed familiar to him. Then the flashes of light were back and he was hearing screams. *Demons waiting to accept me? Perhaps the souls of the men I sent there early?* God, how he hoped preempting the Reaper so many times wasn't coming back to bite him. For he'd been holding onto the thought—even as the short PLA officer with the eye patch punched him about the head and neck—that a reunion with Brook was coming soon.

He was drifting toward a bright light when he heard, over the distant sounds of gunfire and explosions and bass-heavy beat of rotor blades, voices speaking in English. Something tugged at his chin and the light grew brighter. Then, speaking with an accent he knew all too well, a man said, "Christ, Wyatt. Never thought I'd be rescuing *you*. Figured you woulda been the one doin' me the favor."

Piercing pain flashed through him like lightning as fingers probed his wounds. Then the voice was back. Gone was the jovial tone from before. In its stead, fear had creeped in. And the pitch was all over the place. Cade couldn't ever remember Griff being scared *or* rattled, let alone both at once. But it showed in his tone as he said, "Oh man. Wyatt's lost a lot of blood."

Unable to keep his eyes open, Cade felt a gloved palm on his cheek.

Griff said, "We need a dust-off helo standing by. Who's got Quik-Clots? I need all ya got."

Cade felt pain in the crook of his arm. Just a little pinprick, followed by a prolonged burning sensation.

The light was back and someone was pumping his chest in measured cadence when another voice he recognized said, "Bastion, this is Whiplash Actual … ready the med-surg unit"—Lopez drew a sharp breath—"We have a friend in need on the way. He's touch and go right now. And we're going to need lots of units of blood. What's his type … anyone know?"

Another familiar voice laced with Southern California chill said, "Wyatt's O-Positive."

The light was growing brighter now.

Now Cade felt the palm slapping his cheek. The added pain made him wince and draw inward, toward the light, and those he missed.

The distant gunfire, explosions, and screaming ceased.

At just the moment Cade thought he was about to see Brook again, the ringing in his ears went away and his whole world turned to black.

###

To be continued in a new *Surviving the Zombie Apocalypse*
novel in 2019

Thanks for reading! Reviews help us indie scribblers. Please
consider leaving yours at the place of purchase. Look for books in
my bestselling series everywhere eBooks are sold. Please feel free
to Friend Shawn Chesser on Facebook. To receive the latest
information on upcoming releases, please join my no-spam
mailing list at ShawnChesser.com.

Shawn's Facebook Author Page:
www.facebook.com/SurvivingTheZombieApocalypse/

Shawn on Twitter: http://twitter.com/@sdchess

ABOUT THE AUTHOR

Shawn Chesser, a practicing father, has been a zombie fanatic for decades. He likes his creatures shambling, trudging and moaning. As for fast, agile, screaming specimens ... not so much. He lives in Portland, Oregon, with his wife, two kids and three fish. This is his thirteenth novel.

CUSTOMERS ALSO PURCHASED:

JOHN O'BRIEN
NEW WORLD
SERIES

JAMES N. COOK
SURVIVING THE DEAD
SERIES

MARK TUFO
ZOMBIE FALLOUT
SERIES

ARMAND ROSAMILLIA
DYING DAYS
SERIES

HEATH STALLCUP
THE MONSTER
SQUAD